How To
EAT
FRIED
WORMS

THOMAS ROCKWELL
ILLUSTRATED BY TONY ROSS

ORCHARD

ORCHARD BOOKS

First published in Great Britain in 1997 by Orchard Books
This edition published in 2016 by The Watts Publishing Group

10

Text copyright © Thomas Rockwell, 1990
Illustrations copyright © Tony Ross, 2014

The moral rights of the author and illustrator have been asserted.

*All characters and events in this publication, other than those clearly
in the public domain, are fictitious and any resemblance to
real persons, living or dead, is purely coincidental.*

A CIP catalogue record for this book
is available from the British Library.

ISBN 978 1 40832 426 4

Printed and bound in Great Britain by
Clays Ltd, Elcograf S.p.A.

The paper and board used in this book are
made from wood from responsible sources.

Orchard Books
An imprint of
Hachette Children's Group
Part of The Watts Publishing Group Limited
Carmelite House
50 Victoria Embankment
London EC4Y 0DZ

An Hachette UK Company
www.hachette.co.uk

www.hachettechildrens.co.uk

CONTENTS

THE BET

"Hey, Tom! Where were you last night?"

"Yeah, you missed it."

Alan and Billy came up the front path. Tom was sitting on his porch steps, bouncing a tennis ball.

"Old Man Tator caught Joe as we were climbing through the fence, so we all had to go back, and he made us pile the peaches on his kitchen table, and then he called our mothers."

"Joe's mother hasn't let him out yet."

"Where were you?"

Tom stopped bouncing the tennis ball. He was a tall, skinny boy who took his troubles very seriously.

"My mother kept me in."

"What for?"

"I wouldn't eat my dinner." Alan sat down on the step below Tom and began to chew his thumbnail.

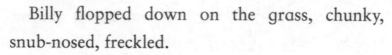

"What was it?"

"Salmon casserole."

Billy flopped down on the grass, chunky, snub-nosed, freckled.

"Salmon casserole's not so bad."

"Wouldn't she let you just eat two bites?" asked Alan. "Sometimes my mother says, well, all right, if I'll just eat two bites."

"I wouldn't eat even one."

"That's stupid," said Billy. "One bite can't hurt you. I'd eat one bite of anything before I'd let them send me up to my room right after supper."

Tom shrugged.

"How about mud?" Alan asked Billy. "You wouldn't eat a bite of mud."

Alan argued a lot, small, knobby-kneed,

nervous, gnawing at his thumbnail, his face smudged, his red hair mussed, shirt-tail hanging out, shoelaces untied.

"Sure, I would," Billy said. "Mud. What's mud? Just dirt with a little water in it. My father says everyone eats a pound of dirt every year anyway."

"How about poison?"

"That's different." Billy rolled over on his back.

"Is your mother going to make you eat the leftovers today at lunch?"
he asked Tom.

"She never has before."

"How about worms?"
Alan asked Billy.

Tom's sister's cat squirmed
out from under the porch
and rubbed against Billy's knee.

"Sure," said Billy. "Why not? Worms are just dirt."

"Yeah, but they bleed."

"So you'd have to cook them. Cows bleed."

"I bet a hundred pounds you wouldn't really

eat a worm. You talk big now, but you wouldn't if you were sitting at the dinner table with a worm on your plate."

"I bet I would. I'd eat fifteen worms if somebody had bet me a hundred pounds."

"You really want to bet? I'll bet you fifty pounds you can't eat fifteen worms. I really will."

"Where are you going to get fifty pounds?"

"In my savings account. I've got one hundred and thirty pounds and seventy-nine pence in my savings account. I know, because last week I put in the five pounds my grandmother gave me for my birthday."

"Your mother wouldn't let you take it out."

"She would if I lost the bet. She'd have to. I'd tell her I was going to sell my stamp collection otherwise. And I bought that with all my own money that I earned mowing lawns, so I can do whatever I want with it. I'll bet you fifty pounds you can't eat fifteen worms. Come on. You're chicken. You know you can't do it."

"I wouldn't do it," said Tom. "If salmon

casserole makes me sick, think what fifteen worms
would do."

Joe came shuffling up the path
and flopped down beside Billy.
He was a small boy, with dark
hair and a long nose and big
brown eyes.

"What's going on?"

"Come on," said Alan
to Billy. "Tom can be your
second and Joe'll be mine,
just like in a duel. You
think it's so easy – here's
your chance to make fifty quid."
Billy dangled a leaf in front of the cat, but the
cat just rubbed against his knee, purring.

"What kind of worms?"

"Regular worms."

"Not those big green ones that get on the
tomatoes. I won't eat those. And I won't eat them
all at once. It might make me sick. One worm a
day for fifteen days."

"And he can eat them any way he wants," said Tom. "Boiled, stewed, fried, fricasseed."

"Yeah, but we provide the worms," said Joe. "And there have to be witnesses present when he eats them; either me or Alan or somebody we can trust. Not just you and Billy."

"OK?" Alan said to Billy.

Billy scratched the cat's ears. Fifty pounds. That was a lot of money. How bad could a worm taste? He'd eaten fried liver, salmon pie, mushrooms, tongue, pig's feet. Other kids' parents were always nagging them to eat, eat; his had begun to worry about how much he ate. Not that he was fat. He just hadn't worked off all his winter blubber yet.

He slid his hand into his shirt and furtively squeezed the side of his stomach. Worms were just dirt; dirt wasn't fattening.

If he won fifty pounds, he could buy that minibike George Cunningham's brother had promised to sell him in September before he went away to university. Heck, he could gag anything down for fifty pounds, couldn't he?

He looked up. "I can use ketchup or mustard or anything like that? As much as I want?"

Alan nodded. "OK?"

Billy stood up.

"OK."

DIGGING

"No," said Tom. "That's not fair."

He and Alan and Joe were wandering around behind the barns at Billy's house, arguing over where to dig the first worm.

"What do you mean, it's not fair?" said Joe. "Nobody said anything about where the worms were supposed to come from. We can get them anywhere we want."

"Not from a manure pile," said Tom. "That's not fair. Even if we didn't make a rule about something, you still have to be fair."

"What difference does it make where the worm comes from?" said Alan. "A worm's a worm."

"There's nothing wrong with manure," said Joe. "It comes from cows, just like milk." Joe was sly, devious, a schemer. The manure pile had been his idea.

"You and Billy have got to be fair, too," said Alan to Tom. "Besides, we'll dig in the old part of the pile, where it doesn't smell much any more."

"Come on," said Tom, starting off across the field dragging his shovel. "If it was fair, you wouldn't be so anxious about it. Would you eat a worm from a manure pile?"

Joe and Alan ran to catch up.

"I wouldn't eat a worm, full stop," said Joe. "So you can't go by that."

"Yeah, but if your mother told you to go out and pick some daisies for the dinner table, would you pick the daises off a manure pile?"

"My mother wouldn't ask me. She'd ask my sister."

"You know what I mean."

Alan and Tom and Joe leaned on their shovels under a tree in the apple orchard, watching the worms they had dug squirming on a flat rock.

"Not him," said Tom, pointing to a nightcrawler.

"Why not?"

"Look at him. He'd choke a dog."

"Geez!" exploded Alan. "You expect us to pick one Billy can just gulp down, like an ant or a nit?"

"Gulping's not eating," said Joe. "The worm's got to be big enough so Billy has to cut it into bites and eat it with a fork. Off a plate."

"It's this one or nothing," said Alan, picking up the nightcrawler.

Tom considered the matter. It would be more fun watching Billy trying to eat the nightcrawler. He grinned. Boy, it was huge! A regular python. Wait till Billy saw it.

"We let you choose where to dig," said Alan.

After all, thought Tom, Billy couldn't expect to win fifty pounds by just gulping down a few measly little baby worms.

"All right. Come on." He turned and started back toward the barn, dragging his shovel.

TRAINING CAMP

"Six, seven, eight, nine, ten!"

Billy was doing push-ups in the deserted horse barn. He wasn't worried about eating the first worm. But people were always daring him to do things, and he'd found it was better to look ahead, to try to figure things out, get himself ready. Last winter Alan had dared him to sleep out all night in the igloo they'd built in Tom's backyard. Why not? Billy had thought to himself. What could happen? About midnight, huddled shivering under his blankets in the darkness, he'd begun to wonder if he should give up and go home. His feet felt like aching stones in his boots; even his tongue, inside his mouth, was cold. But half an hour later, as he was stubbornly dancing about outside in the moonlight to warm himself, Tom's dog Martha had come along with six other dogs, all in a pack, and Billy had coaxed them into the igloo and blocked the door with an orange crate, and after the dogs had stopped wrestling and nipping and barking and sniffing around, they'd gone to sleep in a heap with Billy in the middle, as warm as an onion in a stew.

But he hadn't been able to think of anything special to do to prepare himself for eating a worm, so he was just limbering up in general – push-ups, knee bends, jumping jack – redfaced, perspiring.

Nearby, on an orange crate, he'd set out bottles of ketchup and Worcester sauce, jars of piccalilli and mustard, a box of crackers, salt and pepper shakers, a lemon, a slice of cheese, his mother's tin cinnamon-and-sugar shaker, a box of Kleenex, a jar of maraschino cherries, some horseradish, and a plastic honey bear.

Tom's head appeared around the door.

"Ready?"

Billy scrambled up, brushing back his hair.

"Yeah."

"TA RAHHHHHHHH!"

Tom flung the door open; Alan marched in carrying a covered silver platter in both hands, Joe slouching along beside him with a napkin over one arm, nodding and smiling obsequiously. Tom dragged another orange crate over beside the first; Alan set the silver platter on it.

"A chair," cried Alan. "A chair for the monshure!"

"Come on," said Billy. "Cut the clowning."

Tom found an old milking stool in one of the horse stalls. Joe dusted it off with his napkin, showing his teeth, and then ushered Billy onto it.

"Luddies and gintlemin!" shouted Alan. "I prezint my musterpiece: Vurm a la Mud!"

He swept the cover off the platter.
"Awrgh!" cried Billy, recoiling.

THE FIRST WORM

The huge nightcrawler sprawled limply in the centre of the platter, brown and steaming.

"Boiled," said Tom. "We boiled it."

Billy stormed about the barn, kicking barrels and posts, arguing. "A nightcrawler isn't a worm! If it was a worm, it'd be called a worm. A nightcrawler's a nightcrawler."

Finally Joe ran off to get his father's dictionary:

nightcrawler n: EARTHWORM; esp: a large earthworm found on the soil surface at night.

Billy kicked a barrel. It still wasn't fair; he didn't care what any dictionary said; everybody knew the difference between a nightcrawler and a worm – look at the thing. Yergh! It was as big as a souvenir pencil from the Empire State Building! Yugh! He poked it with his finger.

Alan said they'd agreed right at the start that he and Joe could choose the worms. If Billy was going to cheat, the bet was off. He got up and started for the door. He guessed he had other things to do besides argue all day with a fink.

So Tom took Billy aside into a horse stall and put his arm around Billy's shoulders and talked to him about George Cunningham's brother's minibike, and how they could ride it on the trail under the power lines behind Odell's farm, up and down the hills, bounding over rocks, *rhum-rhum*. Sure, it was a big worm, but it'd only be a couple more bites. Did he want to lose a minibike over two bites? Slop enough mustard and ketchup and horseradish on it and he wouldn't even taste it.

"Yeah," said Billy. "I could probably eat this one. But I've got to eat fifteen."

"You can't quit now," said Tom. "Look at them." He nodded at Alan and Joe, waiting beside the orange crates. "They'll tell everybody you were chicken. It'll be all over school. Come on."

He led Billy back to the orange crates, sat him down, tied the napkin around his neck.

Alan flourished the knife and fork.

"Would monshure like eet carved linghtvise or crussvise?"

"Kitchip?" asked Joe, showing his teeth.

"Cut it out," said Tom. "Here." He glopped ketchup and mustard and horseradish on the night-crawler, squeezed on a few drops of lemon juice, and salted and peppered it.

Billy closed his eyes and opened his mouth.

"Ou woot in."

Tom sliced off the end of the nightcrawler and forked it up. But just as he was about to poke it into Billy's open mouth, Billy closed his mouth and opened his eyes.

"No, let me do it."

Tom handed him the fork. Billy gazed at the dripping ketchup and mustard, thinking.

Awrgh! It's all right talking about eating worms, but doing it!?!

Tom whispered in his ear. "Minibike."

"Glug." Billy poked the fork into his mouth, chewed furiously, gulped!...gulped!... His eyes crossed, swam, squinched shut. He flapped his arms wildly. And then, opening his eyes, he grinned beatifically up at Tom.

"Superb, Gaston."

Tom cut another piece, ketchuped, mustarded, salted, peppered, horseradished, and lemoned it, and handed the fork to Billy. Billy slugged it down, smacking his lips. And so they proceeded, now sprinkling on cinnamon and sugar or a bit of cheese, some cracker crumbs or Worcester sauce, until there was nothing on the plate but a few stray dabs of ketchup and mustard.

"Vell," said Billy, standing up and wiping his mouth with his napkin. "So. Ve are done mit de first curse. Naw seconds?"

"Lemme look in your mouth," said Alan.

"Yeah," said Joe. "See if he swallowed it all."

"Soitinly, soitinly," said Billy. "Luke as long as you vant."

Alan and Joe scrutinized the inside of his mouth.

"OK, OK," said Tom. "Leave him alone now. Come on. One down, fourteen to go."

"How'd it taste?" asked Alan.

"Gute, gute," said Billy. "Ver'fine, ver'fine. Hoo hoo."

He flapped his arms like a big bird and began to hop around the barn, crying.

"Gute, gute. Ver'fine, ver'fine.
Gute, gute."

Alan and Joe and
Tom looked worried.

"Uh, yeah – gute,
gute. How you feeling,
Billy?" Tom asked.

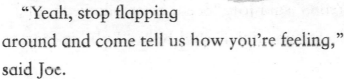

"Yeah, stop flapping
around and come tell us how you're feeling,"
said Joe.

They huddled together by the orange crates as
Billy hopped round and round them, flapping his
arms.

"Gute, gute. Ver'fine, ver'fine. Hoo hoo."

Alan whispered, "He's crackers."

Joe edged toward the door. "Don't let him see
we're afraid. Crazy people are like dogs. If they
see you're afraid, they'll attack."

"It couldn't be," whispered Tom, standing his
ground. "One worm?"

"Gute, gute," screeched Billy, hopping higher
and higher and drooling from the mouth.

"Come on," whispered Joe to Tom.

"Hey, Billy!" burst out Tom suddenly in a hearty, quavering voice. "Cut it out, will you? I want to ask you something."

Billy's arms flapped slower. He tiptoed menacingly around Tom, his head cocked on one side, his cheeks puffed out. Tom hugged himself, chuckling nervously.

"Heh, heh. Cut it out, will you, Billy? Heh, heh."

Billy pounced. Joe and Alan fled, the barn door banging behind them. Billy rolled on the floor, helpless with laughter. Tom clambered up, brushing himself off.

"Did you see their faces?" Billy said, laughing. "Climbing over each other out the door? Oh! Geez! Joe was pale as an onion."

"Yeah," said Tom. "Ha, ha. You fooled them."

"Ho! Geez!" Billy sat up. Then he crawled over to the door and peered out through a knothole. "Look at them, peeking up over the stone wall. Watch this."

The door swung slowly open.

Screeching, Billy hopped onto the doorsill! – into the yard! – up onto a stump! – splash into a puddle! – flapping his arms, rolling his head.

Alan and Joe galloped up the hill through the high grass, yelling. "Here he comes! Get out of the way!"

And then Billy stopped hopping, and climbing up on the stump, called in a shrill, girlish voice,

"Oh, boy-oys, where are you go-ing? Id somefing tare you, iddle boys?"

Alan and Joe stopped and looked back.

"Id oo doughing home, iddle boys?" yelled Billy. "Id oo tared?"

"Who's scared, you punk?" called Alan.

"Yeah," yelled Joe. "I guess I can go home without being called scared, if I want to."

"But ain't oo in a dawful hur-ry?" shouted Billy.

"I just remembered I was supposed to help my mother wash windows this afternoon," said Alan.

"That's all." He turned and started up through the meadow, his hands in his pockets.

"Yeah," said Joe. "Me, too." He trudged after Alan.

THE GATHERING STORM

Alan and Joe stopped in the orchard by the pile of fresh dirt.

"You think he'll be able to do it?" asked Alan, biting his thumbnail.

"I don't know," said Joe.

"He can't do it," said Alan. "How could anybody eat fifteen worms? My father'll kill me. Fifty pounds? He ate that one awfully easily."

"Forget it," said Joe. "If he doesn't give up himself, I'll figure something out. We could spike the next worm with pepper. He'd eat one piece and then another, talking to Tom – Then all of a sudden he'd sneeze: *ka-chum!* Then he'd sneeze again: *ka-chum!* Then again: *ka-chum ka-chum!* A faint look of panic would creep over his face; he's beginning to wonder if he'll ever stop. He clutches his stomach; his eyes begin to water. *Ka-chum! Ka-chum!*"

"Billy's awfully stubborn," said Alan. "Even if it was killing him, he might not give up."

"*Ka-chum! Ka-chum!*" cried Joe. "He falls to the floor. I bend over him. 'God,' I say. 'Call his mother. It's the troglodycrosis.' His eyes bleat up at me. Ka-chum!"

"Remember that business last summer?" said Alan, gnawing on his thumbnail. "When it was thirty-two degrees in the shade and I dared him to put on all his winter clothes and his father's raccoon coat and his ski boots and walk up and down Main Street all afternoon?"

"*Ka-chum! Ka-chum!*"

They went off through the orchard, Joe sneezing, sighing, rolling his eyes – pretending to be Billy suffering from a dose of peppered worm; Alan moaning to himself about how stubborn Billy could be – fifty pounds!

THE SECOND WORM

Billy sighed. On the plate before him lay the last bite of worm under a daub of ketchup and mustard.

"What's the matter?" asked Tom.

"I don't know," sighed Billy. He picked up the fork again.

"Does it taste bad?"

"No," said Billy wearily. "I just taste ketchup and mustard mostly. But it makes me feel sort of sick. Even before I eat it. Just thinking about it." He sighed again and then glanced at Joe and Alan, talking to each other in whispers over by the window.

"What are you whispering about?"

"Nothing."

"Then what are you whispering for?"

"Nothing. It's not important. Just something Joe's father told him last night."

"What?"

"Come on. Finish up. It was nothing. We'll miss the cartoons."

Billy shut his eyes and popped the last piece of worm into his mouth, chewed, gagged, clapped his hands over his mouth, gulped! gulped! toppled backward off the orange crate. Sprawling on his back in the straw, he gazed peacefully up at the ceiling.

Joe and Alan stood over him.

"Open up."

Billy opened his mouth.

"Wider. See any, Joe?"

"Nah, he swallowed it."

"OK, let's go."

RED CRASH HELMETS
AND WHITE JUMP SUITS

After the cinema, Tom walked home with Billy.

"Tomorrow I'll roll the crawler in cornmeal and fry it. Like a trout."

"It's not really the taste," said Billy. "It's more the thought. When I start to eat it, even though it's smothered in ketchup and mustard and grated cheese, I can't stop thinking worm. Worm, worm, worm, worm, worm, worm: gaggles of worms in bait boxes, drowned worms drying up on sidewalks, a worm squirming as the fishhook gores into him, the soggy end of a worm draggling out of a dead fish's mouth, robins yanking worms out of a lawn. I can't stop thinking worm."

"Yeah, but if I fry it in cornmeal, it won't look like a crawler," said Tom. "I'll put parsley round

37

it, and some slices of lemon. And then you can concentrate, think fish. All the time you're waiting in the barn, all the time you're eating it, keep saying to yourself: fish fish fish fish fish fish fish fish; here I am eating fish, good fish.

"Trout, salmon, flounder, perch,
I'll ride my minibike into church.
Dace, tuna, haddock, trout,
Wait'll you hear the minister shout.

"Fish fish fish fish fish fish fish fish
fish fish fish.

"Shark, haddock, sucker, eel,
I'll race my father in his automobile.
Eel, flounder, bluegill, shark,
We'll race all day till after dark."

Billy cheered up.

"Think how they'd all stare. I'd rev up the aisle, zip around the front pew, down a side aisle under the stained-glass windows. My parents would kill me. Rev. Yarder would peer down over the bible stand. 'William,' he'd cry. 'William, you take that engine thing out of here this minute!'"

"Yeah, and then they'd come chasing out after us," said Tom.

Billy laughed. "Waving their arms and yelling. And we'd lead them zigzag round and round and in and out among the gravestones and monuments in the cemetery and then roar off down the Sandgate Road, leaving them draped over tombs, panting and shaking their fists."

"Hup hup!" yelled Tom, dancing around and boxing the air.

"And that Monday we'd smuggle it into class disguised as Raymond Dwelley, because he's so fat, and hide it in the coat cupboard. And then when Milly Butler said anything, anything

39

at all, even something like 'excuse me', or if she sniffed, we'd dump a whole bottle of ink over her head and run for the coat cupboard, overturning chairs and desks behind us to slow up Mrs Howard. She'd come after us, fuming and shouting threats, and suddenly the doors of the coat cupboard would slam open, and out we'd roar on our minibike in blood-red crash helmets and white jump suits, our scarves streaming out behind us! And we'd roar round and round the classroom while Mrs Howard knelt among the overturned desks and chairs, sobbing helplessly into her hands, and then rhum-rhum out the door and up the hall, thumbing our noses at the monitors. Brackety-brackety-brackety up the stairs, stiff-arming tacklers, into Mr Simmons's office – up onto his desk! Broom! Broom! – a backfire into his face, and zoooom! out the window as he topples backward in his chair in a hurricane of quiz papers and report cards. And then, crunch, landing on the driveway, we roar off down the motorway to Bennington and join the Navy so Mrs Howard and Mr Simmons and our parents can't punish us."

THE THIRD WORM

Tom ran out of the kitchen of Billy's house holding the sizzling frying pan out in front of him with both hands, the screen door banging behind him.

Alan threw open the barn door when he saw him coming. Tom thumped the frying pan down on the orange crate.

"There!" he said breathlessly. "Done to a T. Look at her, all golden-brown and sizzling. It looks good enough to eat."

"Yeah," said Billy. He poked the worm with his fork.

Tom took off the pot-holder glove he was wearing. "Think fish," he said. "Remember: think fish.

"Trout, salmon, flounder, perch,
I'll ride my minibike into church.
Eel, salmon, bluegill, trout,
Wait till you hear the minister shout.

"Clam, flounder, tuna, sucker,
Look out here we come, old Mrs Tucker.
Lobster, black bass, oyster stew,
There goes New Orleans, here comes Peru."

He leaned over Billy and whispered in his ear,
"Fish fish fish fish fish fish fish fish fish, go on,
take a bite, fish fish fish fish fish, OK, second bite,
fish, fish, fish, fish..."

THE PLOTTERS

"Geez, you think it'll work?" said Alan to Joe. "Suppose it doesn't? He didn't seem to pay much attention today."

"Don't worry," said Joe. "We got him thinking. It takes time. I've got it all planned out. Trust me."

THE FOURTH WORM

Billy ate steadily, grimacing, rubbing his nose, spreading on more horseradish sauce. Tom bent over him, hissing in his ear, "Fish fish fish fish fish fish."

Billy paused, watching Alan and Joe whispering by the door. He swished the last bite round and round in the ketchup and mustard. All of a sudden he said, "That's not fair. They can't act like that anymore. Every time I swallow they lean forward as if they expected me to keel over or something! And then when I don't, they look surprised and shrug their shoulders and nudge each other."

"Come on," said Joe. "Cut it out. We can watch you, for goodness' sake. We're just standing over here by the window watching you."

"No, you're not," said Billy. "You're whispering. And acting as if you expected something to happen every time I swallow."

"It's nothing," said Joe. "Forget it. Look, we'll turn round and look out the window while you swallow."

"What do you mean, it's nothing?" said Billy. "What's nothing?"

"Oh, come on," said Alan. "It's just something Joe's father told him the other night. It's nothing."

"What? What?"

"It'll just worry you," said Alan. "It's crazy. It's nothing. Forget it."

Billy tore the napkin away from his throat.

"Tell me!"

"It's nothing." said Joe. "You know how my father is. He's always yelling about something."

"Tell me or it's all off."

"Well, look, it's nothing, but the night before last, I was telling Jane about you eating the worms and my father was on the porch and heard us. So he threw down his newspaper and says, 'Joseph!' So I says, 'Yes, Dad?' And he says, 'Have you eaten a worm, Joseph?' And then he grabbed my shoulders and shook me till my hands danced at the ends of my arms like a puppet's. 'It's for your own good,' he says. So I stuttered out, 'It'ssss nnnnot going to ddddo me any ggggood if IIII sssshake to pppppieces, is it?' Janie was wailing; my mother was chewing her apron in the doorway. 'Alfred,' she cries, 'what's he done? You'll deracinate him. Has he hauled down the American flag at school and eaten it again? Has he—'"

"So what's the point?" yelled Billy. "Get to the point! What's it all have to do with me?"

"I'm coming to it," said Joe, wiping his nose. "But I wanted to show you how important it was, my father nearly killing
me and all."

He sneezed. And then Alan began to sneeze and finally had to hobble off into one of the horse stalls, hugging his stomach, to recover.

"Anyway," said Joe, wiping his nose again and hitching up his jeans, "so my father told my mother he thought I'd eaten a worm. 'A what?' says my mother, dropping her apron and clutching the sides of her head. 'A worm,' says my father, nodding solemnly. So my mother fainted, collapsed all helterskelter right there in the doorway, and lay still, her tongue lolling out of her mouth, her red hair spread out beautifully over the doorstep. So I—"

"Will you cut it out?" Billy yelled. "Who cares about your mother? What does it have to do with ME?"

"I think he's lying," said Tom. "Whoever heard of someone's mother fainting and her tongue hanging out?"

"All RIGHT!" yelled Joe apoplectically, stamping around. "ALL RIGHT! Now I won't tell. You can die, Billy Forrester, and you'll have to carry him home, Tom Grout, all by yourself! Nobody says to me: 'Who cares about your mother.' ALL RIGHT! I'm going. Alan," he yelled, "they're insulting my mother. I'm going."

"Don't," said Alan, running out of the horse stall and grabbing Joe by the shirt-tail. "Don't. You've got to tell him. Even your mother would say so. Mine, too. No matter what he said. Isn't it a matter of life and death?"

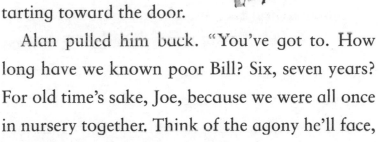

"I won't," said Joe, tarting toward the door.

Alan pulled him back. "You've got to. How long have we known poor Bill? Six, seven years? For old time's sake, Joe, because we were all once in nursery together. Think of the agony he'll face, Joe, the pain and the blood and the gore."

Billy was on his
knees by the orange
crate, wringing his
hands, not daring to
interfere. But when
Joe glanced sullenly
back at him,
he whispered,
"Please, Joe? For
old time's sake?"

"Well, will you apologise for insulting my
mother?"

"I do," said Billy. "I do. I apologise."

So Alan and Joe began to sneeze again and
this time had to bend over and put their heads
between their legs to recover.

Tom, who had been watching them suspiciously,
trying to make out what was going on, started
to say something. "Shut up!" hissed Billy fiercely,
turning on him. "You keep out of it!"

So Joe went on with his story: how his mother
had been carried upstairs to her room; how the

doctor had come, shaking his head; how his aunt had sobbed, pulling down all the shades in their house; how that morning his mother had finally come downstairs for the first time leaning on his aunt's arm, pale and sorrowful; how...

"Yeah," said Tom. "Sure. So why? What does eating worms do to you?"

"Nobody will tell me," said Joe, opening his eyes wide. "It's been three days now, and nobody will say. It's just like the time my cousin Lucy got caught in the back seat of her father's car with the encyclopedia salesman. Nobody will tell me why there was such an uproar." He wiped his mouth. "But one thing's sure: it's worse than poison. Probably—"

"Crap," said Tom.

"Oh, yeah?" said Joe.

But then he and
Alan had another
sneezing fit,
sprawling helplessly
against each other.

"Look at them," said Tom to Billy. "They're not sneezing – they're laughing. Come on. Eat the last piece and let's get out of here."

"You really think so?" said Billy doubtfully. The sneezing did look an awful lot like giggling.

"Sure. Look at them."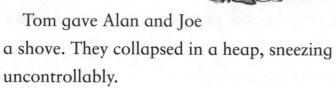

Tom gave Alan and Joe a shove. They collapsed in a heap, sneezing uncontrollably.

Billy watched them. Yeah, sure, they weren't sneezing – they were laughing... Weren't they?

"Hay fever," gasped Alan, "hay fever."

"Um, you've never had hay fever before," said Tom. "How about yesterday or the day before? Come on, Billy. Open up."

So Billy, half believing Tom and half not, glancing doubtfully at Alan and Joe, allowed

Tom to poke the last bite of worm into his mouth and lead him out of the barn.

Alan and Joe sat up.

"It didn't work," said Alan.

Joe began to brush the straw out of his hair.

"You wait. He wasn't sure. Tom was, but he isn't eating the worms. You wait. Billy's worried. He was before, that's why he said he felt like he was going to throw up. But now he's really worried. Suppose I wasn't lying? Did you see his face when I said my father shook me? I thought his eyes would pop right out of his head."

Alan laughed. "Oh, geez, yeah. And when you said your mother fainted."

Joe stopped brushing the straw out of his hair. "Except why'd you laugh so much, for goodness' sake? If you'd kept a straight face even Tom wouldn't have guessed."

"Aw, you laughed first. What do you mean?"

"Me? I laughed first? I did not."

"You did so. You laughed when he yelled at you the first time. You wiped your nose."

They went off through the meadow, arguing.

TOM

Billy pushed the frying pan towards Tom.

"OK, cheat. If it's not supposed to hurt you, you eat a piece."

"Oh, no," said Alan. He and Joe were lying on their stomachs in the hayloft, watching. "If he eats a piece, you lose, Billy. The bet was you were going to eat fifteen worms, not you and him together."

Billy didn't look up, his eyes fixed grimly on Tom.

"All right. Then I'll go dig another worm, just for him. He's so big, telling me: 'Hurry up, hurry up, I can't wait around all day – don't be a sissy.' All right. Now—"

"I didn't say sissy," said Tom uncomfortably. "I

just said if the first four worms didn't kill you, this one wouldn't. I can't help it if my mother told me to be home by two today. She's going shopping, so I have to mind my brother."

"Yeah?" said Billy. "OK. So we'll just have time for you to eat a worm before you go. Come on. Where's the shovel?"

"Here," said Alan from the loft. "We brought an extra today."

A worm dangled squirming from his fingers. He dropped it to Billy.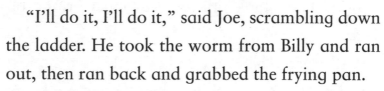

"It's not cooked," said Tom.

"I'll do it, I'll do it," said Joe, scrambling down the ladder. He took the worm from Billy and ran out, then ran back and grabbed the frying pan.

Tom sat down on an overturned pail to wait. He didn't want to eat any worm. It wasn't his bet. He glanced at the door creaking in the wind. Maybe he should make a break for it.

Of course, he could see Billy's point. Billy didn't believe Joe's story, but still…he'd find it reassuring if Tom ate some worm, too.

"He'll eat it," Billy was saying to Alan.

"If he don't he's chicken," said Alan. "After all his talk."

Why don't I eat it? thought Tom. I mean, it's a yucky thing to do, but it wouldn't kill me.

He scratched his neck, shifting his seat on the pail.

I don't know, thought Tom. I just won't. I guess.

He gagged, imagining what it would be like to bite down on a soft, fat, boiled worm. He glanced at the door again.

Billy kicked the door shut.

"Leave it open," said Tom.

"Why?"

"Because I said so."

"Yeah? Well, you don't own this barn."

"Neither do you. Your father does."

Billy rubbed his nose, watching Tom, thinking: he's trying to pick a fight so he won't have to eat the worm.

"OK."

Billy opened the door and set a brick against it.

Tom shifted his seat on the
pail again. He couldn't
stop thinking about
what it would be
like to bite down on
a soft, fat, boiled
worm. He scratched
his ear. Who did Billy
think he was, trying to order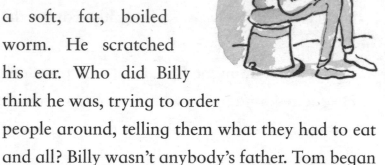
people around, telling them what they had to eat
and all? Billy wasn't anybody's father. Tom began
to feel put-upon and indignant and stubborn.

A screen door slammed: Joe coming back
with the worm. Tom licked his lips. He heard Joe
running across the barnyard toward them...

"Billy!" Alan shouted.

Billy spun around just in time to catch a glimpse
of Tom pelting out the door, the door banging
shut. He flung to the window: Joe sprawled in

the middle of the barnyard on his back, Tom was clambering over the wall into the meadow, the frying pan lay upside down beside the horse trough.

THE FIFTH WORM

Look, said Billy to himself, staring down at the
fried worm on the plate. Be sensible. How can it
hurt me? I've eaten four already. Tom was just
scared. He's like that. He eggs other people on,
but he never wants to do anything himself.

"Give up?" asked Alan.

"Come on," said Joe. "We haven't got all day."

"Five more minutes," said Alan. "Then I win."

"There's no time limit," said Billy. For the first
time he wondered what he'd do if he lost. Where
could he ever get fifty pounds? But how could he
eat ten more? Big, fat, ugly, soft, brown things.
He couldn't ask his father for fifty pounds.

He heard Alan and Joe whispering together.

"He's gonna quit."

"Yeah. I knew he'd never make it when I bet with him. He talks big. Him and Tom are just the same. But they never do anything."

Billy gritted his teeth, glopped on ketchup, mustard, salt, grated cheese, whatever was on the crate, anything, everything, and then grabbed up the worm and tore it apart with his hands, stuffing it into his mouth, chewing and chewing and swallowing, gulping...

Then, panting, he reached out and wiped his gooey hands on Alan's trousers and grinned messily up at him and said,

"There. Five."

NOTHING TO WORRY ABOUT

That night Alan asked his father to show him fifty pounds.

After that, he couldn't sleep, tossing and turning in his rumpled bed. Suppose he lost? He could just see himself asking his father for fifty pounds – begging for it, on his knees, tears streaming down his cheeks; and then, at a holiday family dinner, cringing while all his aunts and uncles and cousins roared over his father's story of "Alan's bet".

He slid out of bed and snuck down the carpeted hall to his parents' bedroom.

"You've got to wake him, Mrs O'Hara, you've got to," he whispered into the phone. "It's an emergency. I've got to speak to him." Pause. "I've got a sore throat, Mrs O'Hara, that's why I'm whispering. Please." Pause. "Oh, thanks, Mrs O'Hara. No, I won't ever call this late again, it's just, it's—"

He waited, gnawing at his thumbnail. A board creaked on the stairs. He stiffened. Silence.

"What do you want?" said Joe suddenly over the telephone. "Geez, I was sleeping. You woke me up."

"Joe, suppose I lose? My father'll never let me take the money out of my savings account. I know he won't. You think I'll lose, Joe? Huh? Huh? Joe, tell me. Give it to me straight. Joe, I got to know. I can't sleep."

Joe sighed. "Look. I told you this afternoon. You've got nothing to worry about. He's cracking. Sure, he ate that one today. Sure, he might—"

THE PAIN AND THE BLOOD AND THE GORE

Four blocks away Billy suddenly found himself in a brightly lit butcher's shop, jostled by a crowd of enormous, pigeon-breasted, middle-aged women, shouting to make himself heard over the din of their chatter and the roars of butchers ordering about the weasel-faced boys who were lugging haunches and tubs of meat in and out of the refrigerator room at the rear. Then a butcher saw Billy jumping and jumping among the women and asked for his order and Billy gave it, and suddenly he was shoved up close to the chopping block and the butcher slapped down ten black worms as big as snakes and Billy tried to say they were too big, he'd choke on them, but the butcher couldn't hear him over the thumps of his cleaver and the din of the women and the hoarse shouts of the other butchers, and before Billy knew what was happening, he was seated at a table in Longchamps Restaurant on Times Square in New York City with a large napkin tied under his chin, and a waiter was uncovering a platter on which lay one of the huge black worms, coiled snakily, a red, red rose wobbling in the centre of its coils.

"How can I ever finish it?" said Billy and cut into a mammoth coil. Steaming pink juice flooded out. Billy ate and ate and ate and ate and then looked...and...and...he must have eaten more than that? And then he looked again and there was no hole at all. He had eaten and eaten and eaten...nothing at all!

And then he felt something cold on his ankles

and looked under the tablecloth and there were two more of the huge worms wound around and around his ankles. And then he felt something weighing down his arm and he looked and there was another worm wound around his arm, glaring hungrily at him, with its bloodshot eyes, and from everywhere in the vast room, winding between the tables, waiters approached carrying huge silver serving platters...

Billy opened his eyes.

For the first moment, in the moonlight flooding his bedroom, his two bare feet, sticking up out of the bottom of the covers, 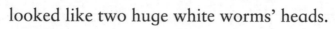 looked like two huge white worms' heads.

And then he realised that he had been dreaming and sank back onto his pillow, the nightmare melting away. There were no huge worms as big as pythons, he was home in bed, his parents were asleep in the next room...

His stomach rumbled.

But suppose Joe hadn't been lying?

The hair stood up on the back of his neck.

Or suppose Joe had made it all up but had been right anyway, without knowing it?

A shutter banged. Billy glanced out the window and saw the moon riding among the tossing leaves. His stomach rumbled and gurgled.

He groaned.

Suppose he was dying? He'd heard of people waking up in the middle of the night with pains in their stomachs, and then, as the windows turned grey in the dawn, they died. Toadstools, soured lobster, tainted pork.

That was a pain!

He clutched his stomach, and groaning, half fell, half staggered out of bed and hobbled toward the door, bent double. Maybe there was an antidote. He whimpered. It didn't hurt a lot, but nothing ever did to begin with, did it?

3:15 A.M.

His mother reached out and switched on the light. "What kind of pain, Billy?"

He stood beside the bed, clutching his stomach. "In my stomach. Oooo, there it goes again, I think."

"Did you eat something before bed?"

She was pulling on her bathrobe. "John, John." She shook her husband's shoulder. He mumbled sleepily. "Did you eat sweets or something before bed, Billy?"

"Worms," groaned Billy.

"Worms? John! John! Billy, what kind of worms?"

"Regular worms, nightcrawlers."

She felt his forehead, lifted his chin to look in

his face. "You don't have a temperature. How many worms did you eat?"

"Five. Two boiled and three fried. With ketchup, mustard, horseradish, salt, pepper, butter. To make them taste better."

"Fried? Ketchup? Taste Better? John! Wake up."

"I had this bet with Alan. Ohhhh." He groaned again.

"Take your hands away. Where does it hurt now? Show me."

"It doesn't really hurt so much now. It's just rumbling and gurgling something awful. It's—"

"Then why are you groaning?" asked his father, sitting up.

"Because I'm afraid it's going to start hurting. Do you think I'm going to die, Daddy?"

"Worms?" his father asked. "Ordinary worms? Earthworms?"

Billy nodded.

"And how many did you eat this evening?"

"One this afternoon. I've eaten one every day for the last five days. But they weren't little ones; they were nightcrawlers, huge ones, as big as snakes almost."

His father lay back down, pulling the covers up around his shoulders. "Don't worry. Eating one nightcrawler a day for six weeks wouldn't hurt you. Go back to bed. It's probably all the ketchup and mustard that's upsetting your stomach. Drink a glass of warm water."

"John, are you sure?" said Billy's mother. "It doesn't seem to me that worms could be a very healthy thing to eat. John?"

His father snuggled deeper under the covers. "I didn't say eating worms would turn him into a prize athlete. I just said they wouldn't hurt him. Now let's go to sleep."

Billy's mother glanced at Billy, shivering beside the bed in bare feet and pyjamas, and then shook her husband again. "John? John, wake up. I think you should call Dr McGrath. You don't really know whether or not eating worms is harmful. I know you don't."

Billy's father groaned and sat up. "Now, look. am not going to call Dr McGrath at three thirty in the morning to ask if it's all right for my son to eat worms.  That's final. Secondly, I do know that Billy's not going to die before morning. If worms were poisonous, which they're not, he would have been laid up before this. Billy, you've been eating worms for five days?"

Billy nodded.

"All right. And thirdly, I ate a live crayfish when I was in college and have suffered no discernible ill effects. And fourthly: I am going to sleep."

Billy's mother slipped her feet into her slippers, stood up and buttoned her bathrobe, and then leaned over the bed and shook her husband's shoulder. "John? John, I won't be able to sleep until you call. John? John, what about tape worms or a fungus? John? Wake up. Billy, you go back to bed. Your father will call Dr McGrath. John? John?"

Billy lay in bed listening to his mother and father arguing in their bedroom. He could only make out a word here and there, usually when his father started to shout, only to be shushed immediately by his mother. Billy got sleepier and sleepier. His stomach had stopped rumbling and gurgling. It was warm and cosy under the covers after standing on the cold floor in his bare feet. Then, in the midst of a foggy drowse, he heard someone dialling the phone in the hall outside his parents' bedroom, and then his father say, "Poison Control?" and explain the case.

Then there was a silence. Billy heard the water

running in the bathroom. And then his father said, "You're sure? These weren't little ones. These were nightcrawlers." Pause. His father laughed. "A bet, I think."

And the next thing Billy knew, sunlight was streaming through his window and Janie was skipping down the hall past his door singing,

"Half a pound of tuppenny rice,
Half a pound of treacle,
That's the way the money goes—"

His father shouted down the stairs, "Helen, do you know where my green tie with the red stripes is?"

THE SIXTH WORM

Billy gulped it triumphantly, serene, untroubled.

By the door Alan glowered, his mind racing: He's gonna do it, he'll win, what'll I do? Fifty pounds.

Joe sat on an overturned pail, whistling, gazing carelessly about...sneaking a glance now and then at Billy. What had gone wrong? Why hadn't he cracked?

Outside, Tom lurked sheepishly in the bushes behind the stone wall, peering at the barn.

THE SEVENTH WORM

Billy ate it offhand, sideways, reading a comic book.

Alan and Joe squatted glumly in the barn door, watching him.

As Billy was dabbing horseradish sauce on the last bite, Tom's head appeared in a corner of the grimy window. He waved tentatively at Billy.

Ignoring him, Billy gulped down the last bite, wiped his mouth, and tucking his comic book under his arm, strolled airily out of the barn, remarking over his shoulder, "See you tomorrow, fellas."

THE EIGHTH WORM

"Where's Joe?" asked Billy, spreading mustard down the length of the fried worm.

"He wouldn't come," said Alan sullenly. "It's not fair putting on that much mustard."

"Ha, ha," said Billy. "Who says? I can put on as much as I like of whatever I like, and you know it. Why wouldn't he come?"

"How should I know?"

Billy swooshed a bit of worm around in ketchup and horseradish sauce. "I know why he didn't."

"Yeah. You're so smart. Big deal." Alan couldn't get the fifty pounds out of his head. What was his father going to say when he told him he'd bet fifty pounds and lost? Geez! He gnawed his thumbnail.

"He wouldn't come because he knows I've won. He knows I could eat twenty worms if I had to."

"Yeah? Yeah? Well, you haven't won yet. There's still seven to go. You act so big. Wait'll you begin to feel it in your stomach. You think you know everything. Yeah. You'll see. You wait."

"Ha, ha," said Billy. "You think you can scare me talking like that?" He strolled past Alan out into the sunlight.

"Hi," said Tom, popping up from behind a barrel.

"Pfffffft!" said Billy disdainfully and walked on.

THE NINTH WORM

"That's not a worm!" yelled Billy. "How can it be a worm? Geez, it must be two feet long!"

"It's a worm," said Alan stubbornly. "It's just like all the others. I rolled it in cornmeal and fried it."

"It's over two feet long!" screeched Billy.

He knew something was up. Otherwise Joe wouldn't have come back, slouching in the doorway pretending to be gazing up at the clouds. But Billy noticed he kept glancing at Alan and him. And Tom was peering in the window again. Something was up.

"Look," said Alan. "I'll cut it. You can see for yourself it's a worm. There. See? Come on. Eat up. We haven't got all day. Joe and me have to go to Shushan with his father."

Billy poked at the huge worm with his fork. Something was definitely up. He ate the piece Alan had cut, looking the rest of the worm over carefully as he chewed. He ate another bite. Fauh! He'd forgotten to dip it in the horseradish sauce.

"Come on, come on, come on," said Alan.

"Yeah," said Joe. "Eat up, Billy, we got to go."

I'll never be able to eat the whole thing, thought Billy. It'd choke me; it's too much yuck at once.

"Half," he croaked. "I'll eat half. This is some sort of ringer. There's never been a worm this long."

"OK," said Alan. "Then the bet's off. Suit yourself. Come on, Joe, he chickened out. Let's go."

"All right, all right," said Billy, playing for time. "The whole thing."

"You'll make yourself sick," said Alan.

He's too anxious, thought Billy. What's going on?

"Leave him alone," said Joe. "Let him eat it. It's his stomach."

He's trying to cover for Alan, thought Billy. He ate another bite. Then he began to scrape the cornmeal carefully off the worm with his knife. "What are you doing?" said Alan. "I think I'll have it plain today. No cornmeal."

"That's not fair! You can't—"

"Glue!" screamed Billy all of a sudden. "Glue! You glued two crawlers together! Geez! You bunch of lousy cheats! Tom! Tom, look what they tried to pull! Glue!"

Panting. Tom bent over the plate. "You're right. Geez!"

Alan kicked a pail, clattering it against the wall. "I told you it wouldn't work!" he screamed at Joe.

"All right. So it didn't work. You couldn't think of anything better."

"That's cheating!" said Billy. "I ought to win right now. You cheated."

"Fifteen worms in fifteen days!" yelled Joe. "You haven't won yet!"

"But you cheated!" shouted Tom.

"So what?"

They argued and yelled, striding here and there about the barn, sprawling against posts, flinging up their arms, kicking walls, banging down on a pail or orange crate and squeezing their heads between their hands.

"It doesn't make any difference!" Joe yelled at Billy. "It didn't work! You didn't fall for it! If you'd eaten the whole thing and then found out it was two worms glued together, then you could have claimed to win because Alan was cheating."

"Big mouth!" shouted Alan from the horse stall, where he was kicking the slats in. "Who thought it up? Not me!"

"Who cares who thought it up?" shouted

Tom. "It's still cheating!"

A pig looked in at the door and then wandered away.

Joe ran out and stuck his head under the tap by the kitchen steps. A minute later he came running back dripping, yelling, "That's not true!"

"What's not true?" said Billy, turning round from shouting at Alan.

"Whatever you said."

"What'd I say?"

"It doesn't make any difference. You're a liar and a cheat and so anything you say isn't true."

"You're crazy. Even Hitler or – or Jack the Ripper – sometimes said things that were true. It's impossible to lie all the time."

Behind them Tom lay down on his back and said, "Arrgh!"

Alan and Joe and Billy turned to look at him.

"What's the matter with you?"

"ARRRGH!"

"Argh?"

"ARRRGH!"

Silence. A bird flew in and then out through a broken window in the loft.

"Well," said Billy. "Yeah. I see what you mean."

He and Alan and Joe sat down on the overturned orange crates. After a while Joe said, "Anyway, I was right. If Billy'd eaten it, it would have been cheating. But he didn't so it's not. The bet's still on."

The pig looked in at the door again.

"A pig's loose," said Alan. "Look."

"Where?" said Billy. "Oh boy, come on. We gotta catch it." He jumped up. The pig bolted.

"Whooooeeeeee!" yelled Billy, dashing out. Tom and Joe and Alan scrambled after him.

83

BILLY'S MOTHER

Billy slumped at the kitchen table on one elbow, pawing in his bowl of Wheaties with his spoon. His mother was washing the breakfast dishes at the sink.

"But why isn't it good to eat hot dogs for breakfast? I know nobody does. But why don't they?"

"Oh, Billy," said his mother. "Stop it. Finish your cereal."

"Well, but—"

A knock on the screen door.

Billy's mother glanced around. "Oh, hello, Alan, Joe. Is your sister better, Joe?"

"Yes, thank you."

"Billy can't come out until he's finished his

breakfast. Would you like to wait for him on the front porch?"

"We came to see you, Mrs Forrester."

"Oh? Come in."

"Mrs Forrester," said Joe, as Alan shut the door carefully behind them. "I don't know if you know about it already, but see, about a week ago Alan made this bet with Billy about eating worms. If Billy could eat fifteen worms, one each day for fifteen days, then—"

"Billy! You're not still eating them?"

Billy stuffed a spoonful of Wheaties into his mouth.

"Not just worms, Mum. I been eating lots of other stuff, too. Look at me. I'm healthy. Dr McGrath told you the worms wouldn't hurt me."

"But Billy, Dr McGrath didn't think you were going to keep on eating worms."

Joe nudged Alan and grinned.

"Oh, Mum, if five worms wouldn't hurt me,

a few more won't either. They're little worms. Besides, it's a bet. If I—"

"They're big worms, Mrs Forrester," said Joe, looking virtuous. "We won't lie to you. My mother told me never to tell a lie."

"Manure," said Billy. "Mum, it's a bet. I told you. If I win, Alan's got to pay me fifty pounds."

"Fifty pounds! Young man, don't you move from that chair." She went off into the front hall.

"Cheats!" whispered Billy. "But you'll see. It won't work."

Alan and Joe gazed nonchalantly at the ceiling. Billy's mother's voice came from the front hall. "Dr McGrath, I'm awfully sorry to bother you again, it's such a ridiculous matter, but since I spoke to you, Billy has continued to eat worms." Pause. "No, no, it's nothing like that. He's acting perfectly normal otherwise. It seems he made a bet with some other boys." Pause. "One every day. He has to eat fifteen to win his bet." Pause. "Oh, thank you, Dr McGrath. I'm so sorry to bother—"

She returned to the kitchen. "But no more bets after this one, Billy. Alan and Joe, don't you egg him on any more. He's far too eager to do wild things."

Billy yukked silently at Joe and Alan. Alan made a rude gesture at him.

"Mrs Forrester," said Joe, "what we really came about is that Alan and me are going up to Lake Lauderdale today with my father to fish. And we won't be back till tomorrow night, so we wondered if you'd make sure Billy eats the worms today and tomorrow. It's not that we don't trust Billy, Mrs Forrester—"

"No," said Billy's mother, smiling.

"—but it's always better if there's a referee. You know, like Mr Simmons says at school: to save arguments and hard feelings. We brought the two worms." He held up a paper bag. "We boiled them already, so you can just keep them in the refrigerator."

"Well," said Billy's mother. "This is quite a responsibility. Are you sure I'll be neutral enough? I am his mother."

"Yeah, we thought of that," said Joe, "but we figured, well, you're usually pretty fair, and besides, parents almost never cheat kids if it's just something between kids. They're usually pretty fair until they get into it."

Billy's mother laughed. "And how does he eat them? Just cold boiled?"

"Well, we've been frying them, Mrs Forrester. We roll them in cornmeal and then fry them like a fish. But he can do whatever he wants. Except that Alan and me have decided it's not fair to make soup out of them or chop them up really small or in a chicken salad sandwich. He's got to eat them piece by piece."

"Who said?" yelled Billy. "When was that ever in the rules?"

"We said!" shouted Alan.

Billy jumped up, kicking his chair over. "Well, then I win! Because it's cheating to make up new rules in the middle."

"Oh, yeah?" shouted Alan. "Then you lose! Because anybody knows it'd be cheating to mash it up."

"You think you're going to weasel out of it after I've already eaten nine!"

"Who's weaselling? You're cheating!"

"Yeah?"

"Yeah!"

"Boys! Boys! Billy! Alan!"

Silence.

"Please. Now Billy, I think – no, let me speak first. I do think Alan and Joe are right. It wouldn't be fair to cut the worm all up. You can just think of some other way of fixing it. Thank you, Joe."

She took the paper bag and looked inside.

"Pew. Billy, are you sure—"

"Mum, you've eaten eels; you ate eels last summer in Long Island. These are just smaller. They're the same thing."

"Well." She put the paper bag in the refrigerator. "I guess if Dr McGrath says it's all right. Now why don't you all go outside?"

"I wouldn't go across the street with those cheats," said Billy. "They can—"

"Yeah?" shouted Alan. "Well, who'd want to go anywhere with you, either?"

"Yeah?" shouted Billy.

"Boys!" cried Mrs Forrester. "Stop it! All right. Alan and Joe, you had better go."

The screen door banged behind them.

"Pffffft!" said Billy scornfully.

Joe's face appeared at the screen. "Thanks for saying you'll help out, Mrs Forrester."

THE TENTH WORM

"What's for dinner?" said Billy's father, coming into the kitchen.

"Well," said Billy's mother. "You and I and Janie are having hamburgers and string beans and mashed potatoes. Billy is having a fried worm."

"More worms? The bet's still on?"

"Look." She took a small plate covered with cling film out of the refrigerator.

"And you've eaten nine of these already, Billy?' He poked the worms curiously. "What do you do, use a lot of ketchup and mustard?"

Billy nodded. "And horseradish and other things. And we fry them."

Billy's father lifted a corner of the cling film and smelled the worms. "Helen, you ought to be able to do better than fried. Use your cookbooks."

"I'm not the cook. I'm just the referee."

"Oh, come on. Think of the challenge."

He took a cookbook from the shelf under the spice rack. "Let's see. Mastering the Art of French Cooking." He leafed through the cookbook. "Here. How about Poached Eels on Toast?"

"No," said Billy's mother. "It calls for chopping up the eel in little pieces, and that would be against the rules."

"How about Spaghetti with Wormballs then? Or a Savoury Worm Pie? Creamed Worms on Toast? Spanish Worm? Wormloaf with Mushroom Sauce?"

"Wait," said Billy's mother, putting down her cooking spoon. "It might just—" She took the cookbook and turned to the index. "Here." She read: "Alsatian Smothered Worm: dredge the worm with seasoned flour. Saute in three tablespoons of dripping until browned. Cover with sliced onions, pour over one cup thick sour cream, cover pot closely, and bake in a slow oven until tender."

"Bravo," said Billy's father. "Put the hamburgers back in the refrigerator. We'll all have worm tonight."

"I won't," said Janie.

"Ha," said Billy, grinning in the midst of chewing. "Wow, Alan and Joe thought they were doing me in when they came to you, Mum, but this is better than steak. It really tastes good."

"Yuck," muttered Janie, making a face.

"Let me have a taste," said Billy's father.

"No, no," said his mother. "Billy has to eat every bit himself. Alan and Joe were very firm about that, and I'm the referee."

"Wow," said Billy. "I don't mind if it tastes like this."

THE ELEVENTH WORM

"How'd you do it?" said Billy. "What's it called?"

"My word," said his father.

"Gosh, Mrs Forrester," gasped Tom. On a silver dish in front of Billy lay an ice-cream cake bathed in fruit syrups – peach, cherry, tutti-frutti, candied orange – topped with whipped cream sprinkled with jelly beans and almond slivers.

"It's called a Whizbang Worm Delight," said Billy's mother proudly. "I made it up."

"Is the worm really in there?" said Billy, poking about with his spoon. And then, scraping away a bit of whipped cream at one end, he glimpsed the worm's snout protruding from the centre of the cake.

"Snug as a bug in a rug," said his mother.

"I still wouldn't eat a worm," said Janie, eyeing the Whizbang Worm Delight with envious distaste.

"I would," said Tom. "At least, maybe I would."

ADMIRALS NAGUMO AND KUSAKA ON THE BRIDGE OF THE AKAIGA, 6TH DECEMBER, 1941

"It won't work."

"Look," said Joe, "even if he remembers the worm while we're at Shea, he can't get one. Where's anyone going to find a worm at Shea Stadium? Don't worry, we'll say, you've won; we'll find a worm after we get home. And we keep right on stuffing him: peanuts, hot dogs, hamburgers, Cracker Jack, ice cream, fizzy drinks, gum, Mars Bars. You know how he loves to eat. You ever seen him refuse something to eat? By the time we start home he'll be bloated, drowsy, belching. Remember the last time? When his father took us?

He was asleep by the time we hit Peekskill. Your father will carry him in from the car; his mother and father will put him to bed; next morning he'll wake up – TOO LATE! You've won! Fifteen worms in fifteen days! He missed a day!"

Alan gnawed at his thumbnail. "What about Tom?"

"We'll ask him along and then just not pick him up. We can tell your father and Billy that Tom's mother called, he was sick, his grandmother died, anything, just so we don't have to bring him with us."

Alan sighed. "Geez, it'll probably cost me eight pounds just to buy all that food – Cracker Jack, hamburgers—"

"Yeah, but it'll cost you fifty pounds if he wins."

"Yeah, well – oh Geez, how'd I ever get into this? If my father finds out—"

Alan slumped on the porch steps, gazing down at his sneakers, gnawing his thumbnail.

"Come on," said Joe, slapping him on the

shoulder. "Cheer up. You haven't lost yet. Go ask your father."

THE TWELFTH WORM

"You think Alan really meant it when he said he'd given up?" asked Billy, turning down the flame under the frying pan. He was cooking a toasted-cheese-and-worm sandwich.

"I don't know," said Tom, looking in the refrigerator. "I suppose so. He asked us to the baseball game – say, is that chocolate pudding?"

"Yeah, but don't take any. It's for supper."

"I could just scrape some off the top, and then you could tell your mother it fell out upside down on the floor by mistake while you were getting the cheese out, so you scraped the dirty part off into the garbage."

"Welllll—" said Billy doubtfully.

"Thomas Grout," said Billy's mother, coming

99

in from the hall. "I'm surprised at you."

"Aw, Mrs Forrester, I wouldn't really have done it. I was just, you know, talking. Everybody talks: my father, Billy's father, Billy, my sisters Suzy, Charlotte, Polly," he was backing toward the door. "Betsy, Agnes, Columbus—"

"I didn't know you had a sister named Columbus, Tom," said Billy's mother. "Would you like some chocolate ice cream instead?"

"Oh, sure, Mrs Forrester," said Tom, relieved. He sat down at the table. "It's my cousin who's named Columbus." He grinned. "Columbus Ohio. He's a capital fellow, Mrs Forrester."

And then he had to grab the edge of the table to keep from rolling off his chair laughing at his own joke. Billy looked disgusted. His mother opened the refrigerator, shaking her head.

PEARL HARBOR

The car slid quietly to a stop under the streetlight outside Billy's house.

"Shh," whispered Alan to his father. "Billy's asleep."

His father glanced back at Billy, snoring peacefully in the back seat, his plump cheeks sticky with orange Tango.

"Alan, run up to the house and tell them I'm bringing Billy in."

Billy's father met them at the front door, and taking Billy, whispered his thanks. Alan and his father went down the path. Behind them the porch light clicked off.

In the back seat of the car Joe and Alan wrestled gleefully.

"We did it!"

"We've won!"

"He'll never wake up now!"

Alan struggled out of Joe's grip and asked his father what time it was.

"Late. Almost midnight, I think."

Joe pulled Alan's head down and tried to sit on it.

"He couldn't do it now even if he woke up. How could he find and cook and eat a worm in the dark? Hee, hee. We've won! We've won!"

GUADALCANAL

But slumped on the bathroom stool, his mother holding up his chin while she washed his face, Billy was waking.

"Hold still, dear. Did you have a good time? You're certainly home late. Is this part of winning the bet?"

Billy's eyes blinked sleepily. He had a gnawing feeling he had forgotten something. He hiccuped, gazing dopily down at the fuzzy blue bathmat... yawned... He'd remember in the morning. It couldn't be that im—

BET!?!

BET!?!

He hadn't won yet! There were still three to go! Fifteen! Fifteen worms in fifteen days! Today was...

He jumped up.

"Mum, I haven't eaten my worm today!"

And suddenly it all came to him. The whole trip...all the chocolate bars, hot dogs, hamburgers, popcorn.

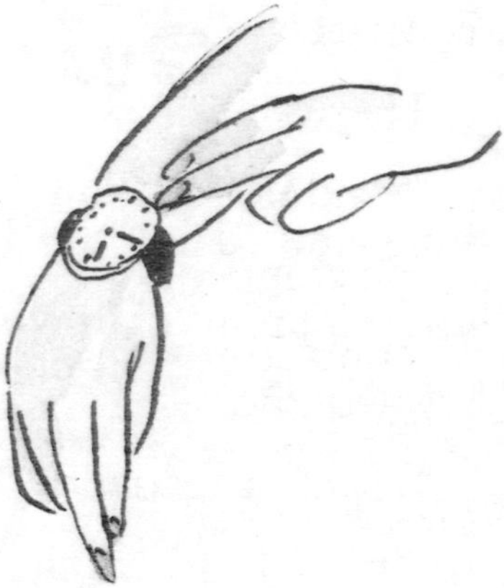

"What time is it, Mum? Quick!"

"About quarter to twelve."

"It was a trick!" He snatched his trousers off the floor. "They were trying to make me forget!" He tumbled and slid downstairs, through the dining room, his shirt-tail flying, yanked open the drawer in the kitchen table, snatched out the torch, the drawer spilling out with a clatter and crash onto the floor, and slammed out the back door.

"The cheats!"

He scuttled across the back field toward Tom's house, searching the ground with the flashlight as he went.

"There! Darn, a stick! Geez, what if I can't find one?"

He stopped.

"There won't be time to cook it!"

He ran on.

"And no ketchup."

He stopped.

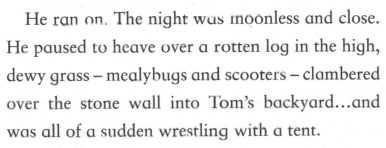

"I bet Tom wasn't sick at all."

He ran on. The night was moonless and close. He paused to heave over a rotten log in the high, dewy grass – mealybugs and scooters – clambered over the stone wall into Tom's backyard...and was all of a sudden wrestling with a tent.

Muffled grunts and thrashings.

"Tom!" he yelled. "Tom! It's me! Billy! They're trying to trick us."

Tom and his younger brother Pete crawled out from under the tent.

"It was a trick," panted Billy. "Alan and Joe were trying to make me forget. Fifteen worms in fifteen days. If I don't eat one in the next ten minutes, Alan'll say he's won. It's almost midnight."

"And they left me home so I wouldn't remind you?"

Billy nodded.

"Have you got a worm?"

"We'll have to find one."

Tom dug back into the tent and came up with two flashlights. They zigzagged back and forth across the lawn, bent over, searching.

"I got one!" cried Pete.

"Shhh."

"I'll have to eat it raw," said Billy. He threw back his head.

"Wait," whispered Tom, grabbing his arm. "You should do it where Alan and Joe can see you. Pete, run and get your siren out of the garage."

THE THIRTEENTH WORM

Under the streetlight in front of Alan's house Tom and Pete knelt over the siren. Billy stood beside them, the nightcrawler squirming in his fingers.

"Now wait till lots of lights come on all over, in all the houses," said Tom. "Then chomp it down. Ready, Pete? Now."

The siren growled, winding slowly up and up until it SCREEEEEEEEEEEEEEEEEEEECHED! across the sleeping neighbourhood, sending birds squawking and chirping into the air from trees and rooftops; dogs began to bark; windows lit up; there were confused shouts, bangs of windows slamming up.

"Ladies and gentleman," shouted Tom through the dying whine of the siren, "Alan Phelps and

Joseph O' Hara, through their craftiness and cheating, their lies and dirty—"

"Come on," muttered Billy, his head thrown back, dangling the worm over his open mouth. "We haven't got much time."

"Alan Phelps and Joseph O'Hara," shouted Tom, "have forced us to wake you all up so that you may now witness, ta-ratta-ta-ratta-taratta-ta-ta: THE EATING OF THE THIRTEENTH WORM!"

He dropped to his knees; the siren wound slowly up to a SCREECH! Billy dropped the crawler into his mouth and chewed furiously, his eyes closed; fell to his knees, still chewing, his face turning beet-red; toppled over on his side, still chewing; rolled and writhed about the sidewalk, clutching his stomach, still chewing – Tom and Pete kneeling by the streetlight, working the screaming siren...

Billy threw open his arms and lay still on his back under the glare of the streetlight, his mouth wide open.

"TAAA–RAAΛAAAAAAaaaaaaaaaa!" announced Tom, springing up and pointing to Billy.

The three boys ran off into the darkness. As they went, Tom yelled, "Remember: Alan Phelps and Joseph O'Hara."

HELLO. WE'RE...

A confused murmur arose up and down the street. Suddenly a boy shouted from the Phelps's house.

"Cheats!"

Alan's father dragged him back from the window.

"Is that why you were stuffing Billy with candy and junk all day?"

"Leave me alone. Yeah. We were trying to trick him. The cheat. CHEATS!" he yelled at the top of his voice, lunging toward the window.

"Quiet!"

His father sat him down hard in a chair.

Joe peered furtively out through the fringe of the bedspread. As soon as he had heard the siren and Tom's yells, he had crawled under the bed.

"And that's why Billy woke the whole neighbourhood up? To show you he hadn't been tricked?"

"Yes."

His father let go of Alan's pyjama collar. In the doorway Alan's mother threw up her hands and went off to the bathroom to take two aspirin.

The next day Alan and Joe tramped from house to house in the neighbourhood, knocking on each door and then reciting in chorus:

"Hello. We're Alan Phelps and Joseph O'Hara. We're the reason you were woken up in the middle of the night last night, and we're sorry." Breath. "You'll be happy to know our parents have punished us we can't watch television or have any dessert for a month and our pocket money has been taken away for two weeks we promise that it will never happen again."

"At least not in this neighbourhood," muttered

Joe as the last door closed behind them.

"And Alan," said his father at dinner that night, "I don't want to hear that there has been any repetition of this incident at Billy's or Tom's house or anywhere else. Do you understand that?"

"But we can't let them get away with it, Mr Phelps," called Joe from the living room, where he was waiting for Alan to finish dinner.

"There will be no repetition of this incident or anything like it," repeated Mr Phelps. "You tried to trick Billy and lost. That will be the end of the matter."

29

"You know what you are?" said Alan, his nose almost touching Billy's. "You're a jerk."

"And you're another," sneered Billy through clenched teeth. "And a cheating, lying, dirty, snot-nosed, cheating, lying one."

"If you say two more words," said Alan, "you know what? I'll beat your head in."

Billy breathed hard.

"I'm right behind you," muttered Tom, peering grimly over Billy's shoulder, his fists clenched.

"Yeah?" said Joe from behind Alan. "So what? We can beat both of you with our hands tied behind our backs and paper bags over our heads."

"You couldn't beat a flea."

"Yeah?"

"Yeah."

Spiffle!

Whack!

Thump!

"Someone's choking! No fair!"

Thwomp!

Gouge!

Joe crawled off behind a tree, nose bleeding.

Womp!

"He's pulling hair!"

"He's scratching!"

Twist!

Twist!

Alan crawled weeping behind a bush. *Thump! Whack! Donk!*

"Billy! It's just you and me!"

"Where are the others?"

Tom and Billy untangled and sat up, bruised, scratched, dusty, shirts torn, hair tousled. Tom's nose was bleeding, Billy's shoe had come off.

"Yaaaaaa ya!" sassed Alan and Joe from behind the tree.

Billy started to shake his fist at them and clamber up, but then sank back. Tom panted beside him, bleary-eyed.

"Yaaaaaa ya, all worn out? Can't fight any more?"

Alan scooped up a handful of mud and flung it at Tom and Billy. Then Joe did the same. Billy and Tom scrambled up and pelted back. Mud splatted against trees and bushes. Alan began to cry. A rock hit Billy over the eye. He sat down backwards in the mud, covered his head with his arms, sobbing. Joe and Tom stopped throwing. Joe grabbed Alan. "Come on."

Tom knelt beside Billy. "Lemme see, Billy. Is it bad? Take your arms away so I can see." He tried to pull Billy's arms apart. Billy wrenched away.

"Come on," said Tom in a scared voice. "I'll take you home. Come on. Your mother can take you to the doctor."

THE PEACE TREATY

Alan and Joe sat on the sofa, Tom and Billy on two straight chairs opposite them.

"Now," said Alan's father. "What's this all about?"

The four boys all began talking at once, accusing, recounting, explaining.

"All right," said Alan's father after a while. "That's enough. Now we know it's got something to do with this bet Alan and Billy made, but Mr O'Hara and I aren't going to get involved in that. You'll have to settle that among yourselves."

"You four boys have been friends too long to start fighting now," said Mr O'Hara. "You really hurt each other. Look at yourselves, your faces all bruised and muddy. Talk it over, work things out, and then you can shake and be friends again."

Joe muttered under his breath, "I couldn't be friends with those rats."

"We'll be out in the kitchen," said Alan's father. "When you've settled it, call us, and we'll all go down to Friendly's for some ice cream. OK?"

Billy and Alan and Tom nodded. The two fathers left the room. The boys gazed silently at each other. After a while, Alan said, "It wasn't us that scratched Tom, Billy did it."

Another silence.

"Did you have stitches?" Billy asked Alan.

"Nah. Did you?"

Billy shook his head.

More silence.

"You tried to cheat," said Billy.

"That wasn't cheating. We were just trying to trick you."

"Yeah, but before that. When you glued the two worms together. That was cheating."

"You would have cheated, too, if you'd been losing."

Billy thought about it.

"OK. But look, no more cheating. I've already eaten thirteen worms; you know I can eat two more. Heck, if I buy George Cunningham's brother's minibike, we can all use it – we'll all have fun with it."

Joe and Alan glanced at each other.

"OK," said Joe. "You win. He wins, Alan."

"Yeah, but—"

"What's the use?" said Joe. "We've tried everything. I'm sick of it. Geez, we've done nothing else for almost two weeks."

Alan scratched his eyebrow, glancing at Joe. "Yeah, but—"

Joe stood up. "Come on. At least we'll get a milkshake out of it."

THE LETTER

Billy lifted the worm out of the frying pan with the cooking tongs and curled it back and forth on his peanut butter sandwich.

"I bet they try something," he said. "Joe won't give up. Alan might, but Joe won't."

Tom was carving his initials in the leg of the kitchen table. "Yeah, but it's not Joe's bet. What does he care?"

"Just the same I bet he tries something."

Billy sat down at the table, turning the sandwich this way and that, looking for the best spot to take the first bite.

Janie came in from the dining room.

"You and Mum got a letter."

Chewing, Billy opened it...

Charles M. McGrath, M.D.

34 Beechwood Drive

Gratton, New York 12601

Midnight, August 15, 1993

Mrs John Forrester

7 Manchester Road

East Gratton

N.Y. 12603

Dear Mrs Forrester:

I have just made a distressing discovery. ~~Ehilr lrsginh yhtouh s~~ medical journal before going up to bed, I noticed an article entittled "Poisons in the Home Garden", a subject which necessarily fascinates me. As I glanced through the article a phase caught my eye: "Lumbricus terrestris, the common earthworm." I read on.

Mrs Forrester, let me assurre you, first of all, that there is no cause for undue alarm. However, you will, I am sure, be concerned to learn that "especially in the months of July and August parents must beware of the

120

common earthworm, some varieties of which are know to secrete a substance (Lumbricus coreopsis), which, though not malignant to the skin, is sometimes harmful if swallowed. Dr A C Roosevelt of Hyde Park, New York, reports that 10% of the boys studied reported no ill effects except induced paralysis of the lower fulmar region; 40% reported abdominal cramping, triple vision (lasting from two to three years and imparing school performance) and extreme lussitude; autopsy reports have not yet been received on the remaining 50%, and so no final conclusions can be drawn, but extreme caution is urged since the blackened and pimply faces of the subjects lead one to suspect the worse."

Mrs Forrester, as your friend and family phisician, I would strongly recommend that your son William eat no more worms until I return on Thursday from New York City and can give him a thurough examination.

Yours sinccrely,

C, M. McGrath, M.D. CMM/ac

CROAK

His hand trembling, Billy laid the peanut butter and fried worm sandwich down on the table.

"Do you think—"

"Wow," whispered Tom.

The screen door banged.

Billy's father came into the kitchen, his tie loosened, his jacket over his arm. He laid his briefcase on the table.

"It's hot," he said cheerfully.

Billy staggered to the sink and feebly poured himself a glass of water.

Tom and Janie watched him, awestruck.

"What's the matter?" asked Billy's father.

Water dribbled down Billy's chin and onto his t-shirt as he drank. His mind swam. Poison?

Paralysis? Extreme lussitude?

"Tom," said Billy's father, "what's going on?"

Tom pointed at the letter lying on the table.

Billy's father read it, smiled, glanced at Billy, and getting a beer out of the refrigerator, sat down at the table.

"Well," he said to Billy. "So it fooled you, eh?"

"Fooled me?" croaked Billy.

THE FOURTEENTH WORM

"But how could Alan and Joe know all those medical words, Mr Forrester?" said Tom. "Lumbricus coreopsis? Fulmar?"

"Do you know what fulmar really means?"

Tom and Billy shook their heads.

"It means a bird, a seabird, I think."

"Wow," said Billy, disgusted. He sat back down at the table and picked up his sandwich.

"They could be arrested, Mr Forrester," said Tom. "Couldn't they be arrested for defrauding the post? Couldn't they?"

Billy grinned and bit down on the peanut butter and fried worm sandwich.

THE FIFTEENTH...

Standing on a rusty pail, Billy peered through a crack into the horse barn. Joe was wandering about lashing at cobwebs with a stick; Alan was slumped on a barrel, gnawing his thumbnail.

Billy went around to the door.

"Hi," he said.

Alan didn't look up.

"Hi," said Joe.

Billy glanced around suspiciously.

"Take it easy," said Joe. "We concede. At least I do. He's still trying to think up something." He pointed at Alan with the stick.

"Where's Tom?" said Billy.

"He wouldn't eat his lunch, so his mother kept him in."

Billy leaned over the platter on the orange crate and smelled the steaming Southern fried worm.

"He wanted to load it with red pepper," said Joe, "but I wouldn't let him."

Billy forked ketchup, mustard, and piccalilli onto the platter, cut a piece of worm, dipped it in the glop, stuck it in his mouth, chewed nervously... swallowed...cut another  piece... The worm tasted better than usual, sort of like kidney beans, Southern fried kidney beans.

"Where'd you get this one?"

"Down behind Bannerman's," said Joe.

"From the muck!" yelled Alan. "The muck! Gooey, slimy, stagnant muck!"

Billy grinned. "Yeah? You'll have to show me. This is the best one yet."

Alan jumped up and kicked the barrel clattering

into a stall. Joe shrugged at Billy, grinning. Billy held up the last bit.

"Ta-rahhh."

He swallowed it.

"OK, lemme look," said Alan. "Come on." He peered into Billy's mouth.

"Oh, no. Come on. There's some still stuck between your teeth there."

Billy sucked noisily at his teeth.

"OK?"

Alan's shoulders slumped.

"I can't get the money till tomorrow," he said. "Oh, geez. You know my dad will make me work every Saturday for six months to pay it back into my savings account."

He trudged slowly toward the door.

"Comin', Joe?"

"Yeah, maybe your father won't act so bad if I'm there when you tell him."

Alan stopped at the door.

"Tomorrow?" he said without turning. "Ten o'clock?"

He sounded as if he was going to cry.

"Yeah, sure," said Billy. "Make it later if you want."

"Nah. It's not going to do any good putting it off. Come on, Joe."

BURP

Left alone in the barn, Billy hugged himself.

"I won! I won! Fifty pounds. Ha, ha."

He sat down on the crate, grinning.

"Heck, I knew I could do it. Ha. I was so scared at first, waking everybody up in the middle of the night."

He burped – beans.

"I should have made it thirty worms and one hundred pounds. That stupid letter. Joe knew when he was beaten though. Ha. Geez."

BEANS?!!?

He stood up.

How come that burp had tasted like beans? He'd had a hamburger for lunch. And a glass of milk. Then the worm. Say...they couldn't have... ?

He snatched up the platter. Nothing left, just a few crumbs of cornmeal. Craning his neck, his eyes popping out, straining, he...he...burped: beans!

Again: beans!

He burst out of the barn, stumbling over the sill, yelling. Across the field Joe and Alan turned. Alan started to run; Joe grabbed his arm.

"It was a fake!" panted Billy, coming up to them. "You faked it! It wasn't a real worm!"

"Real worm?" said Joe. "What're you talking about?"

"You made a worm!" yelled Billy. "Out of beans! Then tomorrow you were going to say I'd lost. I hadn't eaten fifteen worms – the last one was fake."

"Oh, geez," said Alan. "Come on, will ya?"

"He didn't do it while I was around," said Joe. "You sure? What did you have for lunch?"

"A hamburger and milk."

"Yeah, but where'd you get the hamburger?"

"I don't know. My mother bought it. What difference does that make?"

"Yeah, well, a lot of the hamburgers you get these days has stuff mixed in them. You know, sausage meat, soybeans, bread crumbs. So the butcher makes more money."

"Yeah, yeah, yeah," said Billy. "Sure. But anyway, you come on back. Just to make sure, I'm going to eat another worm."

"Geez, suit yourself. Eat four more. Come on, Alan, let's go. Let him eat what he wants."

THE FIFTEENTH WO...

Billy threw back his head, lowered the worm...
Alan charged around the door! Leaped on
Billy's back! Flung him to the ground! Punching!
Yelling! Jumped up! Grabbed Billy's feet! Dragged
him *bump-bump-bump* across the rough straw-
covered floor to the tool closet! Bundled him
inside! Slammed the door! Locked it!

Silence. Water trickling into the trough outside.
Alan panting...

"What are you gonna do with him?" Joe asked
hoarsely from the doorway.

"IF HE'S IN THE CLOSET, HE CAN'T EAT
THE WORM, CAN HE?"

"You're crazy. He'll start to yell. His parents'll
hear him."

"YEAH? YEAH?"

Alan's hair was mussed; his shirt-tail hung out.

"Yeah," said Joe, eyeing him. "He will. He'll start to yell and his parents will hear him."

Alan glanced wildly about...started toward the door...turned...

"Not if we put him down the cistern."

"The cistern?" Joe wiped his mouth. "Alan, cut it out. It's only fifty pounds. Come on. Face it. You've lost. You can't put Billy down in that cistern all by himself. Suppose there's water in it? It's fifteen feet deep."

"We can lower him down with a rope."

BANG! BANG! BANG! BANG! BANG!

Billy was kicking the tool closet door.

"LEMME OUT! HELP! LEMME OUT! IT'S CHEATING! HELP! I wanna get out, I wanna get out, I wanna get out—"

BANG! BANG! BANG! BANG!

He chanted rhythmically, kicking the door with both feet in time with his chant.

Alan ran across the barn and grabbing hold of a beam, skidding to a stop, began to kick aside the hay and trash which littered the planks over the old cistern.

BANG! BANG! BANG! BANG!

"I wanna get out, I wanna get out, I wanna get out—"

"Come on!" Alan yelled at Joe. "Help me! We were all down in it last year. How's it gonna hurt him? Come on. It'll work. I'll split with you. Get some rope."

BANG! BANG! BANG! BANG!

"I wanna get out, I—"

OUT OF THE FRYING PAN INTO THE OVEN

On his knees, yanking at the planks which covered the old cistern, thinking, I've got him. I've got him. I win. He'll never... Alan felt a hand grip his shoulder, glanced up,

"WHAT THE DEVIL IS GOING ON IN HERE?" Mr Forrester shouted down at him.

BANG! BANG! BANG! BANG! "I wanna—"

A confused babble of voices, dying out suddenly.

"Now," said Mr Forrester. "Alan and Joe: home! Scoot."

Alan and Joe crowded out the door.

"I've won!" crowed Billy. He danced towards the platter. "Nothing can—"

"Billy! Up to your room!"

"I've just got to eat this worm, Dad. Ho, ho, I've won! I've won!"

"BILLY! Up to your ROOM!"

"Dad, I—"

His father pointed.

"Dad, if I don't eat what's left, I'll lose; Alan'll win. It's just two—"

"Now. The bet is over. You know what I've told you about that cistern. NOW!"

"Dad, I'll lose! I'll lose! Alan'll—"

"Then you will learn something. March!"

"You mean I can't even eat that last little bit? How long could it take me? What could—"

"Billy. Now."

$%//!?B<small>LIP</small>*/&!

Billy kicked the bed.

He'd won. All he'd had to do was eat two more bites, two bites.

He kicked the wall.

What had his father got so mad for? Alan had started opening the cistern, not him.

Geez, he hadn't even let him explain. Twice. Twice he'd won and then something had happened.

And now he was going to lose? After all he'd gone through? Nightmares, fights, thinking he'd been poisoned? All for nothing?

He kicked the bed.

THE UNITED STATES CAVALRY RIDES OVER THE HILLTOP

"Mrs Forrester?" said Tom, peering through the screen door. "Could I see Billy for a minute?"

"He's up in his room being punished, Tom. He and Joe and Alan were very naughty this afternoon."

"Yeah?" said Tom. "No kidding? What did they do?"

THE FIFTEENTH WORM

Billy kicked the wall again.

Two minutes. What difference could two minutes have made?

He leaned his forehead against the windowpane, gazing dejectedly out into the backyard.

That's what always happened – somebody...

Tom's younger brother Pete appeared suddenly around the corner of the house, running, holding up a little yellow Easter basket...gesturing?

THE WORM! TOM! Pete had brought him a worm! The fifteenth worm!

Billy slammed up the window.

"Catch!" yelled Pete. "Hurry! Tom's talking to your mother!"

He heaved a brick with a string tied to it up to

Billy; Billy caught it, hauled the string up hand over hand, the basket came bobbing up the side of the house. Alan and Joe plunged out of the bushes... Billy snatched the tin can out of the Easter basket, plucked out a huge, squirming night-crawler...

"MRS FORRESTER! MRS FORRESTER!"

Alan and Joe shouted at the top of their lungs, dancing about on the lawn, waving their arms.

"MRS FORRESTER! MRS FORRESTER!"

"TOO LATE!" yelled Billy gleefully.

Throwing back his head, he dripped the squirming nightcrawler into his mouth...chewed and chewed. Tom and Mrs Forrester appeared around the corner of the house.

"Too glate!" Billy yelled, still chewing. "Too glate! I gwin!"

CONTENTS

FOREWORD

S IR Stanley Unwin is universally regarded, along
with Alfred Knopf and a handful of others, as one
of the most important publishers who ever lived.
In a career of over a half century, Unwin launched one
of Britain's greatest publishing houses and published
such books as Thor Heyerdahl's best-seller *Kon Tiki*;
introduced the work of Sigmund Freud to English-
speaking readers; published Gandhi, Nehru, and other
leaders of the Indian independence movement; and was
a close associate and longtime publisher of the great
English philosopher and humanist Bertrand Russell.
No small part of Sir Stanley's reputation rests upon this
classic testament to his craft—*The Truth About Publishing*.

Born in 1884, Unwin first learned publishing under
his step-uncle, T. Fisher Unwin; he ran the sales functions of the elder Unwin's publishing house but left after
a falling-out with his patrician relative. After a trip
around the world (spending much of his time studying
publishing practices abroad), Unwin returned to England on the eve of World War I and purchased the assets
of the near-defunct George Allen & Co.—publisher of
Ruskin. The firm became George Allen & Unwin and
under his stewardship became increasingly profitable
and influential. Unwin was president of the Publishers
Association of Great Britain from 1933 to 1935, and
twice president of the International Publishers Association, from 1936 to 1938 and from 1946 to 1954. He
collected a dazzling assortment of honors: member of

the French Academy, Officer of the Order of Orange Nassau, Order of the White Lion of Czechoslovakia, and many others.

Throughout his career he was well known even outside publishing circles for his resolution in widening the influence of books in general, and for his commitment to publishing freedoms around the globe. He was knighted in 1946.

But to call Sir Stanley Unwin a great publisher sidesteps the key question of just what a publisher is. It is harder to define than one might think. For in the course of a day a publisher may decide to publish a manuscript, reject a half dozen others, conclude a jacket design is all wrong, tell an author why his book has been remaindered, argue with a customs official, read a sub-licensing contract, sign checks, encourage an employee, exhort a salesman to push a book harder, write catalog copy, object to a typesetting bill, ponder where to advertise a new book, and long for a crystal ball to tell him how many copies a book will sell, and how many therefore he should print. A publisher, then, is the sum of many, many parts, all having to do in some way with the business of creating and selling books. No one better embodied the figure of book publisher than Sir Stanley Unwin. He remains "the publisher's publisher."

The first edition of *The Truth About Publishing* appeared in 1926. It was quickly hailed as something of a classic—wide-ranging, detailed, and brimming with wisdom on the central questions of the business. It was translated into fourteen languages from German, Spanish, and French to Czech, Turkish, and Bengali.

The book was updated periodically by Sir Stanley until 1960, and updated again—after Sir Stanley's death in 1968—by his nephew Philip Unwin, in 1976. The present edition reprints the 1960 edition exactly, this being the last edition to which Sir Stanley Unwin himself set his hand. Since that time the nature of getting books before the public has changed even more than it did during Unwin's illustrious career; yet the publishing wisdom underlying this book—the "truth" about publishing—remains fresh as a new-bound book.

Many of the technical aspects of book publishing Sir Stanley describes are relevant no more. His comments on typesetting, for example, are curiosities now in an age of computer design and page makeup—such as the notion that a manuscript may be "simultaneously set up by half a dozen compositors" or that printers charges are based upon setting 1,000 en's; or the complexities of "moulds and stereoplates" used to render illustrations. Despite the many changes in the process of making books, however, *The Truth* still delivers a rich lode of publishing fundamentals: a cast-off is still what it was for Sir Stanley, and is still called that today; although the Monotype machine has gone the way of the manual typewriter, his comments on the esthetics of type (". . . it is as easy to detect whether the design of a book has been thought out as to decide whether a man's suit has been specially cut for him") remain golden; so too his observations on the competing forces of handsome, open design, and economy.

Likewise, Unwin's advice on publishing agreements—when especially detailed—is largely irrelevant today. The sale of copyright, for example, is almost unheard of now, as is the notion of a profit-sharing arrangement with an author, in lieu of a royalty contract. You will no longer find "Colonial edition" printed on the title page of an English book sold in America, nor would many publishers today state that Portuguese rights are readily marketable. But such issues make up the minutiae of the publishing business, subject to change all the time. Any technical obsolescence in *The Truth* has no effect on the book's abiding good sense.

For if Unwin's advice about many such issues is outdated, he is unerringly right—and his counsel is timeless—in matters of publisher-author relations, on the instincts that should guide marketing and promotional campaigns, on the "role" of the publisher, and many other concerns. Publishers, authors, and booksellers all face the same set of problems today as they did in Sir Stanley's time: the competition for media attention in a crowded marketplace, the unpredictability of public taste, the suspicion that often overhangs the dialog between publisher and author. Most remarkable of all is the keenness with which Sir Stanley identifies and analyzes the key problems of book publishing—the ones that echo in the minds of book people today. His "Preface to Authors," for example, remains some of the best advice to new and would-be writers ever given, for it strikes a sympathetic balance between the concerns of publisher and author:

"Your manuscript is your baby, maybe your only child, but the publisher finds a dozen or so new babies on his doorstep every morning . . ."

"A 10 per cent. royalty that arrives the day it is due is better than a 20 per cent. royalty that is never forthcoming."

"The fact that a best seller or a cheap reprint is on a railway bookstall is no reason why your book should be. It will not become a best seller just because it is put on a bookstall. . . ."

His advice for fellow publishers is even more telling. Many publishers must often wish they could have remembered the following words:

"If an edition of three thousand copies represents the demand there is for some book, there is obviously no point in printing thirty thousand, even though the thirty thousand copies could each be produced infinitely more cheaply than would be possible were one-tenth the number printed."

Or these:

"The best [sales] representative is the man who, having interested his customer in the books that are being offered to him, persuades him to take the maximum he can safely buy, and no more."

"Not until the book is produced does the chief work of publishing begin."

"The wise publisher realizes there is an individuality behind each book, just as the wise schoolmaster realizes the different individuality of every boy in his school."

"The amount of [review] space devoted to a book is sometimes more important than what is said about it."

"If a book is not selling and shows no sign of selling, no amount of advertising will make it sell to any extent commensurate with the expenditure."

The Truth About Publishing is chock-full of similar nuggets that showcase Unwin's wide-ranging mind. One reads this book amazed at the breadth of Sir Stanley's knowledge of his craft. The subtleties of handling an author's ego, the hard-headed realities of paper costs and binding prices, the minute details of publishing agreements not only in his native Britain but in the United States, Scandinavia, Japan, and elsewhere—all were grist for his insatiable curiosity about the book business. How many publishing people in our specialized world know as much about contracts as they do about how type is set or how signatures are folded? Sir Stanley Unwin did—but still believed that "it is not till after a wide experience of ten or fifteen years that a publisher realizes most keenly how much there is to learn."

No one can learn all there is to know about book publishing from this book, or from any other. Publishing is at once an art, a craft, and a business, in equal and often competing measures; like parenthood, it must be experienced to be appreciated. Publishers find themselves continually hopping back and forth across the dividing line between a book that does good and one that does well, striving to have the book do both. Well-written books often sell poorly, and many best-sellers are not fine literature, but the capable publisher recognizes the need to bring all sorts of books into the world without burdening them with moral judgments. Publishers know all too well that commercial and artistic success is never awarded evenhandedly. One thing *is* certain—the first job of any publisher is to stay in business, and the field is littered with the remains of publishing houses that have failed. Publishers who have learned how to make the book business profitable often have the scars to prove it.

Ideally, at the end of the day, the publisher can tell himself that he has left some fair number of people a little better informed, entertained, or even moved, and his company enriched—the better able to publish the phenomenal new author whose masterpiece might arrive in the next day's mail. It is an endlessly fascinating job, propelled by the competing forces of art and commerce—of how worthy are the books you publish, and how many you can sell. The best publishers seem born to it, loving every minute of the busy publishing day. Sir Stanley Unwin was such a publisher, and his spiritual descendants exist today in countless publishing houses, large and small, "corporate" and more personal, in every country. But if you can't learn publishing from a book, *The Truth* will do more than any other to foster the hard, gut publishing sense that every maker of books ought to have. It serves as a field guide for anyone involved in the publishing process—authors, editors, marketers, agents, rights or publicity or production people—to learn more about how essential they are to the complex machinery of a publishing house. Above all, *The Truth* is a revealing glimpse into the mind of the publishing creature who most defies definition, yet who acts as the linchpin of the entire world of books—the publisher. Read from one of the great ones, and learn.

—Peter Burford

PREFACE TO AUTHORS

PUBLISHERS are not necessarily either philanthropists or rogues. Likewise they are usually neither lordly magnates nor cringing beggars. As a working hypothesis, regard them as ordinary human beings trying to earn their living at an unusually difficult occupation. (It is easy to become a publisher, but difficult to remain one; the mortality in infancy is higher than in any other trade or profession.)

Remember that it is in your work that the publisher is primarily interested. Let your manuscript therefore be your ambassador and do not mar its chances by insisting upon a quite unnecessary interview. The publisher will request you to call fast enough if he finds your work attractive.

Your manuscript may be a masterpiece, but do not suggest that to the publisher, because many of the most hopeless manuscripts that have come his way have probably been so described by their authors. The works of genius are apt to arrive unheralded, and it is for those that the publisher is looking.

Your manuscript is your baby, maybe your only child, but the publisher finds a dozen or so new babies on his doorstep every morning and has several thousand older children over-running his warehouse and his entire establishment, all of them calling simultaneously for his undivided attention.

With the best will in the world, therefore, there is a definite limit to the time he can spend on yours. Every moment of the publisher's time you waste on needless interviews may be a moment less for the more important task of attending to your offspring.

If you want your manuscript to make a good impression, bestow some care upon it and don't ask the publisher to look at it in instalments. Outward appearances do not matter, but slovenliness and inconsistency do. The fact that a manuscript is dog-eared does not distress a publisher, but the fact that a proper name is seldom spelt twice running in the same way; that a word capitalized on one page is not capitalized on the next; that the first and third chapters have headings, but the second none; that quotations are inaccurately given; that, in brief, the author has skimped his job, makes the worst possible impression upon the publisher as well as upon the publisher's reader. A little extra time spent on the preparation of the MS is worth more to the author than the longest interview with a publisher, or any letter of introduction.

Bear in mind that in common with all human beings, publishers are fallible. They all, I imagine, wish they were not, but they all know (and admit) that they are. 'Publishing fallibility' is too expensive an item in his trading account for any publisher to be in danger of overlooking it. If a publisher declines your manuscript, remember it is merely the decision of one fallible human being, and try another. Don't try to bully the first publisher into telling you why he declined it. He would, in most cases, be a fool to tell you, because, despite fervid assurances to the contrary, not one author in a hundred wants aught but praise for his offspring. One common error may be worth mentioning—the failure of the author to make up his mind at what public he is aiming. Consistency in this matter is essential.

If a publisher accepts your manuscript, remember that in the long run it is the public which decides what the reward of authorship shall be; that the public is a fickle paymaster, and that if it decides to reward handsomely some disher-up of scandal, and to grant the learned historian or philosopher nothing, the publisher is not to blame. If the public will not buy your book the publisher cannot make money either for you or himself. The source of profit, strange as it is to be compelled to reiterate the fact, is the difference between what a book costs to manufacture and what the booksellers pay the publisher for it. A profit cannot be made out of selling a book for what it costs to produce. It is astonishing how many authors think that it can; who assume, in fact, that the laws of arithmetic do not apply to publishers.

All that glitters is not gold. The most effective advertiser is not usually the most showy, just as the most efficient doctor is not often the one with the largest doorplate. The widespread distribution of a book in every corner of the globe does not begin and end with advertisements in two Sunday papers. It is a process laboriously built up brick by brick. It is one thing to be able to sell a book for ten or twelve weeks— quite another to do so for ten or twelve years. These are points to bear in mind when choosing your publisher, but there are others. Does he *really* know his job? If he does, trust him to get on with it; if he does not, do not go to him. Is he financially sound—beyond a peradventure? If he is, the hardest bargain he may drive is likely to prove more profitable to you than the most alluring contract with an insolvent firm. A 10 per cent royalty that arrives the day it is due is better than a 20 per cent royalty that is never forthcoming.

The most stable firms are usually those which have a strong back list of publications with a continuous and profitable sale and who therefore have no need to gamble to secure new business.

Having chosen your publisher, co-operate with him, but do not start out to teach him his job. It is not co-operating, but positively hindering him, to ring him up on the telephone when a post card or a letter would be equally or probably more effective. Never bother the head of a firm with a departmental job. If lengthy instructions must be given over the telephone (they should in any case be confirmed in writing) ask a shorthand-typist to take them down.

Just as you can take a horse to the water but cannot make it drink, a publisher can take a new book to a bookseller, but cannot make him buy. Over twenty thousand new books are published every year, and booksellers can of necessity only stock a selection of them. Because your friends affect surprise that your book is not in stock at the local newsagent, there is no need for you to do so.

The fact that a best-seller or a cheap reprint is on a railway bookstall is no reason why your book should be. It will not become a best-seller just because it is put on a bookstall; it is much more likely to become soiled stock. The railway bookstall proprietors, who see all the new books, know better than anyone else what they can and cannot sell, and if they decide against yours, the chances are at least a hundred to one upon their being right.

Every new book issued by a well-established publisher is shown before publication to the London booksellers and either before publication or shortly thereafter to all the principal booksellers in the provinces. This process takes time which it is most unwise to curtail. The fact that the particular bookseller's assistant you interviewed had never heard of your book is no evidence that your publisher was negligent. On the contrary, it may merely mean on the one hand that when the book was 'subscribed' the bookseller declined it, or on the other that the assistant is not following the lists of new publications in the book trade papers as carefully as he might. But any bookseller or bookstall ought to be able to execute an order for your book promptly, and if any difficulty is experienced your publisher should be immediately informed.

Despite all impressions to the contrary, the selling of new books is seldom a lucrative business; too few people *buy* them. Possibly you have observed that even your own friends and acquaintances unblushingly try to 'cadge' copies of your books. Pocket your pride (or your snobbery!) and tell them boldly that if they don't think the book worth buying, you would rather they did not read it; and do your part in educating the public into a deeper appreciation of books by joining the National Book League and working for it.

In writing this book it has been my endeavour to examine controversial questions as impartially as possible, and always with the hope of finding common ground, rather than points of disagreement.

The growing commercialization of literature—inevitable though it may be—does not tend to promote more harmonious relations between authors and publishers. It is based on the assumption that manuscripts and books are mere commodities; dead, not living things. Such an assumption ignores the peculiar and indeed parental relationship of the author to his work, the realization of which is the beginning of wisdom in a publisher.

I hope that in my zeal to explain the publisher's difficulties I have not shown any lack of sympathy with authors. I can truthfully say that this book would have been a good deal easier to write had I not seen their point of view so clearly.

It was primarily in the hope of helping inexperienced writers to understand some of the technicalities of publishing and thereby to assist them that I allowed myself to be persuaded by several of their number to provide this brief account of book publishing.

If I have succeeded in making the path of the beginner a little smoother, and contributed in any way towards the promotion of pleasanter and more intelligent relations between authors and publishers, I shall be well rewarded.

Two last points: If a publisher has had enough faith in you to go on losing money over the publication of your early and possibly immature work, it is not cricket either to take your first readily saleable MS elsewhere without submitting it to him or to expect him to bid for it in competition with others who have not spent a penny in helping to establish your reputation. It is even more unsporting to ask a literary agent to kick away on your behalf the ladder which has enabled you to climb.

Finally, read your contract and remember that your publisher is just as much entitled to expect you to honour your signature as you are to insist upon him honouring his.

———————

Of all the inanimate objects, of all men's creations, books are the nearest to us, for they contain our very thought, our ambitions, our indignations, our illusions, our fidelity to truth and our persistent leaning toward error.

JOSEPH CONRAD IN 'NOTES ON LIFE AND LETTERS'

INTRODUCTION TO THE SEVENTH EDITION

THE changes there have been in the publishing world since this book was first published in 1926, let alone since I began my book trade career in January 1904, are startling. If the publishers of those days could come back they would be overwhelmed by its present-day complications. They would find it no longer a comparatively simple occupation, but a highly technical one, and they would be appalled by the interminable form-filling and endless governmental regulations. The amount of unpaid work carried out at the behest of authorities, of some of whom they had never heard, they would find incredible.

By comparison the westward move from Paternoster Row to the neighbourhood of the British Museum, and even the westward trend in publishing and the worship of best-sellers, would seem unimportant, though some aspects of the commercialization of literature would be distasteful to them.

What I hope they would appreciate are the improved typography, the brighter jackets and the higher standard of translations, even if they could not immediately reconcile themselves to the fact that the book trade is now beginning to be efficiently organized instead of having no organization at all.

In this seventh edition the most important changes are due to the Brussels revisions of the Berne Convention, the Universal Copyright Convention, the

British Copyright Act of 1956, the new American Copyright Act, the Defamation Act 1952, the Restrictive Trade Practices Act 1956, the alteration in markets, in the terms and conditions of supply, and the new book-production processes. There can have been few periods when the book trade has been so affected by legislative activities as in the last ten years, mostly, I am happy to say, beneficial.

The importance of books has been increasingly recognized, and their status correspondingly enhanced, which is the most important thing of all, because so many of our troubles have arisen through their treatment as 'just another commodity'. Even today, that is the cause of the persistence of many of the obstructions to 'the free flow of books' against which UNESCO and the International Publishers Association are continually waging battle.

The statement is so often made that 'Publishers don't deserve considerate treatment as long as they continue to produce so much trash', that it seems desirable to inquire 'What is trash?' Has a minority of intelligent people—let alone a censor—any right to impose its literary judgments upon a less intelligent or even unintelligent majority?

We all know that 'one man's meat is another man's poison'. Is it not possible that one man's treasure is another man's trash, and that it is best for each of us to choose our own mental diet? There are doubtless officials who in connection with our daily fare would like to prescribe the precise foodstuffs of which our 2,700 calories, or whatever it may be, should consist. In theory it might even be good for us, but in practice we all recognize the desirability and necessity of individual choice.

If those who complain would take the trouble to examine the imprints of books, they would have a clearer insight of the problem. Happily it is still the publishers of distinction and repute who are responsible for the major part of British book production. It has been estimated that if the term be used in its widest sense, 70 per cent of book paper consumption is for educational books. Of much of this vast stream the public is completely unaware. There are, in fact, important educational publishers whose output is never seen except by teachers and their pupils or university professors and their students. But does anyone suggest that we ought to confine ourselves to books of purely educational value? Even people of outstanding intelligence, like the late Earl Balfour, feel the need of mental relaxation, even though it does not necessarily, as it did in his case, take the form of a regular dose of detective fiction. The strictest censor would not, I imagine, regard 20 per cent as an unreasonable margin for good quality books of what may be termed entertainment or escapist type; and it is probable that under present conditions that is just about what we get. Somewhere between 8 and 10 per cent consists of the wide category of books, including poetry, essays, plays, which does not come under either of the previous headings.

This means that the percentage of books which some regard as trash is trifling—certainly less than 2 per cent, probably not even 1 per cent.

We are unduly conscious of this minute percentage

because it represents the scum on the surface of the stream, visible to all, but without significance in relation to the deep current below.

Now that we have defeated one form of totalitarianism only to be confronted with another, is the existence of a little trash too heavy a price to pay to avoid censorship and to retain that '. . . liberty when free born men having to advise the public may speak free'? One thing is certain: if we decline to pay that modest price our days of liberty are numbered.

Publishing, or perhaps I ought to say, Book-Publishing, is quite different from what most people apparently suppose. The young man who regards it as a pleasantly dilettante occupation suitable for someone who does not know what he wants to do but likes books, is under an illusion. If it is not a profession, it is as Mr Raymond Mortimer aptly said, 'at once an art, a craft, and a business', for which a curious and unusual combination of qualifications is desirable.

There is, of course, the literary background; the knowledge of the literature of the subject with which the publisher is dealing, and, equally important, where to turn for that knowledge. But something much more than knowledge is needed, namely judgment, and what for want of a better word I can only call *flair*, in the selection of the MSS to be published and the number of copies it is expedient to print.

Then there is the technical knowledge of paper, printing, binding, blockmaking, etc., connected with the physical production of books—a knowledge which needs to be associated with taste.

But if the publisher is to do justice to the books he

has selected and produced, he must finally be able to market them, not merely at home, but throughout the world. The publisher who is without knowledge of book trade organization is gravely handicapped. Furthermore, just as an adequate knowledge of printing cannot be acquired without spending time in a printing works, a really effective knowledge of overseas markets cannot be acquired without visiting them.

Then there is a certain legal equipment which is almost indispensable—an ability to draft agreements— some knowledge of the law of copyright, which, surprising as it may sound, very, very few lawyers possess, and (otherwise you will pay for it dearly) some knowledge of the law of libel.

In brief then the publisher's task is no simple one; the whole process of book publication has become, as I have said, highly complicated. It is more exacting and calls for technical knowledge of a wider range, and for a higher standard of efficiency than is generally realized.

This will, I think, become clear if I set forth as simply as possible the whole process of book publishing from start to finish. My object is not to teach publishing (it cannot be learnt so easily as that!), but to give information to those outside the trade, and particularly to all devoted to literature, whether as writers or readers.

CHAPTER I

THE ARRIVAL OF MANUSCRIPTS

LET us begin at the beginning: the arrival of the MSS—the solicited and the unsolicited—which pour in daily upon the successful and the old-established publishers, at times in almost overwhelming numbers. For that is the real beginning, as I never cease to tell prospective authors, and not, as is generally assumed, an interview with the publisher at which the author holds forth—often at great length—about the merits of his work. Such interviews are almost invariably a waste of time, and should be deferred until the publisher has had an opportunity of studying the MS. An unknown author, who insists upon a personal interview beforehand with a principal of the firm, is prejudicing, not advancing, his cause. The best and the only introduction needed to a book publisher is a marketable MS, or, if not readily marketable, a work of intrinsic merit. If any explanations are called for, they should be stated as concisely as possible in a letter accompanying the MS. That letter, which will probably be handed or sent to the 'reader' with the MS, and will subsequently be attached to his report, affords an opportunity to summarize any relevant facts likely to influence the publisher's judgment. A statement that the author's aunt thinks him a budding genius is not helpful, but the information that she could ensure the adoption of the work as a textbook in several important schools or colleges might be.

The fact that Mr Smith has promised to review the book (if published) in the *Daily Blank* is probably not worth mentioning at that stage, because the publisher is accustomed to having most of his books noticed by Mr Jones, if not by Mr Smith, in the *Daily Blank*, and is therefore not impressed. But the statement that 2,457 copies of the author's previous book were sold in India in the first six months following publication, because of his wide connections over there, would be of great significance.

Now as to the MS itself—first and most essential, it should have the author's name and address clearly written upon it, preferably both at the beginning and the end. If there is a folder or outer case it should also bear the title of the MS and the author's name. This sounds obvious, but more than half the MSS that reach a publisher bear no address upon them, and an appreciable number no author's name; still more remarkable, some have no title or title-page. When on August 4, 1914, my firm—George Allen & Unwin Ltd.—took over the assets of the late firm of George Allen & Co. Ltd., among my first discoveries were half a dozen or more manuscripts which it was not possible to identify and for which there were no claimants.

I have said that an author's MS is the best introduction, but that presupposes that some little attention has been given to the condition of the MS. An author would not, I imagine, feel it essential to visit a publisher in a new silk hat and a coat of the latest cut, but most authors at least would consider it undesirable to

approach a publisher in a dirty and incoherent condition. But that is, in effect, what they do when they
submit a dirty and dilapidated MS, in bad writing, or
so besprinkled with corrections and alterations as to be
indecipherable. Any MS that has been much handled
is bound to show signs of wear, but if the first and last
sheets are occasionally retyped—and all MSS should
be typed and a carbon copy retained—there will be
nothing to prejudice a reader. Theoretically, of course,
nothing concerns the reader except the substance of the
work; but he would scarcely be human were he not
influenced, unconsciously at any rate, by the illegibility
of the MS. It is a purely utilitarian standard I advocate
for MSS, i.e. fitness for their purpose. A spotless, typed
MS is a nightmare to all who handle it, if it consists of
several hundred unattached sheets or if it is on paper
of some awkward size. Ordinary quarto paper is the
recognized size, and there would seem to be no need in
most cases to depart from it. Stiff, slippery paper or thin
tissue paper should be avoided, and the typing should,
of course, be on one side of the paper only and be in
double spacing. Although the pages should be numbered 1 to the end consecutively it is wise to fasten
together each chapter, not binding the whole MS up in
one tight fastening, which makes the book irksome to
read and tiresome to turn over. A complete MS taste-
fully bound in morocco would fill me with as much
distrust as would an overdressed dandy. I should feel
confident that that was the only form in which the
manuscript was destined to be preserved.

In many publishing businesses the receiving of
MSS and the recording of their dispatch to readers is

entrusted exclusively to one assistant, because divided responsibility would be fatal. It is this assistant's function—

1. to acknowledge receipt of the MS on a form setting forth that, whilst every care is taken of MSS, the publisher does not hold himself responsible in case of accidental loss, etc.;
2. to record the day of receipt and the name and address of the sender;
3. to enter any special instructions regarding the return of the MS, e.g. whether sufficient postage had been pre-paid to cover registration;
4. to fill in the name of the reader to whom it was sent;
5. to record the date on which it was sent to the reader, and the date of its return;
6. to enter other details such as: the initials of the partner or director who is to see the MS after it has been reported upon by one or more readers; whether the reader's fee has been paid; the name of the printers, if the MS has been sent them for 'cast off', etc.;
7. to make an independent record of any illustrations which accompanied the MS, as it is wiser to treat them as a separate item.

So important is it that this record should be both complete and accurate, that many publishers never handle a manuscript until it has been properly entered. The first thing I do after the departure of a visitor who has left a MS with me, is to send it to the proper department, so that it may start its journey aright— and I do this, even though I intend taking the MS home with me that evening. Even when the utmost punctiliousness is observed, manuscripts go astray; and, in view of the number that pass in and out of a big publisher's office, it is astonishing, not that a few are temporarily mislaid, but that it is a rare event in a well-managed concern for one to be irretrievably lost.

The most frequent cause of trouble is two MSS being treated as one in the packing department—a thing that is liable to occur in rush hours, when two short MSS which resemble one another happen to be placed together. On the only two occasions when I really thought a MS was lost, this had occurred, and in both cases it took over three months and more than a hundred letters to track down the missing MS. Everyone to whom the MS could conceivably have been sent was written to. In one of the cases, the recipient was abroad, and our letter and the parcel had remained unopened; but in the other—will anybody believe it?—the author who received the strayed MS deliberately kept it and said nothing; in order, as he boasted, to see how long it would be before we found out!

The MS, having been duly entered, has now to be read, and the exact procedure varies according to the publisher's organization and the nature of the MS. Some publishers keep a permanent reader or readers on the staff, others have outside readers; many have both. Some MSS require no 'reading' at all in the ordinary sense. If Bertrand Russell writes a new book on Philosophy, his publisher does not need to take advice about the competence of the work. Similarly, MSS by established clients of the firm, or solicited MSS, do not need any 'sifting'. They are usually accepted without more ado, and are generally looked through at once by one of the heads of the firm.

Where there is a reader on the staff, the task of sorting the MSS is apt to fall to him—those on special subjects are sent to specialist readers—e.g. works on philosophy would be sent to some leading professor of philosophy in whose judgment the publisher had learnt to place confidence.

In the case of my own firm, every MS which comes in is actually handled by myself when in London or by our editor or one of my fellow directors when I am abroad. In every case there is a written report from our editor or an outside reader. In doubtful cases there may be as many as three or four written opinions. These reports are filed with the relevant correspondence, so that they are readily available years later, if need be.

Special attention is given by the better publishers to the work of beginners. If it shows promise but is not up to publication standard the wisest advice the publisher can give to the author may be to put the MS aside for six months and then to read it again. Three months may suffice. Such advice is, however, seldom taken. Artists do not expect their first immature drawings to be immediately acquired by a gallery for permanent exhibition; but it is astonishing how many would-be authors expect their first prentice work to be immortalized and how few are prepared to exercise the patience of Robert Louis Stevenson. If they could be persuaded to wait until their books were good enough to be accepted by a publisher of repute, instead of, as sometimes, paying a firm of no standing to rush them out, they themselves would benefit and much would be gained all round.

The quality of the unsolicited MSS is not high. The large proportion of hopeless and indifferent material makes any merit stand out. Under present conditions, it is improbable that any really promising manuscript fails to find a publisher in the long run, for the competition to detect any sign of genius is far too great.

The idea that publishers return MSS unread and are *not* interested in the work of beginners is a delusion that I suppose will never be eradicated from some minds; but that it is a delusion a day spent in any competent book publisher's office would effectually demonstrate because a supply of MSS is the life-blood of the business.

Some authors have most elaborate devices whereby they can prove that such and such a page has never been read. They overlook Dr Johnson's wise remark that 'it is unnecessary to eat the whole ox to find out whether the beef is tough'. Others are sufficiently foolish to submit a brief article on, let us say, 'Make-up for teen-agers' to a publisher of learned historical and philosophical works. How long, I wonder, do they think it takes that publisher to decide that the MS is unsuitable?

My own firm publishes no magazines, but scarcely a week goes by without our receiving MSS much too short for anything but magazine publication. Even some literary agents, who obviously should know better, are not altogether immune from similar absent-mindedness, though in their case there is more often failure to single out the particular firm or firms most likely to be interested in any given class of book. I recall, in particular, a MS by a distinguished author, which was never published merely because his autocratic agent offered it to almost every publisher in London except the two who because of its character would have taken it. I would therefore impress upon authors the wisdom of the late W. B. Maxwell's advice to study publishers' lists and to take pains themselves to choose a suitable firm for their work. Information as to the standing of the firm should be sought from the Authors' Society, rather than from an agent, because there are bad and indifferent agents as well as a few exceedingly good ones; and with some even of the better known, several of the most successful publishers have as little to do as possible.

Few authors, I imagine, realize that on an average each MS received by a publisher, whether rejected, as the majority are bound to be, or accepted, costs the publisher *at least* two guineas, and, indeed, a great deal more, if the working expenses could be accurately computed. If the MSS summarily rejected on the ground of hopeless illiteracy, unsuitability of subject or length, were disregarded in arriving at the average, the cost per MS would be still larger. But, despite this fact, it is rarely that a publisher will refuse to consider a MS that sounds at all possible. There could, I think, be no better evidence of the keenness of the competition to secure good literary material.

The number of people who consider themselves fully qualified for the post of publisher's reader is unlimited. The number of those really competent to fulfil that function is extraordinarily small. It is not easy to define precisely what is required. Some firms would say 'ability to spot winners', and leave it at that; but a list consisting of nothing but fifth-rate best-sellers, though highly profitable, would be a depressing business. To most publishers who are keen on their job the sound literary judgment of an Arnold Bennett would be the first and chief ingredient in an ideal reader, though they would not underrate both the necessity and desirability of throwing in a little of Bennett's commercial acumen and *flair*.

I imagine that the best and most successful readers, almost without exception, have either had actual experience in a publisher's office, or have acquired an intimate knowledge of publishers' needs. Absence of such experience greatly lessens a reader's value and involves endless additional work for the publisher in explaining why this is practicable and not that, and, in fact, in teaching the reader his job, which is governed by technical and commercial, as well as literary considerations.

Publishers' readers seldom, if ever, get the praise they deserve. The public knows little or nothing about their conscientious and exhausting work, and few are the authors who are prepared to recognize publicly the benefits they have derived from their friendly suggestions and criticisms. The number of MSS completely recast, or improved out of all knowledge, at a reader's suggestion is far greater than is commonly supposed. Usually his advice is accepted and acted upon, as was the case with one of the most successful first novels of this century. Occasionally, to recall an actual experience, the author rejects with scorn a long list of suggested additions and amendments to his MS on the ground that not a comma needs altering, and then a few months later proceeds to publish the book elsewhere with every single suggestion incorporated, and, needless to say, without any acknowledgment. If authors were as prompt to recognize the services of publishers' readers as they are to criticize them, the public would learn with surprise how much it owes to a group of conscientious workers, of whose existence it is barely aware. I had occasion to show one of our reader's reports on a first novel to Sir Compton Mackenzie; to his letter in reply, he added the following postscript:

I wish reviewers would write as good criticism as publishers' readers!

But, let me emphasize, publishers' readers cannot as some folks imagine turn illiterate and worthless MSS into literary masterpieces. The number of would-be authors who expect publishers to give them free tuition in the elements of their craft is astonishing. If a publisher allowed himself to be drawn into correspondence about the thousands of MSS he declines in the course of a year he would have no time left to attend to those he accepted.

The number of reports on any given MS naturally depends upon its character. The very good and the very bad give little trouble, but there is so much that comes between: the competent, but uninspired; the MS that is brilliant in parts; the book that is too good to pass by, but not quite good enough to take. On all these the publisher is called upon to give his casting vote—and how often the publisher's reader thanks heaven that the final decision rests with his employer and not with him. In this connection it is worth remembering that the most successful publisher is the one who makes the fewest mistakes, i.e. incurs the fewest losses.

The considerations which weigh with a publisher are manifold. If his business is a personal one, his list will, in the long run, reflect his own temperament and character. If there are many influences at work, the list will be like one of those composite photographs which are produced from time to time. But there are other factors; the tradition of the house, which influences the character of the mss that are submitted; any sudden success, which will instantaneously give the publisher a reputation for books of the character of the successful one; the enthusiasm of travellers or senior members of the staff for any particular class of book, and, above all, chance, which may bring the most unlooked-for favours. Every publisher hopes that tomorrow will bring him a *Jane Eyre* or some equally undisputed masterpiece.

It is by books that mind speaks to mind, by books the world's intelligence grows; books are the tree of knowledge, which has grown into and twined its branches with those of the tree of life, and of their common fruit men eat and become as gods knowing good and evil.

C. KEGAN PAUL

CHAPTER II

'CASTING OFF' AND ESTIMATING

I N most publishing offices, the next procedure is to negotiate with the author. That is probably due to the fact that in many cases businesses are built up on the publication of novels; and with fiction issued at a uniform price and in a uniform style, rule-of-thumb methods can be followed without great risk. To me this has always seemed an instance of 'putting the cart before the horse', because, until one has made out a fairly accurate estimate of the cost of production and publication, it is impossible to tell what margin there is to share with the author. In theory, it is, of course, possible to have any margin you want by increasing the published price; but, in practice, there are sharp limitations to any such increase. Frequently a book is worth publishing if it can be issued at not exceeding such and such a price, but most certainly destined to failure if issued at a higher price. It has always seemed to me necessary, therefore, and, in fact, a quite obvious procedure, to ascertain *at this point* exactly to what extent the publication is commercially worth while. This involves delay, but leaves one in the happy position of knowing the facts instead of guessing at them. Many propositions which appear tempting before they are tested in this fashion, cease to be attractive thereafter. I could cite plenty of concrete examples, but perhaps it is sufficient to point out that many a good book

32

cannot be published except at a loss solely because of price limitations. For example, in pre-war days 7s 6d was generally recognized as the top price at which any 'juvenile' could be expected to have a substantial sale. There were, of course, exceptions, but, generally speaking, it was fatal, as some of us found at that time, to publish a book intended for children at even such a slightly increased price as 8s 6d. This is typical of books in many categories. Very occasionally the reverse is true, and one can fix a higher price than is really essential without, in any way, impeding the sale, but this is much more rare now than it used to be. Were it a more frequent occurrence, publishers would have greater justification for issuing books which show an insufficient margin. In brief, there is often a 'right price' for a book, and in such cases publication at any other figure would spell failure.

Recognition of this fact often prompts publishers to meet it by the simple but unwise expedient of printing a larger first edition than the probable sales warrant. It must be borne in mind that the cost of composition remains the same whatever the number printed; if therefore, for example, the initial cost of type setting is £200 the cost of that item will be:

£200	per copy if			10	copies are printed
£2	,,	,,	,,	100	,, ,, ,,
4s	,,	,,	,,	1,000	,, ,, ,,
5d	,,	,,	,,	10,000	,, ,, ,,
½d	,,	,,	,,	100,000	,, ,, ,,

any books for which there is a restricted market will for this reason of necessity appear expensive compared with a mass-produced article. With this in mind the production manager probably points out that if double the number were printed, or even if only an extra thousand were printed, there would be no difficulty about publishing at the desired price.

The production manager may well be correct; but to let the desire to publish at a given price determine the number to be printed, instead of the probable demand, is both a snare and a delusion. The amateur publisher constantly makes this mistake and even the most wary publisher is occasionally led into it. In the long run, the sounder policy is to base all estimates upon the probable number required, and to let the cost per copy control the published price regardless of other considerations.

This presupposes a definite and precise ratio between the cost per copy and the published price, and the strength of mind resolutely to pass by any publications where that ratio is unobtainable; an obvious procedure but adopted by few, even in theory.

Preparing Estimates.—Clearly, whatever method be adopted, it is wise to ascertain the exact cost of production. But just as an architect must make his plans before calling in the quantity surveyor, so a publisher must—mentally at any rate—design his book before proceeding further.

Today, far more thought is given to design than thirty or forty years ago. The difference is startling. There is, for example, the striking improvement in type design, for which we owe so much to the far-sighted action of the Monotype Corporation and recently the Linotype Corporation in seeking and following the best advice. It is no more costly to set a book in a good fount of type than in a bad one and there is no longer any excuse for not using good type faces. The final appearance of the book is more influenced by the right selection of type, and the right proportions of the type area and 'leading', than almost any other single factor. To secure even and regular word-spacing the compositor needs to give a moment's thought at the termination of most lines to judge whether or not a further word can be got in or suitably broken.

The selection both of the format and the fount of type will be influenced by the character of the MS and the number of pages it is desirable that the book should make. A type face suitable for a work of belles-lettres may not be the best for a scientific book, and a MS set in, let us say, Baskerville will run to far more pages than if set in, say, Fournier. Again, a novel will probably be set in Crown 8vo size whereas a biography or work of considerable length is more likely to be Demy 8vo.[1]

The whole question of quality of printing will be referred to at greater length in the chapter on Production. Here it will suffice to emphasize that, except in the case of 'series' where a prescribed style has to be followed, each book should be regarded as having an individuality of its own. A certain degree of standardization is inevitable, but the mechanical

[1] During the war period 1942–45 established British publishers (*not* the war-time newcomers) were bound by the stringent terms of the *Book Production War Economy Agreement* which prescribed the permissible size of type, width of margins, words per square inch, weight of paper, weight of boards and a hundred and one other points affecting book production; a fact readily noted by an examination of any books produced during that period.

production of books will yield no better results than does the mechanical production of clothes, and it is as easy to detect whether the design of a book has been thought out as to decide whether a man's suit has been specially cut for him. The experienced publisher knows when to use the advantages of standardization and how and where the individual touches can be added without excessive cost.

The estimate may be based upon calculations made in their entirety in the publisher's office—a 'House estimate'—or upon precise quotations from printers. Our 'Call for Estimate' form provides for both, and it is for the 'sponsor', i.e. the director or editor who is dealing with the particular book, to say which is wanted. On that form the sponsor prescribes the size of the book, e.g. Demy 8vo, the number to be printed; whether it is to go to a printer in the first class or a less expensive firm; whether it is to be bound in cloth; whether a picture jacket is needed or plain lettering is more appropriate, and lastly the degree of urgency.

In the case of a house estimate, it is seldom that more is attempted than to provide approximate figures, a process that is very simply accomplished by counting the number of words in a few typical pages, multiplying the average by the total number of pages in the manuscript, and then basing the calculations upon a previous publication of the same length, etc. It is a rough-and-ready method which has its temporary uses, but it contains pitfalls for the unwary. If more exact figures are needed, as they always are in the end, the production department make the necessary inquiry from the printer, providing him at the same

time with a specimen page lay-out. When the typescript comes back from the printer with the estimate
and printed specimen page, and it is decided that the
book is to go in hand, the typescript receives editorial
and full typographical treatment to ensure that it is
in proper shape for the printers to proceed. The
amount of work this involves varies enormously.[1]

There is no standard procedure; each publisher has
his own methods. Our production department when
sending the prepared typescript to the printer for
'cast-off' sends with it a 'Style Directive'—a printed
statement of our House Rules, plus points about the
particular typescript in question, such as any special
requirements of the author.

Apart from the more obvious considerations, the
standard of knowledge and taste of the assistants in
the publisher's production department may have considerable influence upon the final appearance of a book,
because in a large business it is not always possible for
the publisher himself to settle every detail. But so long
as books are erroneously regarded as 'dear', financial
considerations will be the biggest factor, and many
desirable improvements in production will be sacrificed
on the altar of cheapness.

'Casting off' technically means calculating how
many pages a given quantity of matter that has been
set up in type will make; but the term is now generally used in a wider sense as covering an estimate
of the number of pages a manuscript will make, if set
in such and such a style. This is a very laborious task,

[1] See page 106.

if it is accurately done, and a 'cast-off' that is not accurate may be very misleading.

Until comparatively recently the number of words was counted, and if a manuscript has been heavily corrected, or is made up of a mixture of cuttings, handwriting and typescript, a word count is still useful. But there are today several recognized modern methods involving the use of Copy Fitting Tables and the Castell Demegraph Slide Rule, and it is characters, not words, that are counted. The printer provides in his elaborate calculations for any matter set in smaller type, such as extracts or footnotes, and in estimating allows for special accents, Greek, Hebrew, tabular matter, etc., all of which 'extras' add materially to the cost. It is highly skilled work, and whichever method is adopted much practice is needed if the desired accuracy is to be attained. The thoroughness with which the work is done by a good firm is to be seen in the extensive list of queries which often accompanies the estimate. Some printers send out with their estimates a printed questionnaire, of which the opposite page is an example.

Our 'Style Directive' anticipates all these points and many others which are largely matters of taste but which it is essential to settle before the printing is started rather than after the whole book is in type.

The requirements of authors differ considerably. Some prepare their manuscripts so perfectly and with so much thought and pains that they would be rightly annoyed if even a comma were altered. Others would be equally annoyed, and perhaps just as rightly so, if their manuscripts were literally followed, for ability to

POINTS RAISED BY THE PRINTER   *Reply*

1. PUNCTUATION: Are we to follow copy exactly, or use our discretion so as to obtain uniformity?

2. CAPITALIZATION: Is the author to be followed exactly, or shall we follow our House Style in details, making any alterations that may be necessary to secure consistency?

3. QUOTATION MARKS: Are double or single to be used, and points inside or outside?
      Our House Style is double quotes and points inside.

4. TITLES OF PUBLICATIONS in Text and Footnotes: Are they to be in italics or roman quoted?
      Our House Style is italics.

5. PRONOUNS REFERRING TO THE DEITY: Are these to begin with capitals?
      Our House Style is capitals.

6. IZE or ISE in such words as recognize, civilize, etc.: Which is preferred?
      Our House Style is ize.

7. SCRIPTURE REFERENCES: Are these to be printed thus: Exod. xv. 24; Psa. iv. 4–vi. 10; Isa. li.–lv.; 2 John 11?
      Our House Style is as printed above.

8. DATES: Shall we print December 9, 1905; December 9th, 1905; or 9th December, 1905?
      Our House Style is the first-named.
   (*a*) nineteenth century; (*b*) 19th century; or (*c*) XIXth Century?
      Our House Style is (a).

9. EXTRACT MATTER in smaller type? Is the extract to be quoted?
      Our House Style is without quotation marks.

10. LATIN AND OTHER FOREIGN WORDS AND PHRASES when used in the text: Are they to be in italics or roman?
      Our House Style is italics.

11. INDEX: Will one be supplied?

write does not always include ability to spell or to punctuate correctly.

Some of the most serious troubles with authors arise from neglect to find out in advance whether the author wants his manuscript followed literally, or if he is willing to adopt his publisher's 'House Style'.

Unless an author has prepared his MS most carefully and knows his way about very well, and comparatively few have a sufficient knowledge of the technique, he would be well advised to permit the publisher's House Style to be used throughout. Any kind of compromise is seldom successful and is never to be recommended because a manuscript may be simultaneously set up by half a dozen compositors. It is quite easy to instruct them to follow 'copy', or to follow the 'House Style', but it is difficult to get uniformity if variations are introduced. This must not be taken as excusing any discrepancies, because the printer's reader is responsible for consistency of style, punctuation, capitals, etc. None the less it will be found advisable in practice either to follow the House Style (except possibly the optional points raised by the printer) or to prepare the MS with sufficient care and forethought to justify the instruction 'follow copy'.

Into the printers' methods of arriving at their estimates and the basis upon which their costs are ascertained we need not delve very deeply. Actually, printers' charges for composition are almost invariably based upon a standard of one thousand 'ens', i.e. what it costs to set up one thousand of the letter 'n', which is midway between the broadest and the narrowest letter of the alphabet. It is obvious that a page full of the letter 'm' could be set up more quickly than a page full of the letter 'i', because a compositor would have to handle three times as many of the letter 'i' to fill the same type space. The actual form in which the estimate reaches the publisher is usually somewhat as follows:

Specification: i.e. the approximate number of words: so many pages containing so many lines and so many 'ems'[1] wide: allowing x pages for an index, if any, as also for any illustrations which are to be included in the actual text of the book.

Machining is usually as per scale, for most printers have a fixed rate which is recorded at the publisher's office, and, when once agreed, is applicable in all cases where exceptional circumstances do not arise.

Together with the estimate, the printers usually send an actual specimen page. Occasionally they merely preface their estimate with the remark, 'if set on the lines of such and such a book'; but, personally, I prefer to have a specimen set up from the manuscript itself, which can be submitted to the author for approval. In this specimen page the printers include, at our request, the title of the book, the approximate number of words, the approximate number of pages, their name, and the date on which the specimen was set up. This has many advantages in connection with the internal working of a publisher's office, and saves any possible confusion between the many such specimen pages which are constantly passing through a publisher's hands.

When completing the total cost it is so very easy to omit some item, that most publishers have a printed form, of which that on page 43 is an example. My

---

[1] 'Pica' or '12-point' ems are the printers' standard of measurement: if set solid, six lines = one inch.

firm's present form is much more elaborate in that it
has

(*a*) a second column to provide a more exact costing
at page proof stage to enable the published
price to be fixed and the jacket to be printed.
(*b*) a third column to enable the final costs of each
item to be compared with the estimate—a
most salutary check.

§ 1 and § 2: *Composition, small type, etc., and make-up*,
are merely copied from the printer's figures.

§ 3, *Paper*, needs careful thought; the weight and
bulk vary greatly according to the nature of the book.
It is also necessary to calculate the quantity of paper
required, which needs care. Even the expert occasionally makes the mistake of halving or doubling the
number of reams required. When the printing is put
in hand we call for an estimate from the stationer,
together with a 'dummy' of the size and specifications
prescribed and his confirmation of the quantity
needed.

§ 4, *Machining*, is 'according to scale', as previously
mentioned, and it is, therefore, merely a question of
knowing how many copies are to be printed, and
filling in the figure accordingly. The number of reams
usually corresponds to the paper ordered and is
repeated from the previous entry on the estimate.

§ 5, *Blocks*, depends, of course, upon whether the
volume is to be illustrated either inside or out. Practically all novels have picture jackets—a costly item, of
which more later.

ESTIMATE   *FOR OFFICE USE ONLY*

for producing   copies of '   ,
to form   volume of say   sheets of 32 pages   8vo size,
approximate number of words   thousand.

		£	s	d	£	s	d
(1) COMPOSITION .... sheets @							
SMALL TYPE, ETC.							
(2) MAKE-UP OR RE-IMPOSING							
(3) PAPER ...... SIZE ..... × ...... WEIGHT							
.... reams @							
(4) MACHINING .... ,, @							
(5) HALF-TONE OR LINE BLOCKS							
(6) PAPER FOR ILLUSTRATIONS							
PRINTING ILLUSTRATIONS							
(7) MOULDING .... sheets @							
STEREOTYPING FROM MOULDS							
(8) BINDING .... copies @							
PAPER BOARDS OR COVERS							
(9) BINDER'S BLOCKS							
(10) JACKETS, INCLUDING PASTE-ON (if any)							
(11) CORRECTIONS .... %							
(12) ARTIST'S OR TRANSLATOR'S FEES							
(13) AUTHOR'S ROYALTY							
(14) ADVERTISEMENTS .... @ scale prices							
(15) Insurance .... @ per £100							
(16) WORKING EXPENSES							
EXTRAS (if ordered by Author)							
....							
£							

SUGGESTED PUBLISHED PRICE...............

§ 6, *Paper for and the Printing of the Illustrations*. Art paper, used for the printing of most illustrations (though it is used more often than it need be), is of a different texture, character, and weight, and has to be separately ordered. The machining of illustrations is calculated from a scale agreed upon with the printers. It is a higher rate than ordinary machining, owing to the greater care required and the additional time consequently occupied.

§ 7, *Moulds and Stereoplates*. These no longer have their earlier importance because there are now other methods of reproducing books of which the type has been distributed. It is uneconomic to take them unless many unaltered reprints are certain to be wanted in which case nickel-faced stereos are desirable. The records of most British publishers would reveal what a startling amount of capital had in the past been invested in moulds which were never used and have no value. In America books are usually printed from electroplates (not type) which are almost invariably included in the original cost. Roughly speaking, the printer's charges are based upon the superficial area of the type of which moulds (papier-mâché impressions of the standing type) or stereos (metal plates cast from the moulds) are to be made.[1] For further information regarding these processes see the section on methods of reproduction in Chapter V.

§ 8, *Binding*. The cost varies enormously according to the number to be bound at one and the same time. The binders make what is known as a 'starting charge'

---

[1] To be precise, plates are charged by back measurement, to include the bevel; moulds by type area plus $\frac{1}{4}$ inch all round to include clump.

to cover the warehouseman's time looking out the sheets, and the 'making ready', which in some of the processes takes almost as long as the work itself—e.g. when once a case-making machine is running, the cost of an extra hundred cases is little beyond that of the materials involved. This tends to make the charge for binding small numbers almost prohibitive. For estimating purposes it is necessary to strike an average— the first number to be bound may be substantial, whereas subsequent binding orders may be smaller. The price is usually per 100 or per 1,000 copies. Some binders prefer orders to be in units of 250, i.e. 500, 750, 1,000 which is how the sheets are usually packed. When calling for an estimate and dummy from the stationer we also ask the binders for their price.

§ 9, *Binder's Blocks*. It is usually impossible to get satisfactory results unless lettering is specially cut, at any rate for the shelf back of the binding. It is cut in brass at a cost of about £4, and can be made to fit the available space, which is rarely possible with type. Nothing disfigures a book more effectively than bad lettering on the binding, so that to begrudge this expense, as some do, is false economy. Brass blocks are also good for their hardness to stand up to heavy pressure on cloth and board under heat. The polished surface gives a good gloss on gold.

§ 10, *Wrappers, Jackets, or Dustcovers*, as they are often called, are today a necessity, and any estimate that omitted them would be incomplete. The cost may be anything from about £30 for, say, 2,500 of the plainer variety to £60 for the same number of picture jackets in four colours, such as are frequently used for novels. This latter figure includes the making of the blocks, but *not* the artist's fees. It is expedient to print a substantial number of overs for publicity purposes and the refurbishing of soiled stock.

§ 11, *Corrections*. Under this head will be included whatever free allowance it is the particular publisher's custom to make his authors. It may be a fixed sum: more often it is 10 per cent of the cost of composition.

§ 12, *Artist's Fee for Jackets* or illustrations, is self-explanatory.

§ 13 and § 14, *Author's Royalty* and *Advertising*, are not, as a rule, included in a Production estimate for the publisher's own use, but are dealt with separately. It is none the less desirable to have them on the printed form as a perpetual reminder.

§ 15, *Insurance*, is usually covered by a floating policy, but individual cases arise where, because of the exceptional value of the MS or illustrations, special policies are called for.

§ 16, *Working Expenses*, or 'Overhead', as they are often called, will be dealt with elsewhere in this book.

If the estimate has been carefully completed, we now have a fairly accurate idea of the cost of producing a MS of which we have formed a favourable opinion.

The next questions to decide are the published price at which the book is to be issued and the amount of the margin of profit available for division with the author. How these questions are answered will be considered in the next chapter.

CHAPTER III

THE PRICE OF BOOKS AND OVER-PRODUCTION

ANYONE having the temerity to suggest that books are cheap would probably be met with a flat denial, or at best an incredulous smile. Yet the slightest study of the question would reveal that there are few, if any, directions where better value is given.

The price of books is a matter of such importance to the book-reading public that it ought to be more widely known not only what are the chief factors controlling their price, but also the proportions in which they operate. As we saw in the chapter on 'Casting Off' and Estimating, the number printed affects the cost per copy more than any other individual item.

But if we confine ourselves to the ordinary run of new books, of which a first edition of from 2,000 to 3,000 copies is printed—this excludes reprints, the big sellers, and educational books—the published price can be divided into three fairly equal parts, viz.:

1. The actual cost of manufacturing, i.e. paper, printing, and binding.
2. The cost of distribution, which includes booksellers' discounts and travellers' commissions.
3. The balance, which has to cover:
    (a) advertising;
    (b) the author's remuneration;
    (c) the publisher's working expenses;
    (d) the publisher's profit.

47

No two cases are alike, and the proportions will vary in special circumstances, e.g. where there is no author to pay, as in reprints of the classics; where there is a popular author commanding large royalties; or where there is less discount given to the trade, as with most educational books; but for general purposes the division will be found accurate enough. I propose to examine each separately.

1. Cost of Manufacture

Book production costs fluctuated so violently during the last forty years, particularly during the two war periods, and are still so far from being stable that it is impossible to give figures of even semi-permanent validity. But I do not think anyone would dispute that the cost of book production is at least five times what it was in 1914 and more than three times what it was in 1939. There has, however, been no proportionate increase in the published price of books.

2. Cost of Distribution

When 'net' books were first introduced, booksellers were glad to secure an admittedly inadequate $16\frac{2}{3}$ per cent, with an extra 5 per cent on settlement of their account. The pendulum has now swung in the opposite direction, and today they demand a clear $33\frac{1}{3}$ per cent *under all circumstances*, even on an order which they have done nothing to obtain for a single copy of a book they have never stocked.

The merits or demerits of their contention are discussed in Chapter VI, and the question is referred to here merely because it is a factor, and a decisive factor, in fixing the price.

If in the future the *minimum* discount is $33\frac{1}{3}$ per cent, the average receipts of the publisher will be reduced, because the wholesaler and exporter will want additional discount beyond the *minimum* allowed to the retailer, i.e. in addition to the $33\frac{1}{3}$ per cent; then the travellers' commission has also to be deducted. At present many publishers give a lower percentage on orders for single copies merely passed on by booksellers, and this keeps up the average net receipts; but if discounts are further increased, published prices will also and inevitably have to be increased. It is to this vital point that so many turn a blind eye. In brief, is the publisher to base his estimates on the assumption that his average gross receipts are going to be two-thirds or only about half the published price? It makes just all the difference.

But booksellers are not the only channel of distribution the British publisher has to consider, because some books are issued for sale primarily to circulating libraries. Here we have another factor to consider, viz. that a smaller number of copies will meet the demand, and the smaller the edition, the higher the price.

But such higher prices affect only a tiny minority of books published, and their influence is fleeting, because any such book for which there is a substantial demand at the circulating libraries is invariably issued subsequently at a lower price for general sale. Unfortunately, however, these 'circulating library books' can sometimes be cited as evidence that books are dear.

3. ADVERTISING: THE AUTHOR AND PUBLISHER

(*a*) Few authors think their books have been sufficiently advertised, and yet it is a common thing for over £75 to be spent on a book whose sales do not reach one thousand. That means an expenditure of more than 1s 6d per copy. Advertising rates have increased alarmingly, and little can be accomplished with £75, unless the daily and Sunday papers are excluded. The cost of advertising is certainly a factor which affects book prices.

(*b*) The author's remuneration nowadays is usually in the form of a royalty calculated on the published price. The royalty system has many advantages, but the plan of basing the royalty on the published price, though equitable enough theoretically, has the effect of necessitating a greater increase in the published price in certain circumstances than would otherwise be the case, e.g. if an extra 4d is spent on production it is necessary to add at least 1s to the published price, in order to cover not merely the additional expenditure and the booksellers' discount, but also the author's royalty upon this increased outlay. I am not contending that this should not be so (there is much to be said on both sides), but state it as a factor affecting book prices. If an author gets 10 per cent royalty on a 7s 6d *cloth* book, and it seems advisable to do a *leather* edition at 10s 6d, ought he to expect 10 per cent on the increased cost of the leather binding?

There is no need for me to refer to the 'ruinous policy' of paying too high royalties, because it has been dealt with so trenchantly in *A Publisher's Confessions*, by the late Walter Page, one of the many distinguished publishers America has sent to Europe as ambassadors. It is obvious that the royalty, whatever it is, is payable out of the difference between the cost of production and the net proceeds received by the publisher. Short of skimping the production, a policy pursued by some, or restricting the booksellers' discount, as is done by others, there is no way of increasing the margin except by increasing the price.

(c) The publisher's working expenses are extraordinarily high. It is not that publishers' businesses are extravagantly run—most of them, I believe, are fairly economically run; but because at best the turnover is small compared with that of any staple commodity such as tea, and the detail involved is out of all proportion.

I do not know of any book-publishing businesses whose working expenses are under 22 per cent—most are over 26 per cent; but I do not ask any reader to accept my statement. Let him refer to the case of *John Murray* v. *The Times*,[1] where the actual overhead costs were closely investigated, and remember that they are now very much heavier.

(d) The publisher's profit, if any, need not detain us, for it does not play as important a part in the fixing of prices as might be expected. This is not because the publisher is a philanthropist, but because his margin on subsequent editions is usually larger,[2] so that if reprints are called for as the result of his moderation, he will reap a greater reward than he could by any artificial enhancement of the published price of the

[1] May 5–8, 1908.
[2] The difference is not so great as it was.

first edition. Apart from this fact, pressure is constantly being brought to bear upon the publisher from more directions than one to keep prices down, and, speaking generally, it is in his own interest (there are plenty of exceptions) to do so.

This completes the list of factors that influence the price of books other than the paramount one of the number to be printed.

It will, I think, be clear to anyone who has read this statement carefully:

(1) That if a publication is to be economically self-supporting the published price must usually be fixed at not less than three and a half times the cost of production, i.e. the cost of the paper, printing, binding, and jackets.

(2) Whereas if allowance had to be made for any increase in the item 'distribution', the published price would have to be at least four times the manufacturing cost. In the USA it is five if not six times.

Despite the foregoing—despite the undoubted facts that production expenses are more than treble what they were in 1939 and that the costs of distribution and advertising have increased—there has so far been no proportionate addition to published prices. *Books are thus relatively cheaper.* The explanation is:

1. That more books are being sold (it has been possible to print larger editions). The bigger the demand for books the cheaper they can be—always provided there is no paper shortage.
2. That publishers are working on a smaller margin (often insufficient to cover the inevitable proportion of losses).

This brings me to the question of—

THE OVER-PRODUCTION OF BOOKS

'Fewer and Better Books' is one of those American slogans that sound so well, but upon examination mean so little. If the phrase were 'Fewer and Better Novels', which is what many people intend, there would be a good deal to be said for it, except that it is not usually the *best* novels which are most wanted by the public. 'Fewer duds and more best-sellers' is the interpretation that many in the book trade would give, but that, again, would lead us away from, rather than towards, the production of good literature. If put into practice this slogan would result in the publication of fewer scholarly works and of more ephemeral quick-selling rubbish.

An analysis of the new books published discloses the fact that fiction forms a much smaller and books on the many new subjects which come to the front a much larger proportion of the total output than most people suppose. There is the vast literature on both electronics and aeronautics, to mention but two such topics. The very diversity of the subjects in which people are interested represents an important factor which those who call for fewer books are apt to overlook. Most of us have never read a book on nuclear fission; but is that any reason why those who want books on that, or any other subject under the sun, should not have them?

Is it not well that anyone who feels he has a contribution to make to the common stock of knowledge should be as free as possible to make it?—that new ideas should be given full consideration? In a tree, is it not a sign of vitality that it sends out endless shoots that ultimately achieve no apparent purpose?

Unwanted Books.—All this brings me to the really unwanted books. Most of them are published at the author's expense, or 'on commission', as it is generally called, and this accounts for the usual condemnation, as a class, of all books published on commission. Certain old-fashioned publishers even boast that they *never* publish anything on commission, probably forgetting that some distinguished authors like the late Bernard Shaw take the sensible line that they do not require any publisher to finance them, preferring to pay the publisher for whatever services they do desire him to render, and to retain the entire profit for themselves. Many famous and very successful books have been published on commission. Two of the best-sellers in my predecessors' list—books that have been selling merrily for years—were, until quite recently, commission publications. If, on the other hand, we attempt to confine our condemnation to commission books for which there is no demand, I am reminded of Edward Carpenter's description of his experience with *Towards Democracy*. I quote his own words[1]:

I have spoken elsewhere about the considerable period of gestation and suffering which preceded the birth of this book; nor were its troubles over when it made its first appearance in the world. The first edition, printed and published by John Heywood of Manchester, at my own expense, fell quite flat. The infant showed hardly any signs of life. The Press ignored the book or jeered at it. I can only find one notice by a London paper of the first year of its publication, and that is by the old sixpenny *Graphic* (of August 11, 1883), saying—not without a sort of pleasant humour—that the phrases are 'suggestive of a lunatic

[1] *My Days and Dreams,* by Edward Carpenter (George Allen & Unwin Ltd, 1916).

Ollendorf, with stage directions', and ending up with the admission that 'the book is truly mystic, wonderful—like nothing so much as a nightmare after too earnest a study of the Koran!'

If we limit ourselves yet further, and say that under no circumstances ought unwanted novels to be published at the author's expense, I feel bound to point out that John Galsworthy's first effort was published under those conditions (it was under a pseudonym). Probably it would never have found a publisher otherwise, because it was immature work, had no sales, and has never been reissued. But had it not been published, would that distinguished writer have been encouraged to take up authorship as a profession?

Anyhow, I think it is clear that we must not be too hasty in condemning even unsuccessful commission publications, if it is the interests of literature we have at heart. Furthermore, we must not overlook the many learned works of research which would never be made available for future students if they had to wait for a publisher willing to finance their publication on their commercial merits.

We are left with the publications which have no intrinsic merit, which show no promise, and for which there is no demand. Despite the very great pressure that is often brought to bear, such books do not, with rare exceptions, appear under the imprint of any of the more reputable publishers. They certainly are a burden to the overworked literary editor who has the task of weeding them out, but a mere glance at the publisher's imprint will usually tell him all he needs to know. They do not occupy much of the bookseller's time or space, because he never subscribes to them, but merely procures them when they are definitely ordered. Usually only a small proportion of the edition is bound up, and, apart from the review copies, and perhaps forty or fifty sold to friends and relatives of the author, very few copies get into circulation. After the lapse of a year or two, the unbound copies are pulped, or, more probably, used for packing up other publications. It is doubtful, therefore, whether the few hundred books of this kind which are published yearly really present any great problem, or even a problem at all. As a method of spending money it does not seem to me to be any better or worse than many others about which no one is unduly troubled. And the fact remains that, whatever provisions were made to suppress this class of book, there would always be with us a few hundred people under the erroneous impression that their literary efforts were masterpieces which must be printed regardless of the consequences or cost. Often they are under the delusion that it is merely due to a secret conspiracy on the part of publishers that their MSS are returned to them.

There is, however, a form of over-production which is seldom mentioned, but which is in some respects more serious in its consequences. If an edition of three thousand copies represents the demand there is for some book, there is obviously no point in printing thirty thousand, even though the thirty thousand copies could each be produced infinitely more cheaply than would be possible were one-tenth that number printed. I have in mind one particular firm, now out of business, which recently ran through £30,000 largely as the result of over-production of that kind. The bookselling trade would have been swamped had the whole of their surplus stock been flung upon the market. A large proportion of it had to be pulped, not because it did not consist of excellent books—some of them were first-rate and most beautifully produced—but because the supply was altogether in excess of what the market could absorb.

Insufficient Sales.—But although I am bound to admit that there are far too many worthless books published, the problem is seldom over-production, but much more frequently under-consumption, or, to be more precise, insufficient sales. Most people have not yet learned to regard books as a necessity. They will beg them, they will borrow them, they will do everything, in fact, but buy them. People who would be ashamed to cadge for anything else they wanted, who will unhesitatingly pay 15s for a meal or even more for seats at a theatre, will think twice, if not three times, before spending even 7s 6d upon a book which will last a lifetime. The fact that we in England do not spend on books—per head of population—anything approaching the amount spent in the Scandinavian countries, and that, relatively speaking, we have not nearly so many well-stocked booksellers' shops, demonstrates that, despite the increase in demand, there is still room for expansion.[1] Book-

[1] How much room is revealed by Mr Harold Raymond's calculation that whereas the average British individual of both sexes, including infants, spends 4⅗d per week on books, the corresponding expenditure on alcoholic beverages, tobacco and cigarettes combined is 14s, i.e. 36 times as much. Though the national expenditure on books has increased from £10 millions in 1938 to £50 millions in 1956, the expenditure on drink and tobacco

lovers would do well to ignore idle chatter about over-production, and to concentrate attention upon encouraging the new reading public which is growing up around us, and in this connection to support the excellent work of The National Book League, 7 Albemarle Street, London, W.1. For the fact that more and better books are not read, we are all in a measure responsible. When during the Second World War the younger generation woke up to the realization of the joys of reading and the inexhaustible treasures of English Literature, and clamoured for books and wanted the best, the best were unobtainable or in short supply.

But this is a digression from our theme. We have now seen how the probable published price is determined and can pass on to the negotiations with the author which, as explained, often precede all the careful estimating, etc., outlined in Chapter II.

advanced in the same period from £462 millions to £1,830 millions, i.e. more than £5 millions *per day*. This formidable figure demonstrates the enormous spending power of the population as a whole, even on non-necessities, a point which is further illustrated by the fact that the expenditure on cosmetics amounted in 1957 to nearly £62 millions.

CHAPTER IV

AGREEMENTS

Is a formal agreement desirable? Is not a verbal
understanding sufficient—confirmed, if need be,
by an exchange of letters? I do not think that
anyone who has had considerable experience of publishing would have any hesitation about answering that
question. A formal agreement is not only desirable, it
is *essential*, and for more reasons than one. In the first
place, if the agreement is properly drawn up, it defines
in the most concise form possible the nature of the
arrangement. It is thus the best and most practical
form of record for the guidance of the many people
concerned in carrying out the understanding between
author and publisher. If no such record existed in the
form of an agreement, it would have to be created for
the efficient administration of the publisher's own business. I speak with no little feeling, because amongst the
businesses with which I have at one time or another
been associated was one where formal agreements were
the exception rather than the rule, and even when formal agreements were signed, they were so 'simple' as
to tell you nothing. The proprietor of the business said
he never had any trouble, his authors always trusted
him, which, indeed, they had every reason to do, for he
was an exceptionally honourable man, who paid his
firm's creditors 20s in the £ when he was under no
legal liability to pay them one penny. But he never

paused to think what would happen when the author's executors and his own successors were confronted with one another, neither having the dimmest notion of their respective rights or obligations! A few score tangles of that kind to unravel would convince anyone of the necessity of a formal agreement. But there are other reasons. It is essential that both parties should know precisely what rights are being conveyed. There is no more fruitful source of trouble than vagueness on such points, and yet agreements by letter almost invariably leave them undecided. It is very easy to say, 'We will deal with this or that question when it arises', but quite another thing to do so when the time arrives. A formal agreement compels both parties to face the issues at the outset; if they cannot agree then, the probability is they never will.

That authors should understand the arrangements into which they are entering is of the utmost importance, and now that they have what G. Bernard Shaw rightly called their 'Trade Union'—The Society of Authors—behind them, they have no excuse for not knowing all there is to know; but there is one point that is apt to be overlooked, viz. that an unfavourable agreement with an honourable firm is at all times to be preferred to an impeccable agreement with an unscrupulous one. An agreement which is ideal from the point of view of one of the parties is likely to be unsatisfactory to the other party. A publisher who habitually enters into agreements with which no theoretical objection could be found, from the author's point of view, either has no real intention of carrying out the agreements or, granted he has the best intentions, will inevitably find himself in the long run—failing some endowment or inexhaustible resources—unable to do so. I shall have occasion to refer to this subject later.

With the Authors' Society's demand for 'The inspection of those account books which belong to the author', I can but express my wholehearted agreement, and deplore the fact that the 'right' is not more frequently exercised. Nothing would promote a greater feeling of confidence than an authoritative statement from time to time that such and such a publisher's accounts had been examined and found not only correct, but very well kept.[1] The Publishers Association recommends the inclusion of a clause specifically according the right. But may I suggest one qualification? The person exercising the right should possess an elementary knowledge of book-keeping. It does not seem to me to be part of a publisher's obligations to teach authors the elements of book-keeping, though I have spent many hours in the process. Authors cannot be expected to bother personally about such things. I merely suggest that if accounts are a mystery to them, they should delegate the task of investigation to someone accustomed to figures. The object of the Authors' Society in running an accounts department is presumably to save authors trouble and responsibility of this kind.

For some reason I have never been able to fathom, many authors have an instinctive feeling that publishers

---

[1] Many American and a few British publishers issue their royalty statements formally certified by a chartered accountant; but if the statement does not include a stock account, such a certificate might in some cases have little value.

are immune from the laws of arithmetic; that, whilst with anyone else 'Expenditure £500, Gross Receipts £400' means a loss of at any rate £100, with publishers this is supposed to mean a thumping big profit. Probably this is due to a very natural disinclination on the part of authors to admit even the possibility of any kind of shortcoming in their offspring. It is just this fact of the unique relationship between the author and his book which makes publishing so different from any purely commercial pursuit, and at once more interesting and more difficult.

Agreements between authors and publishers are of four kinds; any other forms are combinations of these four. They are:

1. THE OUTRIGHT SALE OF THE COPYRIGHT

This may prove an exceedingly bad arrangement for the author and is almost certain to be for the publisher, because if the book is a failure the publisher will get no sympathy, let alone a refund of any excess payment from the author; on the other hand, if the book is a success the author is sure to denounce the iniquity of such an arrangement and clamour for royalties. The method is seldom used nowadays. But there are points in its favour.

No alternative gives a publisher such a free hand to make any and every use of literary material and to exploit every possibility of finding markets for it. No other plan gives a publisher so much inducement to advertise. In fact, it is quite conceivable that an author would gain, on balance, as much as he would lose by the outright sale of, say, one or possibly even two of his earlier works, if the deal were made with a really enterprising firm of good standing. His reward would come with the publication of his subsequent books, for which a market would have been established.

2. A PROFIT-SHARING AGREEMENT

This method has been described by the Authors' Society as 'a bad form of agreement'. That statement seems to me too sweeping. It is a method which has been abused by publishers in the past, and has therefore, and naturally, fallen into disrepute. In so far as it lends itself more readily to abuse than the royalty system, it is a bad form of agreement; but, honourably carried out, there is much to be said in its favour *for some classes of publications*. It gives the publisher more work in connection with the rendering of accounts, and the author a great deal more information about costs of production, etc., than any other method. In fact, if the accounts are made out in the detailed form in which I consider the author is entitled to have them presented, they are so instructive to a young author that he misses much if he never has a book published under this system.

Theoretically, at any rate, the basis is equitable, because there are no profits until the actual costs of production and advertising are covered, and the only question thereafter is the proportion in which the profits are to be divided. It is, in effect, a partnership in which the interests of both parties are identical; but the author has to face the disadvantages as well as the advantages of being in partnership with his publisher. (I am assuming that the agreement is being honourably carried out. I will refer to possible abuses in a moment.) One of the greatest drawbacks seems to me the un-evenness of the flow of the profits. This is best illustrated by an actual example. Under the royalty system, in the case of a book selling steadily at the rate of 500 per annum, of which 2,000 copies were printed at a time, the author's income would be constant. Under a half-profits agreement the first year would show no profit, all the proceeds of the sales being absorbed by the cost of printing 2,000 and binding about 1,000. Towards the end of the second year, it would be necessary to bind up the second thousand copies, and this would eat into the available profits. The third and fourth years, however, would show bumper profits, and both author and publisher would have their reward. But, in the meantime, the author has to live, and the fact that in the long run this method might yield him more would be poor consolation, if he had no other resources.

For this reason, a profit-sharing agreement is not generally applicable, but there are many cases where it is the ideal arrangement for both parties. There are, for instance, many learned works, written without any thought of direct pecuniary reward, whose publication may bring great indirect return to their authors in the form of academic distinctions or appointments. One such author, the sales of whose masterpiece had taken thirty years to cover the printing bill, called the day after he had received the first share of profits to tell me that it was an amusing coincidence that the payment should have reached him on the very day of his retirement from the Professorship the publication of the book had secured him. The patient publisher had been out of pocket for thirty years without any comparable recognition of his part in such uncommercial activities.

At this point it seems apposite to mention that all the criticisms of agreements I have ever read assume that the printed forms were intended to apply to novels. In fact, all discussions on matters connected with the book trade seem, consciously or unconsciously, to be based on the assumption that novels are the only books published, or, at any rate, the only ones that need be taken into account. How great a fallacy this is, a glance at the statistics of new books published will show. It is true that fiction heads the list as the biggest individual class, but novels represent at most about one-fifth of the total new books. Criticism that may be fair when applied to an agreement for a novel, may be grossly unfair when applied to some other kind of book. A profit-sharing agreement may thus be an unfavourable form of agreement for an unsuccessful novel, but a suitable one for a work on philosophy.

Abuses.—1. The charges for production may be excessive. The agreement should accordingly provide that the charges for printing, paper, binding, etc., should be as per printer's, stationer's, and binder's invoices, and should represent the publisher's actual out-of-pocket expenditure. If the publisher is his own printer or binder, an assurance should be obtained that the prices shall be at competitive rates.

2. In the past, when most book publishers issued one or more magazines or periodicals, they were in a position to put profits into their own pockets by

charging for advertisements in them. This is a point that the author is entitled to control.

3. The charge (if any) for 'office expenses'. This is definitely controversial, and there is a great deal to be said on both sides. I thought at one time that the Authors' Society's contention that this expenditure should *not* be included was just. Certainly the publisher is no more entitled to charge his full 'overhead' than the author. On the other hand there are many out-of-pocket expenses, such as commission paid to a traveller for securing an order for the particular book, which the publisher would not incur if he refrained from publishing the work. After forty years' study of the problem I am of opinion that a charge to cover such items of at least 10 per cent of the proceeds of the sales is not merely defensible but just.

Turning to the other side of the account, it is important to see that the agreement provides for full credit to be given for the proceeds of the sales. It is a question of determining a fair average, because the trade terms fluctuate according to the quantity ordered and the time of ordering, viz. before or after publication, and it would be an almost impossible task to treat each individual sale separately.

So much for the possible abuses. They will not arise with a really good firm; and, unless the publisher's honesty is above suspicion it is wisest for authors to avoid a profit-sharing arrangement, useful and equitable as it often is.

3. THE ROYALTY SYSTEM
This method of dealing with literary property is the

one most frequently adopted and is the best form of agreement for common use. In the chapter on 'The Price of Books', information will be found concerning the best way of ascertaining what royalties are, and are not, practicable. Because it is possible to pay this or that royalty in one case, it by no means follows that it is possible, or expedient, to do so in another. It might be a sound method of reasoning were novels of 65,000 words in length, issued at 12s 6d, the only books to be considered; but, as I have pointed out before, novels represent at most but one-fifth of the new books published. Furthermore, a publisher accepting a first novel containing 130,000 words probably has not the same margin (if he has any margin at all!) as he would have were the length 65,000. Although this is quite obvious, it is a point almost consistently overlooked by authors.

If the question is examined at all, it is from the point of view of the established novelist. When you are going to print over 15,000 copies, it does not affect the cost by as much as twopence per copy whether the composition amounts to £120 or £240, but if the first edition consists of 1,500, the difference is over 1s 6d per copy. Perhaps I may be permitted to take this opportunity to point out that the increases in costs of production discussed in detail in Chapter III all tend to make it harder for the writer at the bottom of the ladder and, by comparison, easier for the writer who has arrived at the top.

To return to the amount of the royalty, we have already seen that in a self-supporting publication the only source whence the royalty can come is the margin between the costs of production and the amount received by the publisher from the book trade. Many authors fail to grasp this obvious and elementary fact, and give themselves and others much unnecessary tribulation through their failure to do so. It sounds very nice to say, 'Here is my manuscript: it must be published at 10s and I must have a 15 per cent royalty'; but, if the book is going to cost 6s 8d per copy to produce, and the receipts will not amount to more than 6s 8d per copy, the author is crying for the moon; and however 'enterprising' the publisher, the fact remains that he cannot provide it. As matters stand, there is far too much guess-work in fixing the amount of the royalty. There are times when it is inevitable that chance should enter in; but in most cases it is possible to calculate in advance exactly what margin any particular undertaking will show. If the margin is insufficient, and the cost of production cannot be reduced, the question of increasing the price has to be considered. Will such an increase kill or curtail the sale? In many cases a publisher is bound to advise that it will; in others, that it will not have any serious effect. These situations arise more constantly now than they did, owing to the increase in production costs being out of all proportion to the increase in published prices. Many books are too cheap, and leave no adequate margin for author and publisher, though this fact is seldom realized, even by authors whose interests may thereby be prejudiced.

The impression that there are unsuspected margins out of which higher and yet higher royalties can be paid is so widespread that, in advocating the substitution of careful calculation for guess-work in arriving at the amount of the royalty, I should like to place on record that, whatever the position may have been in the past, publishers today have nothing to lose and everything to gain by courting inquiry into facts and figures; the present tendency is to attempt to work with an insufficient margin, a policy which, in the long run, can only prove disastrous. It is my opinion that an impartial investigation would result today in the scaling down of royalties in many more cases than it would increase them.

In the opening chapter of *A Publisher's Confessions*, the late Walter H. Page, the famous Ambassador publisher, dealt with the whole question of royalties most succinctly. Here is a brief quotation:

The rise of royalties paid to popular authors is the most important recent fact in the publishing world. It has not been many years since 10 per cent was the almost universal rule; and a 10 per cent royalty on a book that sells only reasonably well is a fair bargain between publisher and author. If the publisher do his work well—make the book well, advertise it well, keep a well-ordered and well-managed and energetic house—this division of the profits is a fair division—except in the case of a book that has a phenomenally large sale. Then he can afford to pay more. Unless a book has a pretty good sale, it will not leave a profit after paying more than a 10 per cent royalty.

He is, of course, referring to American conditions, and in America a publisher's working expenses are greater than in England, but that is met to a large extent by the fact that 'a pretty good sale' in the States would mean about double what we should consider 'a pretty good sale' over here. If applied to books published at less than 12s 6d and having a sale of less than 3,000 copies, Mr Page's diagnosis unquestionably holds good for English publications. It is not until the 3,000 mark is passed that profits begin to be made.

A rising royalty met this precise difficulty, because with some publications (by no means all) there came a stage where the available margin increased, and it is equitable that the author should share the benefit, as he would do *ipso facto* under a profit-sharing agreement. But now that paper is five or six times the pre-war price and is such a big factor in the cost of a reprint, the increased profit margin has largely disappeared. It must be remembered that the cost *per copy* of paper is always the same regardless of the number printed, and if the number bound at one time decreases the cost of the binding increases. Many publishers must have been badly caught out by the application of the sliding scale under conditions in which it was no longer justified. It has prompted some of them to make provision in their agreements that the increased royalties shall not apply to small reprints. In some contracts they do not apply if the sales drop to less than a stated number per annum.

The fact that royalties are almost invariably calculated upon the published price is apt to mislead authors as to the proportion of the proceeds they are being paid. Most authors who were receiving a royalty of 10 per cent on the published price would be surprised were they told that they are having about one-sixth of the publisher's gross receipts. Yet it needs only a simple calculation to demonstrate that 10 per cent on the published price is 15 per cent on two-thirds of the published price, which, on an average, represents the maximum the publisher obtains for his wares.

Agreement Forms. —There is no longer any need for detailed comments upon the clauses to be found in most printed forms of royalty agreement because a committee of the Publishers Association, of which I was a member, has prepared a 'Guide to Royalty Agreements' which covers the ground and is readily obtainable.[1] But upon some of the more controversial points further comment may be useful.

1. *Exclusive Right or Exclusive Licence.*—Lord Justice Scrutton at the end of his judgment in the case of *Barker* v. *Stickney* (Law Reports [1919] 1 K.B. 121) definitely advised authors against assigning their copyrights. Now an assignment of an exclusive right of publication in book form is an assignment of a portion of the copyright. The Authors' Society therefore insisted upon the substitution of the word 'licence' for 'right'. But compliance with this quite proper advice had one drawback. It deprived the publisher until recently of the possibility of taking action if there was an infringement of the copyright. The action had to be taken by the author. But the British Copyright Act of 1956 makes it clear that the holder of an exclusive licence can prosecute an infringer of his licence.

2. *Terminable Licences.*—It is sometimes suggested that the licence should be for a restricted period of years. Here the weight of the evidence is against any such restriction. How much time and attention, let alone capital, would you expect a man to expend upon a house or other property of which he only had a short lease? Obviously the more permanent the publisher's interest in a book, the greater inducement

[1] Publishers Association, 19 Bedford Square, London, W.C.1

he has to exploit its possibilities, and experience has demonstrated that he could not rely upon retaining the right to publish merely by satisfying his author. Without adequate security, the better kind of publishing—the publishing of books of permanent rather than ephemeral interest—would become even more difficult than it is at present.

What publisher could, for instance, embark upon such an undertaking as the 'Muirhead Library of Philosophy' if the occasional volumes that proved financial successes were liable to be transferred to his competitors? As well ask a fruit-grower to plant an apple orchard in ground of which he was only offered a five years' lease as expect a publisher of serious books to accept a short terminable licence. There are, doubtless, exceptional cases; but in general and in the long run an agreement for the duration of copyright is advantageous and equitable to both parties, and essential to the publisher.

The only serious objection to be encountered is that a change in the ownership of the publishing business might inflict hardship upon the author. This, however, is a point that could be met by some less drastic provision than a short terminable licence.

3. *American Rights.*—(Or to be more precise the Right of publication in book form in English in the USA.) The advice sometimes given to authors to restrict the territory in which the British edition of their works may be sold is thoroughly unsound. The one possible exception is the USA, and then only in the comparatively few cases where separate production is certain. Apart from fiction not 3 per cent of the

British books issued in any year are thus separately printed in the USA. What about the other 97 per cent? Every English publisher worth his salt tries to secure an offer from an American publisher to print his authors' work in the States; if he fails, he sells sheets, or bound copies, which is usually less profitable to the author. Are agreements to be drafted with the 3 per cent or the 97 per cent of cases in the foreground? The Authors' Society and literary agents always have the 3 per cent firmly in mind, publishers the 97 per cent. Therein lies the difference.

But there is another important aspect of the matter which needs emphasis. It is an undisputed fact that American publishers are often influenced by the judgment of their English colleagues in their decisions concerning MSS by unknown or comparatively unknown writers. I do not suggest that all American publishers are favourably influenced by the judgment of all their British colleagues, or vice versa. But there is no question that in a very large proportion of cases the imprint of the British publisher (or the good will of his firm, if you prefer it), may be a deciding factor in placing the American rights. Some literary agents claim that their recommendation has equal value, but a moment's reflection will show the absurdity of such a contention. An agent is solely interested in effecting a sale. The publisher, on the other hand, has backed his judgment with his money and his imprint. Is it not natural that his verdict should carry conviction? To what degree it will do so will vary according to the publisher's success. Sometimes he will even be able to place a book by a new author with an American publisher who has not read so much as a line of it and relies entirely on the English publisher's 'say so'. Here, then, you have the case of an MS becoming readily saleable to an American publisher just because a particular British publisher has decided to take it. The same thing may be true, but to a lesser extent, in the reverse direction. But if the publisher in question suggests that he is entitled to some share of the benefit of his own good will, he will be told that he is most unreasonable.

It has always puzzled me why the Authors' Society, which is rightly insistent upon the claim of the author to benefit by what he has created, should consider it iniquitous for publishers to claim remuneration for what they have created. Of course, many publishers create no good will of the kind I refer to. Their imprint carries no weight, and they are not entitled to consideration. But a firm that has laboriously built up a reputation for publishing nothing but the best in some particular field is in a different category. If its imprint automatically makes a book marketable in the States, it is preposterous that the firm should be condemned because it refuses to exclude the American rights to please an author and enable him to secure the benefit of his publishers' good will without paying a penny for it.

In the olden days the publisher received 50 per cent of American royalties or other rights, and often got more than he was entitled to. The pendulum has now swung in the opposite direction, and, because a publisher receives, quite rightly, no share in the American or other rights in the work of a successful and well-known author which is sold on the author's name, it is assumed a publisher ought never to receive anything (save possibly an agent's commission of 10 per cent), even in cases where the fate of the book in, let us say, the USA is largely, if not entirely, dependent on whether his imprint is on the book or not.

This does not, however, seem to me a case where philanthropy is called for. Sensible authors, like most other people, are ready enough to pay for value received and according to the value received, and it is time a reasonable compromise was agreed upon. There is a simple and effective way of testing the indebtedness, if any, to the publisher, viz. to put the question, 'Would the American or other rights be equally saleable in the reverse order?'—i.e. *before* the English publisher's acceptance had been secured. In the case of most well-known authors, the answer would be in the affirmative: in the case of many of the unknown, in the negative. The extent of the indebtedness would, of course, vary greatly.

Several distinguished authors who started by excluding American and translation rights from agreements with my firm now, of their own accord, include them. One author solemnly excluded this, that, and the other right, and then, as soon as the agreement was signed, requested us to act as if the rights had *not* been excluded!

Here it may be well to add that the one-time practice of throwing in the Canadian market with the American rights is unjustified. The rule is for the Canadian market to be retained by the publisher in the country of origin.

4. *Continental Rights*.—Although even at its zenith the firm of Tauchnitz never published more than sixty

new titles in a year, its effect at one time upon British book distribution on the Continent was almost devastating. There were many reasons for this, but first and foremost because authors considered it a kind of 'hall mark' to appear in the Tauchnitz collection regardless of the financial aspect of the matter. It thus became a fetich on the part of agents to reserve the continental rights whether or not there was the faintest possibility of Tauchnitz acquiring them. For example, in my early days, negotiations for a book on agricultural co-operation in Denmark broke down solely because the agent would not allow me to have the right to sell it on the Continent. The fact that 90 per cent of the books taken by Tauchnitz were fiction, and that he never took a solid work of that character did not weigh in the balance. The sequel to that story was the publication of the book by a fiction publisher prepared at that time to accept an agreement excluding the Continent; its remaindering by him about six or nine months after publication, and the subsequent sale of many of the remainder copies on the Continent. As the author derived no benefit from the remainder sales, but would have received full royalties had I been authorized to sell his book on the Continent, I think it will be agreed that my description of the reservation of continental rights as a fetich was no exaggeration. I emphasize this because it contributed to the lack of enthusiasm shown by some publishers in those days in developing the continental market. But with the advent of Penguins and other attractively produced cheap editions, both fiction and non-fiction, the influence of the special continental edition has ceased.

The important thing is, that if British publishers are to be encouraged to develop the continental market as many of them are so anxious to do, they must be granted the exclusive right to sell their books there.

5. *Translation Rights.*—Presumably what concerns the author most is that these rights should be exploited to his greatest advantage. If that be the case the desirability of their being reserved by the author needs more consideration than it is usually given. The International Publishers Congress of 1938 devoted a special session (over which I presided) to the question of 'Translations'. Publishers from one country after another pointed out that with translations from any language other than English they negotiated for the rights with the original publishers, and knew where they were, but when it came to translations from English they were nearly always referred to an agent, and more frequently to a local sub-agent of a London agent. Whether or not there was justification for the almost violent disapproval expressed it would ill become me to say, but it is a fact of which authors ought to be aware, particularly any who believe as strongly as I do in studying foreign customers' requirements and not assuming that they will want to do business in your way.

And this prompts me to ask how many literary agents have in the past made any effort to establish personal relations with their continental customers. It is true that many publishers have failed to do so, but they have the excuse that agents always 'reserve' the translation rights. Any publisher who is in touch with his continental colleagues is likely to place an exceptionally large proportion of translation rights and to create sales by his personal visits and recommendations. I could cite scores and scores of instances of translations arranged in this way which would never have been achieved had the authors reserved the rights. One literary agent was so frank as to admit that were he contracting with me for a book of his own he would unquestionably leave the translation rights in my hands.

If the author is in a position to do better for himself, by all means let him reserve the rights; but to do so merely for the sake of doing so is quite another thing. Let him first make sure whether the publisher with whom he is negotiating has or has not special facilities for dealing with them.

This is another of the many questions which seem to be judged almost exclusively from the point of view of fiction (and a best-seller at that!), where the sum involved may be considerable. In the case of translations of works of scientific and philosophic interest, the market is of necessity much more restricted, the amounts at issue are often inconsiderable, and, from a purely commercial point of view, no commission, not even the entire proceeds, would make it worth while to devote the time to this side of their work which some publishers do.

But are there never to be any other than commercial considerations?

Is it or is it not desirable that there should be a wider dissemination in foreign countries of English ideas and learning? The authors I have had the privilege to represent have, without exception, though in varying degrees, stressed the importance of having their work available in other languages far above the pecuniary return. Personally, I feel that to assist in the interchange of ideas between the peoples of different nations is one of the most useful services that can be rendered. So strongly do I feel this, that the decisive question to me is who can be the most certain of placing the rights, not who ought theoretically to control them. The question is dealt with more fully in Chapter IX.

6. *Authors' Corrections.*—The allowance made to authors for corrections has been the subject of endless controversy. If a manuscript is typewritten, the typescript can be corrected just as well as the printed proof, though some points needing correction will elude even a vigilant author until he sees the printed page. If the typescript has already been heavily corrected, it will be much cheaper for the author to have it re-typed, and then to revise it finally with great care and attention, than to incur a correction bill. It is doubtful whether there is any direction where there is so little to show for your money as in expenditure on corrections. The printer's charge works out at about 15s per hour, and anyone who has tried his hand at making alterations in standing type, as I have done for days on end, will know how little can be accomplished in an hour. Whether an author exceeds the allowance depends more upon the care with which the MS is prepared before it is handed to the publisher than upon the generosity of the publisher's allowance, strange as this may sound. Ten to twelve per cent of the cost of composition is in my opinion a fair allowance in the case of a typewritten manuscript that has been carefully gone through, but not even 50 per cent will suffice a

careless author. The point is touched upon again in the chapter on Production.

7. *Remaindering* is a frequent bone of contention. A provision, not always included by publishers, though pressed for, with justice, by the Authors' Society, 'That the book shall not be remaindered within two years of first publication', is entirely reasonable. The further provision that the author shall be given the option of purchasing the remainder stock, though equitable enough, is apt to prove onerous in practice. Some of the best remainder buyers are passing birds, who have to be caught on the wing. Even forty-eight hours' delay may mean an opportunity forever lost, and how often can one be sure of an answer from an author, let alone in forty-eight hours?

8. *Copies Free of Royalty.*—In the case of a first novel, or a book that is unlikely to pay its way, it is not unusual for a certain number of copies to be free of royalty, and such an arrangement, despite all that is said to the contrary, is often equitable to both parties. It merely ensures that during the period when the proceeds of the sales have not even covered the printing bill—let alone yielded a profit to anybody—the publisher should not have to add to his loss the payment of royalties to the author. In effect, it makes the arrangement more akin to a profit-sharing agreement whilst still preserving the royalty principle. In some agreements the royalty is payable on the 'free' copies, in the event of over, say, 1,500 copies being sold within a prescribed period, in which case, unless the publisher is considerably out of pocket on the undertaking, the author receives the full royalty.

9. *Special Sales.*—There has been a good deal of controversy about the royalty to be paid on sales at reduced prices, and, as is usual with all such controversies, it has been discussed and judged with novels primarily in mind. Now, with novels it is possible to justify fixing a dividing line at one-quarter, because, in practice, a novel is saleable on the usual trade terms for novels, i.e. above half-price, or failing that, as a remainder, which, in the case of a novel, is below one-quarter of the published price. There is no half-way about it. This is not, however, true of other publications. In the first place the 'remainder' will quite possibly fetch more than a quarter, though less than half the published price. More important still, there may be openings to be exploited for special editions at reduced prices to organizations or societies. Publishers are constantly accused of lack of enterprise in not following up such opportunities, but it is obvious that they cannot do so if their agreements do not give them the power. To the retort that each opening should be referred to the author, my reply is that, if there were time, I should communicate with the author, even though there was no legal necessity to do so, but in many cases there is not time. Supplementary agreements spell delay, and before the negotiations are completed, the opportunity has slipped by. The test is how the thing works out in practice; success is apt to come to the seller who can give a quick decision.

It is easy to demonstrate that any particular dividing line is unfair to one or other party, if not absurd in its incidence. Experience has shown that an equitable solution is:

1. The full royalty on the published price on all copies sold at above half the published price.

2. A 10 per cent royalty calculated upon the exact amount received on sales at or below half-price, but above the cost of manufacture.

3. No royalty on sales at less than the cost of manufacture or upon any copies presented to the author or others or to the Press or destroyed by fire, water, enemy action, in transit or otherwise.

The provision concerning copies destroyed had unusual significance during the war. Some authors maintained that they were entitled to compensation for 'blitzed' stock. Where the compensation was to come from or, in the case of royalty publications, what loss they had sustained if their books were still in print or were being reprinted were points it apparently never occurred to them to consider.

In royalty questions relating to special sales British authors are much more conciliatory when dealing with American than with English publishers. I might go further, and add that if English authors would sign contracts with English publishers on the terms and conditions which they are usually prepared to accept from American publishers, the path of the English publisher would be a good deal rosier.

10. *Thirteen as Twelve*.—The clause referring to royalties used to include a provision that thirteen copies should be reckoned as twelve, in continuance of a very old custom of supplying a 'baker's dozen', i.e. throwing in the thirteenth copy gratis. The method has been discarded, though it had certain advantages which are examined in connection with 'trade terms'.

11. *Special editions for America and the British dominions* are not necessarily specially printed. They

may be separately printed, but are more usually part
of the English edition set aside for the purpose and for
which, if the sale is to America, new title-pages are
printed, bearing the American publisher's imprint.
Most novels and some other books are issued in colonial
editions. At one time they were in cheaper binding and
had the words 'Colonial Edition' printed on either the
title-page or jacket. Today there is nothing to distin-
guish such copies from those sold in England. The
royalties paid on these special editions are almost
invariably calculated upon the exact amount received
by the publisher, though in the case of colonial editions
of novels it was at one time quite usual to fix an exact
sum, e.g. threepence per copy. The purport of these
'special editions' and their importance is examined
elsewhere. Meanwhile I should like to emphasize that
they are not, as a rule, separately manufactured. Many
'grievances' arise from the failure of authors to grasp
this elementary point.

12. *Cheap Editions.*—The Authors' Society contends that no cheaper edition should be published
without the sanction of the author within two years
from the date of first publication, and it is undoubtedly
right in so doing; unfortunately, the Society's wording
went on to say that 'if within three years no cheaper
edition has been produced by the publisher, then the
publisher's right, as far as the cheap edition is concerned, should be determined'. Let us consider what
this means. Take the case of a popular work on psycho-
logy issued at 10s 6d, which at the end of two years
is selling even better than it did in the first year. If the
publisher does not bring out a cheap edition during

the third year, he is not only to lose the right of doing so subsequently, when it might be profitable, but to leave the author free to sell some other publisher the right to step in and undersell. Clearly the original publisher is likely to be in the best position to decide the appropriate moment at which a cheap edition should be issued.

13. *Revision.*—This arises chiefly in the case of technical publications. No publisher wants to make revisions if they can possibly be avoided. The reason is self-evident; revisions, whether in standing type or in plates, are very expensive, in many cases they involve the complete resetting of the work, whereas a mere fresh impression, *without* corrections, whether from standing type, plates, or by photo-lithography leaves the publisher the maximum margin of profit. There is thus no warrant for the assumption that the author needs any other guarantee that the publisher will not make unreasonable demands upon him to bring the work up to date. (There is probably more need for an assurance that the publisher will give the author the opportunity to do so.) On the other hand, it is essential to the publisher to know where he stands in this matter and that he should not be called upon for additional payments, over and beyond the royalty, for revisions which both parties agree are necessary. He cannot afford to run the risk which the publication of expensive technical works involves without looking some way ahead. It may be ten years before there is any return for the initial outlay, and by that time the work may have secured its author the coveted professorship, and he may have lost interest in the subject.

Has the publisher no right to be considered? In point of fact, difficulties seldom arise until after the death of an author, when a third party has to be called in to do the revision. Then, who is to decide (*a*) whether revision is called for, (*b*) to whom the work is to be entrusted; and, equally important, who is to foot the bill?

In the rare cases where the author appoints an executor technically equipped, it is possible to answer, 'The author's executor', but these cases are the exception, not the rule. Usually the executors are without knowledge of, or interest in, the subject of the work, and are often unwilling to make the very slightest sacrifice of immediate interests, however clearly it is to their ultimate advantage. There are other complications, as an experience of my own firm demonstrated. A well-known scientist had told us just before his death that he wanted his books revised before they were reprinted, and a note was accordingly made in our records. Furthermore, in his will he expressed a wish that revised editions of his works should appear, and made the cost of the revision a charge upon his estate. Here it seemed there would be no difficulty, although the written contract contained no such provision. That was many years ago. Within a few months of the author's death, the question of reprinting one of his books arose. The solicitors acting for the executors regretted that they were unable to authorize us to take any action, or themselves to do anything (the beneficiaries were apparently at loggerheads). At the solicitors' request we wrote again after various intervals, but the reply was always the same. To this day nothing has been done. The time has now gone by; the book has been superseded by others, and were the authority forthcoming, the reply would be 'Too late'.

To summarize the position, it is clear that:

(*a*) During the author's lifetime he should be the arbiter as to whether revisions are needed to keep the work up to date.

(*b*) If revision is needed, the author should undertake it, or, alternatively, nominate someone else to do so (the cost in the latter case to be deducted from the royalties).

(*c*) After the author's death, the publishers should have the right to have a scientific or technical work brought up to date by a competent man, and to deduct the cost from the royalties.

In regard to (*c*), the executors should have the right to decide whether they preferred to pay a fee for the revision or to let the reviser share the royalties, and the publisher should be under an obligation to make it clear in the new edition what departures had been made from the original work, i.e. the nature and extent of the alterations.

It will, no doubt, be said that it is wrong that the publisher should have such power after the author's death, but with experience of the effects of withholding it, I can confidently affirm that, with rare exceptions, it is in the author's, quite as much as the publisher's, interest that the publisher should have it. In any case it is essential to the publisher.

14. *Index.*—The preparation of an index is a laborious task, but it is just as much part of some books as a table of contents. If, therefore, one is needed, the author should provide it. Whether it is necessary, the author can be left to decide; if he is wise, he will consult his publisher; if he is not, and he omits an index when one ought to be included, every reviewer will

relieve the publisher of the necessity of pointing out the defect.

For an index, the *via media* is essential. Too full an index, with every slight reference to a subject, is almost as useless as too slight a one. The salient passages should alone be given. It is a mistake in most cases to give *all* the references, printing the important ones in heavily leaded or larger type; this makes the index unnecessarily expensive. Again, in Biblical references so many texts are sometimes referred to that the reader despairs, and if he turns them up he finds that many are trivial and might have been left out.

15. *Illustrations* are an essential feature of many books. The publisher is entitled to assume that the author has the right, or is in a position to secure the right, to reproduce the illustrations which he is submitting with his MS—otherwise, he is offering for sale something which is not his to sell. The practice of 'expecting the publisher to see to that', and leaving him, if need be, to pay a second time for what he is supposed to have acquired from the author, is indefensible.

On the other hand there are cases where from the outset it is clear that illustrations are needed which the author is not in a position to provide, or that to comply with the present high standards of production diagrams or sketches submitted by the author will have to be redrawn. How such expenditure is to be dealt with should be defined in the agreement. Usually it will be wholly or partly deducted from the royalty unless it has been taken into consideration in fixing the amount of the royalty payable to the author.

16. *Author's Free Copies.*—A clause that is common

to nearly all royalty agreements entitles the author to receive on publication six presentation copies, and to purchase further copies for personal use on trade terms. A point which authors often overlook is that, unless there is any provision to the contrary, copies purchased by them carry royalty just like any other sales. The copies thus cost less than they appear to do.

17. *Libel* is a serious matter. At one time the Authors' Society and the Publishers Association jointly approved a most unsatisfactory clause which seemed to throw upon the publisher the onus of proving the intention of the author to libel (an almost impossible feat), whereas the onus should surely be upon the author to show that the libel was unintentional (a much more practicable task).

A copy of our printed form of agreement, which at that time embodied this wording, came into the hands of G. Bernard Shaw, whereupon the following amusing correspondence ensued, which I secured his generous permission to reprint:

Extract from a letter from Bernard Shaw to G. Lowes Dickinson, 2nd December, 1929.

By the way, the draft agreement contained an absurd clause by which the authors were to hold the publisher harmless if the book contained any libels. Now it (POINTS OF VIEW) will be a tissue of blasphemous and seditious libel from end to end (bar, perhaps, Lodge); and in any case an author can no more shield a publisher against an indictment for libel than for murder. What the authors *can* do is to guarantee that there are no *hidden* libels on individuals.

Stanley Unwin to Bernard Shaw, 6th December, 1929.

Mr. Lowes Dickinson tells me that you commented adversely upon the libel clause in the agreements for the POINTS OF VIEW talks. I agree with you that it is an absurd clause—it is the one approved by the Authors' Society. It has recently let us down very badly, and we much regret that we ever agreed to adopt it.

Bernard Shaw to Stanley Unwin, 9th December, 1929.

The difficulty about that clause is that people cannot be persuaded that the law of the land cannot be superseded by private contract. If a publisher commits a murder he cannot put another man into the dock by producing an agreement to that effect which the other man has signed. Similarly, if he publishes a criminal libel he cannot proffer the writer of the libel as a scapegoat on the strength of a private agreement. It is not clear even that the execution of such a document is not an offence. It is a sort of conspiracy, and might even run into maintenance and champerty.

All that is of any use to a publisher is a declaration by the author that the book contains no hidden libel: that is, a libel which the publisher could not discover by ordinary diligence in reading the MS, and an undertaking to indemnify the publisher against the costs of a civil action based on such a libel.

In the case of POINTS OF VIEW all the libels are criminal. In publishing them you will be publishing seditious libels and blasphemous libels, and nothing can shield you from the consequences. However, as there won't be any consequences it doesn't matter. . . .

Stanley Unwin to Bernard Shaw, 12th December, 1929.

It would indeed be unpleasant to be convicted of maintenance and champerty, but as a publisher I run greater risks than that almost daily!

I fully realize the point you make and had you and I been deputed to draft a clause on behalf of our respective trade unions we should, I hope, have achieved something more satisfactory than the one of which you rightly complain. The difficulty of drafting a libel clause that has any *legal* value is doubtless wellnigh insuperable. But to a publisher the legal aspect is seldom paramount, because in practice an agreement between an author and a reputable publisher binds only the publisher. Its chief advantage to the publisher is negative, i.e. it limits what can be demanded of him. Most authors (but by no means all) are incredibly careless—a clause that is legally valueless may be exceedingly useful in practice in making the author think twice, thus saving the publisher from the effects of carelessness.

When I apply your definition 'hidden libel' to a recent case (settled out of court) when my firm had the pleasure of paying about £500 I find a curious situation. The libel was obvious to the author and it was pure carelessness that *he* passed it. It was not obvious to us, but it would be untrue to say that we could not have discovered it. Furthermore, a prompt apology from the author would have averted an action for damages, but he failed either to acknowledge the complaint or to advise us that he had received it. No clause will help over this last difficulty, but anything that gives a careless author some *feeling* of responsibility is by no means without value to the publisher.

All of which is not to deny that theoretically you are perfectly right, and personally I should like to see the Authors' Society libel clause revised.

Since the foregoing was written Clause 11 of The Defamation Act, 1952, has made it clear that:

An agreement for indemnifying any person against civil liability for libel in respect of the publication of any matter shall not be unlawful unless at the time of the publication that person knows that the matter is defamatory. . . .

Clause 4 of the Act provides an opportunity for an innocent offender to make an offer of amends. If accepted it disposes of the action; if not accepted it is a defence to prove that the words complained of were published innocently and that the offer was made as soon as practicable. It thus renders far less attractive the vexatious 'gold-digging' libel actions, from which publishers suffered so badly.

More recent wordings for this Libel Clause will be found in the Guide to Royalty Agreements to which reference has already been made.

18. *Obscene Libel.*—Until recently the publisher's position was most unsatisfactory. Mere obscenity in itself was not held to be a crime until, some hundred years ago, Chief Justice Cockburn laid down that the test of obscenity was 'whether the tendency of the matter charged as obscenity is to deprave and corrupt those whose minds are open to such immoral influences, and into whose hands a publication of this sort may fall'.

Now the trouble about this definition (the validity of which was never tested in a higher court) is that it leaves the publisher to demonstrate in effect that all his publications are suitable for innocent schoolgirls, a point made by Mr Justice Frankfurter of the Supreme Court of the USA.

Fortunately the Obscene Publications Bill, 1959, redefines obscenity as an offence if its effect, *taken as a whole*, tends to deprave and corrupt persons who are likely, having regard to all the relevant circumstances, to read, see or hear the matter complained of.

Moreover, a person will not be convicted if he can prove that his publication is in the interests of 'Science, literature, art or learning, or other objects of general concern', and on this the courts will hear expert evidence.

This is a great relief to the reputable publisher whose position under the Cockburn test was an impossible one.

19. *Options.*—The frequency with which authors who expect one to handle all their unsaleable and un-profitable books turn elsewhere immediately they have anything everybody wants and the attempts of the

predatory publisher to reap where others have sown has necessitated the securing of an option on the author's next work. No man would be expected to 'take in' uncultivated ground if he had no certainty of reaping more than the first crop. To suggest that he ought thereafter to be satisfied to bid in open competition with those who did nothing to prepare the soil would be palpably unjust.

That these options are frequently abused is common knowledge; but that they are often necessary must, likewise, be admitted. The question to be decided is the kind of option that is fair, and that question has to be answered in relation to the circumstances and, in particular, the risks which the publisher is running. The author of a first novel could reasonably be expected to bind himself to the extent of two further novels, but that he should bind himself to the extent of five or six seems to me indefensible. Properly worded, an option need by no means prove onerous. If the publisher intends spending a great deal of money on advertising a first novel and on establishing the author's reputation, the terms the author would receive for the second book would obviously have to be rather less favourable than those a publisher who had not spent that money could offer, because capital outlay of that kind has to be spread over two or three books to justify the expenditure and prove remunerative. In practice, it is not the first and perhaps most popular book by an author which pays the publisher best, but the second or third, in the publication of which he is reaping the benefit of his earlier work and expenditure. Certain publishing houses are so well aware of this fact that they will resort to almost any expedient to entice away from his original publisher a novelist whose work has been, or is being, specially boosted.

In some circles this blatant exhibition of the predatory instinct is considered 'enterprising', but fortunately it is now realized that it is not in the long run beneficial to the author, the publisher, or the book trade.

What is important is that the option clause should be properly worded; various alternatives will be found in the Guide to Royalty agreements.

20. The *Out of Print* clause is the last to be considered, and is of a much more controversial nature, so much so that some publishers refrain from including it, unless specifically asked to do so. Let us admit at once that it is eminently just that an author should be able to regain control of his work when out of print, if, after due notice in writing, the publisher declines or neglects to reprint it; but, and here comes the controversy, if the book is to be transferred to another publisher should not the author provide for that other publisher (*a*) to refund to the original publisher any royalties advanced but unearned, (*b*) to take over upon an agreed basis any plates, negatives or blocks made exclusively for the work in question. The Authors' Society contends that the author should have the *option* of taking over such material on advantageous terms, but should be under no obligation to do so—in fact, that it would be unfair to make it obligatory.

If the publisher protests, he is told that as he was not prepared to reprint the book in conformity with the notice, it is clear that he has no further use for the blocks, etc., and, therefore, has no grievance. This is based upon a fallacy. The fact that a publisher is unwilling to reprint a book immediately it goes out of print is no evidence that he will not desire to do so later. My firm has reprinted scores of publications that have been out of print over three years, many that have been out of print over seven or even over ten years. There has seldom been a year when we have not had occasion to reprint some old book. Yet the Authors' Society contends that it is equitable that the potential value of material, made in the hope of a reprint, should be taken from the publisher without the very smallest consideration or compensation. I can only say that in this matter the Society is not so fair as its members, because I have never yet found an author, to whom I have fully explained the position, who endorsed its view.

There are two points to be remembered:

(1) The author is under no obligation to give notice that he wants to take over the book.

(2) The question of the amount of the compensation is a matter for negotiation.

Experience shows that to reprint a very slow-selling book immediately it goes out of print is to court an almost certain loss, whereas a year or two's delay may make the venture a commercially practicable one, and, incidentally, give the reprint a much better send-off. There are sufficient reasons for this; the stock on hand at the booksellers' gets absorbed; the book gets advertised and asked for in the second-hand trade, and the supply of second-hand copies becomes exhausted; the publisher accumulates orders, so that, when the reprint does eventually come, there is a market awaiting it. The difference is considerable, because, in addition to supplying the outstanding orders, the publisher is usually able to induce book-sellers to stock the work again—particularly if the book has been frequently demanded. This gives it a fresh send-off, which, otherwise, would have been impossible. We see, therefore, that in many cases the reprinting of an out-of-print book resolves itself into a question of the appropriate moment to reprint.

At the same time, I end where I began, viz. that it is essentially fair that an author should be able to regain control of his work, if it is out of print and the publisher declines or refuses, after due notice, to reprint it.[1] I merely add that, as in most cases it is a question of the right time for reprinting, the author, if he wishes to back his own opinion (or some other firm's opinion), should not expect to do so at his publisher's expense.

COMMISSION AGREEMENTS

'He who pays the piper calles the tunc.' There is thus no legitimate ground for any publisher to take exception to the Society of Authors' recommendations in connection with commission publications, viz. to be careful to obtain a fair cost of production and keep

[1] It must unfortunately be recorded that during war-time a few authors and literary agents tried to take advantage of this clause by threatening publishers with the removal of books which were out of print *solely* because of the paper shortage. In effect they said to publishers unless you give *our* books a bigger share of your limited paper ration (at the expense of your other authors) we shall take them elsewhere. This unpleasant form of intimidation, if not extortion, resulted in publishers taking counter-measures which the Authors' Society resented.

control of the advertisements and sale price of the book. In a contract of this kind, the author assumes entire liability for the cost of production and advertisement and is the owner of the stock; the publisher is merely called upon to put his organization at the author's disposal in exchange for a lump-sum payment and a commission on sales. The publisher is entitled to the exclusive sale in the territory he is expected to cover, for a specified period of time, but to no other rights. All such rights as well as the stock remain vested in the author.

The author is entitled in the first place to an exact estimate of the cost of everything for which it is possible to give an estimate in advance; it is desirable that the specifications in the estimate should be as complete as possible, and that an actual specimen page showing the style of typesetting should be submitted. The particulars should include:

(*a*) The number of copies to be printed and the number to be bound.

(*b*) The format of the book and number of pages.

(*c*) The kind of paper to be used.

(*d*) The style of binding, and, if cloth, whether ink or gilt, and whether special lettering is to be cut.

(*e*) The amount to be spent on newspaper or other advertising and the number of review copies for the Press.

The contract should prescribe:

The period within which the production should be completed (excluding time occupied by the author in proof correcting, and, if the corrections are at all heavy, the time occupied by the printers in giving effect to them).

The published price (the author would be well advised to consult the publisher about this).

The basis upon which the publisher is to account for copies sold and the commission he is to be entitled to deduct from the receipts (the amount the publisher receives depends upon the discount he allows the booksellers and the commission he pays his travellers).

The commission payable to the publisher if, with the author's authority, he effects the sale of any rights.

The dates upon which accounts are to be rendered (half-yearly during the two years immediately following publication and yearly thereafter is a reasonable basis).

The publisher will probably protect himself by the addition of several other clauses, e.g.:

(a) That after the lapse of x years he shall be at liberty either to return the stock to the author or to sell it off as a remainder, whichever course the author may desire, etc.

(b) That he may store the stock at his printer's or binder's, and shall not be held accountable for copies destroyed by fire or accidental damage, in the absence of negligence, but shall take out a fire policy at the author's cost, if the author so instructs.

(c) That he shall be entitled to debit the author's account with any warehousing charges incurred, provided that such charges shall not exceed the scale rates fixed by the Bookbinders' and Printers' Associations.

(d) That he gives no guarantee of securing separate production in the USA, but will endeavour either to place the rights with, or sell part of the edition to, an American publisher, if the author so desires.

(e) That he does not undertake to send out copies 'on sale or return', and any copies so sent at the author's request shall be at the author's risk.

(f) That the author warrants that the work does not violate any existing copyright, and that it contains nothing libellous, etc.

These, in brief, cover the main headings of the agreement, but a further word is necessary about the advertising and the distribution of review copies. The amount to be spent and the number of copies allocated for the Press have probably been settled at the outset, and in most cases the author will be well advised to take advantage of his publisher's experience in deciding the directions in which the money is to be spent and whither the copies are to go. At the same time the control should, theoretically, be vested in the author.

The publisher's remuneration is a much more contentious question. As already stated, it takes two forms: a publication fee, which in many cases is included in a lump-sum estimate of the costs of production and publication, but is sometimes charged as a separate item; and a commission on sales. Speaking broadly, authors tend to get about as much or as little service as they pay for. At one time or another I have been consulted about, or shown, the agreements and accounts of a score or more commission publications issued by firms of the highest standing. In each case it was clear the author was, if anything, getting *more* than was being paid for. In one of the instances the author was bitter in his complaints. The publisher, he thought, was obviously 'doing him down', and had made thousands [*sic*] out of him, because the book had run into six or seven editions and he, the author, had scarcely had a penny. Careful investigation showed that all the publisher had charged was 10 per cent commission on the sales, i.e. less than half his working expenses. The absence of profit was due to the book being published at such a figure as would bring back the original outlay and little more in the event of the entire edition being sold. When I asked who fixed the selling price at such a low figure, the author replied that he stipulated that the book should not be published at more than 3s 6d, because he thought it would do him good professionally.

I give this illustration because, if a distinguished

engineer, such as this author, accustomed to every kind of calculation, could misjudge the position so hopelessly, it is more than probable that others will do so.

To the uninitiated it would appear that a publisher must obviously make money out of a book which the author has paid to have published. Actually, the better firms with an elaborate and costly organization find it extremely difficult to make commission publications pay at all. The reason is simple: such a publisher's working expenses inevitably *exceed* 20 per cent of his turnover, but how often is he allowed as much as 20 per cent commission by an author? Anything in excess of 15 per cent would usually be considered extortionate.[1] This deficiency is, of course, to some extent made good by the amount included in the original estimate by way of publication fee, but what an amount of work, correspondence, interviews, and technical supervision that fee has to cover! Were a publisher paid one-third of what a solicitor would charge, he would indeed be fortunate.

Why then do the better publishers ever handle books on 'commission'? The answer is, many do not, and none accepts more than a small fraction of those offered on a commission basis. To the question, 'Why do they take any at all?' the answer is, 'There are many reasons'. First and foremost, it may be a book that will bring kudos, or open up some useful connection. Secondly, although a commission publication may not bear its full share of working expenses, it may help to meet that part of the overhead charges, such as rent,

[1] It would help matters were the publisher's commission, like the author's royalty, calculated upon the published price.

which has, in any event, to be faced; in other words, it may help as a 'fill up', particularly in a concern which has either its own printing works or bindery.

In brief, the proportion of books published on commission by the better firms is usually small, and there is generally some good and sufficient reason for acceptance in each individual case. With firms of no particular reputation the position may be very different. Such firms have little or no organization to keep up, and may merely want the use of the author's money and the opportunity of snatching a quick profit in exchange for a minimum service.

In publishing, as in other walks of life, the best and therefore the more costly is usually the cheapest in the long run.

Authors would be well advised to take as much care in choosing a publisher as they would exercise in selecting a solicitor or a doctor (no wise man would choose either on the score of cheapness), and, above all, to refrain from handing over money to firms of which they know nothing without first making proper inquiry regarding their financial standing.

It should be obvious that if a publisher is unwilling to assume the responsibility for financing any particular venture, he is doubtful about its commercial prospects. No author, therefore, should step in and take the risk in such circumstances, unless he is willing to lose a substantial part of his outlay. The publisher who shows any sign of wanting authors to provide him with capital is probably one to be avoided.

Here let it be said that there are two or three harpies masquerading as publishers who do untold harm to the book trade. Timely inquiry at the offices of the Authors' Society, or even from a responsible book-seller, would prevent any author getting into their clutches.

For my own part I always discourage inexperienced authors from paying for the publication of their own books. If the work has intrinsic value, and the author, with his eyes open, chooses to run the risk and is in a position to lose his money, that is a different question.

One last word before concluding an already over-long chapter.

We have seen that a formal agreement between publisher and author is essential; that a bad agreement with a good publisher is better than a perfect agreement with a bad one. We have discussed how the agreement should be drafted, but we have not commented upon an interesting fact, viz. that *in practice* the agreement is only binding upon the publisher. I do not want any unpleasant insinuations read into that remark. A publisher covenants to do things that are readily enforce-able; an author often covenants to do things that are not readily enforceable. Publishers have their place of business, and an action can be brought against any firm of standing without the slightest difficulty, with the knowledge that, other things being equal, sympathy will be with the author, and with the certainty that if damages are awarded they can be collected. Authors, on the other hand, may be rolling stones, or resident abroad; but even if they were not, a publisher would probably be considered vindictive, however good his case, if he took action, and in the end might well lose more than he could possibly gain. But although in this respect it may be a one-sided affair, a contract is a great protection to the publisher, for it defines and limits the claims that may be brought against him.[1]

At the same time, without wishing to stress the point or to bring any charges against authors as a whole, it is fair to publishers that I should place on record that there must be few firms who have been in business for any considerable length of time who could not produce a score or more unfulfilled or broken contracts which, however bitterly they may have felt about them, they have taken no steps to enforce. The black sheep are not all in the publisher flock, even if they are the only ones of which the public hears.

[1] Since this book was written, my attention has been drawn to a suggestion made many years ago by the late Major G. H. Putnam, which I heartily endorse. It occurs on page 121 of the 7th edition of *Authors and Publishers* (1897): 'I trust that it may at some time prove practicable to establish a kind of literary court or board of arbitration, before which court could be brought the various questions and issues that arise between publisher and author. The most important of the issues to be considered in this way would be those which, while distinct breaches of good faith or of justice, are not of necessity infringements of contract or breaches of law.'

CHAPTER V

PRODUCTION

I T is not possible, even were I competent to attempt such a task, to give in a chapter anything approaching a complete account of the numerous and highly technical processes, such as paper-making, block-making, printing, and binding, which are employed in the making of a book. Nor is it necessary, because there exist popular handbooks and learned treatises on all these subjects from which the reader can get more expert and detailed information than I could impart.[1] All that will be attempted here is to put authors in a position to follow intelligently those parts of the processes with which they are likely to come in contact.

It will probably simplify matters if we take each process separately, though in practice several of them are often being dealt with concurrently.

Printing.—In an earlier chapter we discussed the process known as 'casting off' a manuscript, i.e. calculating, after making due allowance for such variable factors as 'small type', etc., how many pages the book will make if printed in such and such a style. But we did not stop to consider a question which arises still earlier, viz. the choice of a printer. To the uninitiated, any printer is a potential book printer, but this is no more

[1] e.g. G. A. Glaister: *Glossary of the Book* (London: George Allen & Unwin Ltd., 1960).

the case than that any tailor is competent to make a lady's costume. Either a printer is a book printer or he is not a book printer; the commercial printer who has occasionally printed a book (probably a local directory or a glorified catalogue) is a person to be avoided, if you want a presentable article. The firms which specialize in book printing may be divided roughly into two classes: (1) the competent, but often uninspired; (2) the incompetent, but cheap.

Most of the firms in the first category are to be found in the provinces and Scotland, and between them they do the bulk of the book printing other than perhaps novels. Their prices do not vary greatly—partly because the introduction of a careful costing system[1] has shown them what their working expenses are, but chiefly because the rates of wages do not vary very greatly. The difference between the rates payable, say, at Edinburgh, Plymouth, and Colchester is negligible compared with that between those three places and London. Wages represent at least half the printer's bill, so that the rate paid is one of the chief determining factors in the price. It is not, however, the only one, because almost as important is the completeness and the competence with which the work is done.

It is obvious that if part of the process be omitted or skimped, a saving of wages may be effected, and it is here that the printers in category 2 come in. They are to be found, for the most part, in the smaller provincial towns. Their output is not considerable, and it is seldom that they are trusted with the printing of

---

[1] Some day publishers may be wise enough to follow their example and compare notes more freely.

anything less straightforward than a novel. It is apt to prove disastrous when they are, because they pay no competent reader to check the proofs; have no one able to make a trustworthy 'cast off', and spend no adequate time upon 'making ready' before machining, without which satisfactory results are unobtainable. The extent to which some publishers employ firms of this kind has always surprised me. In my judgment it is false economy, and the practice of devoting unlimited time and energy to tracking down some printer who will cut his price a few pence further is surely based upon a wrong assumption, viz. that printing prices, except perhaps under war-time conditions, show an undue margin of profit to the printer. There are a few firms of book printers who, because of special circumstances, make considerable profits, but they are the exception, not the rule. It is a point upon which I happen to possess inside information. Furthermore, the employment of incompetent firms lowers the standard of printing. The only way better firms can compete is to skimp their work and, in effect, this is what they are often made to do, instead of being encouraged to improve their standard.

Many authors think it is a great advantage to a publisher to possess his own printing works. This is a delusion. It may even be a positive disadvantage. To be run economically and therefore profitably, a printing plant needs an even supply of manuscripts to print. No one firm, however large, can ensure that the supply will arrive sufficiently regularly to keep all the machinery steadily employed. If there is a lull, either the machinery is idle or, in order to make full use of his plant, the publisher is tempted to embark on some new publication which he would otherwise have declined. There is thus a perpetual conflict between the requirements of the printing and publishing sides of the business. The ideal arrangement is probably entire independence, but close association with one or at most two firms of printers, coupled with perfect freedom to go elsewhere at times of pressure. Many of my fellow-publishers, however, would disagree with this opinion and pronounce in favour of unlimited competition.

Preparation of MSS.—However excellent the printer selected, it is necessary for the publisher to 'prepare the manuscript for press', more so today than ever. The main task of the assistant in the editorial department undertaking this important task is to apply House Rules and to eliminate as far as possible all cause for subsequent corrections. With machine composition, where the operators are highly paid and the capital value of the machinery involved is high, the saving made by well-edited typescript is considerable.

Manuscripts are almost invariably typed, but unfortunately, few typists fulfil the barest minimum of what might be expected of them when producing the typescript of a book. Is it unreasonable, for instance, to suggest that they should have a 'Rule of the House' as a book printer does, and thus preserve some measure of uniformity in such matters as the spelling of proper names and the use of capital letters; that they should know that single underlining indicates 'italics', double underlining 'small caps', and treble underlining 'large capitals'; that they should single space and indent quoted matter and, obvious though it would seem, type out a proper title-page and list of contents? I would urge any typist, who happens to read this, to go a step further and to take note of the preliminary pages of any well-produced book and see what more is needed, e.g. a bastard title (or, as it is more generally, though inaccurately, called, a half-title) and a page corresponding with the back of the title on which the bibliography, copyright notices, etc., are given. If it is known that the book is to be illustrated, it is quite simple to include a blank page headed 'List of Illustrations', even though the illustrations have not yet been selected. Similarly, blank pages headed 'Preface' or 'Introduction' should be added, if either is contemplated, but not yet written. These details have an added importance now that it is customary, where possible, to paginate the 'prelims' with the text.

Instructions to printer should be precise and comprehensive. Our own form includes a delivery schedule[1] and Style Directive as well as general or specific instructions on all the matters dealt with in the following pages. It takes care of everything that can possibly be foreseen, e.g. the number and character of proofs required, whether a precise number of copies is to be printed, or whether the number is to be controlled by the amount of paper delivered by the stationer, and innumerable other points. One of special importance is an instruction to hold the type and to give us a month's notice of the date when type rental becomes payable.

A similar comprehensive form with a delivery schedule gives detailed instructions to the binder, thus

[1] If this is to be adhered to it is vital to ensure that there is no delay in the provision of the 'copy' for the index if there is to be one.

obviating last minute inquiries about our requirements.

These delivery schedules enable us to maintain 'Progress Cards' recording the exact position of each book and automatically revealing any delay.

The choice of the Size of the Page to be used is governed by various considerations. Most novels are produced crown 8vo size, i.e. $7\frac{1}{2}$ in. × 5 in., and are printed on sheets of what is termed quad crown paper, i.e. 30 in. × 40 in. (with the advent of ever larger machinery, double quad crown, i.e. sheets measuring 60 in. × 40 in., is now frequently used, particularly when large numbers are to be printed). Similarly, a biography will probably be printed on demy paper, though if it is a particularly long book a still larger size may be selected. For the sake of reference I give below the standard sizes in use.

Name	Size of Page	Size of sheet most usually printed	Purpose for which it is usually adopted
Foolscap	$4\frac{1}{4}$ × $6\frac{3}{4}$	27 × 34 (Quad Fcp)	Pocket editions
Crown	5 × $7\frac{1}{2}$	30 × 40 (Quad Crown)	Novels
Demy	$5\frac{5}{8}$ × $8\frac{3}{4}$	35 × 45 (Quad Demy)	Biographies,
Royal	$6\frac{1}{4}$ × 10	40 × 50 (Quad Royal)	Books of Travel, History, etc.

Intermediate sizes are often adopted when the paper is being made specially. A publisher may, for instance, have his novels printed on paper measuring 31 in. × 41 in. instead of 30 in. × 40 in., thus giving them a more handsome appearance. My own firm often uses paper 32 in. × $42\frac{1}{2}$ in., which is half-way between crown and demy (called large crown), and is the size of the paper on which the earlier editions of this book were printed.

But all departures from standard sizes, attractive as they may be and often are, automatically involve the special making of the paper, and it is well that authors should realize what that may mean. It is seldom practicable to make less than a ton, or to be sure of doing so in less than three weeks; furthermore, the quantity may vary as much as 10 per cent, so that when you order paper for, say, 2,000 copies, you may receive, barely sufficient for 1,800, or be compelled to take enough for 2,200. These things may not be particularly inconvenient when the first edition is being produced, but might easily prove disastrous were reprints wanted in a hurry, or were only a small impression called for.

The question will be asked why publishers do not carry stocks of paper in the sizes they favour. The answer is that many of us unwillingly do so—unwillingly, because even if the size is right, the weight and bulk of the paper may be wrong, and these vary just as much as the size. There is the further trouble that, despite the utmost forethought, the paper is sure to be in stock at the wrong printer's when it is urgently wanted, thus involving double expense for carriage.

The use of crown and demy papers obviates all these difficulties, because they are always obtainable at a moment's notice from the wholesale stationers and in varying weight and bulk; in practice, therefore, they are the sizes most frequently used, even though a large crown would often look better.

About twenty-six countries now use a standard size

based on a square metre (AO) and known as DIN (=Deutsche Industrie Normen).

The following table shows the description and the dimensions of seven trimmed sizes in the DIN A series which correspond most nearly to British sizes, from 8-demy down to demy 8vo.

	Millimetres	Inches (approx.)	Demy sizes
2A	1189 × 1682	$46\frac{13}{16}$ × $66\frac{3}{16}$	45 × 70
Ao	841 × 1189	$33\frac{1}{8}$ × $46\frac{13}{16}$	35 × 45
A1	594 × 841	$23\frac{3}{8}$ × $33\frac{1}{8}$	$22\frac{1}{2}$ × 35
A2	420 × 594	$16\frac{1}{2}$ × $23\frac{3}{8}$	$17\frac{1}{2}$ × $22\frac{1}{2}$
A3	297 × 420	$11\frac{11}{16}$ × $16\frac{1}{2}$	$11\frac{1}{4}$ × $17\frac{1}{2}$
A4	210 × 297	$8\frac{1}{4}$ × $11\frac{11}{16}$	$8\frac{3}{4}$ × $11\frac{1}{4}$
A5	148 × 210	$5\frac{13}{16}$ × $8\frac{1}{4}$	$5\frac{5}{8}$ × $8\frac{3}{4}$

The Kind of Type and the type area of the page are the next points to be considered. Fifty odd years ago books were hand set; nowadays machine setting is the rule.

The Monotype machine, which is now so frequently used for bookwork, is in two parts. The first, like a large typewriter, punches holes in a roll of paper. In the second machine the roll is unwound and acting upon the pianola principle casts individual pieces of type for each letter and space, and quite uncannily, in fact almost miraculously, arranges them in correctly spaced lines. In the Linotype the whole line of type is cast in one piece called a 'slug', and the subsequent addition of so much as a comma, therefore, involves the resetting of an entire line.

When machine setting was first used for books the results were generally deplorable, but today a wide range of the best type faces is available.

Fifty years ago people who would have been shocked at a mixture of two schools of architecture looked complacently upon typesetting in which half a dozen styles of lettering were mixed. Fortunately for the general standard of typography in England, those days have passed and there is an insistent demand for good type with a definite character about it. Whether it be Caslon or Bembo, an old-face type or old-style, is a matter of personal taste and fitness for the particular purpose for which the type is wanted. The important thing is to have a type that is both readable and beautiful, as are all those which have stood the test of time.

Even so, vigilance may be needed, because the most beautiful page of type may so easily be marred by the use of a headline of some different fount. It is thus necessary not only to select a suitable type, but to see to it that it is used throughout the book.

Type Sizes, of course, vary; those most frequently used in books are:

12 point, formerly called PICA (pronounced pi'ka),

11 point, formerly called Small Pica

10 point, formerly called Long Primer (prim-er)

9 point, formerly called Bourgeois (burjoyce)

8 point, formerly called Brevier (bre-veer)

The Type Area of the page is often governed by economic as well as aesthetic considerations. We most of us like wide margins and generous spacing of the type, but if good value in books consists in giving the maximum length for the minimum price, wide margins and generous spacing are not compatible with good value. For instance, many of the original volumes in the

Everyman Library, which represented the last word in good value, were 'set solid', that is, without leads[1] between the lines of type, and have margins which leave much to be desired; but the books are not to be condemned on that account. None the less, it is of the utmost importance that full consideration should be given to the desirability of good margins, sufficient spacing between the lines, and equal spacing between the words, when determining the type area of the page. For that reason it is essential that the specimen page submitted by the printer should be on paper of the size it is intended to use, but—and this is a point for authors to bear in mind—it is improbable that the paper will be of the quality and weight finally chosen, as just then it might well be premature to make the final selection.

The arrangement of the type area on the page, or, to put the same thing the reverse way, the width of the blank margins at the top, bottom, and sides of the page, needs most careful attention, and is not a matter that can be left to chance. The technical term used is 'imposition'; it covers not only the arrangement of the individual page, but the whole sheet, of which the page may only be a $\frac{1}{32}$ (a thirty-second) part. This is a much more complicated matter than it seems at first, and we shall come to it in a moment.

Galley Proofs.—Before the question of imposing the type arises, it has to be composed, and it is not at first broken up into pages, but is set in long galleys. Only a few years ago it was a customary thing, and still is in

[1] The width of leads is measured by 'points' (see type measurements above). A one-point lead is one seventy-second of an inch. This page has the equivalent of a one-point lead between the lines.

America, to send out first proofs in this form. Such proofs, called 'galley' or 'slip' proofs, are still necessary where extensive additions or deletions will be made in the proof, which will involve changes in the pagination, i.e. will involve carrying matter back or forward to another page. Contrary to the current opinion among authors, galley proofs afford no economy if, as is usually the case, the corrections do not materially alter the number of words in any given page. Furthermore, should the additions or deletions happen to come at the end of a chapter, it may be quite as simple to deal with them in page proof as in galley proof. It is usual, therefore, nowadays in England for the first proofs to be sent out in page form. The custom has been accentuated by the printers' practice of making a more formidable charge for 'making up' if they have first to submit proofs in galley and then subsequent proofs in page. The advantages of 'going straight into page' are many, and the disadvantages in most cases negligible. There will always be a few instances in which galley proofs are essential, but they will remain the exception. Page proofs are easier to handle; they are more serviceable as advance material to travellers; more useful for Press purposes; and, above all, more economical. Two further advantages are that the index can be made as the proofs are first read (which helps in the detection of inconsistency); and that one has no anxiety about errors made by the printer during pagination. But if galley proofs are eliminated, a little more forethought is needed about various minor matters. The importance of preparing the manuscript for press has already been emphasized; extra care needs to be exercised if the book is to be paged right away, particularly if the preliminary pages are paginated with the text.

The 'Prelims', the expression used to designate these preliminary pages, means in practice the first eight or sixteen pages of a book, and covers the Bastard Title, the Title-page itself, the Bibliography, Dedication, Contents, Preface, etc. The 'lay out' or arrangement of this part of a book, and particularly of the title-page, calls for considerable typographical skill. A glance through the prelims of a book at once reveals whether or not an expert has been at work. There is a prescribed order in which such things as Contents and Lists of Illustrations, Prefaces, and Introductions should appear. Upon some points there are divergencies of opinion, but the principles laid down by the late Dr Ballinger might with advantage be generally adopted. In the course of an interesting letter in *The Times Literary Supplement* of April 6, 1922, he wrote:

When a Preface exceeds two or three pages it should be treated as an introduction. If this could be agreed, the following order for the preliminary pages might be used without inconvenience: I. Title (with bibliographical note on the verso); II. Preface; III. Contents; IV. List of illustrations; V. Introduction; VI. Text.

Many publishers print on the title-page their 'mark' or 'colophon'; it is doubtful whether this is the most suitable place, as it leads to a certain monotony and may often be an obstacle to a good piece of setting; the bastard title is better, but even here it may be too prominent or overpowering; probably the traditional position of the colophon at the close of the book would be more appropriate, if any general rule is to be laid down.

Whether the date is given on the front or back of the title-page is unimportant *so long as it is given*. Were it certain that the book was never going to be reprinted there would be much to be said in favour of putting it on the front. But if it is desirable—as I feel most strongly it is—to ensure the giving of the completest possible bibliographical information in the case of reprints, it is much wiser to begin by giving the date on the back.

If the date is on the front and a reprint is hurriedly ordered, the new date will be substituted for the old, and the desirability of a bibliography may be forgotten. Should the date be given on the back in some such form as

First published in 1955

the mere addition of the words 'Second impression 1956' automatically forms the desired bibliography, whether anyone happens to think about it or not. All librarians and others to whom bibliographies are of special importance would therefore be wise to advocate the printing of the date on the *back* of the title-page.

This brings us to the use of the words 'Impression' and 'Edition'. It cannot be too strongly urged that the word 'impression' should be confined to reprints in which there are no alterations of any kind, and similarly the word 'edition' should not be used unless the reprint contains revisions or additions or represents a change of format. The republication at a different price or in a different form of part of an impression which has already been placed on the market is best described as a 'reissue'. It should not necessarily be inferred, because the word 'edition' is used, that the alterations are extensive. If a book is 'considerably enlarged' the publisher may usually be trusted to say so. An impression or edition may consist of any number of copies; a book that is in its fifth impression may not have sold to the extent of one that has not been reprinted. But the fact that most printers now charge for machining any number less than 1,000 at the scale rate for 1,000 makes it unprofitable to print less than that quantity; in fact, there is a tendency today to feel that if it is not worth reprinting 1,500 it is not worth reprinting at all, except in the case of some big and expensive work. On the Continent, and particularly in Germany, an edition usually means 1,000 copies, and a publisher printing 5,000 copies may even announce them as 1–5 editions.

The back of the title-page serves other purposes, most important of all—the copyright notices. In the case of all books first published in Great Britain copyright can be claimed under the Berne Convention. It may be followed by some such wording as the following:

Apart from any fair dealing for the purpose of private study, research, criticism or review, as permitted under the Copyright Act, 1956, no portion may be reproduced by any process without written permission. Enquiry should be made of the publisher.

But if United States copyright is desired and the work has been published since September 26, 1957, and is not by a citizen of or a resident in the USA, it is essential to add ©, followed by the name of the owner of the copyright and the year of publication.

Last but not least in importance is the printer's imprint, preceded by the words 'Printed' or, as some people prefer it, 'Made in Great Britain', or whatever the country of production may be. The inclusion of the printer's imprint is compulsory in any case;[1] but it is the import or export of copies without the country of origin clearly printed upon them that brings the fact home and gives the inexperienced publisher his first acquaintance with the Merchandise Marks Act or American customs regulations.

The inclusion of such things as dedications, short prefaces, etc., in the 'prelims' is a simple matter, if thought of in time, but apt to prove troublesome and expensive after the type has been made up *if no pages have been left for them*, as well as to cause delays at the printer's if settled at the last minute. It is a safe rule, when in doubt, to leave an extra two blank pages in the 'prelims', because if they are not wanted, they can be left as two extra blank pages at the beginning of the book. Whereas, should an extra page for which no provision has been made be added, it may have to be separately printed and specially 'tipped' or 'pasted in' as a frontispiece often is.

Head-lines also need forethought; few things are more annoying to the intelligent reader of a serious work than to see the title repeated at the top of page after page on both the left (verso) and right-hand (recto) sides. To avoid this, the publisher often gives standing instructions to his printer that, failing any advice to the

---

[1] Few people seem to be aware that under the Newspapers, Printers and Reading Rooms Repeal Act, 1869, it is the *printer's* imprint and *not* the publisher's imprint which is obligatory.

contrary, the title of the book should be used as the left and the title of the chapter as the right-hand head-line. This is a good serviceable arrangement, and has the great merit of enabling the printer to complete the work at once. Furthermore, it facilitates the identification of loose sheets, a point emphasized by Dr Ballinger. Some authors, however, prefer the title of each chapter as the left-hand head-line, and a running head-line, descriptive of the contents of the actual page, on the right. If this plan is adopted, the right-hand head-lines have to be left blank for the author to fill in when he receives the proofs. This means an extra item on the correction bill, and it should be clearly agreed between author and publisher whether it is to be regarded as a 'correction' or not. Whichever method of dealing with head-lines is adopted, it would be helpful to the printer if authors who favour long titles to their chapters would indicate on the MS an abbreviated version for use as the head-line of the page. Printers are usually very clever at finding the best abbreviation, but as it often means putting special emphasis on part of the chapter title, it is a point much better settled by the author, and preferably before the typesetting begins.

Authors often suggest that they shall deliver *part* of their MS, so that the printers may make a start. This is seldom, if ever, advisable, unless the complete MS has already been 'cast-off' and has merely gone back to the author for verbal polishing, or for some purpose which will not change its final length. For the printer to go ahead with an instalment would, in most cases, be making a false start and mean loss of time. It would almost certainly prove uneconomical.

Modern Single-Sided Printing Machinery is constructed to print 32 or 64 pages of an octavo book on one side of a sheet. The maximum advantage is thus secured by making a book consist of so many sheets of 32 pages each—in other words, a multiple of 32. Hence, when we speak of a novel being a ten-sheet book, we mean that it contains $10 \times 32 = 320$ pages. Perfector printing machines print both sides of a sheet in one operation, giving 64 or 128 octavo pages at the time.

A sheet is printed to fold, and the number of times it is folded determines whether it will contain 4, 8, 16, 32, or 64 pages. Sixty-four pages may be machined as one sheet, or, at the most, two sheets of 32 pages each; on the other hand, the printing of 56 pages involves the machining of not less than three sheets, of 32 pages, 16 pages, and 8 pages respectively, unless eight superfluous blank pages are added, thus making a 64-page sheet. This explains why nearly all books, whether the fact is revealed by the pagination or not, consist of an even number of pages, usually a multiple of 32, in almost every case a multiple of 16.

Now, if it is desirable to make the book consist of an 'even working' of 32 pages (the separate machining of an odd four- or eight-page section would be termed an 'uneven working'), it follows that a page must be chosen which will produce this result. It is easy to realize that the addition of a line to each page will reduce the number of pages, or that the making of each page an 'em' narrower will increase the number of pages, but as we have seen two founts of type of the same nominal size may produce different results, some founts having a broader face than others and tending to occupy more space and thus run into more pages. Very exact adjustments are therefore possible if the *complete* MS is in the printer's hands and there are no variable factors. The printer should, for instance, know before he starts work whether there is to be an index and how many pages to allow for it. It is better to over-estimate rather than under-estimate the number required, because it is easy to fill up blank pages with advertisements, whereas an extra two pages would have to be specially printed; and if less than four pages were included, they would have to be 'pasted in' at the end of the book.

To show at a glance some variations in type I have asked the printer to give three specimens below, all of them in 11 point (small pica) type.

These few lines are set in eleven-point Baskerville, which is a very broad-faced type. Note the number of letters and words in each line.

These few lines are set in eleven-point Fournier, which has a narrower face. Note the extra letters which can thus be included in each line.

These few lines are set in eleven-point Perpetua, which has a narrower face. Note the extra letters which can thus be included in each line.

For clarity some volumes need chapter sub-divisions. These can be:

Cross-heads, usually even small caps or bold face upper and lower case centred.

Shoulder-heads, usually even small caps or italic upper and lower case.

Side-heads, usually italic upper and lower case. Examples of all three are given below.

THE SIGNALMAN'S CONTROL

(Cross-head)

THE SIGNALMAN'S CONTROL

(Shoulder-head)   Always a separate line, full out.

The Signalman's Control.—This is a specimen of a Side-head.   Indented 1 em,.and run on, not a separate line.

At this stage other questions may arise such as mar-
ginal notes.[1] These materially increase the cost because, *A Marginal Note.*
apart from the additional typesetting involved, they
either increase the area of the page and thus the cost
of 'making up' the page (the compositor's remuneration being based upon the superficial area), or, if the
page be made narrower to allow for them, increase
the number of pages. Another method is the
A Cut-in Note 'cut-in note', which avoids increasing the
area of the page, but complicates the typesetting and is rather more costly than a marginal note.

Proofs.—Although it is usual to print 32 pages and
even 64 pages in one sheet, the proofs are almost
invariably sent out in sections of 16 pages, and the
book, when finally bound, will probably be in 16-page
sections (it is not convenient to sew larger sections
together). Each of these sections is numbered on the
first page, sometimes with the ordinary arabic numerals,
but more usually with the letters of the alphabet. Most
people have at some time observed stray letters of the
alphabet on pages 17, 33, 49, 65, etc., of a book, but

---

[1] The term 'side note' is ambiguous and should be avoided.

few, except the initiated, have realized their purpose, which is to facilitate the 'collating' or gathering together of the folded sheets preparatory to sewing them. These letters or 'signatures', as they are called, have an added use as a name for each section of the book. Authors are sometimes mystified when told by their publisher that he is sending them proofs of sigs. A and B of their book to pass for press; it means, of course, the proofs of the two sections containing pages 1–16 and 17–32, respectively.

Proofs are almost invariably printed on proof paper, usually some cheap paper upon which it is possible to write, and *not* upon the paper to be finally used, which may be, and often is, quite unsuited for writing. Furthermore, proofs are 'pulled up' on a hand-press merely to enable the author to check the accuracy of the typesetting, and for that purpose it would be waste of time to bother about the evenness of the printing. These two points cannot be too much emphasized; every publisher receives all too frequently the most pathetic letters from authors, who have just received their first proofs, expressing the hope that better paper is going to be used and that more care will be taken over the quality of the printing.

The number of proofs provided varies with the printer and the instructions of the publisher. Six sets are supplied by most printers gratis, but if more are wanted, some small extra charge may be made. The publishers themselves require proofs for various purposes, e.g. (1) to check the quantity of paper to be ordered; (2) for their travellers all over the world; (3) for publicity purposes; (4) to show American and foreign publishers in connection with the sale of the American and translation rights; (5) to lend to the artist, if a design is needed for the cover; (6) to look through themselves and possibly pass on to a lawyer to vet for libel. It is usual to send the author two sets— one of them a marked set stamped 'to be returned', the other an unmarked duplicate for the author to retain and use, if need be, for the preparation of an index. The 'marked' set has generally been gone through by the printer's reader, whose encyclopaedic knowledge and eagle eye have saved many authors from pitfalls.

It is the duty of the printer's reader to draw attention to any doubtful points as well as actual mistakes which he observes. A question mark in the margin, which some authors seem to regard as 'an impertinence' (I quote from an author's letter), is merely an indication that the passage queried should be carefully read by the author. It may be that the grammar is a little shaky, that the meaning is not clear, that there has been some inconsistency, or that the reader thinks a slip may have been made. If the passage is found to be correct as printed, the question mark should be struck through and the 'reader' relieved thereby of further responsibility. The query mark should not be left undealt with. The question mark, as used by the printer's reader, is a method of drawing attention to a particular phrase or paragraph, and an inquiry as to whether it represents the author's intentions; it is not an expression of any doubt about the author's views.

Authors' Corrections and Alterations.—In Appendix II will be found particulars of the proper way of marking proofs to show any corrections or alterations it is desired to have made.[1] Before making any corrections let alone alterations authors should pause and count the cost. There is no escape from the fact that they are exceedingly expensive, and that there are few directions where there is so little to show for the money spent. (There is only one thing worse than making alterations in standing type, and that is correcting stereoplates; but to that we shall come later.) As alterations are charged at so much per hour for the time expended upon them, it is important for authors to know the kind that is most troublesome. This last aspect of the matter deserves more attention than it usually receives. In the first place, it is well to keep steadily in mind that each letter is represented by a little piece of leaden type which can neither expand nor contract. When some words are struck out, a gap is created which must be filled somehow. If words containing an equal number of letters are substituted, the minimum of inconvenience and expense is caused; on the other hand, should nothing be substituted for what is deleted, every ensuing letter has to be moved along, either until the end of the paragraph is reached or until, thanks to additional spacing between each word in several successive lines, the gap has been filled. This is known as 'putting the type through the stick', as it has to be taken out of the forme in which it has been made up and actually handled again by the compositor.

On a larger scale the addition or deletion of several lines may give quite undue trouble and involve the transfer of type from one page to another, unless, as

[1] See also *Author's Alterations Cost Money and Cause Delay*, produced by the British Federation of Master Printers.

already mentioned, it happens to occur at the end of a chapter, where space is available and there is in consequence a measure of elasticity. Similarly, instructions to make a fresh paragraph may involve the disturbance of many lines. Two questions, therefore, the inexperienced author should always ask himself or herself: Is the correction *really* necessary? Have I made it in a way which involves least trouble?

Printers' charges for corrections are often the subject of dispute because they are not easy to check, and certain unscrupulous firms have occasionally sought to

CORRECTIONS AND ALTERATIONS

Title...

Signature..   *Stage*..

The Compositor's and Reader's charges on this amount to £   :   :

For UNWIN BROTHERS LTD

Date...   ....

make up in this way for 'price cutting' in their estimates. Others may have, whether by accident or design, included in their charges the cost of correcting their own errors. The remedy for these ills is threefold: First and foremost, to employ an honest printer with a reputation to lose; secondly, for authors to correct printers' errors in some distinctive way, by the use (say) of different coloured ink; thirdly, for the publisher to insist upon a correction ticket or docket for each batch of corrected proofs. Such a slip, of which the above is an example, enables the publisher to keep a much closer watch upon the expenditure being incurred.

It is obviously much easier to check the cost of the corrections on a few sheets than those in the whole work.

In all cases where the corrections are heavy and the author's allowance is likely to be exceeded, it is wisest to obtain an estimate of their cost *before* giving effect to them. There is then time for the author to decide to do without the corrections or alterations, to authorize them to be made, or to obtain an independent estimate of their cost; and the publisher will have the satisfaction of avoiding one very common cause for grievance.

Imposition.—Immediately the first sixteen pages are imposed, the printers may submit a special proof for the approval of the imposition. In some cases a slip is attached of which the following is an example:

URGENT

Kindly say if the margins of this page are satisfactory.

Also, does your Binder require any special imposition to suit his Folding Machine?

Progress is delayed pending your answer.

There are two distinct questions to be answered. As has already been pointed out, the arrangement of the margins is one of the most important factors in determining the appearance of a book. It will be found in practice that where the margins of a book are correct they are twice as broad at the bottom as they are at the top; and the outside margins and what you see of the two centre (or inside) margins will represent the mean between the top and bottom margins as shown in the simple diagram opposite. A book is held at the bottom or side, never at the top. Here we have another proof of the statement that 'fitness for use' results in a pleasing appearance.

The imposition sheet sent for approval will not, however, correspond exactly with this formula, because allowance has to be made for trimming or cutting the

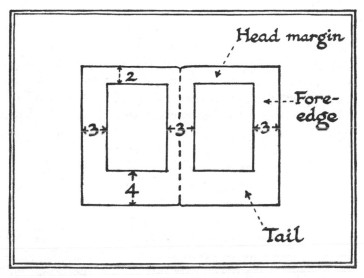

edges in the process of binding, and for the amount of the centre margins or gutter[1] which will be hidden out of sight when the sheets are sewn. The amount so hidden tends to increase with the thickness of the book. The trimming or cutting of the edges—and comparatively few books nowadays are left completely uncut—will be affected by the nature of the folding, and this

[1] The margins of a printed sheet which, after folding, form the inner margins between adjacent pages. (Printers regard the furniture between adjoining fore-edges as gutters.)

brings us to the second question asked by the printer, which should have been answered at an earlier stage.

Today most of the folding hitherto done by hand is done by machine. The two processes are not the same, and different folding machines demand different arrangement of the pages. It is, therefore, necessary for the printer to know which way the sheet is going to be folded before he can arrange the pages, i.e. impose them. Any reader who wants to understand this question of imposition will find it very easy to do so if he will take a piece of paper and fold it three times, thus forming a 16-page section; then, without cutting the edges, number the pages one to sixteen in words. When unfolded he will be surprised to find what unexpected positions some of the pages occupy—still more is it the case with a 32-page section. (See page 129.)

With hand-folding the majority of the uncut edges, or 'bolts', as they are technically called, appear at the top of the book, with some machine-folding the bolts appear at the bottom. Hand-folded sheets may thus have more trimmed from the top, whereas machine-folded sheets (to make sure of clearing the bolts) may have more cut off the bottom of the book. Though theoretically perfect, machine-folding is never in practice so accurate as hand-folding.

The Revision of Proofs.—If the author's corrections are few and clear, there will be no need for a 'revise', and the proofs should in that case, before their return, be marked 'press' and initialled by the author. If one section is heavily corrected, that section can be marked 'revise' and the rest 'press'.

It saves both time and expense to do without revised

proofs, and in most cases they are unnecessary, except possibly for the first and last 'sigs.', which contain the prelims and the index. The latter cannot be completed until page proofs of the whole work are available; so what technically is a 'revise' of the last 'sig.', and of such matter as it may contain, is actually a first proof of the index.

IMPOSITION FOR HAND FOLDING

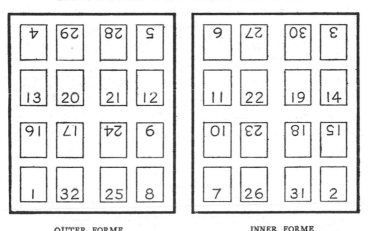

OUTER FORME

Containing amongst others, the first and last pages which appear 'outside' of the signature when folded.

INNER FORME

Containing amongst others, the second and third pages of the signature when folded.

Despite all precautions a few errors are sure to escape notice. The proportion, if the proof-reading has been skilfully done, should not be high. However irritating the mistakes, it is much better to keep a careful record of them in readiness for a second edition than to print an errata slip which nobody bothers to read, essential as it occasionally may be.

Authors often suggest sending, and sometimes even do send, proofs back direct to the printer. Except in the rare instances when the publisher has felt it expedient to arrange for this, it is one of those short cuts which prove the longest way round. The printer either sends the proofs, or writes, to the publisher before doing anything with them, as it is to the publisher he has to look for payment for any work done, and it is only from the publisher, therefore, that instructions can be accepted. Apart from that fact, it would be quite impossible for the publisher to keep a watch over the production, let alone the correction bill, if he did not know whether and when and in what condition the proofs had been returned.

On the 'Progress Card', to which reference has already been made, the movements of proofs are carefully recorded. At one time individual 'sigs.' were sent to the printers as and when passed for press, but in practice no time is saved thereby, on the contrary complications often arise if machinery is started on isolated 'sigs.'. It is wiser to send the printer the press proofs complete.

Many book printers send their more important clients a weekly report showing the position of all 'work in progress'. Although useful they should in theory be unnecessary if the clerk in charge of the Progress Card is making a daily check to see whether the printers are adhering to the schedule prescribed when the work was put in hand. If they are 'slipping' immediate action can be taken.

The Press Work, or machining, as it is now called, for it has long since ceased to be done by hand, is the next process to be considered. Bookwork is largely done on 'flat-bed' machines, i.e. the type is on a flat surface, whereas newspapers are, for the most part, printed on rotary presses, i.e. the type, or rather plates cast from the type, are on a cylindrical surface. Most cheaper books are produced by the latter process. The evenness of the printing is largely dependent upon the evenness of the surface of the type. The bed of the machine is exactly level, the composition rollers that carry the ink are easily adjusted, but the thousands of little pieces of type may not present a true surface. The process of preparing the surface of the printing machine cylinder so that even pressure is given on every part of the 'forme' and type, together with other minor adjustments, is called 'making ready'. It is a most laborious affair if the work is conscientiously done, and it is here and in the quality of the ink that the cheap printer is apt to economize.

It is well, however, for authors to remember that just as the rubber tyres of a motor-car suck up loose stones from the best macadam road, so the ink rollers passing over the type occasionally draw out any isolated letter which is not firmly held by the pressure of its fellows. Punctuation marks, which are very slim pieces of metal, are particularly liable to be drawn out in this way. It is thus not due to malevolence on the part of the printer, as I found one author thought, that stray commas and full stops disappear from the end of so many lines of verse. Even if they are not entirely removed by the suction of the rollers, they may sometimes be broken off.

Theoretically, if any letter gets misplaced in course

of machining, a proof of the page affected is, after correction by a compositor, re-examined by the printer's reader; but, in practice, the machine-minder, wanting to get on with his job, occasionally puts the letter back where he 'thinks' it comes from. Very often he thinks right, but if he does not, there arises one of those tiresome misprints which the author complains—quite correctly—were not in the proofs he passed. The remarkable thing—and authors and publishers would do well to bear the fact in mind—is, not that errors of this kind occur, but that they happen so comparatively seldom in really good printing offices.

A more serious matter is the 'greyness' of much modern printing. The causes vary: the paper may be unduly absorbent or fluffy, bad ink may have been used, or pressure may have been brought to bear upon the printer to expedite delivery, in which case he may find himself compelled to run the ink thinner to ensure its drying more rapidly. In any case it is a point which needs perpetual vigilance, because otherwise the appearance of a book may so easily be marred.

Paper.—Hand-made and mould-made papers and the best quality writing-papers are still made from cotton and linen, but both these materials, even in the form of rags, are too costly for ordinary commercial purposes, and other products of plant life have long since been substituted. The three materials now chiefly used in book papers are esparto, a coarse grass which grows wild in Spain and North Africa; wood pulp, in the form of what is known as either chemical wood or mechanical wood, the latter being of the poorest quality, and straw.

The best antique papers, more particularly the 'featherweights', are made of esparto, and it is on antique papers, whether 'laid' or 'wove', that most British books are printed.

One technical point in paper production must be mentioned. The swift flow of pulp in the web of the paper machine causes the fibres to lie mainly in one direction—this is termed 'grain direction'. The term 'long grain' is used to describe paper in which the fibres run parallel with the length of the sheet. 'Short grain' means that they run parallel with the width. The fibre of paper tends to swell more in width than in length. This is apparent in a bound book where the grain runs across the page; such a book will not open flat. If the grain runs from head to tail the book opens well. Thus for an octavo book from a quad size sheet, the binder prefers short grain paper. Most printers nowadays will accept paper with whatever grain is sent to them; but ideally they would like to print along the grain of a page or on long grain paper. In this con-flict, the publisher puts the binder's requirements first, except in colour litho work, where the unevenness across the grain could affect precise colour registration.

Whether the paper should be pure white, heavily toned, or preferably some shade between is a matter of taste, apart from the fact that some type faces call for a whiter paper than others. Unless some measure of uniformity in colour and weight is aimed at, a pub-lisher may find himself in difficulties when it comes to using 'over makings' or surplus stock. To have part of a book printed on one shade or thickness of paper and the balance on another is deplorable. When paper is specially made a percentage of $7\frac{1}{2}$ per cent over or under the amount ordered has to be 'tolerated'.

For some quite inexplicable reason the public in pre-war days measured the value of a book by its bulk; its cubic dimensions were apparently more important than its literary contents. The identical book which was 'poor value' when it bulked half an inch became 'good value' when it was printed on fluffy paper which bulked an inch, and the sad or amusing thing about it—take your choice which—is that the chief difference between the two books is the amount of air left in the fluffy paper. It is rather like saying that the white of an egg is better value when beaten up because it occupies so much more space. A firm, well-rolled paper can be bound more securely, will last longer and is in every way better than a fluffy one which incidentally gives the printer trouble by choking up the type, covering the machine, and worse still the ink rollers, with a deposit of the loose fluff and thus seriously affecting the quality of the printing.

If line illustrations are to be printed in the text, papers with a smooth surface have to be used, such as a 'machine finish' (MF), which is smooth without being glossy. Unfortunately the paper on which the text is printed is seldom suitable for photographic illustrations. These have usually to be printed separately on a still smoother paper, viz. 'art' or a machine coated paper. The glossiness of the art paper, which is both bad for the eyes and an abomination to the artist, is obtained by coating the paper with china clay. A degree of sharpness satisfactory for some photographic or 'half-tone' blocks is, however, often obtained

on a well-rolled uncoated paper, which is of a more
pleasant appearance.

The various sizes in which paper is usually made
have already been mentioned. The standard of quantity
is the ream, which is nominally 500 sheets, but may be
as few as 480 or as many as 516. Book papers are nearly
always supplied in reams of 516, thus giving the printer
some allowance for spoilage and ensuring that if paper
for 1,000 copies is ordered, not less than a thousand
and possibly a few more will be forthcoming.

In earlier days the printer always supplied the paper,
but at the present time nearly all publishers do their
own paper-buying, and instruct the paper merchant
where to send it. It is most desirable that he should
submit an out-turn sheet *before* making delivery. In
addition, in order to avoid mistakes, the printer usually
sends a specimen sheet to the publisher for verification,
with a printed slip attached giving the size, the quantity delivered, etc.

Naturally publishers listen sympathetically to their
printer's views on paper quality, and in case of any
doubt consult them before placing an order.

Calculating the quantity of paper required is apt to
prove very troublesome to the uninitiated, because it is
so easy to make the mistake of ordering half or double
the quantity needed. Not only does the number of
sheets in a book vary, but the number of sheets that a
ream will give varies according to whether it is ordered
in the double or quad size. Take as an example a novel
of 320 pages: for one thousand copies 10 reams will
be required if the paper is ordered in quad crown
(30 × 40), 20 reams if double crown (30 × 20) paper

is used, and only 5 reams if, to take advantage of larger machinery, double quad crown (60 × 40) is needed. The difficulty will be lessened if the new standardized measurement of 1,000 sheets is generally adopted (at present it does not apply to papers made for book publishers), but there will still remain the confusion between 'pages' and 'leaves'.

Illustrations.—There are innumerable methods of reproducing illustrations, but with the more costly it is unnecessary to deal, as they are not used extensively in commercial book-production. Progress is continually being made; new processes are evolved, or old methods improved almost out of recognition. Two of the more costly processes used in expensive books, 'photogravure' and 'collotype', give the most satisfactory results, and the former is now frequently adopted when the number to be printed is sufficiently large to justify the use of a rotary machine; unfortunately, however, cheaper and much less satisfactory alternatives have generally to be used.

For certain classes of colour printing, hand-drawn lithography, on stone or plastic, is still adopted; the printing thereafter being done from a normal litho plate. But for the most part modern reproductions are made by either half-tone or line processes.

The half-tone process can be used for the reproduction of almost any type of original, but principally those in graduated tones, such as photographs, wash-drawings, or paintings; it has the great drawback that the best results are dependent upon the use of glossy 'art' papers, which are so heavy to the hand. Hence the frequent necessity of printing illustrations separately from the text and—in that case—inserting them, if possible, between or in the centre of signatures.

It can easily be seen if an illustration is printed from a half-tone block, either by observing the little dots in the reproduction with the naked eye, as one can do in the illustrations in a daily paper, or by looking at the reproduction through a magnifying glass, if a finer screen has been used and the dots are too close together for the eye to detect them.[1]

Most modern coloured illustrations, if not printed lithographically, are produced by this process, in which case three blocks for the three primary colours, yellow, blue, and red, are used. Better results and finer shades are, of course, obtainable by using four or more blocks, but this adds materially to the expense. It will readily be understood that the difficulty of accurately superimposing the printing of one set of blocks upon another, technically called 'registering', automatically increases with the number of colours. It is not surprising, therefore, that it costs more to print one illustration in two colours than two illustrations separately in two different colours. In the first case a great deal more care has to be exercised than in the second. Naturally, therefore, if economy has to be studied, the number of colours used has to be reduced to the minimum. In colour printing, the order in which the colours are printed, and the shades of yellow, blue, and red used, greatly affect the results, and it is customary, therefore, for the blockmaker to provide 'progressive pulls' for the printer's guidance. The blockmaker should be instructed to pull

[1] See pages three and four of the specimen illustrations inserted between pages 144 and 145.

his proofs upon paper similar to that upon which the blocks are to be printed. Such proofs can then be used as a standard to check the final results.

If any 'legend' or 'caption', i.e. descriptive matter below an illustration, has to be printed, the printer pulls up a rough proof for the lettering to be checked. When this rough proof is sent to the uninitiated author to make sure that the wording is correct, it often calls forth a remonstrance and an expression of hope that the illustrations are not going to look quite as bad as that! Once again, therefore, it is necessary to emphasize that such proofs are submitted only for the purpose of checking the wording. If any alterations are going to be made, it is obvious that the paper must be of a kind on which it is possible to write. Furthermore, nothing would be gained by the expenditure of time upon careful printing at that point.

The line process is a cheaper method, and where it can be adopted is generally to be preferred. It is useless for the reproduction of photographs or wash-drawings, but is suitable for the reproduction of line drawings, diagrams, woodcuts, or very simple coloured illustrations where the colours do not intermingle.

A new standard has recently been set in the illustration of scientific text-books, and this we owe to the happy collaboration of a scientist and artist. Their technique is to make the diagram self-contained; there is no need to refer back to the text for explanations. This can be seen, for example, by comparing a drawing of the Star Triangle from a standard college text-book on astronomy with the drawing of the same subject in Lancelot Hogben's *Science for the Citizen*. This new style calls for the fullest collaboration between author and artist.

It has always surprised me how few of the many artists who earn their livelihood by drawing for reproduction ever make any real effort to study the media through which their work is to reach the public. For instance, it is astonishing what a small proportion of the designs submitted for the jackets of novels are drawn in such a way as to be suitable for reproduction with three line blocks instead of three half-tone blocks. Not only is the line process cheaper, but it is more effective for such purposes and does not have to be printed upon glossy art paper. For this reason line illustrations can be, and generally are, printed with the text of a book; whereas half-tone illustrations, as we have seen, usually have to be printed separately on art paper unless the whole book is so printed, in which case the volume will feel like a lump of lead. As a matter of fact, half-tone and type can be printed on a well-rolled esparto, or MF paper, if a screen of 133 dots is used and a good pressure.

Wherever illustrations are printed in the text it is nearly always essential that galley proofs of the latter should be provided, as it is seldom possible to arrange for the placing of the illustrations beforehand.

The 'Offset' Process.—There is one further method of reproduction to which reference has not yet been made and which has come increasingly into vogue, and that is the 'offset' process which is particularly useful for the photographic reproduction of an existing book, illustrations, maps and line or pencil drawings. It is a form of lithography, using, in the place of stones, thin zinc plates, which can be attached round the cylinder of a rotary press. This development from stone to metal, giving higher printing speeds, opened the way for the use of photography which in turn enabled fine and intricate work to be reproduced on the plate. Subsequently it was discovered that if the design on the metal plate was printed first on a sheet of smooth india-rubber and from there on to a sheet of paper, an impression of a greater degree of sharpness, and yet one having a softer quality, could be obtained. In offset this is what is done. The image is first printed on to a cylinder covered with india-rubber and passes from that immediately on to the paper. The smooth rubber blanket permits the image to be built up more perfectly than is possible on a grained plate, and because of its perfection of surface less ink is necessary, thus reducing the risk of the still damp ink smudging the page next to it, technically known as 'set off'; furthermore, the resilient rubber also presses into the grain of the paper, giving unbroken lines on moderately rough-surfaced papers.

As the method involves the use of photography it is most suitable for facsimile reproduction. Alterations can, however, be made by re-setting the passages or pages affected and photographing the corrected version. But exceptional care has to be taken with the machining of the corrected matter (rough pulls will not do) and it is essential to use paper as similar to that of the book to be reproduced as can be obtained. Further, the pasting of the new matter over the old must be done most accurately because the slightest deviations from the straight would mar the final appearance. An advantage of the process—often overlooked—

is that the type can be photographed smaller, or larger, so that, for example, a Demy 8vo book can be reproduced Crown 8vo size, or vice versa.

Half-tone colour offset lithography has the advantage over letterpress half-tone that it does not necessitate the use of art paper. On the other hand it must be admitted that a job which could be printed in three colours from half-tone blocks would call for at least one additional colour in photo-lithography. Granted the extra colour, photo-lithography gives the more pleasing result. Another point worth bearing in mind is that negatives used in photo-lithography are easily stored, and each time they are used give a perfect result, whereas half-tone blocks get worn and are easily damaged.

Photo-lithography is a process calling for expert workmanship which is dependent upon the careful training of employees. The proportion of firms claiming to be photo-lithographers who are capable of producing first-class work remains and probably will remain comparatively small.

Blockmaking.— The position was most unsatisfactory. The leading English blockmakers adopted a fixed scale of charges by the square inch from which they would not depart by a hairbreadth. A scale which may be appropriate for rush work, often at overtime wage rates, done for newspapers and periodicals is not necessarily appropriate for book work carried out at leisure. How inappropriate may be judged from the fact that it was at one time possible to have blocks made in Holland and sent to London by air mail (an expensive procedure) at less than the English blockmakers' tariff.

An interesting and disconcerting feature of this situation was that an independent firm paying full trade union wages but satisfied with a lower margin of profit ran the risk of having pressure brought to bear upon it *by the relevant trade union* to charge the full scale. On the 7th January 1960 the Federation of Master Process Engravers announced that it was *not* going to defend its price agreement in the Restrictive Practices Court, and would no longer maintain a minimum scale.

To estimate the price of a block all that is needed is to calculate the number of square inches thus:

One illustration to be reproduced

$$5 \text{ in.} \times 4 \text{ in.} = 20 \text{ square inches}$$

and consult a blockmakers' sliding scale, which gives the cost according to area. There is, however, one important point to be remembered: that, under the prevailing scale, blocks measuring less than 14 square inches are charged as if they were 14 square inches—a provision which particularly penalizes book publishers.

Methods of Reproducing Books.—The cheapest method of reprinting a book is to do so from standing type. In America comparatively few books are printed from type at all, as the custom over there is to make a set of electroplates of the type and to print from the plates. The process of electrotyping is much more frequently used in America than in England. It consists of depositing a thin layer of copper upon a waxen mould and backing it with a metal composed of 93 parts of lead, 4 parts of antimony and 3 parts of tin. This is a more costly process than the making of stereoplates, to which we shall come in a moment.

Most printers in England allow the type to be kept

standing free of charge for six months, from the time
the printing is completed, and nearly all will keep it
longer on payment of the standard rental of 1s per
16 pages per month (1s 4d if the size exceeds demy
8vo). Even thirty years ago the holding of type in this
way was a serious matter, because, in effect, it was
locking up the printer's capital. Now that books are
machine set, it is merely a question of holding up so
much metal, for as soon as the type is done with it is
melted down again. None the less, the amount of metal
thus required in a large printing office is very substantial, and at the expiry of the six months the publisher will be faced with a request for permission to
break up the type in order to release metal. He has then
various courses to consider. If it is improbable that a
further edition will be called for, he will give instructions for the type to be distributed. If he feels that the
point will be decided one way or the other in the
immediate future, say within the next month or six
weeks, he will probably agree to pay rent for the standing type. If he is certain that several unaltered reprints
will be wanted in years to come, he will give instructions for the type to be 'moulded', i.e. for papier-
mâché impressions of the type to be made from which
subsequently—when they are wanted—stereoplates
can be cast. But it is no longer economic to take moulds
if only one or two reprints will be needed.

Stereoplates are made of stereo metal, which consists
largely of lead. They are thus rather soft, and it is
impossible to print unlimited numbers from them.
When they are likely to have specially hard wear, it is
usual to have them nickel faced. If care is taken in the

process, it is possible to cast two sets of plates from one set of moulds.

It is dangerous to generalize, because the cost and character of the typesetting of a book may vary so considerably, but roughly speaking, the cost of taking a set of moulds and subsequently casting a set of stereoplates from them is about three-quarters the cost of composition, assuming that the composition is fairly straightforward. There is thus no economy unless many reprints from the plates will be required.

This is such an infrequent occurrence that today publishers seldom spend money on moulds which in any case would be useless if alterations were unexpectedly called for since corrections would have to be made in the stereoplates. When it is realized that these are solid pieces of metal of the same size as the area of a page of type and that to make alterations in them necessitates cutting out the parts affected and accurately soldering in the new matter, it will be seen that this is an undertaking to be avoided.

Fortunately for publishers there is the alternative of photo-lithography, a development of 'offset', to which reference has just been made. The chief drawback is the blurred effect of lithography as against the sharp impression of letterpress.

It ought, perhaps, to be mentioned that British printers charge slightly more for printing from plates than for printing from standing type, because more care is needed in the 'make ready'. This is specially the case if there are any illustrations in the text. American printers, on the other hand, prefer machining from plates, and charge extra for machining from type.

New Processes.—Since 1950 there have been many technical developments affecting book production which must in the long run make for speed and economy. Notably, there has been the introduction of various machines for photo-composition, replacing metal-type composition for the impressions on which intaglio and lithographic printing depends. Typewriter composing machines for the same purpose have appeared. In Linotype, teletypesetting reduces composition to almost typewriting simplicity and even makes possible setting by remote radio control; so far this applies chiefly to newspaper printing, but with further technical development and improved operational skill will speed and cheapen book printing. Electronic photo-engraving machines for the production of half-tone printing plates depend upon the conversion of varying light intensities into the movements of a cutting or burning stylus. Dow and similar etching machines for line blocks not only make cheaper line blocks possible, but also the reproduction of an entire book from printed copy for letterpress printing at costs which compare well with photo-lithography. In blockmaking, however, the full economic advantages of these amazing developments have yet to be passed on to the customer.

Warehousing.—In the happy days of my youth warehousing was a minor problem to publishers. Both printers and binders were nearly always ready to hold printed sheets free of charge and almost indefinitely. There is no doubt that the privilege was greatly abused. It is so unusual to get 'something for nothing' that few publishers realized it was a privilege until they lost it.

Today there are very strict limitations to the length of time a printer will hold stock, and immediately the pre-scribed period of three years has elapsed, rent becomes payable at so much per 1,000 books per annum. The figure varies from 4s 6d for a crown 8vo pamphlet of 64 pages or less to £2 14s for a demy 4to volume of 256 pages. These charges rapidly become formidable and are doubled in the seventh year. The renting of an independent warehouse is not necessarily a remedy, because the biggest item is apt to be the warehouse-man's wages and not the rent. It will be seen, therefore, that with the exception of those rare birds, the steady sellers, the time inevitably and all too soon arrives when the cost of warehousing the surplus stock of a book exceeds the proceeds of the sales. Publishers thus have a far greater incentive than heretofore to dispose of unsaleable books. It was bad enough to have capital locked up and unfruitful; it is now worse because in addition it is a source of expense.

This aspect of the matter indirectly concerns authors, many of whom appear to think publishers excessively perverse if they show any anxiety to 'remainder' a book, or to pulp surplus sheet stock which it will never pay to bind, even though several years have elapsed since the work was first published and it has entirely ceased to sell. This question will be considered more fully in Chapter VI in the section on Remaindering.

The form in which books are stored varies. They may be in flat sheets as originally printed and baled up by the printers, or the sheets may have been folded and collated by the binder, and packed in parcels of from (say) twenty to a hundred copies in readiness for binding. Even if the binding has been completed the books have to be carefully packed and labelled just the same, or they would soon become dusty and unsaleable.

Looking out a single copy of a book that is stored in flat sheets may be a lengthy business, if each sheet is in a separate bale. The warehouseman has not only to move each of these heavy packages from its rack, but to unpack and repack each of them and subsequently restore them whence they came. For this reason it is usually an expensive matter for a publisher to supply single copies in sheets, unless he has had some packed up in readiness for a possible demand in that form, or happens to be giving a binding order which will necessitate the bales being opened.

Binding.—The two kinds of binding which chiefly concern the book publisher are cloth binding and paper binding, if in those two categories are included the many compromises that lie between. Vellum and leather bindings may be needed for special editions and special occasions, but their use as 'publishers' bindings' is too restricted to detain us.

Some printers have fully equipped binding plant, many are competent to tackle paper binding, but much binding is still carried out by independent bookbinding factories in and around London and, to a lesser extent, Edinburgh. It may be convenient to *print* books at some distance from the centre of distribution, but it is seldom wise to bind them too far away, because if there is an unexpected demand for the book, every hour's delay in the delivery of further supplies may be a serious matter. Although the larger the number bound at once the cheaper the price of the binding, it is often unwise to bind up the whole of an edition at the outset. The cost of printing five hundred copies more than are needed is little more than the value of the additional paper, whereas the cost of binding in excess of one's requirements would be a substantial item. Most publishers, therefore, restrict their binding orders to their immediate needs, and this presupposes the proximity of the binder if more copies are wanted in a hurry, and, equally important, the closest possible watch from day to day upon the movement of the stock.

The efficiency of a publishing business may often be tested by the care with which this side of the work is supervised. Booksellers would not have cause to complain that so many of the books they needed were 'binding', if the principals of publishing houses more frequently called for an explanation why their books were being so 'answered'. In war-time it is inevitable, but under normal conditions the trouble is usually due to lack of forethought, carelessness, or want of co-ordination between the relevant departments, though there are, of course, unexpected occasions when the best regulated houses will be caught napping.

Lettering.—As far as outward appearance goes, the most important part of the binding is the lettering. Here the second-rate publisher and the amateur almost invariably give themselves away. Good lettering can seldom be obtained without incurring the trouble and expense of having a brass block engraved at a cost of about £4 for the average spine lettering. It is a complicated process which cannot be started until the final thickness of the book is known. Guessing will not do because an eighth of an inch too much or too little will mar the effect. It is usually possible to make use of the stationer's dummy sent as a sample of the paper and to show its bulk. Alternatively, if there is no great urgency, an advance copy taken from the actual printed sheets is used. The precision and final finish given to the brass block by the hand engraver render it far superior to the cheaper soft metal zinco, cast from type, which is sometimes used as an alternative.

Many publishers attend to their own letterings and deliver them to the binders; others leave it to the latter. In either case it is important to see that a good model is followed. There is neither necessity nor excuse for bad lettering on a book. It should be legible, beautiful, and in keeping with the book. On the Continent, great store seems to be set upon variety. In this there seems to me no point. There is ample room for variation in the style of the binding, the colour of the cloth, etc., without artificially introducing it in the lettering.

The question of whether the lettering is to be in gold or in ink is largely governed by the price. Good plain ink is always to be preferred to any imitation gilt. The main thing to remember is that gilt is most effective on dark-coloured cloths and ink on light ones, but even to this rule there are exceptions, as coloured inks can often be used on dark cloths with good results.

Book Cloths.—Many authors have pronounced likes and dislikes about the colour and grain of the cloth to be used on their books. Most publishers are ready and willing to put themselves to considerable trouble to please authors in matters of this kind, particularly when the authors are specific and not vague in their requirements. It costs no more to bind a book in one colour than in another, and if a publisher has his own idiosyncrasies in such a matter, he has plenty of opportunities of indulging them, and has no need to begrudge an author one such chance. My advice to authors who have set their hearts upon binding of a particular colour is either to send a pattern of the colour, or, better still, to name a book issued by the same publisher bound in the cloth approved. There will be some obvious limitations to what the publisher can do in the matter of the quality of the cloth—buckram, for instance, costs considerably more than an art vellum. Cloths of an honest 'cloth' texture are preferable to those 'grained' to simulate watered silk, crocodile skins, etc., and it is important that the cloth selected should be fadeless.

Fortunately we are no longer tied to cloth. There are today cheaper materials such as Linson which is much used and to the uninitiated is indistinguishable from cloth and Fabroleen which is still less expensive.

If the sheets reach the binders imposed for machine-folding, they will probably all be folded and collated forthwith, whether all are to be bound or not. The folding has already been described; the collating is the gathering together of the folded sections of the book in the right order. Until this has been completed, the binder does not know and cannot report to the publisher how many 'perfect', i.e. complete, books the sheets will yield.

Imperfect books are mostly due to mistakes made in this process. Either a section is missed altogether, or two of the same signature are inserted, or a wrong one substituted. Despite careful checking, slips of this kind are bound to occur, and in view of the speed with which the work is done, it is astonishing that the proportion of 'imperfect' books is not larger. It certainly would be but for an ingenious method of marking each signature at the point where the outside fold comes. If a signature has been missed the omission automatically reveals itself. Binders rectify imperfections without charge and without demur, and will often, in addition, refund the cost of posting back the imperfect copy. The best plan is to send it to the publishers, when they will usually forthwith exchange it for a perfect one if it is otherwise in good condition 'as new'. If, however, it has been inscribed or marked in such a way as to render it unsaleable, the actual copy will have to go back to the binders to be put right, and this may mean from three to four weeks' delay, particularly in the busy season of the year.

When the work of folding and collating has been completed, the binder reports to the publisher that he has so many perfect copies. If a good printer and binder have been employed, this represents the full number of sheets advised, or possibly a few over. When there are shortages, the binder sends an 'imperfection' note showing exactly what sheets are missing. Should the trouble be due to the default of the printer, it will then be for the publisher to take the appropriate action to secure the missing signatures.

The 'cases' in which books are bound are produced nowadays by machine, and the binder requires to know, therefore, before he starts just how many are needed. As with the printing machine it is the 'making ready' that occupies so much time, so with a case-making machine it is the preliminary adjustment that is the

THE TRUTH ABOUT PUBLISHING

trouble. After the machine is once started the process is more or less mechanical.

Jackets.——When the binding is completed and the books have been pressed and given time to dry, they have still to be inserted in dust-covers or 'jackets'. The evolution of this 'dust-cover', because that is precisely what it is, would take too long to describe. People who talk as if jackets were an unnecessary innovation over-look the fact that some form of protection is essential. Fifty years ago it often took the form of plain paper, waste printed sheets or glassine. Then, for convenience, the name was printed on the shelf-back or side; then on both. Some descriptive matter was subsequently added, and later, illustrations. The question is not whether we can do without a dust-cover but whether it shall be dull or decorative—uninteresting or utilized to give information. A mere protection from dust or an attractive and integral part of the book, and incidentally a most important sales factor.

Certain firms specialize in the printing of jackets, and so are able to keep prices down. The usual practice, therefore, is for a publisher to employ such a firm and to deliver the jackets ready printed to the binders.

Here again there is apt to be trouble and delay over 'thickness', and much as the publisher would like to push ahead with this part of the work, he usually can-not do so until a 'thickness copy' is available and it is possible to ensure that the jacket will fit.

The realization that some of these costly modern picture jackets will immediately be discarded without having served any purpose sometimes makes pub-lishers pause. But the fact that booksellers both at home and abroad regard attractive jackets as essential for any book that is to be displayed is decisive and no publisher therefore, let alone one who takes his export business seriously, now hesitates to describe them as indispensable.

Alternative Bindings.—We have thus far referred solely to ordinary cloth bindings with gilt or ink letterings. There are many alternatives, but they mostly have one drawback, viz. that they are unsuited to the requirements of public and circulating libraries, and so long as people insist on borrowing books instead of buying them, this will remain an important consideration.

A cloth binding with a carefully printed label, and binding produced in every way as a cloth binding, but with some strong and suitable paper substituted for the cloth in the making of the case, are both attractive. For small and cheaper books, many developments of paper bindings are now used; e.g. the paper cover is pasted on and turned over a 'stiffener', or, cheaper still, merely turned over the end paper. Any method which gives the paper binding an added feeling of solidity seems to help to make it acceptable to the British bookbuyer accustomed to having his books in cloth.

The many people who periodically write to the Press advocating paper-bound books on the continental model, overestimate the extent to which this would affect the price where small editions are concerned. However desirable paper bindings may be, the fact remains that, owing to the use of modern machine binding, the difference between paper and cloth binding is not substantial. In both cases the sheets have to be folded, collated, and sewn. The saving is in the provision and fixing of a case which a case-making machine produces at an incredible speed. On an average the maximum gain in substituting paper for cloth would be between 5d and 7d. This would justify a reduction of about eighteen pence in the published price. Now, any publisher who made the experiment found that the cloth binding was chosen in nine cases out of ten, unless the difference in price was enhanced to an uneconomic and unjustifiable extent, leaving the loss on the sale of the paper bound copies to be borne by the increased price of the cloth bound copies. It must be remembered that in the case of most new books a large part of the first edition is destined for public and commercial lending libraries, and must therefore be bound in cloth. This leaves merely a residue available for paper binding. It is interesting to note that even on the Continent, where publishers are not so dominated by the requirements of libraries and paper binding was the rule, there is an increasing tendency to use cloth bindings.

The mass-produced paper-back is very different. Here is no question of binding up a portion of a small edition in paper covers, but of taking advantage of the fact that the cost of composition remains the same whatever the number printed, and that large editions can be economically machined on a rotary press. As we have already seen, the size of the edition is the biggest factor in the cost per copy.

Cheap paper-bound editions are not, as many suppose, an innovation. At the end of last century, Cassells published the National Library in a small format at threepence in paper covers, and during the first dozen years of this century most publishers issued ill-produced super royal 8vo paper-backs in double column setting at sixpence; in fact, many publishers' cellars were full of them just before the First World War. The pressure brought to bear upon publishers by authors to issue sixpenny editions of their novels was such that many were published for which there was no real justification. In brief, the choice was not sufficiently selective. In consequence, although the total sales remained substantial, they were spread over so many different books that the publication of many of them at sixpence became uneconomic.

With the advent of firms like Penguin, which not merely concentrated upon this type of publishing, but devoted great pains both to the quality of the production and to the selection of titles, the position changed. But inevitably the published price of these cheap editions has increased more rapidly than other publications. So long as a minimum sale of 35,000 of popular titles is assured all may be well. Trouble arises when the total number of titles available increases more rapidly than the total sales and in consequence the sale *per title* decreases. There is no margin for unsold stock.

That the mass-produced paper-back has stimulated the reading of, and demand for, books, there is no doubt; but they are a welcome and valuable adjunct to, not usually a substitute for, the conventional clothbound book. Today, however, we are witnessing an interesting intermediate stage, taken from the USA of original productions or reprints of serious works in attractive, but not necessarily cheap, format, designed for their large college population. These 'egg head' paper backs, as they have sometimes been called, produced in editions of 10,000 to 15,000 by a number of British publishers (including Penguins), appeal to a younger generation who have the means and seem prepared to buy them in adequate quantities. It is a promising development.

Binding for America.—Reference has been made elsewhere to the sale of 'special editions' to the USA, and it may be well to explain the binder's part in their production in the event of the edition being supplied bound and from the existing stock of sheets. The first thing is to have fresh title-pages printed bearing the American publisher's imprint on the face and the essential words 'Made in Great Britain' or 'Printed in Great Britain' on the back—essential, because without this the books would not pass the American customs. The binder then cuts away the original title, as well as any advertisements, and substitutes these 'cancel titles' bearing the American publisher's imprint, inserts the American publisher's name on the binding when making the cases, and with that the 'special edition' is achieved.

The Time Occupied.—We have now examined in turn all the more usual processes employed in the making of a book, but no mention has been made of the important question of the length of time occupied. It is a point upon which it is especially dangerous to generalize, because no two books are alike—not only are some long and some short, but some are straightforward, others the reverse: one book may not contain a footnote, another may be smothered in them and have Greek and Arabic letters into the bargain. But for the benefit of any authors who are under the impression that books are printed, like newspapers, in a matter of hours, it may be well to give some general indication of the *minimum* time that will probably be required for the production of, say, 2,500 copies of an ordinary and quite straightforward book of 65,000 words in length:

Casting off and estimating	say 2 weeks
Composition	say 4 weeks
Author correcting proofs	say 1 week
Printer correcting type	say 2 weeks
Machining	say 4 weeks
Binding	say 3 weeks
Time lost in transit of paper and printed sheets	say 1 week
Contingencies	say 1 week
	18 weeks

It will thus be seen that assuming the *utmost* promptitude on the part of the author in passing the first proofs and no necessity for revised proofs, nearly five months, and often more, are usually needed for the production of a book.

Even this, as will be seen in a subsequent chapter, does *not* include publication.

Authors should remember that the best workmanship requires time, and that it is seldom wise, therefore, to bring any undue pressure to bear to expedite the printing and binding.

CHAPTER VI

THE ACTUAL SELLING

IT is one thing to produce a book, quite another to sell it, though some authors one meets regard the two as synonymous. I have often had occasion to tell authors that advance copies of their book will be ready on such and such a day, and am still surprised at the frequency with which they reply, 'Then you will be publishing the book on that date'. Authors who are specially insistent upon publishers exercising the greatest possible activity in pushing their books seem often to grudge the time necessary for the process, and are apt to be annoyed when told that not until the book is produced does the chief work of publishing begin. Kliemann starts his interesting treatise, *Die Werbung fürs Buch*, with a little poem by Felix Dahn, which I venture to paraphrase as follows:

> To write books is easy, it requires only pen and ink and the ever-patient paper. To print books is a little more difficult, because genius so often rejoices in illegible handwriting. To read books is more difficult still, because of the tendency to go to sleep. But the most difficult task of all that a mortal man can embark upon is to *sell* a book.

Dahn was attacking the tendency to borrow books instead of buying them, but the quotation is none the less an indication of both the difficulty and the importance of the selling end of a publisher's business.

Publicity in all its various forms is discussed in a separate chapter. Here it is proposed to deal with the relationship between the publisher and his various customers, the booksellers and circulating libraries at home and abroad. In recent times emphasis has rightly been laid upon the importance of a closer and more personal relationship between publishers and booksellers; an aspect of the matter which it would be difficult to over-emphasize. It has been my good fortune at one time or another to call upon the majority of the leading booksellers in Great Britain and Ireland, and practically all those of any importance in all the dominions and colonies, as well as those in other distant countries such as Brazil, Indonesia and Japan, and nearer home from Iceland to Athens and Lisbon. It involved the devotion of over two years to the study of bookselling conditions abroad and three subsequent voyages round the world, but it can truthfully be said in more senses than one that a publisher cannot spend his time more profitably than in the company of booksellers. In practice, however, that contact has to be largely maintained through travellers and by correspondence.

The Daily Orders —Before dealing with the activities of the various travellers a publisher employs, it may be well to give some indication of the usual way in which the day-to-day orders are executed. Some are collected from the 'orders clearing' run by Book Centre. Many come from the booksellers in the form of postcards, or at printed-matter rate in open envelopes, and they are the part of the post first dealt with in most publishing offices. In many cases they are separated and sorted out before the other letters are opened, because there is not a moment to lose if the books are to be invoiced, looked out, and packed in time to ensure their speedy dispatch, whether by rail, carrier or post. The best-run offices pride themselves upon the rapidity and accuracy with which this part of their work is done. Before 1957 the booksellers paid carriage, and usually instructed the publishers to deliver their requirements to a carrier with whom they had a contract and to whom a 'booking fee' of about 3d for each parcel was payable. Now that most publishers pay the whole or greater part of the cost of carriage they prescribe the means of transport. Many have found passenger train the most efficient and expeditious method for parcels weighing over 2 lb. and post for those weighing less.

Orders for substantial quantities of a title may call for different action, as most publishers keep their main supplies either at their bookbinders or at a warehouse situated in some less expensive quarter than their own offices. Such orders may be dealt with in a number of ways. Instructions may be given to the binders over the telephone, or by delivery note, to send in the requisite copies, which are then packed and dispatched exactly as a smaller order would be, though, of course, more elaborate packing, or rather baling, is necessary, and possibly a packing case. Alternatively, and this is a method in constant use if the customer is in London, or employs an agent in London to attend to his packing and shipping for him, the binders are instructed to make delivery direct.

Export orders are usually much more troublesome than home orders, in that they practically all involve three or more copies of each invoice as well as, in some cases, elaborate declarations for customs purposes, and that most tiresome thing a consular certificate. To the exceptional difficulties with which the publisher is confronted by the action of countries like Brazil, and still more the USA, we shall turn later. Many London retail booksellers send to the publisher's trade counter for their urgent supplies, thus saving a day. Whilst at the publisher's counter, the bookseller's collector calls over the titles of all those books he wants but of which he has been unable to trace the publisher's name. It is highly skilled work attending to the busy trade counter of a leading publisher. Many titles are called over daily, and the publisher's assistant has to be able to spot any of his firm's books. This presupposes an exact knowledge on the assistant's part of the titles of all the books in the particular publisher's catalogue. But even that is insufficient, because much imagination is required to identify some of the titles given. It would be a comparatively simple matter were the titles given correctly, but the occasions for error are frequent. In the first place, the customer may not give the bookseller the correct title. He may, for instance, refer to it under the title of an article about the book; he may not even know the author's name. The bookseller's assistant who takes down the order may not do so correctly, and the collector may find the writing indecipherable and make a mistake in copying it into his book. Even when correctly written down, some names prove difficult to pronounce; but in most cases the title is detected, the book is supplied, and all goes well. Occasionally there is failure, but on the whole the work is done astonishingly well. It does not follow that because a book is ordered a publisher is in a position to supply it. It may be that the book is out of print, that it is out of stock, or not yet published. For each of these eventualities there is a definite and correct reply, mostly in the form of initials, viz. o/P = out of print; RP = reprinting; os/USA = out of stock, but on order from USA; Bdg = binding; NYP = not yet published (the initials NO are ambiguous because they could mean 'not ours' as well as 'not out'); NK = not known, etc. A country bookseller ordering three books of which one is available, another out of print, and the third ready shortly, will receive an invoice for the book that can be supplied, with a note at the foot of it that such and such a book is o/P and the other NYP, and he has all the information he needs to explain the position to his customer.

Orders for books that are temporarily out of stock, binding, or reprinting, are carefully recorded by the publisher and are referred to as 'dues'. Should there be no great lapse of time between the receipt of the order and the date when it is possible to execute it, the publisher will probably supply it without more ado, with a note of the order date or order number on the invoice. If, on the other hand, some time has elapsed, it is customary to send the bookseller a post-card advising him that the book is now available and either asking permission to execute the order, or stating that the order will be executed unless the bookseller advises to the contrary. If the publisher's business is efficiently run, an eagle eye will be kept upon the 'dues' by the trade manager, if not by one of the principals of the firm, because it is one of the most effective methods of ensuring that orders are not being unreasonably held

a book. To call upon all the wholesale and retail book-sellers in London, as well as the many export houses, takes from two to three weeks, according to the thoroughness with which the work is done and the number of customers visited. In the case of several of the bigger firms it is necessary to leave for inspection at their offices copies of the books which are being subscribed. It is thus essential for the town traveller to have several advance copies of each book if he is to do his work efficiently. Some of his customers will look through his samples more or less at any time and give their orders there and then. Most of them have their definite hours when they will see travellers, and woe to the man who attempts to disturb them at any other time. Some of the bigger firms supply printed forms for the traveller to fill in, of which a specimen is given on page 166.

The task that confronts the buyer of a big firm like W. H. Smith & Son, which handles every conceivable type of publication, would require divine inspiration to be correctly done. It is very easy for the publisher to criticize. He has seen the reader's report on his MS; he has had opportunity after opportunity of getting to know everything about his books, and it is his own fault if he does not know. But the buyer is daily confronted with scores of books he has never seen, and to each of which he cannot devote more than the most fleeting attention. Many buyers would, I am sure, be thankful if the publishers would settle the numbers to be purchased and accept the responsibility for their mistakes. And where confidence is established either between the publisher and the buyer or the publisher's

W. H. SMITH & SON, LTD.
BOOK DEPARTMENT,
STRAND HOUSE, W.C.2.

The utmost accuracy is requested in completing this form, as the information asked for will be used not only for reference lists for our branches, but will also appear in 'The Bookseller', Whitaker's 'Cumulative Book List', etc.

Date subscribed

Publisher

Publishing date

Classification

Title of book. In the case of a volume of short stories the words 'Short Stories' should be entered after the title.

Format

Binding

Author (Surname first)

Editor (Surname first)

Number of pages

Selling price (state whether net or non-net)

Number of illustrations

Translator (Surname first)

Language translated from

Type of illustrations

Advertising matter available

Name of series

Date of previous edition

---

1. Novels for Library circulation should have trimmed edges. Other books for Library use should be cut or trimmed.
2. Novels ordered for the Library are required to have picture or other wrappers as with ordinary sale copies.
3. Books ordered for the Library must be properly sewn on tapes and lettered on spine.
4. The selling price of all books should be printed on the wrapper.
5. Terms arranged on subscription to be continuous unless otherwise stated.
6. Repeat orders for books subscribed on sale or return, will, it is assumed, also be supplied 'on sale'.
7. In the case of publications taken by them for sale or return, W. H. Smith & Son reserve the right to keep such publications on sale at their branches for at least three months.

Number ordered by Book Department	Date of entry in Order Book	Terms		Terms for Colonial Edition

Number ordered for Export				

	SCALES			NOT-OUT BOOK
	STALLS		SHOPS	Customer's Orders
Number ordered by Library Dept.				Stock "
				Export "
				S S S "

166

representative and the buyer, this is to some extent what happens. It would occur a great deal more frequently if fewer publishers, and for that matter authors, were under the delusion that it is good business to land the buyer with the maximum stock he can be persuaded to purchase, regardless of whether there is any hope of his being able to dispose of it. This is most emphatically not sound business for the publisher, and unless it is the last book he intends writing, it is still less sound business for the author. 'Once bit twice shy' holds good of booksellers as of other people, and the worse they are bitten in connection with the work of any particular author, the more shy they will be about handling his next book.

Some of the bigger firms occasionally seek to protect themselves when buying books of doubtful saleability by marking their order, or part of their order, 'see safe'. If this condition is passed by the publisher it means that, although the books are bought and paid for, and cannot, therefore, be regarded as 'on sale or return',[1] the bookseller has the right to return, within a reasonable period, for credit or exchange, any surplus copies left on his hands. Thus if the firm has bought fifty copies of a new novel and marked the order 'half see safe', the publisher will be paid for fifty, but may find himself obliged to take twenty-five back.

The best representative is the man who, having interested his customer in the books that are being offered to him, persuades him to take the maximum he can safely buy, and no more. Most town and country

[1] The 'on sale or return' method of selling books is examined in Chapter VII.

travellers are salaried employees of the firms they represent, but in addition receive a commission on all orders actually obtained by them, accepted and executed by their firms and paid for by the customer.

Most publishers have a definite publication day, say every Monday or every alternate Thursday, in which case the traveller has so to arrange his work as to ensure that all his orders are handed over before that particular day as it is essential that all orders should be executed simultaneously. To ensure that all book-sellers should be able to supply copies on the day of publication, country orders have to be dispatched well ahead of London orders. Any failure to exercise care about simultaneous supply would have the effect of giving one customer preference over another, and has to be avoided at any cost.[1] This is particularly impor-tant with certain export markets. There is for example a weekly sailing date for South Africa and even a slight difference in the time of delivery in London may result in a customer in South Africa receiving his supplies a week ahead of or after his competitors.

Publication Note.—In some firms, my own amongst the number, the principle of the time-table is carried still further, and a printed form headed 'Publication Note' is issued to all departments about a month before publication, giving the dates when supplies will come in, when the review copies and orders from overseas, country and town are to go out. If this plan is adopted, great care has to be taken by the production and other departments concerned that there is no

[1] Magazine publishers take even more pains over this than many book publishers.

failure on their part to keep to the schedule dates, as any departure from them in the case of even one out of the several books to be published would throw the whole machinery out of gear. The publication note serves a good many purposes other than those indicated. There is, in fact, no department which is not in some way concerned with it. The cashier, for instance, on receipt of his copy of the publication note, automatically sees whether there are any payments due to authors on publication. The advertising manager, if it has not been dealt with earlier, discusses with his principals the amount to be allocated for advertising each particular book on the note, and the invoicing of the accumulated 'dues' starts at once. One of the principals or the publicity manager writes to advise the authors of the date that has been fixed, and considers what special steps each particular book calls for. With certain firms, the whole work of publishing is purely mechanical. The books might be sausages for all the individual attention that is given to them; but the wise publisher realizes there is an individuality behind each book, just as the wise schoolmaster realizes the different individuality of every boy in his school. It is surprising how much can be done for most books by personal treatment of this kind. Usually it can only be done by the publisher himself, and often means much time and thought as well as endless correspondence. How much can be accomplished by the writing of individual letters is astonishing. Naturally, imagination plays a big part. The publisher has to think not only who ought to be interested, but whom he, the publisher, is in a position to interest in the book. If he has made personal contact with many booksellers, he will remember that this, that, or the other one was particularly interested in this or that subject or this or that author, and can make use of such knowledge. It may be that he can persuade some organization to help make the book known. The only limits to what is possible are the limitations of the publisher's own time. Some authors are unwise enough to take up so much of it that they leave him none in which to get on with the pushing of their books.

I may here add that authors who are told by junior assistants in bookshops that their book is 'not known' must not immediately throw the blame upon the unoffending publisher. They may take it for granted, if the bookshop is in London, that a copy of their book has been actually offered before publication to the bookseller, and, in any case, whether in London or not, the bookseller himself probably knows all about it, even if his assistant does not.

Trade Terms.—We cannot leave our town traveller without making some reference to the all-important question of terms. Wherever publishers and booksellers meet, whether in person or by deputy, terms are sure to be among the questions discussed. It is the custom, and from both the publishers' and authors' point of view a good custom, to allow the bookseller a better discount on 'subscription orders', i.e. on orders placed before publication. These better discounts are known as 'subscription terms'. Booksellers ordering copies of a book at that stage are, to a limited extent, sharing the publisher's risk in that they are sinking their capital in an untried venture;

but, equally important, they are ensuring that the book will be readily available (and probably displayed) in their bookshop on the day of publication. This is a proper and equitable ground for special consideration, and nearly all publishers grant specially favourable subscription terms. There is unfortunately a tendency to use all concessions given, and very properly given, on subscription, as a lever for securing the same terms after subscription. All the arguments for granting repeat terms as favourable as subscription terms sound so very plausible. Why should the poor bookseller be penalized and granted less favourable terms when he wants subsequently to buy more copies of a given book, because he finds that there is a substantial demand for it? Why is a bookseller left with so little inducement to go on selling an already published book, etc.? The answer to all these most excellent arguments is just this: that were a publisher to grant the same terms after subscription as before subscription, the book-seller would inevitably and naturally tend to wait and see whether the book was going to 'catch on' before committing himself, and would thus, in a very large proportion of cases, refrain from buying on subscription. If, therefore, a publisher were unwise enough to make a general practice of conceding his subscription terms after subscription, he would soon find himself confronted with the necessity of granting some new concession on subscription orders, and the whole trouble would begin again. Quite regardless, therefore, of what the particular discount should be, it is clear that the bookseller should be given, and is entitled to receive, some special inducement for sharing the risk of publication by ordering books before they are published. On the question of what these discounts ought to be, feeling is very strong. In the chapter dealing with the price of books I have emphasized what seems to me the most important point of all, and the one that is consistently overlooked, viz. that there can be no increase in discounts without a corresponding increase in published prices. The bookseller who in one breath tells you that books are too dear, and that he must have a larger share of the proceeds, is crying for the moon. Just because I emphasized the essential relation of discounts to published prices it was assumed by many booksellers that I begrudged them a living wage. I begrudge the real booksellers nothing; I regret that there are not more of them. But as a friend of booksellers, as one who is furthermore dependent in some measure upon them for his livelihood, I feel bound to call out when I see disaster looming ahead. The claim made by many booksellers to receive a *minimum* discount of $33\frac{1}{3}$ per cent *under all circumstances*, on books of every kind, and even on single copies, is not, in my judgment, a tenable one, and if pursued with success would inevitably lead to an unwarranted increase in published prices, a consequent reduction in sales, and very probably the breakdown of the 'net book agreement', an agreement which booksellers rightly regard as their sheet-anchor and to which reference will be made later. There may be certain classes of books which call for exceptionally favourable terms, but it is no good shutting our eyes to the fact that there is a large proportion of books which could be effectively distributed and sold direct to the public at less

expense than a *minimum* 33⅓ per cent would involve.
As I have pointed out when examining the question
of discount in relation to price, a minimum 33⅓ per
cent discount means in practice that the cost of distribution will be round about 50 per cent of the published
price. A minimum 33⅓ per cent to the bookseller is
a maximum 66⅔ per cent to the publisher. The publisher's average receipts will be much less by the time
the special inducement on subscription orders, the
extra discount to wholesalers and exporters, as well as
the traveller's commission are deducted. So long as the
retail bookseller is pressing for a *maximum* 33⅓ per cent,
he is on much safer ground, and this, I think, most of
the best booksellers realize. They are as a whole better
off today than they have ever been, largely because of
the increased demand for books and partly because,
with the exception of school text-books, they are now
all issued at 'net' prices. Moreover they receive 33⅓ per
cent upon an ever-increasing proportion of their
orders and no longer have the whole burden of carriage.

In practice, discounts will vary to some extent with
the kind of book. With some publications, booksellers
can be much more helpful than with others, and their
remuneration, if it is to be on a durable footing, is
bound to have some relation to the service rendered.
Again, the risk of loss is greater in certain cases than
in others. A standard work, whether it be on philosophy
or economics, even if a ready sale is not effected, can
always be sold at something nearly approaching what
the bookseller has paid for it. On the other hand, a
novel, or a volume of verse, if left on the bookseller's
hands, may not yield a fraction of the bookseller's

initial outlay. For practical purposes, these varying terms fluctuate in the case of 'net' books between a minimum of 25 per cent and a maximum of 33⅓ per cent. There is a growing tendency to grant more generous terms, i.e. 30 or 33⅓ per cent after subscription provided two or more copies are ordered. The claim to increased terms on single copies, which is very insistent, calls for special examination. It is quite true that orders for single copies of already published books are sometimes 'for stock', and such orders may be and are from time to time included with those given to the traveller and executed on subscription terms. But the suggestion that any considerable proportion of such orders, except from a few 'pedigree' booksellers, for single copies of published books are for stock will not bear examination. It is a matter which some of us have had opportunities of testing over and over again. For example we have sent to carefully selected people whom we know from our records were likely to be interested a circular letter drawing attention to some good book on a special subject which had ceased to sell. It would be easy to get the bulk of such business direct, but it is our practice to suggest that the order should be handed to a bookseller, and if an order form is attached the word 'bookseller' is introduced at the appropriate place. About three days after such circularization the orders begin to reach us from all parts of the country, a very large proportion from firms who have never stocked a single copy of one of our more serious books or lifted a little finger to help us to sell them. Can the claim that such a firm ought to receive more than 25 per cent, for merely passing on an order, be justified? Most business men would welcome with open arms any business that they had done nothing to obtain; which involved no risk, very little trouble, and covered their overhead expenses. Should booksellers expect more? Of course, if such an order is passed on by a real bookseller who is not content with merely dealing out cheap fiction, there is a great deal to be said for the contention that he is entitled to special consideration in recognition, not of the particular service, but of what he is doing in general to promote the sale of better books.

Taking it as a whole, trade terms have materially improved, and it is now to increased sales rather than to increased discounts that booksellers should look for increased profits, and with this contention the most far-seeing amongst them are now agreed.

The Wholesaler is a far more important link in the chain of book distribution than many realized until Simpkin Marshall, for many years the leading firm, went into liquidation. The difficult problem is to provide him with a margin sufficient to cover his working expenses and yield a small profit, and at the same time enable him to supply the small bookseller on the publisher's ordinary (*not* 'subscription') terms. It was here that a 13/12 arrangement proved especially useful. The privilege was conceded to all, whether wholesale or retail, who took advantage of it; but the wholesaler, because of the nature of his business, was seldom called upon to pass on the benefit to his customers. He thus had, under a 13/12 dispensation, an additional 8 per cent apart from any increased discount to which he was entitled as a wholesaler. On the other hand, the large retailer had no grievance, inasmuch as he could enjoy the advantage of the free copy. It is unwise, therefore, to assume that the long survival of the baker's dozen in the book trade was due solely to stupidity.

Educational text-books have purposely been excluded from the preceding discussion of terms. They are mostly ordered in large numbers. They are published at cut prices which only permit of a lower range of discounts, usually fluctuating between $16\frac{2}{3}$ per cent and 25 per cent. Any increase in the discount on educational books would automatically involve an increase in the published prices. Anyone taking the trouble to estimate the cost of their production will find that the publisher's margin of profit is of the narrowest. The reason why educational books are a profitable line is that the orders tend to be for quantities and the turnover is often much more substantial than for ordinary publications. Furthermore, if once a particular book is at all generally adopted for class use, it sells itself with very little further effort. Happy is the publisher who has many such books.

Circulating Libraries are amongst the biggest buyers upon whom the home traveller calls, and here we enter upon a very thorny subject. There are some publishers who defend the circulating libraries; some who would like to see them abolished root and branch. In so far as they promptly and efficiently supply the public with the particular books for which the public asks, it is difficult to see that serious objection can reasonably be taken to them; but unfortunately the conditions here laid down are applicable only to what is known as 'guaranteed subscriptions', and they form (alas!) a tiny minority. There is no certainty that what other subscribers ask for they will be given. On the contrary, in practice, such subscribers will at the best have to put up with such books on their list as are not in active demand, but more frequently with inferior substitutes of which the library has surplus stocks. The present system tends to assist the circulation of indifferent and bad books, and to retard the circulation of really good books, especially those by writers who have not yet established reputations. The public has been led to expect that for a penny or two a day the loan of all the new books can be secured, and, having contracted to pay a circulating library less than they willingly pay for a daily newspaper, they either delude themselves or are deluded into thinking that all the latest books are at their disposal and that there is not the slightest necessity ever to buy one. The remedy is not necessarily the abolition of circulating libraries (the circulating-library habit has become far too engrained in England for that), but the educating of the public to see that they get the books they ask for and not substitutes. The subscriber who will uncomplainingly put up with whatever his circulating library is pleased to give him would be the first to protest if his grocer gave him margarine when he had asked for butter. When more people give to the things of the mind a fraction of the thought that they do to food and clothing, they will not be satisfied with anything less than a guaranteed library service. Lest this should be construed as an attack upon the administration of circulating libraries, I think it is fair to add that one or two of the largest are extraordinarily well run, and that neither I personally, nor my firm, have any complaint to make about them. I would go a step further, and say that what they accomplish for the most insignificant sum is remarkable. Let us, however, hope that people will become as insistent upon getting from the circulating library the book they want as they are upon getting the right brand of cigarettes from their tobacconist or a particular kind of soap from their grocer.[1]

The Country Traveller cannot of necessity keep in such close touch with his firm or even with his customers. Whether Scotland, Ireland, and Wales are included in the territory or the ground is divided up between two, three, or more representatives, it is not possible for the country traveller to call upon country booksellers as frequently as the London traveller calls upon his customers. Some of the smaller places will only be visited twice a year, and larger towns four or at most six times per year. It is thus necessary for the traveller to carry a much wider range of samples, and to have with him particulars of all forthcoming books likely to be published before his next visit. Of some recent books he will have with him a proof or finished copies, but of many he will have only jackets and descriptive paragraphs from the announcement list. No bookseller could be expected or would want to read though the entire book while the traveller was there, but he does need to know what the book is about and what its

[1] Further information concerning Commercial Circulating Libraries can be obtained from *Britain Today* (Sept. 1946), the volume *Rapports* (International Publishers Congress, Paris, 1931) and the Report issued by the Society of Bookmen in 1928 (British Book Trade Organization, page 132).

appearance will be. Naturally, the more the traveller has to show the bookseller the better it is for the latter, and the more likely the traveller is to obtain orders. It is customary for the country bookseller to be advised before a representative calls on him.

In the country, and still more in London, the quantities bought are very largely dependent upon the record of the previous book by the same author, with the result that, however bad a book is, it is almost certain to have a good reception at the hands of the trade if it follows a success, or, however good the book, it is likely to have a bad reception if it follows a failure. The predatory type of publisher relies upon this fact when bidding for a new book by an author some fellow-publisher has launched with special success. Where there is no record to go upon, the buying tends to be ultra-cautious,[1] and in view of the large number of indifferent books published this is hardly surprising, though it is extraordinarily annoying at times to the publisher when he finds, despite his representatives' eloquence, a really first-rate piece of work 'turned down' or bought in insufficient quantities by the booksellers.

There is fortunately a growing tendency amongst booksellers, as well as amongst the public, to be influenced by the publisher's imprint. Certain firms have the reputation of publishing the best books on particular subjects. When they come along with new books on these subjects they are considered certain to be good, because the publishers have a reputation to lose, whereas if a fiction publisher suddenly comes along with a book, say, on Buddhism, it is probably because his

[1] Except in war-time when it was often reckless.

travellers have told him that books on Buddhism are selling, and not because a particularly good book on the subject has come his way. It is almost certain, in fact, to be a book rejected by the specialist publisher. A few booksellers specialize, and their buying is then greatly simplified.

Book Tokens have had a marked effect upon the book trade. They have encouraged people who would not otherwise venture to do so, owing to the difficulty of making the right selection, to give books as presents. They have brought into the bookshops many who otherwise would have hesitated to enter, and they have spread part of the Christmas demand into January. Yet, strangely enough, there are still a few booksellers so short-sighted and unimaginative as to look askance at them.

When we turn to the *representatives in the dominions and overseas*, different conditions prevail. Some firms have actual branch houses in India, Canada, Australia, and elsewhere, but for the most part publishers employ representatives living in the different dominions who work on a commission basis; that is to say, that the publisher appoints someone resident, for instance, in Cape Town to act as his South African representative and to call on all South African booksellers on his behalf, and in return agrees to pay a commission, usually of 10 per cent, on all orders obtained by the representative. Such a representative is independent and may act for several publishers as well as for firms in associated trades. The farther the representative is away from his principals, the more important it is to provide him with advance information about forthcoming publications. If, for instance, you do not write to your New Zealand representative about new publications more than three months before their issue, you have not given him adequate time to secure and send you orders in readiness for execution on the day of publication. From overseas, therefore, comes the insistent call for advance information. Home booksellers, on the other hand, object to the announcement of books too far ahead of the date of publication. Each firm has its own particular method of getting over this difficulty.

The practice of my own firm is to put into type, in the form which it will ultimately take in our list, a descriptive paragraph of every book within a matter of hours of the contract being signed, regardless of when the book will be published. A sufficient number of proofs are then printed for all our many representatives overseas and for those distant customers who need this information. In this way, by merely pasting these slips into the latest edition of our announcement list, the overseas representatives have at all times the maximum information about forthcoming books which we are in a position to give them. Uncorrected proofs and jackets of each book follow as soon as practicable, and various other steps are taken of a more personal nature into which it is unnecessary to go. The trade papers from time to time issue special export and announcement numbers, and these are, of course, carefully looked through by overseas customers. In such issues it is customary to advertise books much farther ahead of the publication date than would otherwise be done.

Colonial Editions, to which reference has been made on page 83, are no longer separately produced. They are usually copies of the home edition supplied on special terms; in the case of novels at half price. The theory was that people overseas *bought* new novels whereas we at home only borrowed them. It is no longer valid because the circulating library habit has spread to the dominions and book buyers overseas are all too prone, despite their privileged position, to wait for yet cheaper editions of the novels to appear. It is difficult to justify the continued supply of books on such privileged conditions to dominions, whose standard of living is higher than ours, particularly as it results in the author receiving a lower royalty per copy. These half-price sales yield little direct profit to anyone save the overseas bookseller but may result in an increased circulation, in some cases, and thus enable the publisher to print a rather larger edition which is an advantage.

Each of the *overseas markets* presents some particular problem.

In *Canada* there is the proximity of the USA, the different currency, the excessive cost of distribution and the consequent, almost prohibitive, increase in the price charged for British books.

In *Australia* and *New Zealand* there is the question of 'marketing', i.e. the granting of the monopoly of the sale in Australia and/or New Zealand to one retail bookseller. In practice, this means the sale of more copies than would otherwise be disposed of, but—and it is a very big but—the copies have to be supplied at an exceptionally cut price, and the granting of a monopoly to one customer is apt to cause offence to many, if not all, of the others. A point that has to be remembered is that firms taking markets in this way will only select a book here and there from a publisher's list. The publisher will still be confronted with the marketing of the rest of his list, and the problem is not made easier by the fact that one or two of his best-sellers are excluded.

As in Canada the price charged for British books is substantially enhanced, as may be seen from the accompanying examples from the Australian and New Zealand booksellers' schedules.

English published price	New Zealand price	Australian price
7s 6d	9s 9d	12s 6d
10s 6d	14s 0d	17s 6d
15s 0d	19s 3d	25s 0d

(The above figures assume that the overseas bookseller has been granted a discount of 33⅓ per cent from the English published price.)

Most of the diversity between the prices fixed in Australia and New Zealand respectively is due to the fact that £100 sterling equals £125 in Australian money in which case 6s sterling equals 7s 6d in Australian coinage. In order to keep down prices pressure is continually brought to bear upon publishers to grant special terms if not to supply other books as well as novels at half price. But a moment's thought will make it clear that if the author is not to be deprived of his proper royalty and the publisher of his small margin of profit an increase in published prices to cover the increased discount would automatically be involved. In other words, the publisher would have to charge more for his books, and thereby prejudice their sale, in his principal market (Great Britain) in order to suit the requirements of a section of his overseas market

(Australia and New Zealand). In individual instances it may be a practicable proposal, if published prices are fixed accordingly, but as a general principle it is obviously unsound.

South Africa—where there are fortunately no currency difficulties—is a wonderful market for British books, but it must be judged by its population, not by its size. Few people realize that the white population of that vast continent is only about $1\frac{1}{2}$ millions and that of these about half are of Dutch descent. This leaves about $\frac{3}{4}$ million people—that is less than one of our larger cities contains—spread over a huge area—so huge that it takes days and nights in the train to traverse it. Just because of these distances, and the consequent high cost of freight, the price charged for a book in Rhodesia is not necessarily the same as in Cape Town or Durban.

India is a market of outstanding importance thanks largely to the universality of the English language. The English translation of a work written in one of the many vernacular languages, other than Hindi, may easily achieve a larger circulation in India than the original version, whose sale is necessarily limited to the comparatively few who can understand it.

Three troubles are credit, piracy and, still more important, sterling shortage involving the licensing of imports. In the aggregate considerable business is done by small local firms who are apt to indulge in price-cutting and with whom it is a risky business to grant even the most limited credit. The COD postal arrangement or, to use the initials which designate the Indian system, VPP (Value payable by post) greatly facilitated this class of business, and before the advent of licences it was possible to execute orders from firms to whom it would be unsafe to give credit. The better class of business is, however, done through the score or more of really substantial Indian firms. Piracy arose chiefly in connection with text-books set for school or college use. Information as to what will be required is naturally known locally before the English publisher hears anything about it, and at one time local firms printed and sold unauthorized editions and sometimes were even out of business before the English publisher had time to take action. This difficulty was met and the problem largely solved by the appointment of representatives on the spot empowered by the Publishers Association to take immediate action in the event of infringement of the copyrights of any of its members. To what extent (if any) unauthorized translations in the vernacular languages appear in India it is difficult to say. Probably the matter has not much pecuniary importance, but the same cannot be said of Japan.

Japan is a signatory to the Berne Convention, and, theoretically, at any rate, international copyright prevails there, but it is extraordinarily difficult both to discover and to prevent the type of firm that is here today and gone tomorrow from issuing unauthorized translations and thus forestalling arrangements for authorized ones. Japan was and still is a most important market for English books. Nearly all educated Japanese read English, and their thirst for knowledge is insatiable. The fact that a book was what some people would describe as 'hard reading' does not deter the Japanese; it merely whets his appetite. The Japanese

student is bent upon mastering his subject and is prepared to make the necessary effort to do so. Moreover,
he is encouraged to spend a definite amount per month
on books. The evidence of this is to be found in the
magnitude of orders for serious books that came to
English publishers from Japan. Were I asked what
firm carried the completest stock of books on practically
all subjects and in all the more important languages,
I should have unhesitatingly answered at one time
Maruzen of Tokyo. Today they handle other wares
and have more competitors.

Nothing so adequate has yet been done for the distribution of English books in *China*, but when once
conditions are more relaxed, the demand for them
might prove even greater than in Japan. It is a market
with enormous possibilities; at present only the fringe
of the country is touched, for the most part through
the official buying agency Guozi Shudian of Pekin and
intermediaries in Hong Kong.

Meanwhile, it is a paradise for literary pirates who
shamelessly turn out the most deplorable unauthorized
photographic reproductions of British and American
standard works and pass them off as the publications
of firms of world-wide repute.

Pakistan as a market for books was disastrously
affected by partition. Lahore was probably the third
most important centre of distribution in United India,
but nearly all the most important booksellers were
Hindus who had to take a hurried departure. Most of
those who stepped into their shoes were inexperienced.
Moreover, they were almost immediately confronted
with currency difficulties and a postal customs charge

on every book package they received. The latter was imposed under the mistaken belief that it existed before partition, and I am happy to say that I was instrumental in getting it abolished. But the shortage of sterling persists, and has led to the intrusion of the USA into what was an almost exclusively British market. Pakistan booksellers are enabled by the United States Government to purchase American publications in rupees, so that, although they are much more expensive than British publications, the currency problem is circumvented.

Burma, and still more *Indonesia*, have their currency difficulties which handicap their ability to buy British books. This is particularly unfortunate in the case of Indonesia where English is taking the place of Dutch. Here, as in Pakistan, the United States Government has intervened with their IMG (Informational Media Guarantee) scheme to enable Indonesian booksellers to pay for American publications in rupiahs.

Siam is a small but useful market for British books and has no currency problems to contend with. Bangkok has some pleasing bookshops in addition to its other many attractions.

The *Philippines* is by tradition an American market as far as books in English are concerned. When self-government was granted, free entry for American publications was one of the conditions laid down. This discrimination has recently ceased, and *all* foreign books are now subject to a 10 per cent tax. Most contracts, however, give the United States publishers the exclusive market which they have so long enjoyed.

British books are to be found in appreciable quantities in *Mexico*, *Central America* and in all the leading centres of *South America* despite the language barrier. *Brazil* is a market of special and ever-growing importance. More and more time is being devoted in most of these countries to the study of English, and in medicine, art and many other fields British books are in increasing demand. In certain South American states the European cultural background of their authors seems to make them more acceptable than American publications. The Publishers Association has co-operated actively with the British Council in encouraging interest in British literature throughout this important territory.

Collectively the *Crown Colonies* and newly self-governing members of the Commonwealth are a most important outlet for British books, though individually the demands from some of the more remote islands may be small. It is impossible to enumerate them all. Both *East* and *West Africa* represent an ever-growing market, but there is no doubt that West Africa will be the more important, as the desire for knowledge in such countries as *Nigeria* and *Ghana* is insatiable. *Ceylon* was a substantial customer and one hopes may be again. *Hong Kong*, *Malaya* and *Singapore* are good markets for light literature and educational text-books. The South Sea Islands, such as *Fiji* and *Samoa*, add their small quotas to the demand for English books. In the *West Indies*, including Trinidad, British Guiana and British Honduras, the establishment of Public Libraries has stimulated the West Indians' natural desire for knowledge. The passion of the West Indian children for reading is startling and augurs well for the future of that part of the world.

USA—Few British publishers, unless, of course, they have American branches, make any serious attempt to do business direct with American retail booksellers; it is largely done through American publishers. In many cases the book is independently printed in the States, in which case the English publisher has nothing to do with the American market, except to collect the royalties, if he has effected the sale of the rights. Some English books published in the USA are sold to American publishers in the form of an edition bearing the American publisher's imprint. The edition may be as few as a hundred copies or as many as three thousand. The editions are sometimes supplied in flat sheets, sometimes in folded or sewn sheets, and sometimes bound, with the American publisher's imprint on the binding. The form in which they are supplied tends to vary with the ever-changing American customs regulations. Some years ago the duty was as high as 25 per cent; it was then assessed upon the actual amount paid for the copies by the American publisher. But in due course there came along a Government pledged to tariff reduction. The duty was reduced to 15 per cent, but an artificial method of assessment was adopted which had the effect of increasing instead of decreasing the amount of duty payable. The American customs authorities now disregard the price paid for bound books, but base their assessment upon what they regard as the ordinary wholesale price in the country of origin, which they still consider to be two-thirds of the English published price. The rate of duty is 5 per cent—9 per cent if the author is an American. But since the USA signed the UNESCO-sponsored cultural convention on June 26, 1959, there is every prospect that it will soon be abolished. An American consular invoice is required for shipments exceeding $500 in value. The value is based upon the artificial American Customs Assessment, not upon the actual amount charged for the books.

In order to avoid difficulties with the American customs, it is now the practice of many American firms, when importing bound books, to substitute for the English publisher's invoice an invoice made out by themselves. This is known as a 'replace invoice', and gives the artificial valuation that the American assessors require. It is an extraordinary position, because in London the publisher is called upon to swear before the American Consul that the invoice represents the full valuation of the goods and the full amount charged, and is liable to all sorts of pains and penalties for a false declaration, and yet, having correctly filled in the invoice and truthfully made the necessary declaration in London, he is liable to be fined if some totally irrelevant figures are not substituted in New York.

But then the American customs have always seemed to take a special delight in obstructing the flow of books into the USA—*if printed in the English language.* In this matter they apply that 'discrimination' against which the USA inveighs so vehemently when the position is reversed. They have found, for example, that the wording of the Universal Copyright Convention affords them excellent excuses for holding up shipments from Britain of which they readily avail themselves. Incidentally their requirements seem to vary from port to port.

The maximum price for sheets sold to an American publisher is one-third of the English published price, but for large quantities this price is cut. Occasionally, a very low price is accepted and a royalty paid separately. One-third of the price sounds very little, particularly when it includes a royalty to the author, but it is usually the maximum it is possible for an American publisher to pay. Those who have any doubts about this should calculate the actual cost for themselves, and preferably the cost of an edition supplied bound, where the price would be one-third plus binding. First there is the cost of the packing-case and consular fee; then there is the freight—a very substantial item, little less, in fact, than the cost of posting the copies would amount to. Then 'duty' based upon the official assessment of two-thirds of the published price must be added. This would leave the American publisher actually out of pocket (allowing nothing for advertising) by the time he had granted American booksellers the 40 per cent discount they are accustomed to receive, unless the American publisher fixed the American price at considerably more than the dollar equivalent of the English published price. There is a definite limit to the amount of increase that it is practicable to charge. It is this limitation that restricts the amount it is possible to pay for the sheets. Many of the editions are purchased by American publishers visiting London before the books are produced. Most British books of importance are published in America in some form.

Books not so published in the USA are bought in

single copies on behalf of American libraries and others by firms of exporters. The total quantity so ordered of any one book is seldom substantial. The United States public libraries are entitled to import without restrictions but private people who order books from England are liable to have them held up by the American customs. Over and over again when we have received complaints at the non-fulfilment of such orders inquiry has shown that the packages were waiting for the consignees to call and open them in the presence of a customs official. The consignee was usually unaware that his book-packet was being thus detained and in some cases the customs office was not even within easy reach. The United States of America is one of the few countries in the world thus to restrict intellectual intercourse and tax knowledge. Incidentally, as already stated, it is only books in English that are taxed.

The Remainder Market.—All publishers presumably try to gauge their requirements as accurately as possible when giving printing orders for books. Some are much more successful in doing so than others. There are firms that are conservative and very cautious in deciding the number to print, whereas there are others, as we have seen in an earlier chapter, that are reckless. It does not always follow that a book has been a failure because it eventually reaches the remainder market, although this is nearly always presumed. It may have been issued by the wrong firm, or alternatively the book has been a success, has gone through three or four editions, and has done so well that the publisher orders too many when reprinting for the fourth or fifth time. Sales have a way of dropping off suddenly, and often at the most inconvenient moment, when a substantial reprint has been completed. If a publisher has printed conservatively and gauged his requirements accurately, the stock of the book is eventually sold on the ordinary trade terms, and the book is then answered 'Out of print'. But with many books there comes a stage, whether it be sooner or later, when sales at the original price cease while there is still some stock on hand. If the number is small it presents no urgent problems, but if the number is considerable the publisher is compelled to consider the best means of disposing of the stock. As we have seen in the chapter on Production, the pressure upon the publisher to deal with surplus stocks is much greater than it was.

Whether his contracts give him power to 'remainder' or not, the publisher who is in friendly touch with his authors would want to consult them on such a point if the particular author in question is readily accessible and has not, as so often proves to be the case when he is most urgently wanted, changed his address without notifying his publisher. Some firms have a special file for the many letters addressed to authors and returned by the Post Office marked 'Gone away; no address'. It is quite natural that when an author's book has ceased to sell he should lose interest in it and its publisher, but it is, to say the least, a little surprising when such an author turns up a year or two later (sometimes after having changed his address two or three times without intimation) and complains bitterly that he has not heard from his publisher. In the majority of cases where the author is consulted, he has no suggestion to make regarding the disposal of the stock, though often indignant at the mere thought of his book being 'remaindered'. Then the problem is left for the publisher to face. There are several courses he may take.

The first and important question is whether the stock is bound or unbound, because the difficulty may be met, or rather partially postponed, by pulping the unbound stock, if it is clear that it will never pay to bind it; this reduces the stock on hand to more manageable proportions, and may preclude the necessity of taking any further action. Flat sheets can be used as packing material. Folded and collated sheets, on the other hand, are useless except for pulping. It may, however, be a book for which there is a market at a lower price. Unless, however, it has been a success at the higher price it is seldom wise to attempt a reissue at a lower one, although authors often seem to think this course more desirable, or perhaps less *infra dig*.

The reissue of the same stock at a reduced price usually merely postpones the difficulty and makes the stock much more difficult to sell subsequently to a remainder dealer, and the reason for this is clear. To market the reissue at the reduced published price, the publisher has to turn to precisely those same channels, i.e. the 'new' booksellers, through which the book has ceased to sell. The reissue is therefore not likely to be purchased at all freely; there are no reviews to help to sell it, and there is no margin for extensive advertising. On the other hand, the sale of the stock to a wholesale remainder buyer results in the book being offered to the public at the same price at which it was proposed to reissue it but through different channels, with the added inducement that the buyer is apparently securing a bargain. It does not need a draper to tell us that it is easier to sell an article apparently reduced in price from 30s to 15s than to sell the same article as if it were no bargain at its proper price of 15s. The attraction of the remainder buyer's catalogue is that it contains high-priced articles offered at low prices. In fixing the price that he can ask, the remainder buyer has to consider the published price, because the greater the difference between the original published price and the price which he is asking, the bigger the bargain he appears to be offering. The effect, therefore, of the reissue of surplus stock at lower published prices is to depress its value when the time comes, as it almost certainly will come, to remainder it, because the amount then offered will be based upon the lower published price, not the original one.

Why there should be such a stigma attached to a book being remaindered is not clear, because it merely means the sale of the book through different channels and to a different, but none the less very discriminating, public. It would be an exaggeration to say that 'the remainder of today is the rare book of tomorrow', but it is undoubtedly true that the reputation of some books has actually been assisted, if not made, by remainder-ing them. In fact, the remaindering of part of the stock of any book with intrinsic merits will stimulate a demand for it. This is so widely recognized that some publishers deliberately keep back a certain number of copies of any book they are remaindering, knowing full well that as soon as the surplus has been absorbed, a fresh demand for the book will arise. But it does not justify the practice known as *partial remaindering*, that is of selling part of the stock to one privileged book-seller at a remainder price whilst simultaneously supplying all the others on ordinary terms, a practice which happily has now disappeared.

Remainder buyers are extremely fastidious. It is with difficulty that they can be persuaded, except in war-time, to purchase at any reasonable price a book that is not obviously what they would term a 'plum'. The idea that they will make some sort of a bid for any surplus stock is a fallacy, and in some cases a publisher is left to find his own outlet. When the quantity is small and readily absorbed in the second-hand book trade, or by some organization or society interested in some question touched upon in the book, this may work out satisfactorily.

In earlier days, most remainders were sold through second-hand booksellers, but today they represent only one of several outlets. Many new booksellers, for example, are devoting tables, or a section of their shops, to remainders, and not merely at the time of the National Book Sales. Again, stores often handle them, and there is an important overseas demand.

More imagination is called for in disposing of remainders than in selling new books. New outlets have continually to be found, not necessarily connected with the book trade; particularly so in the case of a large remainder house handling several million books in a year. As we have seen, it may have proved expedient to pulp any unbound copies because the remainder buyer naturally takes into consideration the total number of copies that have to be absorbed when placing his order or fixing his price. In America they are much more drastic in dealing with remainders, and usually prefer to pulp the stock or let it go at a nominal price rather than bother much about it. And there is a great deal to be said for that point of view, because the amounts eventually realized are sometimes trifling.

One important point must not be overlooked and that is the understanding with booksellers that allowance will be made on any stock still on their hands if the book is remaindered in less than three years of first publication (two years if fiction), or if they have recently purchased the stock on the ordinary terms. The publisher is thus often in the position of having to give allowances on copies on which the full royalty has been paid, without any hope of recovering the royalty; this may mean that he is worse off than if he had given the book away.

I cannot leave the subject of remainders without mentioning a practice, prevalent forty or fifty years ago, which has recently been revived—that is of manufacturing them. So great is the bargain appeal that a book that is no longer available may be reprinted for sale as a remainder at a reduced price with a jacket showing the original price or even an artificially enhanced price.

The Net Book Agreement.—Reference has already been made to the 'Net Book Agreement' (for the latest wording see Appendix III), and it ought therefore to be explained firstly that it is primarily a statement of terms and conditions of supply and secondly that it came into being as a remedy for 'underselling'—a practice which was steadily undermining the book trade. Anyone interested in the history of the inception of the agreement will find it in Sir Frederick Macmillan's little volume. Endless difficulties had to be overcome, and it was to the persistence of a few publishers and a small minority of booksellers that the trade owes this beneficent reform, which protects it from undercutting and ensures that a book published at a net price shall be sold at that price and not less.[1]

At first, discount booksellers opposed the innovation; few believed in it, but these persevered; today all booksellers regard it as indispensable and are as jealous as publishers about its maintenance. Most publishers now have wording printed on their invoices to the following effect:

NET books are supplied subject to the Publishers Association Standard Conditions of Sale registered under the Restrictive Trade Practices Act, 1956.

Under the original wording collective action could be taken against an offending bookseller but following the Restrictive Trade Practices Act, 1956, it can be taken only by the individual publisher whose terms of supply have been infringed.

Whether a particular firm or organization should be allowed trade terms used to be a source of difficulty. But that and many other problems were thoroughly examined in 1927 by a representative 'Joint Committee of Publishers and Booksellers' whose reports and recommendations are embodied in a volume edited by F. D. Sanders entitled *British Book Trade Organization*[2] which is a mine of information and will repay

[1] *The Net Book Agreement*, 1899. MacLehose, 1924.
Memoirs of J. M. Dent. Dent, 1928.
[2] London: George Allen & Unwin Ltd. (1939).

careful study. Most of the recommendations have been acted upon, though a few of them were strenuously opposed at the time by some of the older publishers and booksellers as being too revolutionary. The work of the Joint Committee (since supplemented by the Report of the 1948 Book Trade Committee published in 1954) probably represents the biggest step the British Book Trade has ever taken towards putting its house in order, and it is perhaps permissible therefore that I should record that it was the direct outcome of the visit of a delegation of British publishers and booksellers to Amsterdam and Leipzig which I initiated.

Here I must confine myself to a few of the more important proposals to which effect was given. First a permanent Joint Advisory Committee of Publishers and Booksellers, known as the 'JAC', was set up to examine all applications for 'recognition' as entitled to trade terms and to recommend the form the recognition (if any) should take.

Previously there had been only one kind of 'recognition'; under the new regulations there were several categories. In addition to the general bookseller there was the 'other trader' with a limited form of recognition. For example the circulating library which required books solely for loan; the coin dealer who wished merely to sell books on coins; the religious or political organization whose facilities were confined to the books the sale of which they were directly concerned to promote and of which, sometimes, they were in a position to sell more copies than the entire book trade. In this connection booksellers often overlooked that sales can be effected at the moment when a person's interest is aroused which could not be secured even one hour later. It is thus possible to sell the book of the words of a play to a person in a theatre who would not dream of buying it when he got outside. Similarly with political literature sold at a political meeting. That one sympathizes with the desire that all business should be effected by and through a bookseller need not blind one to the fact that sometimes it would not be done at all were it not done on the spot and at the time the interest was awakened. Fortunately, there is a growing tendency for booksellers to co-operate to secure extra business of the kinds indicated, and so long as it *is* secured no one will be better pleased than publishers that it should be handled by booksellers. The view that a publisher ought to let golden opportunities slip if he cannot persuade a bookseller to take advantage of them is not, I think, widely held.

In addition to recognition either as a bookseller or 'other trader' handling books in some defined category, provision was made for 'Book Agents' authorized to draw their supplies from a named bookseller and be paid a commission by him, and the opportunity was taken to solve the thorny problem of the supply of Public Libraries[1] who under carefully prescribed conditions, if the magnitude of their orders justify it, may now be granted a licence entitling the booksellers named thereon to make them an allowance of 10 per cent. As a further outcome of the Restrictive Practices Act 'recognition' became, by implication, illegal and the list of 'recognized booksellers' was in consequence

[1] The case for the Public Libraries will be found on pages 216–17 of any of the first three editions of this book.

discontinued. It was found, however, that there would be, as a result, a need for an ordinary directory of bona fide booksellers which is now published as part of its information services by the Publishers Association.

Export Traders (other than Retail Booksellers in the United Kingdom and Eire) were also classified as follows:

CLASS A—Export Booksellers (i.e. Exporters in the United Kingdom and Eire whose main business is buying for overseas booksellers). Full Export Terms.

CLASS B—General Exporters (i.e. Firms in the United Kingdom and Eire whose business includes the buying of books for overseas traders for re-sale and who will, if called upon to do so, produce original orders).

Orders to be scrutinized and divided into (a) orders for books intended for private individuals, schools, libraries and institutions abroad on which the discount is generally limited to 10 per cent; (b) orders for books shown by the destination given on the orders to be for re-sale by traders abroad on which full export terms may be allowed. (By destination is meant the name and address of the Exporter's overseas customer or a shipping mark which is known to be that of a trader abroad.)

CLASS C.—Export Commission Agents, now Book Agents as a result of a re-classification agreed in May 1934 (i.e. Firms in the United Kingdom and Eire buying for organizations and private individuals resident abroad, who are not purchasing for re-sale). Terms: full published prices less a commission not exceeding 10 per cent. Publishers should secure an undertaking that all books purchased are to be exported.

Nowadays Class C Exporters are usually dealt with under the Bookagents' Licensing arrangement at a discount not exceeding half that received by the supplying booksellers themselves.

There are scarcely any parts of the world to which British books do not penetrate, but the publisher is not always aware of the precise destination of those he supplies for export.

A wholesale exporter in the UK may act as the buying agent of booksellers in all parts of the world, and whereas firm AB may buy chiefly for Australia and YZ for South Africa, either or both may, in addition, have a client, or clients, in Valparaiso or Bangkok. The publisher is usually given the 'mark', which more often than not consists of the initials of the overseas booksellers, e.g. the initials T.M.M. stand for T. Maskew Miller of Cape Town.

The prime object of requiring adequate marks from exporters is to ensure that the British edition is not sent into any overseas markets the rights in which have been leased to, or controlled by, some other publisher (e.g. an American publisher).

Unfortunately the new *Directory of Exporters* issued by the Publishers Association in January 1960 does not separately list exporters exclusively supplying booksellers.

The export commission agent may act for private customers (i.e. non-bookselling firms or individuals) in all parts of the world, and however carefully the order is scrutinized by the publisher's trade department (and such orders are more carefully examined by the best publishers than some booksellers believe), it is not practicable to keep a record of the ultimate destination of every book thus supplied. Again, most home booksellers have at any rate a few customers abroad, so that the export of English books is going on all the time through many channels. We now know that export sales represent about 35 per cent of the total turnover of the British book trade. In the case of my own firm it amounts to well over 50 per cent.

The final decision about including a firm in the directory of bona fide booksellers rests with the Council of the Publishers Association.

The Exchange Control Act, 1947, provides that in the case of exports to countries *outside the sterling area* a C.D.3 Form must be filled in if the shipment exceeds £500. Pages 1 and 2 of this elaborate form are retained by H.M. Customs. Pages 3 and 4 are returned to the consignor to be held until payment is received. The form is then surrendered to the consignor's bank together with a copy of the invoice and the buyer's cheque. If payment is not received within the time stated on the form The Controller, Exchange Control (Exports), Customs and Excise wants to know why.

Public Libraries—most unfortunately from some points of view—have practically no direct contact with publishing, but they are indirectly and collectively the most important customers of the better type of general book publisher. Their support of the worth-while book, and their refusal to buy the meretricious, might exercise an even more decisive influence upon the quality of books published if so many Library authorities did not spend such ridiculously inadequate amounts on new books—in fact, if they did not underrate the importance of the very commodity for which public libraries exist. That problem is fully dealt with in Mr Lionel R. McColvin's masterly and exhaustive Report on the Public Library System of Great Britain,[1] so that there is no need for me to dwell upon it. But what is known

[1] Library Association, 1942. See pages 58–60 and 125.

to few is that a small minority of Library Committees actually favour a policy which ensures, if successfully applied, that no authors shall receive any remuneration from the copies of their works which these libraries circulate. This—to them apparently laudable end—the librarians achieve by buying review copies, remainders and even on occasion books that prove to have been stolen. The one criterion is cheapness, and if to secure an illicit $2\frac{1}{2}$ per cent they can persuade a bookseller to break a written agreement they seem to regard it as a meritorious act. I have referred to this minority because I agree so wholeheartedly with Mr McColvin, 'that wherever the local authority was neglecting its duty (in the matter of Library service) it was not only the local community that suffered, but also the whole state . . .'.

The importance, actual and potential, of the work of public librarians and their influence are alike immense.[1] It is impossible to assess how much they have done to spread a knowledge and love of books. Good librarians, and we are blessed with many such, do not need to be told that taking the long view the best books are always the cheapest, whereas the cheapest (apart from reprints) are seldom the best.

Special Editions, supplied to and sold by various societies and organizations, are not welcomed by the trade (why, indeed, should they be?); but most intelligent booksellers recognize their inevitability, if not their usefulness, and realize that they provide an 'extra' market which would not otherwise be tapped.

[1] Their total expenditure on new books in 1945 was probably about £750,000, and in the year ending March 31, 1958, over £3,000,000.

These 'special editions' are usually bound in cheaper style, whether it be in paper covers or limp cloth, and are often printed on cheaper paper. They are distributed by the organization or society in question, and in fairness to booksellers the condition is made (if it is not made, booksellers have every right to complain) that the sale shall be rigidly restricted to their members.[1]

It would be beyond the scope of this work to treat of the developments of bookselling, for which all the best booksellers would readily admit that there is still ample room. Personally I believe there is an increasing opening for the bookseller who will specialize—I do not suggest that he need necessarily give up his general connection, but merely that he should so develop some one field as to become the recognized expert upon it. He would then be in a much more effective position to undertake circularization and the distribution of books on approval.

But I cannot resist the temptation of mentioning another not immediately profitable but useful and interesting method of selling books in which I have long been interested—the CARAVAN BOOKSHOP. There are large sections of the rural population in Great Britain out of reach of any bookshop. If people cannot visit a bookshop, the remedy is to take the bookshop to them. Small towns and villages, particularly mining villages, which could not support a bookseller, ought in a well-ordered world to receive a visit from a peripatetic bookshop every month and preferably on a recognized day each month.

At first, such a caravan bookshop would find cheap

[1] Book Clubs, see page 275.

juveniles and practical handbooks the most saleable, but by degrees it would prove possible to carry a wider assortment. It would be essential for book-tokens to be accepted because as matters stand people in the heart of the country and out of reach of a bookshop often find it a burden to exchange them.

Local co-operation in making the venture known could easily be secured, and popular lectures about books arranged to synchronize with the visit of the caravan bookshop, thus making it a kind of missionary for the promotion of book-reading. Success or failure would largely depend upon the enthusiasm and personality of the man or woman who had the courage to embark upon the venture. It is the old story of finding the right man; but what more delightful occupation could be found by any book-lover who, for reasons of health, wanted to lead an outdoor life?

Many will dismiss the idea as visionary, though it works effectively in Northern Nigeria and something similar has already proved practicable in connection with rural libraries for the *loan* of books. There would thus seem to be no insuperable difficulty about arranging it for the *sale* of books. One most enterprising lady who embarked upon the experiment covered her out of pocket expenses, but was unfortunately unable to continue long enough to benefit from the connection she was building up. Until the monthly visit became a recognized and anticipated event an adequate turnover would obviously not be forthcoming.

The most effective method would probably be for the caravan bookshop to work from a provincial centre where there was accessible untilled ground. It is important both to keep down the mileage and to have a nearby base from which to draw supplies. W. H. Smith & Son are so well equipped to make the experiment that one cannot but wish that they would do so. It might well prove desirable for such a peripatetic bookshop to visit factories during the lunch hour or at closing time. Booksellers are apt to overlook the many workers who now have money to spend but have no opportunity of visiting their shops during the hours when they are open.

Quite apart from the foregoing the question arises whether retail and wholesale newsagents ought not to be encouraged to make use of their exceptionally efficient machinery for supplying newspapers to develop a really speedy and reliable 'get any book to order' business. In the many places where there is a newsagent but no bookseller, this would be a great advantage to the general public who not finding a book in stock in their locality often wrongly assume that it is unobtainable. As matters stand newsagents who neither refer their customers to a bookseller nor offer to obtain books for which they are asked may be a positive hindrance to book distribution. It is all part of the 'single copy' problem and the need of an efficient 'parcels clearing' to which thought is at last being given. Were it more widely recognized that a nominal charge of sixpence for specially obtaining a single book was reasonable, as it is, the economic difficulty would at once be largely overcome.

But to return to existing methods, it would be unjust to finish this chapter without paying a tribute to the increasing number of real booksellers whom the late

Professor Laski described in the *New Statesman* as 'part of the living basis of civilization'. 'It is not that they have about the best commodity in the world to sell. The very fact that they are good booksellers draws about their shops most of the people who have something to say. A town without a good bookseller is like a body without a soul.'

We cannot be too grateful to them.

CHAPTER VII

BOOK DISTRIBUTION ON
THE CONTINENT

NEARLY all the leading continental countries have most carefully thought out book trade organizations and none more so than Germany, whose *Börsenverein* was founded well over a hundred years ago. In 1913 it represented the greatest achievement in book distribution that there has ever been, and the whole mechanism moved with the precision of a well-oiled clock. In earlier editions of this book I included a detailed account of its working, but since that time so much sand has been thrown into the machine first in the shape of currency and other regulations necessitated by inflation, then by the Nazis that it is no longer wholly applicable. Furthermore, the Second World War and the intensive bombing experienced by Leipzig, which fortunately spared the '*Bücherei*', has lead to far-reaching changes, and brought to an end the custom of the German Book Trade to make all deliveries 'free Leipzig'.

Out of the Leipzig ashes a Phoenix has arisen in Frankfurt, an interesting reversal of what happened more than a hundred years ago when, on political grounds, Leipzig was chosen instead of Frankfurt as the centre of the German book trade. The far-sighted municipal authorities of Frankfurt have ensured that Frankfurt shall remain the book centre by (*a*) granting

the *Börsenverein* a magnificent free site in the centre of
the city, (*b*) advancing the cost of substantial new build-
ings on such a favourable basis that the *Börsenverein*
already owns the first block and now has in addition a
large hall (suitable for concerts) in which to hold
meetings.

In Germany, book trade organization began by
embracing the whole book trade. Separate associations
for separate interests came later.[1] It is difficult to
exaggerate the debt which book trade organizations
everywhere (including the *Maison du Livre*) owe to the
example of the *Börsenverein*, even if they had no actual
contact with it.

The distribution of British books on the Continent
is a more important business than many publishers
sometimes think. But it consists very largely of orders
for single copies of many titles. Furthermore, much
of the business is done through exporters and wholesalers, so that the publisher may be unaware of the
ultimate destination of the copies he is supplying. The
British book trade owes a greater debt to the specialized
knowledge and activities of these firms than is usually
admitted. For all practical purposes, before the last
war, the continental booksellers drew their supplies of
books in the English language almost exclusively from
London. American publishers with London branches
or agencies wisely dealt with this specialized business
through London. Geographical proximity was, of
course, an important factor; how important may be
judged from the fact that books ordered at the same
time would as a rule reach Amsterdam more rapidly

[1] In England and America there is no equivalent of the *Börsenverein*.

than Aberdeen. The pre-war continental service was extremely efficient. But geographical proximity is not the only reason for so much of this business being done from or through London. Currency and credit complications frequently compelled it.

For the non-Latin countries Leipzig was, as Frankfurt now is, the main centre of book distribution on the Continent, and those British publishers who took advantage of that unique organization *in addition to* working direct from London, were able to do appreciable extra business. For example, before the Great War of 1914–18 I was able to sell more British books in Budapest, where it was 'good form' to read English books, than in a big provincial town like Sheffield. But let me hasten to add that I should not have been able to do so had I not at that time been the only British publisher carrying stock in Leipzig. Had many firms been doing so it would probably not have paid any of us. The cultivation of the continental market involves more intensive and exhaustive work in relation to possible turnover than any other. To start with, it is not one market but as many as there are different countries, languages and currencies, and each calls for separate study and separate treatment. A bookseller in Amsterdam or Stockholm may know more about British books than many an English bookseller, but that is unlikely to be the case in Sofia or Split. If the continental market is to be adequately looked after, far closer attention than in the past will have to be given to the special requirements of the individual countries. Facilities which may be fully justified in one case may be unwarranted in another.

Turning then to the various countries let us begin with *Holland* which as we have seen can be so rapidly supplied from London: it is a first-rate market from every point of view. The Dutch have an excellent book trade organization with splendid headquarters, the Centraal Boekhuis at Amsterdam. There are many firms handling British books and their credit is almost uniformly good. They keep in close touch with London, buy intelligently and in earlier days did a substantial business with Indonesia.

Taking it as a whole, Northern Europe is a bright spot in the book world. There is probably no better group of booksellers anywhere, whether judged from the point of view of knowledge of their job, credit worthiness, or efficiency of organization. In relation to population, which is comparatively small, these countries must be among the best book markets in the world.

In *Denmark*, about which I have written elsewhere,[1] the unique feature is that nearly all the leading publishers are booksellers and nearly all the leading booksellers are publishers. There is thus a much fuller understanding of each other's problems than is usual elsewhere. Here, as in the other Scandinavian countries, no one is permitted to open a bookshop who has not had a thorough training as a bookseller.

In *Norway*, where the organization is much like that of Holland, the sale of English books is largely in the hands of two firms and many of the country booksellers draw their supplies of English books through them. They do particularly well with medical, scientific

[1] *Danish Book Trade Organization* (London: George Allen & Unwin Ltd.)

and technical books, and books in English have been gradually superseding those in German. One of the interesting developments of the Norwegian book trade, about which I have written elsewhere,[1] is their unique method of dealing with the requirements of Public Libraries, since extended to Ships' Libraries.

Sweden,[1] unlike Norway and Denmark, has separate associations of publishers and booksellers. Distribution is effected for the most part through a Stockholm company (Seelig), owned by the booksellers themselves, which daily receives the orders from the country booksellers and distributes them to the publishers, and subsequently receives and dispatches all the parcels to the booksellers without any expense to the publishers.

All accounts and money, however, are, as a rule, sent by the booksellers direct to the publishers. Much of the business is done 'on sale or return' with a yearly settlement. The question of credit is dealt with most effectively. In 1911 the booksellers formed a kind of mutual insurance society to guarantee the publishers against bad debts, the premium payable by the bookseller being calculated on his turnover. The publishers gave a substantial donation and agreed that no new booksellers should be granted credit who were not accepted as members of the society. Swedish booksellers are thus in effect licensed, because, if a locality is being well served and there is no indication that another bookshop is needed, credit is withheld from the newcomer.

Finland boasts at least two bookshops at Helsinki, one of them probably the largest in Europe, carrying a

[1] See *Book Trade Organization in Norway and Sweden* (1932).

stock of English books which would compare more than favourably with what could be found in many of the largest provincial towns in England. Similarly in *Iceland* there are at Reykjavik and Akureyri excellent booksellers stocking and selling English books, which is more than could be said of some English towns with a population of as little as 65,000, let alone 8,000.

The demands of *Soviet Russia* for British books, which will presumably now steadily increase, are centralized in *Meshdunarodnaya Kniga*. Before the Second World War the Baltic States, and particularly *Esthonia*, were showing an increasing interest in British books. In *Poland* there was always and still is a substantial demand. The limiting factor is shortage of sterling.

The *Czech* booksellers were almost uniformly reliable, and the demand for British books, which was always good, was expanding not merely because of the increasing numbers of Czechs reading and speaking English, but because of the waning interest in French and the antipathy to anything German. This latter is nothing new. I am never likely to forget my first visit to a Czech bookshop over fifty years ago. I addressed the manager in German and received a cold, uncomprehending stare. I apologized that I could not speak Czech and explained that I was English. 'Oh, if you are English', responded the Manager, 'of course we will talk German.' Unfortunately all the buying has now been centralized as in Soviet Russia.

In the days of the Austro-Hungarian Empire Vienna and Budapest were substantial markets for British books, but with its collapse their importance lessened.

In Vienna the demand is still there to a considerable extent, and in Budapest, before the Communists took over, much could be done if one could surmount the currency hurdles. There has never been any doubt about the cultured Hungarian's love of things English.

In Bucharest the sale of British books was leaping forward, until the descent of the iron curtain put an end to it. It was to ensure that the better type of British book should be available in at any rate one bookshop in each of the more important centres in countries like *Yugoslavia*, *Bulgaria* and *Turkey*, and *Greece* that I invented what has become known as the British Book Export Scheme, since adapted, in a modified form, by the USA Informational Media Guarantee (IMG) arrangements in Indonesia, Israel, Turkey, and elsewhere.

As far back as 1918 a Departmental Committee of the then Department of Information had reported at considerable length upon the difficulties of the Foreign Distribution of British Books, but no attention had been paid to their recommendations.

The British Book Export Scheme was much more modest. It provided, with the approval of the Treasury, for the sharing by the publishers, the foreign booksellers and the British Council of such expenses as might be incurred in securing the desired wider distribution of British books in centres where they were not otherwise readily obtainable.

The British Council, working in collaboration with the National Book Council, was to issue monthly lists of such of the new English books as were of cultural importance. These lists were to be sent to the selected foreign booksellers with an invitation to order any books likely to be of interest to their clientele. The invitation was to be accompanied by an undertaking to credit them in full with the actual cost of those books they had not sold within a prescribed period (probably six months). The bookseller's contribution to the cost of the scheme was thus confined to the postage or freight incurred. This was to serve as a deterrent to reckless ordering.

Instead of returning unsold books the bookseller handed them over to the local representative of the British Council. On receiving a notification that this had been done the publisher credited the bookseller with the full amount charged for the returned books (other than postage or carriage) and then invoiced them to the British Council at half price (less an additional $2\frac{1}{2}$ per cent by way of contribution towards the cost of printing the lists). The publisher thus bore a substantial portion of the loss and the British Council acquired the books for presentation purposes, carriage free, on exceptionally favourable terms.

To the bookseller it was an 'on sale or return' arrangement, but to the publisher a sale 'firm purchase', thus complying with the requirements of both!

It must be emphasized that the scheme was not, and is not, a substitute for such methods of distribution as already exist, but was, and is, intended to supplement them by enabling selected bookshops in certain countries to carry a more representative stock of English books than would otherwise be practicable. War prevented the immediate application of the scheme in the territories for which it was specifically devised, and there have been subsequent modifications in it, but the general principles hold good.

It is an arrangement particularly suited, with modifications to meet individual circumstances, to countries acutely short of sterling.

In point of fact in *Turkey* a different method was adopted more adapted to local requirements and run entirely by the British Council. Great interest was aroused in British books but today, 1959, solely owing to currency difficulties, which one hopes will pass, business is more or less at a standstill.

Before 1914 *Germany* was by far the most important market in Europe for British books. The period between the two world wars was most tantalizing. The demand was there but currency and other difficulties virtually suspended contact. Today there is once again an upward trend.

A large part of the business to be done in normal times with *Switzerland* is seasonal, and calls for detailed attention out of proportion to the turnover at all but the larger resorts. The booksellers in the German-speaking parts of Switzerland are in touch with Frankfurt and to a much lesser extent Leipzig; those in Geneva and the French parts look largely to Paris. There are excellent bookshops in all the big towns and an important wholesale firm at Olten.

The demand for English books in *Italy* is fairly substantial, and the same might be said about the credit which some of the Italian booksellers require. It is in fact easier to sell books in Italy than to secure payment for them. A considerably larger business could be done, particularly with scientific and technical books, but for these credit difficulties.

When one refers to the *French* market in relation to English books one means Paris, because all the other French centres put together do not absorb as many English books as Paris, where the sale is largely in the hands of three firms, British, American, and French respectively. All three carry substantial stocks of English books, particularly of the lighter kind, and do a very considerable business. Certain of the other French booksellers attend to the university and scholastic requirements and much business goes through Hachettes.

Belgium, for one reason or another, was never a satisfactory market. If they wanted British books as much as they said they did, W. H. Smith & Son's branch in Brussels would have had to be expanded out of all knowledge. There are now, however, gratifying signs of a real demand.

The desire for British books in *Spain* is considerable, but when the Nazi influence upon the Franco régime was paramount every obstacle was put in the way of its fulfilment. Many Spanish translations from the English have appeared since the war and the supply of British books has been increased, but the sale of both rights and books has been handicapped by shortage of sterling.

In *Portugal* the demand was greatly enhanced during the war, and it remains to be seen to what extent that interest will continue. The success of the British Council's activities here and in Spain in promoting the knowledge of English is materially assisting the demand.

Although they do not form part of the Continent of Europe it is convenient to include here certain adjacent countries.

Israel developed into a market of quite exceptional importance, and during the war it was difficult to comply with all the requirements of the many booksellers in Jerusalem, Tel-Aviv and elsewhere. Unfortunately owing to Israel's acute shortage of sterling little business could thereafter be done and what was an almost exclusively British market was handed over to the Americans under the IMG scheme to which reference has already been made. The American publisher sells in local currency and collects the dollar equivalent from the United States Government which uses the Israeli pounds to finance information services, etc. Although the Israeli booksellers would prefer British books which cost half the amount, they have no alternative but to buy what they can pay for in their own currency. We can only hope that ere long a British Book Export Scheme which will enable British publishers to compete, will be authorized.

Syria and the Lebanon likewise show signs of taking a deeper interest in English literature, instead of confining themselves as in the past to things French. In *Iraq* there is an active bookseller at Baghdad and signs of activity elsewhere. Business is opening up in *Kuwait* where there is no shortage of sterling. From *Iran* orders are now beginning to arrive steadily and there is every reason to hope for an increasing demand because so many young Iranians are learning English.

Egypt, like Israel, developed an insatiable appetite for British books during the late war, and though following the Suez crisis business temporarily ceased the demand is still there and is likely to increase.

Turning to the question of book distribution on the Continent as a whole, if it be true that 'no one can escape from the influence of the books he reads', the wide distribution of English books, whether in their original language or in translation, must be of incalculable advantage in spreading English ideas throughout the world. We are often told that trade follows the flag, but, as I pointed out about thirty years ago, it would be truer to say that 'Trade follows the book'. The book penetrates farther; its influence is more subtle and more far reaching. It moves the hearts and minds of people in their homes by their own firesides, and often at the most quiet and receptive moment. Moreover, is it not probable that foreign nations brought up on British scientific text-books would want the British instruments and machines therein described rather than others of which they had not the same intimate knowledge, and is not this equally true in varying degrees in other directions than science? Certainly the Germans acted upon that assumption. Curiously enough, it is we English who have been slowest to appreciate this, though I am happy to be able to add that the Federation of British Industries now does so.

If, as I believe, 'a nation's literature is the permanent embodiment of the experience of its greatest men and women', could there be any more desirable thing for any nation to offer the world?

A *Clearing House* for books such as is to be found in

the leading continental centres is a piece of machinery and orders are given *through*, not *to*, it.

The use of a 'clearing house' does not involve any change in the ultimate destination of any order, and does not necessarily obviate the need of a wholesale firm. Booksellers who order from a wholesaler today would continue to order from a wholesaler; those who prefer to order direct would still be free to do so. Its sole object is to achieve economically, efficiently and expeditiously the purely mechanical side of a publisher's activities. The principle behind it is to do collectively those routine operations like invoicing, packing and dispatch which are best done collectively and centrally and to leave the publisher free to concentrate all his attention upon the many things from selecting MSS to production, publicity and selling where individuality can be expressed and which in any case call for personal treatment.

The Clearing House as a system is not a foreign institution: English bankers adopted it a hundred and eighty years ago. It is merely its application to the book trade that we owe to Germany. It exists in embryo in London, in the shape of the Book Centre at Neasden. Here we have a co-operative nonprofit-making undertaking equipped to handle for publishers the purely mechanical side of their job and with ground available for expansion. Were some such organization generally used, the convenience and the economy might be great though it has its drawbacks.

1. The orders made out to the individual publishers would be posted in one envelope by letter post to the centre and thus not dribble in at odd times by printed-matter post as at present.

2. The entire requirements of each bookseller (better still the entire requirements of all the booksellers of any one town) would be dispatched from this one source.

3. The publishers would have only one centre to which to deliver goods instead of many.

4. It would be an easy matter to arrange a motor delivery service for an area of 50 or even 100 miles round London.

5. The saving in 'carriage charges' as well as postage on orders and remittances might be considerable.

6. Catalogues, publicity material, etc., could be delivered in bulk to the centre, and for a nominal charge distributed to the entire trade in the daily or weekly parcels.

7. A goods train service for non-urgent orders to distant places where freight is a big item could be arranged. In some cases it would be practicable to send weekly consignments at 'truck rate'.

8. A satisfactory town trade centre service could and would have to be evolved. A co-operative town delivery service would be simple. The present overlapping is pathetically uneconomic.

The suggestion, in brief, is to arrange the purely mechanical side of distribution rather more conveniently and economically than at present, but to leave undisturbed the relationship of bookseller, wholesaler, and publisher. How far this co-operation can be developed without loss to the publisher's individuality is a vital consideration which deserves careful study.

Some of the services mentioned above are to some extent already being operated by Book Centre Ltd. Their 'Orders Clearing' deals with over a million orders per annum. 'Book Deliveries' is a London book delivery service covering not only Book Centre but a number of other publishers and 'Parcels Clearing' is a system of bulking other publishers' parcels with those of Book Centre for more economical and speedy dispatch.

The 'On Sale or Return' System

Any and every one outside the book trade who sets out to investigate book distribution abroad, and in particular how the sale of English books can be increased, invariably prescribes the same medicine, viz. the supply of books 'on sale or return', oblivious of the fact that it has been tried over and over again with disastrous effects on the patient unless taken in homoeopathic doses.

It may therefore be worth while to examine why this advice is given and why it is unsound.

The book trade in most continental countries is organized on the basis of 'on sale or return', and their books are produced in a form which lends itself to that method of doing business. But on balance the movement is away from, not towards, that basis, and an increasing proportion of the books sold are cloth-bound and supplied 'firm purchase'. It is one thing to supply paper-bound books on sale, quite another to supply cloth-bound books. Widespread distribution 'on sale' automatically involves printing larger editions; the amount of capital locked up in the supply of paper-bound books is less, and soiled copies can be rewrapped comparatively inexpensively. The recasing of cloth-bound books, on the contrary, is costly.

Continental booksellers, who are accustomed to receive cheap French paper-bound books 'on sale', quite naturally and truthfully point out to any inquirer that more English books could be sold were they freely available 'on sale'. But English publishers, who have experimented over and over again, will equally truthfully point out that the comparatively few additional sales thereby effected are achieved at an economically disastrous cost. In addition to the direct financial loss, there are technical difficulties, e.g. in connection with authors' royalties. If the system is to have a reasonable chance of success, the stock must remain with the bookseller for at least six months, in which case the 'returns' (invariably unfit for resale as new copies) almost necessarily arrive after the author's account has been made up and paid. Apart from the clerical work, already burdensome in proportion to the trifling turn-over, it is, to say the least, difficult for a publisher to recover money once paid to an author.

In that case, why not issue English books in paper covers? The answer is simple. English people (rightly) simply will not buy new books, at much above 6s, in that form. This is not a mere opinion, but a fact which has been put to the test again and again. No publisher who has made the experiment is likely to forget the extent to which he burned his fingers. Why 'rightly'? Because, unless the cloth edition is made to subsidize the paper edition, the reduction in the published price thereby achieved is ridiculously small—probably about 1s 6d. How many English people confronted with the same book in paper covers at 9s and in cloth cases at 10s 6d would begrudge the extra eighteen pence? Furthermore, on the Continent most books are bought; in England most (alas!) are borrowed. The bulk of the editions must therefore inevitably be cloth bound for supply to Public and Commercial Lending Libraries.

Because it is not practicable to graft 'sale or return' business on to an organization ill-adapted to it, there is no reason why nothing should be done, but it is necessary to make sure that one is not throwing away the substance for the shadow.

In such countries as Denmark, Norway, Sweden, Finland, Holland or, farther afield, Japan, very satisfactory business is already being achieved. For this reason it is necessary to examine the problem from two angles:

(1) The countries where existing trade is not unsatisfactory.

(2) Those, where the business done is negligible.

In the first category a little more elasticity might lead to more sales. By this I do not mean the supply of books on sale or return, but readiness to supply one or at most two booksellers in each big centre with a single copy 'on approval' of any book he wants to be able to examine prior to purchase. This merely places the continental bookseller in the position of the London bookseller, who actually sees and has an opportunity of examining every new book.

Where this practice is not in force there should be greater readiness to help by an exchange the foreign bookseller who finds that what he has ordered from a printed announcement is unsuited to his requirements. This must not be interpreted as making all stock exchangeable but merely as a willingness to exchange where prompt notification is sent after receipt of the goods. Many of the more enlightened firms already act upon these principles, but some of the older and more conservative ones are unduly rigid.

The best way of dealing with Category 2 is the

British Book Export Scheme of which particulars were given earlier in this chapter.

Reverting to the foreign countries in which satisfactory business is already being done, complaints that publishers will not supply 'on sale' will not, as explained above, carry us anywhere, but if any responsible bookseller is experiencing difficulty in getting a single copy of a new book 'on approval' before deciding whether he can stock it, information should be sent to the British Council. It is, of course, essential that the complaint should be specific, i.e. that it should give:

(1) The name and address of the bookseller.

(2) The name of the publisher with whom difficulty has been experienced.

(3) The title (or titles) of the book (or books) which it was desired to inspect.

CHAPTER VIII

PUBLICITY, Etc.

DOES any author think his book has been adequately or properly advertised? The answer to that question will explain how dangerous it is for a publisher to mention, or even to suggest, that there are any limitations to what can be accomplished by advertising. Should a publisher ever be rash enough to do so, it is at once assumed that he does not believe in advertising, and he is dismissed as a bad publisher. Anyone listening to some authors might easily be led to believe that a publisher is good or bad according to the amount of newspaper space he takes, even if it is chiefly used to advertise the publisher's name. Whether the advertisement is well or ill done; whether even the author who is talking merely has his name included in a list of scores and scores of titles, does not seem to weigh in the balance. The important point, consciously or unconsciously, would seem to be the superficial area occupied by the publisher in the particular papers read by the author in question.

Now, the results of this are twofold. In the first place, there is a conspiracy of silence amongst publishers in regard to newspaper advertising. Secondly, there is a tendency to do certain advertising for the sake of appearances and not for the sales it will secure. It would seem, therefore, to be high time to examine the whole question dispassionately and to see whether the most obvious forms of advertising as carried out by the least intelligent firms are necessarily the best, or whether, for many books at any rate, other forms of advertising are not more fruitful of results. When discussing the question of advertising books, we are confronted once again with the trouble that besets nearly all discussions of publishing questions, viz. that two out of three people taking part in the discussion will be thinking about novels, and not about books in general, of which novels only form a fractional part.

'*Blurbs.*'—If our treatment of the question of publicity in relation to books is to be at all complete, we must begin at the beginning, and that is with the writing of the descriptive paragraph which is to appear in the publisher's list, on the jacket of the book, and in advance information sent to the publisher's travellers and to the Press. These brief descriptive paragraphs, or 'blurbs' as they are sometimes called, are most difficult to write. (If anyone doubts the assertion, let him try his hand at writing one of some famous work of the past.) To be read, the paragraphs must be brief; to attract the newspaper editor they must, if possible, have news value; to be of service to booksellers and librarians they must give an adequate description of the contents of the book: possibly indicate the author's qualifications for writing it. In the case of novels, the extent to which the details of the plot should be given is a problem needing special consideration. It does not follow that when an author is asked to write a paragraph the publishers[1] will use it exactly as submitted. The

[1] My own firm sends with such requests a form calling for detailed biographical and other information likely to be helpful with sales promotion.

'blurb' may be much too long; in any case it may contain phrases that would make it unacceptable. Publishers reserve, and most authors willingly concede to publishers, the right to edit and adapt these paragraphs. Even so, the revision has to be done with discretion and due regard to the author's feelings. If the author describes himself as 'the greatest authority' on a question, the publisher is confronted with the necessity of either reducing him to 'one of the great authorities' or being told by the reviewers that the claim made for the author on the jacket is preposterous. Although the words are the author's, the statement when printed becomes the publisher's.

Many authors have the most vague ideas as to what publishers can do in the way of getting paragraphs inserted in the Press. It would indeed be pleasant if publishers had the power that is sometimes attributed to them, but the fact remains that editors please themselves, or rather endeavour to please their public, in deciding what they will include in their columns. They may include a paragraph specially adapted to their requirements which highlights a point of topical interest, and they will most certainly exclude it if it has no news value. A point to be remembered is that a paragraph may have news value for one paper and not for another. Nearly all paragraphs about forthcoming books may be of interest to, let us say, the *Publishers' Circular*, and that paper may therefore use 'blurbs' in the form of a news item. Paragraphs announcing new books of importance were at one time a distinctive feature of *The Times Literary Supplement* and of some of the dailies; but in these cases the paragraphs were invariably the work of a member of the staff of the paper who devoted time to the collection of news of this character. The skill with which it was presented was an object-lesson to the budding paragraphist or the author confronted for the first time with the necessity of writing a 'blurb'. Of course here, as in so many other directions, imprint counts. Newspaper editors know which are the firms that may be said to buy their manuscripts by the dozen, and which are those that carefully select them. A book on some serious subject announced by one firm is sure to be good, and the paragraph about it will receive consideration. The announcement of a similar book from another firm will be as certainly disregarded.

Review Copies.—The publisher's imprint is of still more importance where reviewing is concerned. Review copies pour in upon the literary editors of the leading papers in overwhelming numbers. It is impossible for any ordinary paper to attempt to deal with all of them. In most offices a preliminary classification is made the moment the parcels are opened. Experience has shown that on given subjects the books bearing some imprints will be of importance, and that those bearing others can immediately be discarded. And here be it noted that most literary editors will not be influenced by whether the publisher is a big advertiser or not, but by the intrinsic merits of his publications. It is the best books rather than the best sellers that will attract the editor's eye, unless, of course, the latter have news value and call for attention, as some books do, in the news columns rather than in the literary columns of the paper.

The distribution of review copies is an important function of the publisher. Just because it is a partly mechanical task there is a tendency in some offices to make it entirely mechanical and to delegate the work to a junior. This, I am sure, is a mistake. It does not follow that the publisher need necessarily make out each list himself, but he certainly should cast his eye over most of them. To facilitate the work, many publishers have a printed review list on which are included as far as possible the names of all papers to which they are accustomed to send review copies. This is usually classified under such headings as dailies, weeklies, monthlies, provincial, dominions, etc. In this case, all that is needed is to tick the names of the papers which are to have the particular book. If it is on some special subject, the publisher will almost surely consult his author to make certain that no relevant paper of importance is omitted. In any case, well-informed suggestions from authors are always acceptable. A recommendation that copies should be sent to papers long since defunct does not inspire confidence. On the other hand, there are authors to whom the publisher would unhesitatingly send the printed review list to mark.

The publisher having delivered the review copy at the editor's office, and having obtained a receipt for it, has done his part; he cannot be expected to bombard editors with letters asking when they are going to review the book, or inquiring why they have not done so. What authors do is their own affair, but they will be wise to act with the utmost discretion, for it is more easy to do harm than to do good. Many editors have a most unfortunate habit, when being pestered by authors, of getting out of the difficulty by saying they have not had a review copy. This is distinctly unfair to the publisher, because it is a direct reflection upon his efficiency. In some cases the author goes away and condemns his publisher unheard; more often he sends in a complaint. In every case where such a charge has been made against my firm, and it has been done scores of times, we have had no difficulty in proving delivery and showing the editor a receipt for the book signed by some member of his staff. In some newspaper offices, the review copies are left lying about, and no adequate record is kept of them. In most of the best, however, great care is taken, and the literary editor watches jealously over the books.

Few publishers nowadays deface their review copies by stamping them on the title-page, but many mark them in some inconspicuous way. Reviewers are seldom well paid, and are fully entitled to what they can get by the sale of the copies. At the same time it would seem fair to ask that a decent interval be allowed to elapse before they are sold. In order that notices may appear on the day of publication it is usual to send out the review copies about a fortnight beforehand. There have been cases where the review copies have been on sale at the second-hand booksellers' *before* the book was published. That is indefensible. I think that not less than three months should be allowed to elapse. The organized sale of review copies to Public Libraries is a matter of grave concern to authors and publishers, and could become a serious deterrent to the publication of scholarly work of limited appeal where the loss of the sale of a single copy counts. The trouble, of course, is that the reviewer knows that the sooner he sells his copy the better the price he is likely to get for it.

A printed slip accompanies all review copies, giving the date of publication and requesting that no notice shall appear before that day. Any newspaper infringing the understanding by publishing a notice before the date of publication could not expect to receive further review copies in advance, but there is seldom any difficulty in regard to this. The trouble today is to secure prompt notice. The more reviews on the day of publication, or within a week thereafter, the better for the book. At one time, if a book was not reviewed within a few weeks of publication, it was probable that it would not be reviewed at all. Nowadays there are many instances where none of the best reviews appears within the first three weeks of publication.

The selling value of Press notices is most uncertain. There are cases where a single review in *The Times Literary Supplement*, the *Spectator*, or the *New Statesman* has started a book on its successful course; but excellent notices of another book in all three papers may sometimes be almost without effect. Two things are quite certain, viz. that good reviews do not necessarily mean good sales, nor the absence of reviews bad sales. The amount of space devoted to a book is sometimes more important than what is said about it, but even that is no criterion. The value of reviews in the news part of a paper is not always as great as would be supposed—probably because the news editor takes all the piquant things out of the book and the reader does not feel there is any necessity to bother to get the book himself. Few books have had half the notice given to

Dr Montagu Lomax's *Experiences of an Asylum Doctor*. Practically all the papers with large circulations devoted columns to discussions about it in the days immediately following publication, and it even resulted in a Royal Commission. The suggestion was frequently made that the author had made a fortune out of it and was going to retire on the proceeds. That statement was repeated in my presence at a dinner-party. A discussion of the book ensued, from which you would have gathered that all had read, even if they had not bought it. I asked everyone in turn whether he had purchased a copy. Not one had done so; only two of all those present had even borrowed it from a lending library. This must have been typical of what had happened everywhere, because at the time (about four months after publication) less than seven hundred copies had been sold, and the receipts had not at that date covered the cost of printing, paper, and binding, let alone yielded a penny to either author or publisher. The Press had so 'gutted' the book that few people felt there was any necessity to read it.

Applications for review copies are often received by publishers direct from reviewers; authors often ask that copies of their books should be addressed to a particular reviewer instead of to the editor, or the literary editor, if there be one. Such requests have to be closely scrutinized, if not entirely disregarded. To comply with them is to usurp the editor's function (or at any rate to attempt to do so), and to decide which of his staff shall be entrusted with the reviewing of some particular book. Editors very naturally resent such interference, and in any case it is neither polite nor desirable to 'short-circuit' them in this fashion. It is perfectly simple to ask the editor if it is his wish that the copy should go direct to the particular reviewer, or alternatively to suggest to the reviewer that he should ask his editor for the book.

Press Cuttings.—Publishers expect to receive voucher copies of papers containing notices of their books, and in most publishing offices fairly complete sets of Press cuttings are available for inspection by authors. Should the publisher receive any duplicate cuttings, he is usually prepared to present them to the author, but if a complete set is desired the best plan is to subscribe to a good Press-cutting agency. It is essential that they should be instructed before publication, as it is by no means easy to get cuttings from back numbers of newspapers.

Some publishers take much more pains than others to check the results of the distribution of review copies. My own firm keeps a statistical record from which it is possible to see at a glance what books any particular paper has received, and exactly which of them it has noticed. If the proportion noticed by any paper becomes unreasonably low, fewer books are sent. Should notices cease to appear the paper is dropped from the list and copies are sent only when specifically asked for. On the other hand, if the proportion noticed is considerable, there is a natural tendency to send more books to that paper, even though it is not one of first-rate importance, because a review in print is worth two in prospect. The maintenance of such a record means trouble, but unquestionably saves wastage and enabled us on one occasion to expose an apparently reputable journal which consistently applied for review copies which it as consistently refrained from reviewing—but not from selling.

There is much less connection between reviews and advertisements than is commonly supposed or than some advertisement canvassers would like one to believe. Literary editors are mostly very jealous of their independence, and rightly so. Opinions that can be bought carry little weight, and for this reason, if for no other, the wise publisher welcomes independence in the reviewer. Unfortunately, it would not be true to say that there was never any connection between advertisements and reviews, because in the case of at any rate one important and independent paper such a connection could be traced. How it can arise is easily explained. More reviews are put into type than appear—at the last moment some have to be discarded. The advertisement manager who is interested in the 'make-up' and is on the spot is allowed in some offices to decide which of the less important notices shall go in. But, taking it as a whole, reviewing is very fairly done and the best books seldom get overlooked, particularly if the publisher knows his job.

Other Free Copies.—In most agreements, provision is made for the author to have six presentation copies on publication and to have the right to purchase further copies for his own personal use on trade terms. Authors often ask for these copies to be sent them before the official date of publication. It is seldom wise for the publisher to comply with such a request, because the circulation of copies before publication, particularly among the author's friends, almost invariably causes the publisher trouble. A friend who sees the copy and has one on order wants to know why it has not been delivered to him. When the bookseller tells him it is 'not out', he replies quite rightly that he has seen a copy. The bookseller is charged with incompetence, and, knowing that he is in no way at fault, is apt to suspect unpleasant things of the publisher. This is a frequent, not an imaginary occurrence, and when a publisher shows reluctance to part with copies before publication, he has good reason for so doing.

It is truly said that the best way to start the sale of a book is to get it talked about by the right people. With this end in view advance copies are often distributed to critics and others partly in the hope that they will express opinions which can be quoted by the publisher in his advertisements.

The total number of free copies distributed varies with the book, and might conceivably be as few as twenty in the case of a book with an exceptionally limited appeal, or as many as two hundred in the case of an inexpensive book on a popular subject or an educational text-book. The usual number varies between sixty and one hundred. The figure includes not only the six free copies to the author, but copies required for the use of the publishers' travellers and for the publisher's own file, and, what is a much more serious matter, the statutory copies which the publisher is, or can be, called upon to supply gratis to no less than six different public libraries.

No one could reasonably object to the obligatory copy to the British Museum, but when the principle is extended to the compulsory giving of a copy to the library of an independent dominion, it becomes a serious tax which most publishers strongly resent. No other class in the community has to face a capital tax of this kind. It is an exceptional handicap in the case of costly and learned publications of which only small editions are produced, and works out even more unjustly in the case of small importations. If a book is not imported, libraries can make no claim for a copy, but when for the convenience of English buyers a publisher imports even a few copies of an expensive work published abroad, and has his name associated with it, he can straightway be compelled to hand over five, if not six, of the copies he has bought. It is an obvious injustice, and penalizes the publication of just those books which are often most important and most costly and difficult to produce. It is customary to make light of the burden and talk as if it were only a matter of shillings, if not pence, but in the case of a firm with a considerable output the tax may be many hundred pounds per year.

The British Museum copy is obligatory without application on the part of the Museum authorities. The copies for the four libraries at Oxford, Cambridge, Edinburgh, and Dublin respectively, are obligatory if written application is made for them within twelve months of publication. An agent acts for the four libraries, and in point of fact everything is applied for, including many books to which the libraries are not entitled. Now that the Republic of Ireland is independent, the Dublin library can no longer be considered as having even the pretensions of the other three, particularly as it did not even catalogue more than a fraction of the books for which it applied.[1] The only excuse given is that, were the claim waived, the British Museum and other libraries would lose their right to receive free copies of such few publications as are issued in Ireland. But if British publishers are to be taxed for the benefit of an Irish library, why not tax them to support a Canadian, Australian, or New Zealand library? I have no doubt that the librarians of Toronto, Wellington, and Sydney would welcome the privilege of receiving a free copy of every book published in Great Britain, and that their Governments would not think that they were making a bad exchange in agreeing to send the British Museum free copies of their local publications.[2]

Few people seem to be aware that the Copyright Act does not make delivery of the copies a condition of copyright; the only effect of non-compliance with the requirements of the section is to expose the publisher, upon whom, and not upon the author, the duty is imposed of delivering the requisite copies of the work, to a fine not exceeding £5 and the value of the book upon summary conviction. That is to say, he is liable to a separate fine for each library in respect of which default is made.

The library at Aberystwyth is in a category by itself. The obligation is a comparatively recent innovation. I think I am correct in saying that it arose in the early hours of the morning when the clause dealing with statutory copies in the 1911 Copyright Act was being

[1] Instructions were given to the College Librarian in April 1946 that every book received in future under the Copyright Act should either be catalogued or returned to the publisher.

[2] The British Museum receives an obligatory copy of every book published in South Africa. The Crown colonies also provide them.

considered in the House of Commons. Some enterprising Welsh member observed that Wales did not get a free copy and drew attention to the fact. It was assumed that publishers did not object to being selected for this special form of taxation, and the National Library of Wales was thus suddenly endowed at the publishers' expense. At the moment, the only remedy left to the publisher is passive resistance, i.e. to comply with the Act, but to give not the slightest assistance to those whose business it is to enforce it—a most inconvenient procedure to the aforesaid remarkably patient officials, but a most effective means of registering a continual protest. No official will again be able to say that publishers do not appear to object to these regulations.

But demands for free copies of their publications descend upon publishers from many other directions. It would occupy too much space to attempt to enumerate them; were a tithe complied with, yet more publishers would find their way to Carey Street. Strange as it may sound, never a week goes by without publishers having to explain that they produce books in the hope of *selling* them, and that the widespread impression that they make their living by giving books away is a delusion.

When a library is to be started, no one thinks of asking Maple's to give the furniture and Catesby's to give the linoleum, but it often seems to be considered quite in order to try to cadge the books from publishers. This is all part of the average Englishman's idea that a book is a thing one begs, borrows, sometimes steals, but never buys except under compulsion.

Learned societies and similar institutions always

seem to me especial offenders, both because they exist presumably to promote the study of the subject in which they are interested, and because they ought to know better. So far from encouraging the publication of learned works by the purchase of copies, they seem with one accord to devise means of securing gratis even the one copy required for their own library.[1] One such society, of which I am a fellow, with an income of many thousand pounds, boasted that although it has to spend a few hundreds on rebinding and the purchase of old books, its total expenditure on new books amounts to only about $2\frac{1}{2}$d per annum, because all the review copies sent to its Journal are claimed for the library. Should the publisher object to providing the library in this manner, a letter is sometimes sent to the author asking him to 'present' the book. The very people who act in this fashion are apt to complain of the lack of enterprise of British as opposed to continental publishers, and never hesitate to point out how many more works of research, etc., are issued by foreign publishers. They seem oblivious of their own share of the responsibility. A foreign publisher of a first-rate learned work knows that all institutions interested in the subject will buy copies; the British publisher realizes (alas!) that he will be expected to donate them. If the foreign publisher is sure of selling £50 worth of copies and the British publisher is equally certain of having to give the same £50 worth of books away, the difference between their respective positions is more than sufficient to turn the scale and to make a possible profit a certain loss.

[1] The London Library is the latest to do so.

When wealthy institutions in the USA and at home ask my firm to 'present' them with a copy of some inexpensive book we have the following 'form letter' in readiness to send them:

We have received your letter of ....and are sending you, as requested, a copy of...............................by............................... .

At the same time we cannot but marvel that the funds of...............................
should apparently be unable to stand the strain of purchasing a copy of this inexpensive publication, and we sincerely deplore the circumstances which must have compelled you to appeal to our charity.

It has proved uniformly successful; it brings both the payment and a better understanding of the publisher's position.

Of one such publication, the applications for free copies amounted to three times the number sold, so engrained is the habit of regarding publishers alternatively as philanthropists or endowed institutions.

Newspaper Advertising.—After this digression let us return to newspaper advertising, which represents the one kind of publicity given serious attention by some firms. There is a sense in which we know little or nothing about either the value or the effect of newspaper advertising in its relation to books, and yet there can be no publisher who has been in business for any length of time who has not gleaned a great deal of empirical knowledge. The ordinary advertising expert is of little assistance to the book publisher. On that point, at any rate, most publishers who have made the experiment of employing one will agree. The problems that the ordinary advertiser has to face are different in many essentials, as advertisement agents often discover for the first time when suddenly called upon to apply their expert knowledge to books. In the first place, there are very severe limits to what it is possible to spend on any one book, because the turnover of any one book is so limited. A publisher is dealing with pence where the seller of a staple commodity is dealing with pounds. Again, and this is a most important point, the demand for publishers' wares is seldom repetitive, like the demand which successful advertising can secure for, let us say, soap or cigarettes. If 'No. 13 soap' is actually found to be 'unlucky for dirt', further tablets will be bought and used by the customer who has been induced to try the soap as a result of an advertising campaign. As a rule, one copy of a book satisfies the demand for the book on the part of the particular customer who has bought it, and (alas!) will probably also satisfy the demand of the many friends to whom he is sure to lend it. There is an added difficulty, and that is that we may nearly all be potential buyers of some particular brand of soap, but there are few books of which more than an infinitesimal fraction of the public can truthfully be regarded as potential purchasers. Our requirements in the matter of books are much more personal and individual than our needs in the matter of food or clothing, or even toothpaste. This point is consistently overlooked by those who consider that large advertisements in the daily Press are the only things that count. Advertisement consultants are quite correct when they point out that the papers with the big circulations are sometimes the cheapest, if calculated at per person reached, but their argument, to be valid, presupposes that the person reached is a potential buyer, and this is where the daily newspaper may conceivably be the most costly and least successful medium of all for the advertising of some kinds of books. The advertiser is obviously paying for so much circulation that is useless for his purpose. All successful advertisers know that an appeal addressed to those definitely interested in the article offered is more effective than two or three times the number of appeals to those who 'may be' or 'ought to be' interested. To put the matter in another way, if a book appeals to most of the readers of, let us say, the *News of the World*, it may be sound business to advertise it in that paper, but if it appeals to only 1 per cent of the *News of the World* public, it is a costly and ineffective way of approaching that 1 per cent.

The advertising of half a dozen books may, and probably does, involve half a dozen methods, as well as a variety of channels. The very vulgar type of advertisement may be suitable for vulgar works intended for the vulgar-minded, but such advertisements would merely repel the more cultured bookbuyer. The method as well as the channel of approach has then to be considered. Special intelligence is needed, because with the things of the mind saturation point is much more quickly reached than in other directions, and the attitude of the buyer is more critical. 'Bright ideas' and 'new stunts' for book advertising are all very well, but have to be sparingly used to be effective. They are not easy to maintain at a high level, and they will almost certainly prove to be unsuited to some of the books being advertised. In arranging his advertisements, therefore, the book publisher is usually compelled to fall back upon good plain type, and where appropriate small eye-catching line drawings, even though he may be charged with lack of enterprise; but it must be good type, and the increasing pains now taken with the lay-out of book advertisements may be observed in the advertisement columns of any literary paper. The best results are not obtained without effort and expense.

Some newspaper offices are incapable of setting a book advertisement decently—to begin with, they may not have the right type. To meet such difficulties and secure the best results, publishers are frequently compelled to employ their own typesetters, and to supply the newspapers with moulds or stereos. This adds to the expense of the advertisement, but likewise to its effectiveness. It further standardizes the setting, and thus secures the repetitive impression which is so important in advertising. The importance of attractive presentation is accentuated by the sharp increase in the cost of advertisements. The rates of one Sunday paper, for example, advanced from 15s an inch in 1913 to £15 an inch (single column) in 1958, on which latter basis an eight inch double column advertisement costs £240 for one insertion.

The difference in the effect upon the eye of the style of presentation may be seen in the two examples of good and bad type given below:

𝔓𝔘𝔅𝔏𝔌𝔖𝔥𝔌𝔑𝔊 PUBLISHING
𝔗𝔥𝔈 𝔗𝔯𝔘𝔗𝔥 THE TRUTH

There is a distinct limit to what people will read in the way of descriptive matter. On the other hand, it is often

extremely difficult to give in a few words a really telling
description of a book. The question that ought to be
faced, but seldom is faced, is, What is the advertisement
designed to achieve? Is it expected to make someone
buy the book who has never heard anything about it or
its author before; is it intended to inform those who
know the author or who are interested in the subject
that the book has been published; alternatively, is it
meant to be a reminder to those who have read reviews
of the book, and are interested in it, that they ought to
buy it; is it merely desired to provide a convenient list
of books for subscribers to ask for at their lending
library; or is it to advertise the publisher rather than
the books? The end desired makes all the difference,
or should make all the difference, in the means adopted
to attain it.

Personally—and I am quite aware of the risk I run
in making this statement, that it will be used in a quite
unjustifiable way against me—I do not believe that many
people buy books *merely* because they see them advertised. If the book is being talked about, an advertisement may stimulate them to procure it. Were it on a
subject in which they are interested, or by an author
whose work they admire, advertisements might prompt
them to go to a bookshop and get it when otherwise they
might not do so. Had it been recommended to them
by a friend, an advertisement would perhaps stimulate
them to buy it. This theory that book advertising is
more likely to remind or stimulate people to whom the
thought of buying the book has already occurred, rather
than to create a bookbuyer out of the void, is borne out
by almost every publisher's experience, viz. that if a

book is not selling and shows no sign of selling, no amount of advertising will make it sell to any extent commensurate with the expenditure; whereas if a book shows signs of catching on, careful and discriminating advertising may yield the most excellent results. The contention that books can be made to sell *merely* as the result of an advertising campaign has been tested over and over again. It has often been proved successful in the case of sets of books, when it has been possible to convince the public that they are needed as articles of furniture in their homes, but it has seldom, if ever, been successful in the case of an individual book which the public had not otherwise shown signs of wanting.

One of the most interesting examples of recent years was a certain 2s book upon which about £2,500 was most skilfully spent. The advertising certainly secured it a substantial circulation, but the gross proceeds of the sales only amounted to about £2,800. It is quite true that to sell 40,000 copies of a serious work was a distinct achievement, but publishers can hardly be expected to make a habit of spending £2,500 to secure such a result.[1] They would rightly point out that it would be nearly as cheap to give the books away. On the other hand a succeeding book by the same author would almost automatically enjoy a large sale even were less than a twentieth of the amount spent on advertising it.

This is the clearest evidence that anyone could wish that it is the following books by the same author that derive the maximum benefit from any extensive adver-

[1] Another striking instance was Lord Beaverbrook's *Politicians and the Press*: a careful analysis of the figures will be found in Constable's Monthly List of April 1926 and May 1928 (No. 79) onwards.

tising. What better justification could there be for the claim that a publisher needs a definite option upon subsequent work before embarking upon any big campaign?

When on one occasion the author of an unsaleable book maintained that it could be sold by extensive advertising, my firm challenged him to spend as much as he liked, and where he liked. We offered to carry out all his instructions and do all the work free of charge, and left him free to secure the best expert advice if he desired, on the understanding that if the *gross proceeds* of the sales from then onwards exceeded two-thirds of the advertising expenditure, we would ourselves pay the entire amount, but that otherwise it should be borne by the author. The challenge was accepted; the advertising was very well done, but the proceeds of the sales did not amount to so much as half of the sum spent.[1]

In brief, the conclusion at which we arrive, regrettable as it may sound, is that just as whipping will maintain, and even accelerate the speed of a top that is already spinning, but will achieve nothing with one lying dormant on the ground, so advertising will maintain and even accelerate the sales of a book which is already being talked about, but will do little or nothing for one in which there is otherwise no interest. So that when we are told that a book has sold well because it was extensively advertised, the truth may be that it was extensively advertised because it sold well.

Some advertising, however, is needed in every case

---

[1] Particulars of a challenge made to advertising agents and a much fuller examination of the problem of book advertising will be found in *Best Sellers: are they born or made?* (London: George Allen & Unwin Ltd.), 1939.

in order to inform librarians, booksellers, and others of the existence of the book; but that does not necessarily involve advertising in daily papers. It means advertising in a book trade paper, in *The Times Literary Supplement* and some of the better weeklies. Book advertisements in such papers are often as carefully examined as the text. In advertising in them, one is addressing an audience definitely wanting information about new books; but this, as we have seen, is very different from trying to arouse interest where it does not exist. My beliefs were fortified by some interesting data collected by the late Eugen Diederichs of Jena, who had the happy idea of inserting in all his publications a post-card asking his readers to let him know what prompted them to buy the book. The figures are so instructive that I give them below.

	Men	Women
1. Reviews	18·1	17·6
2. Personal recommendations from friends and others	14·2	17·0
3. Other works by the same author ...	13·8	12·0
4. Special prospectuses	9·8	5·0
5. Window displays	8·6	5·0
6. Publishers' catalogues and lists	6·7	5·4
7. Booksellers' recommendation	5·2	7·0
8. Subject being studied	4·7	3·3
9. Advertisements	4·0	1·2
10. Newspaper articles	3·0	3·3
11. Lectures	2·8	5·0
12. Quotations	2·6	3·3
13. Specimens of the text	2·1	2·5
14. Personality of the author	1·3	1·7
15. Copies received on approval from booksellers	0·8	1·2

16, 17, and 18, all less than 1 per cent, include such items as quality of the production.

I do not wish to suggest that such a limited experiment is in any way conclusive or that the reasons given would be applicable in England, but the results are none the less illuminating. First, in both lists of what prompted people to buy the books, comes 'reviews'; second, 'personal recommendations'; third, other works by the same author; and special prospectuses, fourth. Advertisements only appear ninth on the list in the answers from men, and nearly bottom of the list in the answers from women.

Other Forms of Publicity.—I would draw special attention to the high place occupied in the list by 'special prospectuses', and this brings us to the whole question of circularization as a means of interesting people in books. It is not a form of advertising of which there is much outward evidence. A publisher who spent his advertising appropriation in this way would, in the eyes of many authors, be a 'bad' publisher, whereas the publisher who spent the same amount in the daily Press with far less result would be a 'good' publisher, but the fact would none the less remain that, for many books, this form of advertising and advertising in specialist papers often pay best. If circularizing is to be well done it means the patient collection of the best possible lists of names and addresses of those interested in given subjects. It is always essential to have your target very clearly in view if you are to hit it. The lists will, of course, include libraries at home and abroad, because they are the biggest buyers for serious books. Some firms have built up most profitable businesses almost entirely upon such advertising. Success or failure will depend chiefly upon the care with which the names and addresses are selected, but also upon the attractiveness of the circular, facsimile letter, or prospectus. In some cases, a post card may bring excellent results, particularly as a follow-up or reminder. Some booksellers will give effective help with the distribution of prospectuses, but this side of their activities has not yet been as carefully thought out or as fully developed as it might be. If more booksellers kept a classified card-index of all their customers and potential customers, a great deal more could be done in co-operation with publishers. In some cases, for instance, it would be quite possible for the publisher to produce a circular letter suitable for booksellers to sign and send out, thus making the appeal more local and personal.

One form of publicity which I have often thought desirable is to send out particulars of new books in the form of small cards so printed and arranged as to be suitable for use by librarians and booksellers in a card-index and preferably, therefore, following some recognized form of classification. It would mean trouble, and although the English book trade is possibly not yet sufficiently organized to make the scheme worth while, this method of sending out particulars of books will, I am convinced, some day be generally adopted.

The publisher's complete catalogues, and the announcement lists which he issues two or three times a year, still afford one of the most valuable means of publicity. Few authors realize the number of such lists distributed by some firms, or the care with which they are looked through. The result of the dispatch of a big batch of announcement lists can often be traced in the next week's orders, and it does not follow that the only results obtained by this means are those of which there is immediate evidence. Many firms in addition publish house organs. They vary greatly both in their character and in their cost. It is doubtful whether the most elaborate and expensive are necessarily the most effective. The extent to which they actually affect sales is very difficult to determine. If they are to be consistently well done, much time and energy must be devoted to them. As has already been mentioned, personal letters count for a very great deal in promoting the sale of books. A single letter may be the means of securing much publicity of the very greatest value. It is not always the publicity that costs most that is the most prolific of results, nor, and this must be emphasized again, is the most effective publicity work necessarily the kind most obvious to the author's eye.

Other publications of the same firm are, of course, constantly used as a means of securing publicity. Each book is made, as far as practicable, to advertise its fellows. Not only the jackets, but any spare pages at the end of a volume are devoted to this purpose. The latter have special value, as they confront the reader when he has just finished a book and is most likely to be allured by a new one.

Loose insets were at one time freely used as an advertising medium, but were discarded when the Australian customs, in their zeal to tax all advertisement matter not printed in Australia, decreed that as the duty was assessable upon the weight, either the importer must remove the loose insets or the books themselves must be weighed as part of the advertisement material and included in the assessment. Some publishers, nevertheless, still insert insets, but they run grave risks in so doing, if they do not remove them from any copies destined for Australia.

Authors' portraits are increasingly used; in America they seem to be an essential part of the advertising campaign. With a well-known author this is understandable, as it adds a further kind of personal connection between the author and the reader, but the use of photographs is no longer restricted to established writers. Perhaps it is well to remind authors that photographs intended for this purpose should have been taken at their own expense, not 'free sittings', as otherwise fees will be payable to the photographer, and the extent to which the photograph is likely to be used will be thereby limited. A carefully mounted photograph is not required, a simple unmounted silver print, which the photographer will supply quite cheaply, being much more effective. Small snapshots are seldom of much use for reproduction, because in blockmaking it is more usual to reduce the size of the photograph than to enlarge it.

The small poster at one time had some vogue in connection with popular novels. But it proved uneconomic and is in any case no substitute for other forms of advertising. Booksellers can seldom make space for them.

Show cards on the other hand can often be used by booksellers if they are not unduly large. (12 in. × 15 in. should rarely be exceeded.) They should emphasize one compelling sales point in the fewest words and with the simplest visual impact.

Window displays can also be most effective with appropriate books. Topical, interesting or amusing exhibits can be combined with show cards, photographs and book jackets into a most attractive and efficient sales force. It is a form of publicity which calls for co-operation with the bookseller concerned. In that connection the importance of convincing booksellers that a particular book is readily saleable cannot be exaggerated. Some of the most effective advertising is directed to that end. Of outstanding books it is essential that leading booksellers should receive proof copies well ahead of publication.

Television.—A tremendously influential medium is already publicizing books—sometimes through interviews with authors in a topical news item; at others by presenting the people behind the books. But this development is still (1959) in its infancy, and will doubtless grow as the television authorities find out how many more viewers are interested in books and authors than is usually assumed. Increases in sales can be traced to the presentation of a book in a television or radio programme, but the value of television for advertising is most uncertain. It has the disadvantages of mass circulation papers inasmuch as one is paying a high price to reach an audience containing a small percentage of bookbuyers. Book Tokens Ltd. made use of it in their 1958 pre-Christmas campaign, but apparently with less effect than anticipated.

The Cost of Advertising.—People often ask what percentage of the publisher's turnover is allocated to advertising. No reliable figures are available. My guess would be about 5 per cent of his turnover. When it is borne in mind that a large proportion of the British publisher's turnover consists of the sale of old books upon which little or nothing may be spent on advertising, it will be realized that the percentage on new books is extremely high. The gross turnover of a novel, of which round about fifteen hundred copies are sold, may not exceed £500, and yet on such a book it is usual for a publisher to spend at least £100—in other words, over 20 per cent of his gross proceeds—despite the fact that on a first edition there may be no margin of profit at all.[1] In proportion to the turnover involved, few commodities are so extensively advertised as new books. It is not, however, out of the heavily advertised books that the publisher makes his living, but out of books which continue to sell year after year with little or no expenditure on advertising. Such books, of which the reader may have never heard, are the backbone of many of the older houses. It would be safe to go farther and add that, if some of the old firms had to live on the profits made on their new books in any one year, they would indeed be unhappy.

In the past there has been little disposition on the part of publishers to compare notes regarding such matters as the ratio of the cost of advertising to turnover. In Appendix V is given an analysis of such information as I have been able to obtain concerning working expenses. I hope that publishers will send me criticisms of these figures, and that I may be in a position to give more authoritative information at some later date.[2]

[1] See Appendix VI (page 340).
[2] This was written in 1926. Thus far only one has done so.

Taking it as a whole, book advertising is fairly well done. Criticism is easy; improvement difficult. We could many of us do wonderful things if we had not to ensure that the expenditure on advertising brought a commensurate return.

Co-operative Publicity.—No chapter on the advertising of books would be complete without a reference to co-operative publicity, for which in its early days I fought so hard. In previous editions of this book I related how despite the most perverse and obstinate opposition a modest and tentative beginning had been made by the inauguration of the National Book Council whose objects were the promotion of book reading and the wider distribution of books. Those interested in the history of the movement will find it in the story of The Society of Bookmen,[1] a small but representative body whose one and only object is the advancement of the knowledge and appreciation of good literature.

Here it must suffice to say that the confident hope I expressed twenty years ago that out of this modest beginning much greater things would grow has been amply fulfilled. The National Book Council has expanded into the National Book League with magnificent headquarters at 7 Albemarle Street and thereby widened both its membership and scope. If as Emerson said 'In the highest civilization, the book is still the highest delight', it is not only fitting but essential that there should be a widely representative body, disassociated from vested interests, able to speak with authority and knowledge on behalf of books.

The National Book League is just such a Public

[1] British Book Trade Organization, page 100.

Relations body representing books and will I am confident be eagerly concerned at all times to achieve for them the status which all the wiser elements in the community would wish them accorded and to which they are unquestionably entitled.

In regard to the future of book advertising, my own view, and I know it is shared by few, is that the tendency will be to use the daily Press and television primarily to arouse interest in books in general and to create a feeling of need for books and the recognition of their value in daily life; to concentrate advertisements of individual books in those papers, such as the weeklies, whose readers are definitely on the lookout for information about new books, and to develop the use of facsimile letters, prospectuses, etc., offering specific books to the public definitely interested in them. More of this latter form of advertising ought I think to be carried through by the booksellers working in closer co-operation than heretofore with the publishers.[1] This, at any rate, is what a careful study of what can and cannot be accomplished by the different methods of advertising books would lead one to expect, but even before this new edition has been printed some further and better method of promoting the sale of books may have been devised.

In view of the certainty that I shall be charged with not believing in advertising, just because I have ventured to point out some of its obvious limitations in connection with books, I should like to suggest that it would be equally truthful to charge me with not

[1] The Booksellers Association made an unsuccessful attempt to revive the idea of co-operative book trade advertising in 1956.

believing in ships because I refuse to shut my eyes to their limitations and their unsuitability as a means of land transport. I am, as a matter of fact, a whole-hearted believer in advertising, but at the same time have come increasingly to realize that much of the experience gained about advertising in other fields has less application to books than is commonly supposed.

CHAPTER IX

COPYRIGHT AND 'RIGHTS'

BEFORE discussing the more important 'rights' in books, other than the right of publication in book form in the English language with which this work is principally concerned, it will be well to examine, however briefly, the sources whence these 'rights' are derived.

The British Copyright Act of 1956 embodies the Berne Convention as revised in 1948 at Brussels and provides for the United Kingdom ratification of the Universal Copyright Convention. It is the subject of several treatises, and it will therefore be sufficient for our purpose here to state that it amends and extends the law of copyright so as to cover technical and other developments which have occurred since the passing of the 1911 Act. This defined copyright as: 'The sole right to produce or reproduce the work or any substantial part thereof in any material form whatsoever, to perform, or in the case of a lecture to deliver, the work or any substantial part thereof in public; if the work is unpublished, to publish the work or any substantial part thereof; and shall include the sole right' . . . to publish translations, dramatic versions, and to make films, etc., and secures these rights for the life of the author and fifty years from the end of the calendar year in which he died in every original literary work first published in His Majesty's dominions, without formality other than the delivery of a copy of the work to the Trustees of the British Museum within one month of publication.

The 1956 Act protects for the first time, but for twenty-five years only, the typographical arrangement of a book.

Publication means 'the issue of copies of the work to the public', and for the purposes of the Act 'first publication' is not prejudiced by simultaneous publication elsewhere, *not exceeding thirty days* previously.

This last point, particularly when the period was fourteen days, as it still is in some Commonwealth countries which unlike South Africa and India have not yet adhered to the Brussels Convention, was constantly overlooked by American publishers, and sometimes by English literary agents who should know better. In fact, a careful examination would show that a startlingly large proportion of American books were not copyright, theoretically, at any rate, in Great Britain because of failure to publish them within the prescribed period of their publication in the USA. I say 'theoretically' because, so long as British publishers continue to act, as they almost invariably do, on the assumption that all books in English by living writers are *ipso facto* copyright and the legality is never questioned by anyone else, the works are for all practical purposes 'copyright' *throughout Her Majesty's dominions*. I have purposely emphasized these last four words because elsewhere, before the Brussels Convention, simultaneous meant simultaneous: the original Berne Convention made no provision for the latitude allowed by British law. Furthermore, based on the French text, the Dutch Courts held that 'distribution', even if made by an independent firm in—let us say—Canada does not necessarily constitute 'publication'. Even under British law 'a colourable imitation of publication' is insufficient.

When the position is reversed, and it is a question of British publications in the USA, the assumption is that a work is *not* copyright in the USA unless there is clear evidence to the contrary. This fact has some unfortunate results, as we shall see later.

The Berne Convention, which automatically secures, without formalities of any kind, copyright in all the countries of the signatories, is now so taken for granted that few people realize that this form of protection of literary property has existed for only about seventy years. To be precise, the first Convention was signed in 1886; it was revised in 1896, 1908, 1928, and again in 1948.

Practically all the civilized nations of the world are signatories, the only important exceptions being Russia, the United States, certain of the South American Republics—which have their own convention—and China. The Soviet authorities inherited the position from their Tsarist predecessors, whose example it is to be hoped they will not follow indefinitely. The United States, long debarred from signing by their insistence upon local manufacture as a condition of copyright, have frequently had Bills under consideration so drafted as to enable them to signify their adherence to the Convention. But they have thus far all ended in talk.

Even without these countries, the Convention covers

well over nine hundred million people. Its terms are of such importance, and are so little known amongst authors, that I give below the particulars of the White Paper which contains the official English (and French) versions, including the revisions made at Rome in 1928 and Brussels in 1948.[1]

The 1908 revision, amongst other changes, brought translations into line with original works, whereas under the earlier Conventions translation rights in any language fall into the *domaine public* if no translation in that language is published within ten years of publication in the country of origin. Although acceptance of the revisions was optional, every member eventually ratified the 1908 Convention. Certain countries, however, did so with minor reservations, and in particular Greece, Holland, Italy, and Japan made this ten-year reservation regarding translation rights.

The extent and duration of the copyright protection enjoyed in each country under the Berne Convention is whatever is accorded to its own authors by the country where the protection is being used, provided that in no case shall the *duration* exceed that granted to authors in the country of origin. 'The country of origin' is defined as, 'for unpublished works, the country to which the author belongs; for published works, the country of first publication'; and for works published simultaneously in several countries within the Union (as also in countries without) the Unionist country granting the shortest term of protection.

Most countries, including France and Great Britain, give protection for fifty years from the end of the

[1] The Berne Convention, Cmnd. 361 (Treaty Series No. 4, 1958).

calendar year in which the author died; some give thirty years; Spain grants eighty.

The Universal Copyright Convention[1] which became effective, as far as Britain is concerned, on September 27, 1957, we owe to UNESCO. It does not in any way affect the provisions of the Berne Convention, as amended at Brussels, of which some would regard it as a watered down version drafted to secure the adherence of the USA and various South American countries. The duration of protection under this Convention is (*a*) 'not less than the life of the author and 25 years after his death, or (*b*) for those countries which, like the USA, compute the term of protection as a fixed period of years from the date of publication of the work or from registration prior to publication, not less than 25 years from the date of first publication or registration'. Article 3 is as follows:

Any contracting State which, under its domestic law, requires, as a condition of copyright, compliance with formalities such as deposit, registration, notice, notarial certificates, payment of fees or manufacture or publication in that contracting State, shall regard these requirements as satisfied with respect to all works protected in accordance with this Convention and first published outside its territory and the author of which is not one of its nationals, if from the time of the first publication all the copies of the work published with the authority of the author or other copyright proprietor bear the symbol © accompanied by the name of the copyright proprietor and the year of first publication placed in such manner and location as to give reasonable notice of claim of copyright.

From the foregoing it will be observed that, though the formalities are restricted, the Convention follows the

[1] The Universal Copyright Convention, Cmnd. 289 (Treaty Series No. 66, 1957), H.M. Stationery Office.

American principle that everything is in the *domaine public* unless there is a notice to the contrary. Moreover, the manufacturing clause still applies to the writing of American citizens wherever resident, subject to the *ad interim* copyright provision permitting the importation of up to 1,500 copies. Article 3 thus involves endless complications, besides the necessity of ascertaining the nationality of every author whose work it is desired to protect. It continues the American practice of discriminating against books in the English language. However, we must be grateful for any mercies where United States copyright is concerned. It is interesting to note that according to Act VI of the Universal Copyright Convention 'Publication means the reproduction in tangible form and the general distribution to the public of copies of a work from which it can be read or otherwise visually perceived'.

Of the many rights enjoyed by British authors under both the British Copyright Act of 1956 and the Berne Convention, the first to call for consideration here are *Serial Rights* which may theoretically exist in all publications, although in practice only a small proportion of the thousands issued each year are serialized; similarly, by no means all the serials that appear in newspapers and magazines are published in book form. The best books do not necessarily make the best serials, and vice versa. In fact, it is safe to say that the best serials are specially written for that purpose, in which case care can be taken to ensure that each instalment has a satisfactory 'curtain', and a satisfactory 'curtain' from an editor's point of view is one that compels the reader to buy the next issue of the paper or magazine. Apart from novels, few books, other than personal reminiscences of well-known people, lend themselves to serial issue *in extenso* prior to book publication. The 'reminiscences' may take any form, and would, of course, include personal stories of travel or exploration; to be 'well known' is not necessarily to be favourably known. On the other hand, *parts* of many books can first be used as articles.

Serialization takes time, and even though a story may be adapted for the purpose, the author may not be willing to defer publication in book form to take advantage of the fact. Most newspapers and magazines book up their serials a long way ahead, and to be successful in placing serial rights on any large scale it is necessary to have exact knowledge of such openings as exist at any given moment. Other factors being equal, the more time there is in which to place the rights the greater likelihood there is of doing so to advantage.

In selling serial rights, it is particularly important to define the rights that are being offered and to ensure that the material will appear in *at least* three instalments.[1] Occasionally it is possible to get a favourable offer for the world serial rights; more usually the serial rights for individual countries or States are sold separately. Again, in most cases, all that is sold is the 'first serial rights' or the 'single serial use' in a given paper or periodical *before* the book is published, thus leaving the possibility of securing a further return from the second serial rights. These second rights, which

[1] The publication of a complete novel in *one* issue of a journal jeopardizes book sales, and in a recent judgment has been defined as book rights and not as serial rights.

may be second only in the sense that they are after book publication, are sometimes purchased for 'syndication'; that is to say, a firm buys the remaining serial rights for a lump sum and makes its profit by farming them out to a number of small papers, none of which could afford to buy even the second serial rights for its own exclusive use. In addition to selling these rights to the smaller provincial papers in the United Kingdom, a firm of this kind would expect to pick up £20 here and £25 there in such places as, let us say, Ceylon, Tasmania, or the North or South Islands of New Zealand, because in normal times many of the dominion papers run serials.

Apart from knowledge of openings, to which reference has been made, there is a large element of luck in placing serial rights. An unexpected gap between two serials may leave an editor particularly anxious to secure another in a hurry—at such a moment whatever comes his way will receive unusually favourable consideration —unusual because at most times the supply greatly exceeds the demand.

An important element in success is close and constant contact with editors or the London representatives of those overseas and my own firm has a specialist, who, under the supervision of the directors, concentrates on this task. As so often in publishing imagination and a detailed knowledge of requirements plays a large part in the placing of serial rights, sometimes with unexpected papers in out of the way places. The individual payments so secured may be small but cumulatively are a welcome and often unexpected addition to the author's receipts.

The prices paid for serial rights vary enormously. Big figures are obtained by popular novelists or people much in the public eye. The fiction editor of a popular magazine has often to choose between a story totally unsuitable for serialization by an author with a big name and a first-rate serial at a quarter the price by an unknown writer. In such cases the 'name' is almost invariably selected. I recall one occasion when a famous novelist, who had failed after much effort to place the serial rights in his new novel, offered the book rights to a publisher on the condition that he bought the serial rights. The author was satisfied that the serial rights could *not* be otherwise sold. The novel was over 150,000 words in length and there was very little action in it. The publisher accepted the offer provided he had *carte blanche* to blue pencil for serial purposes, to which stipulation the author readily agreed. A competent journalist was instructed to cut out more than half the book and leave nothing that was not strictly relevant to the thread of the story. In this form, much to the author's surprise, the publisher found an editor willing to pay £400 for its serial use, largely for the sake of the author's name.

This preference of 'names' to quality or suitability in selecting serials is being overdone and will in the long run bring its own nemesis.

Far and away the best prices for serial stories or series of articles are paid by American papers, *if* you are in the happy position of being able to supply exactly what they require. It is well worth while for British authors to study their requirements, for the rewards of compliance are substantial.

The claim that previous serialization helps the sale in book form can sometimes be substantiated. On the other hand, so can the statement that serialization has proved prejudicial. Overseas booksellers tend to object to, home booksellers to favour, serialization. On balance it probably does as much harm as good to a book, but any slight disadvantage may be more than compensated by the financial benefits derived by the author.

The American Book Rights, except in the case of the few favoured authors whose books will unquestionably be separately printed on both sides, are usually best handled by the British publisher. Some of the reasons for this were mentioned in the chapter on Agreements.

American copyright[1] in a British book could only be secured before the ratification of the Universal Copyright Convention in 1957 by its complete manufacture in the States within 60 (or, subject to the deposit of a copy of the English edition at Washington, 60 plus 120) days of publication in Great Britain. These periods of *ad interim* copyright were extended on June 3, 1949, to five years provided a complete copy is deposited in the USA, with an application for registration, within six months of first publication in Great Britain, and that not more than 1,500 copies, which must bear the statutory notice of copyright, are imported. As stated earlier, this last provision still applies to the work of authors resident in the USA, or to United

---

[1] The term is twenty-eight years with option of renewal for a further twenty-eight years; but application for renewal must be made by the copyright owner within the year prior to the expiration of the original term.

States citizens wherever resident, but now extends to the full term of 28 years.

Irrespective of other considerations, the British publisher naturally endeavours to arrange for separate printing in the USA because that gives a book the best chance; but the number of new books so printed, apart from those of the favoured few whose case we are not considering, is exceedingly small. For every other kind of arrangement for publication in the States, whether it be the sale of a set of electroplates, the supply of an edition in sheets or of bound copies with the American publisher's imprint, the use of the British publisher's typography, or, in the case of a foreign work, the use of the English translation, the British publisher *must* be called in.

As one or other of these alternatives is eventually adopted in the case of the greater number of ordinary books, the effect of any reservation of the American rights by the author is, in most cases, merely to make it more difficult, if not impossible, for the publisher to arrange a satisfactory deal when he is eventually asked to negotiate. He is obviously in a better position to do well for the author if he controls the rights from the start. But there is another important factor particularly applicable to new authors or works on a new subject. American publishers visiting London are invariably pressed for time; they want to secure the best material available, but have limited moments or hours in which to examine it. They may listen with attention to the eloquence of authors or author's agents anxious to sell MSS, but it will not carry the conviction of a fellow-publisher's remark, 'Here are our readers' reports; we

THE TRUTH ABOUT PUBLISHING

are taking the book'. There is a simple and effective test. How often will an American publisher buy a book by an unknown author from that author or a literary agent without either reading it or having it read? Never! On the other hand, many an American publisher's big successes have been bought solely on the strength of a British publisher's recommendation. It happens constantly with some British publishers in whose judgment American publishers have learnt to place reliance. Is that of no value to the unknown author? Again, certain publishers have such a high reputation for books on particular subjects that their imprint on any book in that field will at once render the rights easily marketable in the States (or vice versa). Would not good will of that kind be rated and rewarded highly in any other business or walk of life?

To choose the right American publisher is of paramount importance, and in making his selection the British publisher will probably be guided by just those reasons which should influence every author in the original placing of his MS.

First should come financial stability (many authors think about this last, if they think about it at all; but to enter into an agreement with a firm that does not pay its royalties is much worse than useless).

Second, the quality of the publisher's list (most publishers tend to specialize to some extent, and it is nearly always wise to choose a firm noted for the kind of book you have to sell).

Third, the strength of the publisher's selling organization (this would often exclude the very small or new firms).

Fourth, the desirability of securing a publisher likely to take a personal interest in the work (this would sometimes exclude the very biggest firms).

Other less ponderable factors would influence a publisher's final decision, such as his previous experience with the various possible American firms, etc., but, having made his selection, a publisher would realize the advantages of abiding by it for future work by the same author. The advantages of remaining loyal to one publisher are numerous; the disadvantages few. In the same list each book by an author can be made to advertise its fellow. Just as an individual lump of hot coal will soon cease to give out heat, whereas a dozen pieces will maintain a fire, so the individual book will lose momentum, whereas a dozen by the same author in the same publisher's hands will collectively continue to sell. A group of books can be given attention and publicity in many ways denied to a single book. A librarian or a bookseller ordering an author's books may easily overlook some of them if they are spread over a dozen publishers' lists, but is unlikely to do so if they are concentrated in one. Fortunately these very obvious facts are becoming increasingly recognized by authors and, let it be added, by literary agents, who despite their protestations of virtue in this respect, were at one time largely responsible for authors moving from publisher to publisher for the sake of some immediate advantage such as a slightly higher 'advance', regardless of the permanent disadvantage to their clients.

The American market may sometimes prove more important than the home market because, owing to the greater population in the States, a book that 'catches on' sells much more largely over there. As a rule, there are no half-measures about it. The American book-buying public appears to be more easily led than ours, and to exercise less independent judgment. The herd instinct carries all before it, and publishing is both much more and much less of a gamble.

'Working expenses' and trade discounts are greater, and it is therefore comparatively seldom that the scale of royalties paid by American publishers starts at more than 10 per cent for unknown or lesser-known writers, or at more than 15 per cent for the better known, and it now never rises to as much as 20 per cent, however large the sale.

Royalties are often paid on books not legally copyright in the USA, but in that case 10 per cent is usually the limit; such an arrangement would probably be operative if the American publisher decided to print such a book after having imported it.

The importation of 'editions', whether forming part of the English edition or separately printed, is the method adopted by American publishers in cases where a large sale is improbable. Some firms specialize in importations of this kind; others seldom, if ever, take a book if they do not feel it is worth while to print it. It is the British publisher's business, if he has not his own branch in the USA, to know the suitable firms to approach.

Piracy.—We have seen that, unless printed in the USA within the specified time, British literary property was at the mercy of anyone who cared to print it in the States; it is true no reputable American publisher would think of doing so, but there are American firms which make a practice of pirating English books. The price of freedom (from such piracy) is eternal vigilance. It is a great mistake to think, as many do, that because there is no legal protection, nothing can be done. In most cases pressure of some kind can and should be brought to bear. One illustration will suffice, though it would be easy to give many examples.

A new firm of American publishers started a popular series of reprints, and, interspersed among old non-copyright classics, included books by living authors not technically copyright in the States. When, without permission, they included several titles from our list, we naturally remonstrated, though, of course, without effect. The firm in question was both anxious to sell its publications over here and to open up relations with British authors. It employed a well-known firm of literary agents to act for it, and sent certain of its publications for review in English periodicals. When the agent offered us for publication in Great Britain a book containing our own copyright material, it seemed time for our campaign to begin.

1. We wrote to the agent asking him whether he was aware he was acting for a firm which made a practice of taking the work of living authors without paying for it. He very properly replied that he would at once terminate the agency unless they undertook to cease doing so.

2. We wrote to several of the firm's leading customers in New York, pointing out that the series contained many volumes by living authors which had been taken without permission, and asking them to be good enough to write and verify our statement.

3. We wrote to the Authors' Societies of Great Britain and of America, as well as certain publishers, drawing their attention, and asking them either themselves to protest or to get any of their authors whose work was being 'pirated' to do so.

4. Immediately any of the firm's works were reviewed in an English paper, we wrote to the literary editor asking whether he realized these publishers made a practice of appropriating the work of living authors

without paying for it. Several editors wrote to the firm that they could not, in the circumstances, continue to notice their books.

5. In drafting contracts with any American publishers, we included the condition that they should not authorize the inclusion of any of their publications in the offending series, and of course explained why.

6. Finally, we advised the firm what we had done, and said it was only the beginning.

They were very soon anxious to come to terms, and agreed to pay royalties on past as well as future sales, because, as one of the then partners of the firm subsequently explained to me, we had made life such a burden to them that it was much simpler to come into line and pay up. He admitted with delicious candour that it got on their nerves when, every time the telephone bell rang, it proved to be an inquiry whether it was a fact that they were taking English literary property without paying for it.

Unfortunately there are others with thicker skins who persist in their evil ways to the detriment of Anglo-American relations.

One of the most astonishing examples of piracy was in connection with the work of Freud. A hitherto unknown American concern extracted chunks (not necessarily complete chapters) from our publication, *The Interpretation of Dreams*, translated by Dr Brill, mixed them with instalments of at any rate one other work by Freud, published by Heinemann, and announced it under another title, not only as a new book by Freud, but as an 'authorized translation' by Dr Eder, who, like Freud, knew nothing about it—and, still more unbelievable, this remarkable publisher claimed copyright in the book!

But, once again, let it be emphasized, piracy is the exception, not the rule; and few of the many excellent firms of American publishers, whose names are so well known and respected, are ever guilty of taking literary property by living authors without making proper arrangements with whosoever would be the copyright owner were America a signatory to the Berne Convention, as, let us hope, she may be some day.

Dumping of back numbers of American periodicals, cheap editions, and 'remainders' is another trouble with which the British publisher has to contend. Mass production leads at times to mass accumulations, and those holding huge stocks of which it is imperative they should dispose promptly do not always pause to consider in what territories they are entitled to sell their surplus wares. Legislation either to prevent, or to place a tax upon, the importation of back numbers has resulted. Such *ad hoc* legislation is not, however, without its unfortunate results as will be seen from a letter I wrote to *The Times* (May 14, 1934) under the heading 'Duties on Bibliography'.

Book Club Rights.—When I observed how disturbed German booksellers were at the unexpected success of the Buch-Gemeinschaft, founded in 1924 and the first of all book clubs, I urged the Associated Booksellers of Great Britain and Ireland, as the Booksellers Association was then called, to form their own book club before an outsider stepped in. They replied, without hesitation, that a book club would not appeal to British readers or ever come to England. It is true that they have not attained in Great Britain the dominant position that they have secured in the States, where the selection of a book by one of the major organizations could be likened to drawing a first prize in a big lottery. Standardization of book selection carried to such extremes seems to me a disaster. It promotes the worship of the best-seller, and discourages the publication of good books which do not happen to have mass appeal. Book clubs in Great Britain are so carefully regulated that it is difficult to feel strongly about them. They nearly all rely upon 'bargain appeal', a factor of which the book trade as a whole has shied at making appropriate and legitimate use. As the result largely of 'bargain appeal', book clubs have sold millions of books that would not otherwise have been sold by the book trade. If, as most of us believe, the wider distribution of books is in itself a desirable thing, book clubs have certainly justified themselves. Personally I feel that a book club which achieved what 'Readers Union' originally hoped to do, namely the selection of outstandingly good books which had *failed* (like the early Conrads) to secure on publication the sale they deserved, and thus gave distinguished writing a second chance, would be rendering a public service. But that is expecting too much, though it is an ideal worth remembering.

Digest and Condensation Rights are a more recent innovation. The amounts paid for the use of successful books thus selected are often substantial, and like receipts from book clubs and the authorization of cheap reprints are shared equally by author and publisher.

Translation Rights automatically exist in the case of all countries which are signatories to the Berne Convention, though, as we have seen, the duration of the rights may vary. The absence of such rights does not promote the publication of translations, as might be supposed. On the contrary, where anyone may publish a translation without permission, it is usually worth nobody's while to run the risk of doing so. The risk in such a case is threefold, because there is not only the uncertainty of whether the translation will sell, but the possibility that some competitor may simultaneously be preparing one, and the certainty that competing editions will be published, if by any chance the venture proves successful.

The financial benefit to be derived from translation rights varies from country to country and often affords little clue to the importance of a translation appearing. For example, a Swedish publisher could and would probably pay more for Swedish rights in a book in which he was interested than a Greek or Roumanian and a Bulgarian publisher put together; but in view of the number of Swedes who read English, translations into the other languages mentioned may be much more desirable from a national point of view. And it is this national aspect of the matter I should like once again to emphasize. The importance of ensuring the publication of competent translations of the best English books in as many languages as possible far transcends monetary considerations. But here let me hasten to add that the sentimental author who, in consequence, gives his translation rights away in response to a gushing letter from a continental admirer, does not thereby ensure the publication of a translation, let alone a competent one. The only satisfactory method of doing so is to contract with a responsible publisher, who will undertake both to have a faithful translation prepared and to publish it in a prescribed time. *Some* payment is always desirable. The mistake often made is to ask 'more than the traffic will bear'. It is astonishing how difficult most authors, and even some literary agents and publishers, find it to assess the appropriate amount. A moment's thought will bring to mind the paramount considerations. The first, common to all languages, is that the cost of making the translation is a first charge on the item 'authorship'. It is obvious that it must in effect be deducted from the royalty, because, if the royalty be a fair one, it is impossible for the publisher to pay a translator *in addition*. To put the matter in the converse way, it will not be disputed that if a publisher can afford to pay a translator *in addition* to any given royalty, he is in a position to pay a higher royalty, if there is no translator to pay.

The cost of translation must therefore be taken into consideration in assessing the amount of the royalty. One method of doing so is to halve or otherwise divide the royalty until the translator's fee has been covered; another is to accept a lump sum for the first '*x*' copies and the full royalty thereafter. When that point is grasped, and it is fundamental, various questions have to be considered:

1. What is the probable sale (or, alternatively, what is to be the size of the first edition and at what price is it to be issued)? The answer to that question will depend upon the size of the population speaking the language; their degree of interest in things British, and the proportion of the population that is literate. It is clear that a publisher issuing a book in a language spoken by a comparatively small population, most of whom are illiterate, can only make a nominal payment. The

important thing in such cases is to ensure that any payment which is not on account of royalties should cover merely a prescribed number of copies, and that there should be provision for a royalty on sales in excess of that number.

2. What is the purchasing power of the country concerned? This includes not merely the standard of living, but the relation of the currency to sterling.

3. What, *under similar circumstances*, would be a fair royalty in England? because that *less the cost of making the translation* will then give some clue as to what could be asked or expected.

It should be borne in mind that translation rights embrace serial as well as book rights; it is thus important that there should be no ambiguity as to what rights are being offered or purchased. Many foreign newspapers and periodicals make use of translations as 'feuilletons', and the fact that 'rights' have been secured for this purpose does not necessarily secure publication in book form. Most authors will rightly regard actual publication in book form as of the essence of the contract, in which case it is wise to provide for the rights automatically reverting if publication does not take place within a prescribed period. If the author has sufficient linguistic ability to check the quality of the translation, provision may be made for it to be submitted to him. It may also be wise to place on record that there shall be no abridgment or alteration without the author's written consent.

The agreement should provide for half-yearly accounts at the start (yearly thereafter), and show clearly whether the royalty is payable on the full published price of the cloth-bound as well as of the paper-bound copies. Many Swedish publishers calculate all their royalties on the published price of the paper-bound edition. At one time this was unimportant, as the bulk of the sales were in that form, but with the ever-increasing tendency to use cloth binding the difference may be considerable.

In the guide to Royalty agreements, already referred to, there is a supplement dealing with the wording of agreements for the sale of translation rights. There is not the slightest difficulty in ascertaining which publishers in the leading European countries are interested in the publication of translations, because UNESCO publishes an 'Index Translationum', which provides much interesting information as to the European languages from, and into, which books of every type are being translated; but it is doubtful whether a dozen people in Great Britain or the USA bother to study the 'Index'.

As the conditions vary from country to country it will be convenient to treat them separately.

German Translation Rights.—There is no longer any difficulty about arranging contracts upon a royalty basis. There are, however, pitfalls for the unwary. The number of publishers in Germany is legion, and, as we have seen in the chapter on Agreements, an unfavourable contract with a good firm is at all times to be preferred to a favourable contract with an unstable one. An English publisher in close touch with the *Börsenverein* is in a position to ascertain the status of any German firm in a way that no author or agent can do, and as a recipient of the trade paper, the *Börsenblatt*, the circulation of which is restricted to members, has unique opportunities of gauging German and Swiss publishers' requirements. Points of this kind are apt to be overlooked by authors.

All questions not specifically settled in a publishing contract entered into in Germany are governed by the German law regulating publishing; thus, for example, if no mention of either matter is made in the agreement, the author is entitled after the lapse of twenty years (*vide* § 2) to include any of his writings in a collected edition, and the publisher is entitled (*vide* § 6) to use up to 5 per cent of the edition as 'free copies'. There is much in the Act of great interest to British authors and publishers, but it would take us beyond the scope of this book to examine it.

The Danish and Norwegian Translation Rights are now almost invariably sold separately. It is usually possible to secure a royalty arrangement, but a lump-sum payment for a defined number of copies is sometimes substituted. This latter method secures the right to further payments if the translation proves unexpectedly successful. Of necessity, owing to the smallness of the populations of these countries, the amount that can be expected is not very substantial.

The Swedish Translation Rights usually yield rather more than the Danish or Norwegian rights, because the population is larger and there is a substantial sale for Swedish books in Finland as well as in Sweden. Some Swedish publishers make a point of consulting their Finnish agents or collaborators before deciding upon the purchase of any rights. Speaking generally, the sale of the Swedish rights indicates a probable demand for the Danish and Norwegian rights, and vice versa, because the requirements of all three countries are very much alike. This also applies to the *Finnish Translation Rights* for which one can expect about half the amount received from Sweden.

The Dutch Translation Rights in any literary work that proves particularly successful in England are readily marketable; this is surprising in view of the fact that every second person in Holland knows English, if not two or three other languages. The Flemish part of Belgium and to a rapidly declining extent the Indonesian Republic provide an additional market for the Dutch translations, and the amount paid for these rights, though inconsiderable, is often as much as for the Danish or Norwegian rights. Here again the payment should cover a prescribed number of copies, if it is not on account of royalties.

When we turn to the *French Translation Rights* we are confronted by more difficult conditions. French publishers are by no means modest in their valuations of translation rights in their own publications (their requirements are often ridiculous, particularly if they think an American firm is interested in them), but are apt to be timidity itself when it comes to embarking upon French translations of English works, let alone making any substantial payment for the rights. It is usually possible to arrange for a royalty basis, but if that is done, an advance payment and a provision that it shall be forfeited if publication does not take place within a prescribed time are desirable.

The Spanish Translation Rights are no longer an uncertain quantity. Spanish publishers find a ready sale for translations from English and are willing to pay a reasonable and often generous figure for the rights.

One basis favoured is a cash payment of from £35 to £50 for the right to sell 2,000 to 3,000 copies with a 10 per cent royalty thereafter, but for important books £50 or more is obtainable on account of royalties. It is well to remember that Barcelona is an even larger centre of publishing than Madrid. Many of the most enterprising Spanish firms have their headquarters in Barcelona, and some of them publish books in Catalan as well as Spanish. Furthermore there is ever increasing publishing activity in Mexico and South America and it is becoming practicable on occasion to sell the Spanish rights for these territories independently. It is thus essential when disposing of Spanish rights to define the territory covered by the transaction. Broadly speaking the quality of Spanish translations, particularly those made in South America, leaves a good deal to be desired. Some firms take a great deal more trouble than others to maintain a high standard and authors are well advised to take this fact into consideration.

The Portuguese Translation Rights are becoming increasingly saleable particularly to Brazilian publishers most of whom are satisfied with the exclusive right of sale in Brazil and Spanish America and pay good prices. This leaves one free to sell the rights for Portugal and the Portuguese colonies to a Portuguese publisher if he can be persuaded to buy them with the Brazilian market excluded. Of the two territories Brazil is already the more important and in the future will be overwhelmingly so.

The Italian Translation Rights are becoming more valuable. Italian publishers used to be less willing to pay a reasonable sum for translation rights than their

Spanish confrères, but this is no longer true. In fact in 1959 Italy became the more important market.

The Hungarian Translation Rights were readily marketable but their sale is now (1959) largely governed by political considerations.

Polish Translation Rights are becoming of increasing importance. The usual basis for their sale is an outright payment, half in sterling and half in blocked zlotys, for a licence to print a prescribed number of copies varying from 3,000 to 10,000.

Serbo-Croat and Roumanian Translation Rights are also saleable, but to a much more limited extent.

Hebrew Translation Rights would be more readily marketable were Israel not so short of sterling. Nevertheless sales are by no means negligible. The prices paid inevitably reflect the smallness of the market.

The Czech Translation Rights were more important than the population of Czechoslovakia would lead one to suppose. The Czechs are good bookbuyers and translations from English are popular. But State publishing houses limit their buying to what the State approves. A modest advance payment on account of a 5 per cent royalty rising to $7\frac{1}{2}$ per cent after 3,000 copies and to 10 per cent after 5,000 copies is the officially recognized basis.

The Japanese Translation Rights are in increasing demand but the prices paid are disappointing. The number of responsible firms is limited whereas the number of irresponsible concerns from whom it is difficult or impossible to secure regular royalty accounts seems to be unlimited. The trouble is doubtless accentuated by Japanese shortage of sterling. Apart from translation rights there is a demand for licences to print cheap editions of books in English, heavily annotated in Japanese, for the use of students. It is sometimes forgotten that Japan is a signatory of the Berne Convention and that in consequence 'pirated' editions can be seized.

Indian Vernacular Rights.—The translations of English books into the Indian vernaculars ought I feel to be encouraged. The editions, except in Hindi, are often small and the published price low so that the amount that can be paid for the rights may be insubstantial. A fee for a defined number of copies is appropriate.

The Russian Translation Rights are of no commercial value because the Soviet authorities appropriate them without payment unless the author is a good communist or someone they approve, in which case he may be granted some roubles for expenditure in Russia. Their own authors are treated generously.

Other Translation Rights can be placed from time to time, but the amounts usually received do not justify devoting space to each country separately.

DRAMATIC, CINEMA AND OTHER RIGHTS

Dramatic Rights seldom concern the book publisher. There are agents who specialize in the placing of them and the Authors' Society's Associated League of British Dramatists is in a position to give authors expert advice.

Amateur Dramatic Rights, on the other hand, may concern the publisher. The issue of plays in book form, which is often unremunerative, greatly facilitates their sale and an interest in these rights may provide the publisher with an inducement to embark upon publication when otherwise he would not.

The Film Rights are in a slightly different position. They are often excluded from the book publisher's contract, but the fact remains that they are usually unsaleable until the book is published. In other words, in the case of an unknown writer it is the publisher's expenditure that renders these rights marketable. It may easily happen that a publisher, in losing heavily over the publication of a first novel, may give substantial value to the film rights, and also, according to Curtis Brown's one time manager, 'help an author enormously to place his short stories and journalistic work, and probably enable him to get better prices'. But if a publisher ventured to suggest that in such circumstances it would not be inequitable were he to have some quite modest share in this result of his enterprise, he would probably be denounced.[1] The publication of novels by unknown writers is often exceedingly speculative, and there would seem to be no good reason why an author, who chose to do so, should not offer a publisher, by way of additional inducement to take the risk, an interest in the film rights which, but for publication, would remain unmarketable.

'Pictures' soon get out of date. The right granted should therefore be to make *one* picture only, and there should be a time-limit in the contract. Application is

[1] Since that was written my firm lost heavily over the publication of an English translation of a Scandinavian novel of which the film rights were sold for £2,000 to a Hollywood firm who would never have heard of the author or read the work but for our expenditure.

often made for an 'option' on the film rights. In such cases a payment is customary. This is forfeited if the option is not taken up but forms part of the advance if the rights are acquired.

Sound Broadcasting Rights may be a source of direct revenue and in addition have value as publicity. The *minimum* fees payable are governed by an Agreement entered into between the BBC, the Authors' Society, and the Publishers Association.

Television rights are becoming increasingly important and should be jointly controlled by the publisher. It may be suggested that this will prejudice the sale of film rights because all film companies now demand television rights. This difficulty can be overcome by the publisher agreeing to relinquish, *for so long as may be necessary*, his joint control, subject to the payment to him of a suitable sum by way of compensation. Some film companies are content to acquire television rights in their film alone; others are satisfied to control them for a comparatively short period, and in some instances to compensate publishers in respect of their share in the rights. It should be remembered that in many cases the publisher, by the mere fact of contracting to publish a book, apart from his services in its promotion and marketing all over the world, increases the value of these rights, and indeed may even bring them into existence.

The situation is complicated by the fact that television rights are of different kinds. At one end of the scale are readings from the text of the book, at the other dramatized versions in which only some of the author's original works are used. The difficulty is to draw a line anywhere, or properly to define television rights as opposed to dramatic rights.[1]

Anthologies, Compilations, Musical Settings, etc.— With the dictum laid down by the Authors' Society that anyone wanting literary material should pay for it, all who have given thought to the matter are bound to agree, at any rate in theory. There would seem to be no more excuse for any man 'cadging' for material with which to fill a book, out of which profit is to be derived, than for furniture with which to fill his house. The question is thus merely one of deciding what fee is equitable. Each case has to be judged on its own merits; the publisher is usually in a position to gauge what is fair. There is, in most cases, a definite limit to what an anthology maker can afford to pay for copyright material, and the effect of asking excessive fees is to decrease, not increase, the revenue from this source.

Many a poet receives more collectively for the right to use individual poems than from the royalties on the sale of his works, and welcomes the attention of the anthology maker.

It should be remembered, however, that the modest fee appropriate for an anthology of which at most 1,500 or 2,000 copies will be printed is totally inadequate for a newspaper compilation of which anything from fifty thousand to half a million may be sold. It is thus important to know the precise use to be made of the material and the size of the edition as well as the territory the licence is expected to cover.

Prose compilations are in greater favour in America than in England, judging by the number of applications

[1] See *Guide to Royalty Agreements*, Fourth edition, page 25.

received for the use of copyright matter. In such cases the fee usually bears a fairly definite ratio to the length of the extract.

The relative importance of words and music in the case of a musical setting may be a difficult question to decide. Composers are apt to feel that a nominal fee to the author meets the case, whereas authors may claim as much as a half-share in the composer's royalty as their proper due. Each case has to be examined individually, and a settlement arrived at somewhere between these two extremes.

The remuneration claimed by publishers for the placing of rights is almost invariably discussed with a complete disregard of the varying circumstances. Any commission in excess of 10 per cent is *ipso facto* dismissed as extortionate, whereas a charge of 20 per cent in some cases might be as much an underpayment as a commission of 10 per cent on others (e.g. some large and easily effected transaction) might be excessive. Presumably the remuneration should under normal circumstances bear some relation to the service rendered and the labour involved. It seems strange to have to suggest anything so obvious, but authors are as apt to overlook this point today as were some publishers in the past. An amusing indication of the frame of mind engendered by an over-diligent reading of the *Author*, under the late G. Herbert Thring's editorship, was afforded by an experience of my own, when a member of the Society solemnly assured me that one shilling (which, by the way, she never paid) was 'ample' reward for writing three letters and spending some time on the telephone to secure her a fee which but for my initiative would not have come her way. I had been rash enough to suggest half a guinea!

'*Fair Dealing*' with a copyright work is not an infringement if it is (*a*) for purposes of research or private study, (*b*) for purposes of criticism or review, if accompanied by a sufficient acknowledgment.

Sufficient acknowledgment is defined in the Copyright Act 1956, but 'fair dealing' is not. The Publishers Association and the Society of Authors have established a general understanding of what is permissible[1] in normal practice:

> *Prose:* a single extract up to 400 words, or a series of extracts (with comments interposed) up to a total of 800 words but of which no one extract exceeds 300 words.
>
> *Poetry:* an extract or extracts up to a total of 40 lines, but in no case exceeding one-quarter of any poem.

In a review of a newly published work greater latitude than this would be reasonable.

N.B.—A clear distinction must be drawn between such reasonable use and the reprinting of even the briefest quotation in an anthology, which may not be done without permission.

The Literary Agent

As for the question (frequently put to publishers) whether I believe in literary agents, I always feel inclined to reply as I should were I asked if I 'believed'

[1] See the appendix to the Publishers Association's Guide to Royalty Agreements.

in spectacles: 'Yes, if you need them and can be quite sure of getting the right kind.'

To a few authors an agent is indispensable; to some others a great convenience; but to the majority unnecessary. This is clearly demonstrated by the indisputable fact that most publishing contracts have always been, and still are, made direct between the author and publisher without the intervention of any middleman. This may not be true of individual firms, but of the thousands of new books published in any year it is doubtful whether even 10 or 12 per cent are placed by agents.

There are, of course, agents of all kinds—the excellent, the really bad, the indifferent, the reasonably efficient, and the hopelessly inefficient. For this profitable occupation no qualifications seem to be required. It is rare to find one with a thorough knowledge of any foreign language or with continental experience, though they mostly claim to be experts in dealing with translation rights. In point of fact, most of them are out of their depth if they attempt to handle anything but fiction, memoirs, or popular works with a wide appeal, and some of them are honest enough to admit the fact.

Had the placing of MSS for publication in book form remained their principal activity, their business would probably have declined as rapidly as it grew, because the prejudice against intermediaries is fairly general, and because the agent's supposed duty of protecting the 'innocent' author from the 'wicked' publisher has long since been assumed by the Authors' Society, whose function it obviously is. It is amusing to observe that the question of protecting the author from his supposed protector—the literary agent—is now sometimes discussed in the columns of the *Author*.

The trouble would be mitigated if not largely solved if the Authors' Society officially 'recognized' as 'Literary Agents' only those firms who had their accounts properly audited and submitted to the Society a half-yearly certificate that all their liabilities to authors had been faithfully discharged. If they were wise the better agents—and there are some of the highest repute—would welcome such a procedure.

With the advent of new 'rights' of many kinds, the management of literary property has become a much more complicated and technical business. This has greatly strengthened the agents' position and made their services of real value to some authors. Whilst it is quite true that some agents are better than some publishers in placing subsidiary 'rights' of one kind or another, it must not be forgotten that some publishers are better than many agents at so doing.

For many authors today, the right of publication in book form is by no means the most important direct source of income. Film, serial, dramatic, broadcasting, or other rights may yield far more, and it is in these directions that an agent may prove particularly helpful. At the same time it must not be overlooked that, indirectly, book publication is still of paramount importance. The author's prestige—which, translated into cash, means the price his articles or short stories will command—is nearly always dependent upon the reputation made by his books. This fact is increasingly recognized by authors.

In placing book rights, agents tend to turn first to the big fiction publishers, who are, of course, their chief clients, and failing them, to the unimaginative or new publisher bent on building up a list in haste. Whether this is in the interests of authors, or whether the best publishing is done by either class of firm, is, to say the least of it, doubtful; but that agents should give them first consideration is perhaps inevitable. In both cases the decision is likely to be based mainly upon commercial considerations; the intrinsic merits of the MSS will not be examined too closely. The specialist and the literary publisher, on the other hand, are usually more independent. They are more fastidious in their selection of MSS, and not so ready to buy 'blindly'. Nor have they any need to do so, because such firms receive so many MSS direct from authors. Furthermore, their reputation probably rests upon the maintenance of a very high standard.

Authors employing agents should remember that some of the best publishers avoid doing business with certain agents, and vice versa: otherwise they may find, too late, that the most likely firm to take their work has never been approached. It would also be well for authors to bear in mind that a publisher may be able and willing to grant concessions to an individual which fear of creating a precedent would deter him from granting to an agent. This at once introduces a certain rigidity into negotiations with agents.

One other point deserves mention because it is a frequent cause of friction. Its importance was recognized by the one-time manager of Curtis Brown Ltd. and I cannot do better than quote his words:

A publisher likes to have his contracts as nearly uniform as possible, for this simplifies his handling of a book. A certain routine is usually established in regard to publishing a book, and if there are no special points to be observed, the process of production and selling will go along automatically in a well-ordered office; but confusion is apt to occur if the publisher has to stop constantly and refer to his contract to see whether he has the right to do this or that. Book-keeping is also simplified and mistakes are less likely to occur if the contract is on standard lines.[1]

It would certainly help matters considerably were agents to take this to heart.

Copyright Infringements.—The protection of copyright is a matter which concerns both author and publishers of books and periodicals. In the past infringement of copyright was largely confined to unauthorized reprinting, but in recent years, with the development of photographic methods of reproduction, the use of copyright material without permission has greatly increased.

A memorandum on this problem, including microfilming, has been drawn up by the Publishers Association and can be obtained (gratis) on application to the Secretary at 19 Bedford Square, London, W.C.1.

[1] *The Commercial Side of Literature.*

CHAPTER X

OTHER ASPECTS OF THE BUSINESS

THE preceding chapters have left untouched a number of interesting questions and much of the day-to-day routine work of a publisher. I propose here to repair some of these omissions. The efficiency or inefficiency of all the activities previously described depends largely upon the co-ordination of the various departments. The infinite detail makes this a difficult task even where the utmost good will prevails, and a quite impossible one without it. A policy of water-tight compartments is fatal in a publisher's office, because almost everything decided or done in one department has some bearing upon the work of another. The more understanding there is among a publisher's employees of the other fellow's job, the more co-operation there will be and the fewer mistakes. For this reason, if for no other, it has always seemed to me a wise policy to take pains to ensure that all employees should know as much as practicable about the business as a whole, as well as the exact bearing of their work upon that of the other departments. Of course, the larger the staff, the more difficult this is to achieve.

Before 1914, employees in the book trade were for the most part seriously underpaid, and the labour troubles encountered thereafter were an almost inevitable reaction. Few firms had the decency, or should we say foresight? to grant wage increases *pari passu* with the rise in the cost of living; many resisted the most modest demands until they found themselves coerced. Those times are gone, never, I hope, to return. Today a different spirit prevails. Whilst it is clear that it is not possible to pay the exceptional wages earned in newspaper offices, it is generally agreed that a reasonably high standard should prevail, and that so far as practicable the more responsible employees should feel a direct interest in the prosperity of their respective firms. This is the more important because, as in solicitors' offices, there are few highly paid posts in the book trade. The largest firms may have two or three managerial positions; the smaller none, or at most one. A successful publisher's manager is usually tempted to start in business for himself; in any case, publishing profits are usually too precarious to justify high salaries; and, whatever he paid, the publisher who had his whole heart in his profession would want to do the lion's share of the managing himself.

Finance.—It is a commonplace that the financial side of a business is of paramount importance, but it is one that is even more apt to be overlooked in a publishing house than elsewhere. The temptations to do so are great. It is so easy, if your inclinations prompt you to publish a particular book, either to ignore altogether or to judge too optimistically its financial prospects. The danger inherent in giving the benefit of the doubt to every book in which you are personally interested has perpetually to be guarded against. But, apart altogether from these considerations, there is the equally important question of the general basis upon which the business is to be run. In the past it was customary for publishers to rely very largely upon extended credit obtained from stationers, printers, and bookbinders, to finance their undertakings. It was a thoroughly evil system for many reasons, but particularly because of the way in which it bolstered up inefficient and some-times quite insolvent firms, with the result that when the final and inevitable crash came, the losses sustained by all concerned, and authors in particular, were much greater than would otherwise have been the case. The printer and bookbinder, if they held any considerable stock upon which they could claim a lien, might in such cases conceivably recover something from the wreck, and in any case they probably charged sufficiently high prices to cover the risk; but the unfortunate author was almost invariably an unsecured creditor to whom little or nothing was forthcoming. During the two war periods it was impossible for extended credit to be given, and it is to be hoped that publishers as a whole will never again desire or be able to depend so largely upon stationers, printers, and bookbinders for the capi-tal with which to run their businesses. The firms that can pay promptly for their requirements are obviously likely to get the best service, but if publishers are to be in a position to do this without outside assistance, they must, especially in the case of growing firms, place painfully sharp limitations upon the drawing out of such profits as are made. As we have been officially reminded, 'the soundest method of trade—and this applies to individuals, companies, and combines—is to trade on one's own resources and not on borrowings'. But having given this excellent advice officialdom has since made it virtually impossible for most publishers, at any rate, to follow it.

Authors are directly interested in the financial stability of publishers, though it is surprising sometimes how little thought they appear to give to it.

Authors' Accounts.—The efficiency with which these accounts are prepared varies enormously from business to business. There are alternative methods of securing the necessary figures of sales. The most rapid and the simplest is to take the number printed, to deduct from it the stock on hand and the number distributed free to the author and to the Press, and to treat the balance as sold. The alternative and more reliable method is to analyse all the sales, that is to say, to go through each invoice separately and post each transaction to a sales analysis card on which, under the title of the work, are entered exact particulars of every copy sold. How many publishers adopt this method I do not know. It is a most laborious task, but has many advantages. It provides a double check, because freedom from mistakes can easily be ensured by the simple process of adding to the sales shown in the analysis the stock on hand and the number given away, and see that the total tallies with the number printed. Furthermore, it enables the publisher to tell at a glance who have proved the best customers for any particular book.

Whichever system is adopted, the question arises whether an author is entitled to 'stock accounts'. The Authors' Society says 'yes', but foolishly couples with that answer the demand for half-yearly accounts, which shows a lamentable ignorance of the actual working of a publisher's office. The stock account, to have any real value, must be based upon actual stock-taking figures, and no publisher takes stock more than once a year. It is quite bad enough that for one day in the year his entire business should be brought to a standstill. On the other hand, authors very naturally do not want to be kept waiting unnecessarily for payment, and where any sum over £10 is involved an interim account is a reasonable request. It should, however, be clearly understood that it *is* an interim account, and it should not be given the same status as an account based upon stock-taking figures. To press for accounts to be rendered within an unduly brief period after the closing of the year to which they refer, is unwise because it precludes the checking of the author's account with the stock-taking figures.

Some publishers believe in giving the minimum information, a course which breeds suspicion. But the inclusion of stock accounts proved such a rod for our backs when we lost over a million books by enemy action that I can no longer recommend others to provide them. The fact that we did not recover from war risks insurance as much as the sheets would have fetched for pulping, and that all our agreements specifically state that no royalty is payable on copies destroyed, did not deter some authors from making exorbitant demands based on the stock accounts and indulging in acrimonious correspondence. The many publishers who refrained from giving stock figures were completely spared that unpleasantness.

In connection with the preparation of authors' accounts, a card-index summary of agreements is essential. The more standardized the agreement forms are, the more easy the work becomes. At the best, the amount of detail involved is usually out of all proportion to the turnover. Just as I think it is in the publishers' interests to see in what way they can reduce booksellers' overhead expenses, so I believe that if the Authors' Society were wise, it would see what steps could be taken, without impairing efficiency, to reduce the appalling amount of clerical work which authors' requirements inflict upon publishers. It is obvious that the more a publisher is compelled to spend on unnecessary overhead expenses, the less margin he has for either the author or himself.

An example of such economy, in the case of a book that has had its day, is to compound the royalty on the balance of the stock by a single cash payment appropriate to the circumstances. It is the common-sense and practical way of saving the clerical labour entailed in the rendering of innumerable further small accounts.

Stock-taking is a much more complicated process than authors are apt to realize. The stock actually held at a publisher's office generally represents a fraction of the whole, though it will probably include some copies of every book in his list. The balance may be distributed over all parts of the kingdom. Some of the stock, bound and unbound, may be at printers' so far away as Aberdeen or Plymouth, in the publisher's own warehouses, or in those of the binders he employs. The publisher's staff has, therefore, not only to count the stock in the publisher's actual possession, but also to obtain reports from all the printers and binders who hold stock for him. These reports have to be carefully checked with the publisher's own records. It is very rarely that they tally. Long lists of queries go back to the printers and binders, and it may be weeks before all the figures are finally adjusted and ready to enter in the publisher's stock-book.

Liens.—Printers and binders now profess to object very strongly to holding so much stock, and make varying charges, after the lapse of three years, to cover the serious expense of warehousing it. In many cases, however, they would be very nervous if they did not hold it, because practically all of them claim a lien on stock so held; that is to say, they claim the right to regard the stock as security for the payment of their account for printing or binding it. There are two kinds of liens, a general lien and a particular lien. The former, which is much more difficult to enforce, is a kind of floating charge which disregards the question whether the account for the printing and binding of the particular books stored has been paid. A particular lien, on the other hand, which is comparatively easy to enforce, is concerned merely with the printer's or binder's charges for actual work done on the particular book on which the lien is claimed. The question sometimes has the very greatest importance to authors. Let me take an extreme case as an illustration, viz. a commission publication for the production of which the author has paid the publisher, but for which, although the printing and binding have been completed, the publisher has not yet paid either the printer or binder. If, at that stage, the publisher's affairs came into the hands of a receiver, the author might find himself in the unfortunate position of not being able to secure possession of the stock for which he had paid without paying for it a second time, assuming, as might well be the case, that part of the stock was at the printers and part at the binders. What the position of the printer or binder would be if the lien was never cleared still remains uncertain. Both printers and binders usually claim the right to sell such stock so as to use the proceeds to meet their charges. In so far as they are dealing with the publisher's own property, that is to say the physical materials of which the book is made, their claim is probably valid, but it is difficult to see how they can sell the book *as a book* without infringing the rights of a third party, viz. the owner of the copyright, i.e. the author. In practice there is usually some compromise, because the receiver is as anxious to wind up the affairs as the author or publisher is to get possession of the books.

One point printers and binders are apt to overlook is that from the moment they charge for warehousing they cease to be 'gratuitous bailees' and in consequence lose the measure of relief from responsibility that status secures them.

Upon the *Valuation of Stock, Plant, and Copyrights* depends the solvency of a publishing business. It is the easiest thing in the world to show profits if you care to deceive yourself as to the value of the stock on hand. The standards applicable to other businesses are not applicable to publishing. Every book venture would show a profit if the stock left on hand were worth cost. There would indeed be little difficulty were it sufficient to write off 10 per cent or even 20 per cent from cost. But, alas! few books that have ceased to sell are worth anything approaching cost, and many have no value except for pulping. If the book is not a steady and substantial seller, the only safe plan is to face the question what the stock is certain to realize as a remainder; and, in the case of a steady seller, it is essential to make sure that the stock is not in excess of the requirements of, say, the next three years, before accepting cost as a proper valuation. There is no short cut; every item must be separately valued title by title. Practically all publishers agree about the need for drastic depreciation; nearly all impress upon you that they themselves see to it that their own stock is adequately written down; but the fact remains that nearly all publishers deceive themselves—often quite unconsciously—and over-value their stock. Many publishers would be unable to look their profit and loss account in the face if they dealt really adequately with depreciation. This sounds like a very sweeping statement, but there is plenty of evidence to support it. I have in one connection or another been called upon to examine scores of publishers' accounts—it is true that they were many of them firms that had got into difficulties—and I have never found a single instance where the stock was not hopelessly and fantastically over-valued. But there is no need to confine ourselves to private information. The records at Somerset House will show anyone interested what an amazingly large proportion of the oldest and most esteemed publishing houses have been reconstructed in some way or other at some period of their existence, in order to write down their capital and reduce their valuation of stock, plant, or copyrights, which they found themselves unable to do by any less drastic means. There are few publishers who would not be thankful to turn their entire stock into cash at the figure at which it appears in their balance-sheet, and if that is so, it is quite certainly over-valued. Apart altogether from other considerations, there are two points which are almost invariably overlooked when valuing stock:

1. The heavy cost of realization: if the publisher does not receive considerably more than the figure at which the stock is valued, he will be seriously at a loss by the time it is turned into cash.

2. The author's interest in the stock: even if it cost nothing to dispose of the books, the publisher would be out of pocket by the amount of the author's royalty if they merely fetched the price at which they were valued. In the case of profit-sharing books, the author's interest may be 50 per cent.

The extent to which publishers deceive themselves varies greatly, but the most remarkable case I ever encountered was that of a diary publisher long since deceased, who solemnly valued at cost diaries for past years! This sounds incredible, but it is probable that an examination of many publishers' valuation books would disclose some examples which, though less obvious, were equally wide of the mark. There have even been cases of publishers who wrote up the value of their stock when they found the results of the year's trading were not entirely to their liking.[1]

When we turn to the value of plant, which, by the way, is not plant in the income-tax sense, because in

[1] Since the foregoing was written many publishers lost stock by enemy action. Under the provisions of War Risks Insurance cum Excess Profits Tax the provident publishers were heavily penalized because anything received by them beyond the nominal amounts to which they had written down their stock in their balance-sheets was taken as excess profits, whereas the improvident who over-valued, or had artificially written up, their stock were endowed by having it turned into cash at inflated prices which showed no 'profit' on their balance-sheet figures.

a publishing business it refers merely to moulds, stereo-plates, electroplates, negatives, and blocks, there is only one safe rule, and that is to get the valuation on to a metal basis as rapidly as possible. By a metal basis I mean, of course, what the plates, etc., will fetch for melting. In the case of plates of works of a permanent value, from which many reprints will be wanted, the cost can, if necessary, be written off over a period of three or five years, but it should be written off in equal instalments, because to write off say 20 per cent each year does not mean, as so many people innocently imagine, that the whole amount will have disappeared in five years. On the contrary, a third of it will still remain, and after yet another five years only about 90 per cent of the original sum will have been written off. Unless they are already on a metal basis, all valuations of plant should now be drastically overhauled in view of the new processes which enable one to reproduce books of which no plant is available. This is a factor which even income-tax officials cannot ignore.

The overvaluation of copyrights was the pit into which many publishers of past generations fell. In those days, it was much more customary than at present to acquire copyrights for a lump-sum payment, and in such cases it was natural, and indeed often essential, to include a substantial item for copyright in the balance-sheets. But the tradition has survived to an age when a publisher rarely, if ever, acquires any copy-rights. An exclusive licence of the book rights for the duration of copyright may have some value for balance-sheet purposes, but short leases certainly have not. The wise plan is undoubtedly to place 'rights' in the

THE TRUTH ABOUT PUBLISHING

same category as goodwill, and to aim at treating both as hidden reserves rather than as realizable assets.

Correspondence and Callers occupy the greater part of the publisher's day. Both are at times apt to be overwhelming. To deal with correspondence effectively needs, above all other qualifications, imagination. Few people seem to realize the importance of putting themselves in the position of the recipient of the letter. There is an inevitable tendency to assume that what is so familiar to you must be obvious to your correspondent, whereas to the inexperienced author, at any rate, all the technical terms used so lightly by the publisher or his assistants are mysterious hieroglyphics. In the turmoil of the day's work it is not always easy for the publisher to remember that to the author his book is 'the only pebble on the beach'. It may be extremely tiresome at times, but it is none the less natural that authors should be curious to know everything about their offspring, and always inclined, like an overanxious mother, to suspect the worst. The late W. B. Maxwell referred to the publisher's 'awful silence'. To some extent it is, I fear, inevitable, but I think something might be done to break it. One might, for instance, devise a printed card, the most appropriate sentence on which could be underlined. This might, however, arouse more suspicions than it would allay. Letters voluntarily giving information to authors easily become a terrible burden, but I agree that it is well worth while for the publisher to write them, despite the fact that they almost always involve yet further correspondence. The trouble is that if you begin to give information to some authors, there is no end to the correspondence explaining the information and why you gave it.

Much work can be saved by the use of 'form letters'. Any correspondence which is repetitive, such as letters sending proofs to an author, should be dealt with in this way. But if a letter is to be standardized, it should be given unusually careful thought. A 'form letter' need not necessarily be printed. In many cases it is better that it should not, but there is none the less an economy both in time and mental effort in using it.

There are many ways of declining MSS—some publishers take pains about how they do it, others do not. Personally, I think the way it is done is very important, because the communication will reach the author at a moment when he is likely to be particularly sensitive. At the same time it is seldom wise to give reasons for declining a MS. Nearly all would say they desired it, but four out of five would not only resent the explanation when given, but enter into an argument about it. Furthermore, it is wise to remember that though the decision was right, the reason for it may well have been wrong.

Callers are a very great problem: they can rob one of so much time. Many publishers, I believe, refuse to see anyone except by appointment. This seems to me a mistake, and I can say with certainty that it would have lost me a good deal of business. On the other hand, some parts of the day must be kept sacred, and it seems to me indefensible to expect to see a business man before he has had an opportunity of dealing with his morning's correspondence.

If the maximum is to be accomplished, the day's

work must be carefully planned; a certain amount of routine is essential. Contrary to the usual impression, the telephone is a great enemy of efficiency, and the extent to which it is abused is incredible. Information which cannot be given off-hand should never, under ordinary circumstances, be demanded on the telephone; and it is surely unnecessary to insist upon asking a director of the firm a question which could be equally well and perhaps more promptly answered by a junior. An inquiry as to whether a review copy of a book has been sent to the *Little Pemington Gazette*, if written on a post card, can be answered without effort, whereas the same inquiry made through the telephone to the principal of a big publishing firm is like sand in a complicated machine.

The Titles of Books often present one of the most difficult problems a publisher has to face. In some cases, success or failure may depend upon the right choice. It is desirable both that the title should be short and that it should accurately describe the book, two conditions that frequently seem incompatible. The difficulty can sometimes be solved by the addition of a sub-title, which, if necessary, can be longer and convey a more exact idea of the contents. Fanciful titles which convey no meaning and might equally well be used for almost any kind of book are invariably a mistake. Ruskin could use them with impunity, because people wanted to read his books regardless of what he called them, but lesser men should beware of following his example in that particular respect.

Although there is no copyright in titles, publishers do their utmost to avoid duplication, because of the confusion it is apt to cause. If an author experiences difficulty in selecting a title, he will be well advised to supply the publisher with a long list of suggestions from which to make a selection. It may well be that not one in the list will be suitable as it stands, but the selection may suggest to the publisher some other really good name for the book. In the case of

Translations, the title is especially important. It is not always easy to follow the original as closely as might be desired. The rule should be to give the original title on the back, if not on the front, of the title-page, particularly if the English title leaves any doubt as to which particular work by the writer is being translated. The point is so easily overlooked that I would urge translators themselves to draw attention to the desirability of giving the fullest information upon such points as part of the bibliographical information the reader is entitled to expect. In my early days the standard of translations was deplorable, but in recent years there has been a marked improvement. It is now more fully realized that even the most perfect knowledge of a foreign language does not make one a good translator; that there is a definite technique to be mastered; that exceptional conscientiousness is called for, and that no one can be expected to make a really first-rate translation into any other language than his own mother tongue. In fact the greater the literary merit of the original the greater the need for literary gift on the part of the translator.

The publication of translations is highly speculative, much more so than the publication of an original work, because there are in effect two authors to pay instead of one, and both, as a rule, call for immediate payment and are unable or unwilling to let their remuneration depend wholly upon the result. Foreign authors and publishers who have heard of the wonderful sales of some particular translated book are apt to have the most fantastic ideas of the value of the English translation rights, and if the word 'America' is breathed, I have known foreign publishers name a figure for which one would think they would be pleased to sell their whole business. Even thirty years ago, translation rights were almost invariably sold for a small lump sum; today the most impossible royalties are asked. Probably the fairest plan to both parties is a lump sum for a definite number of copies with a royalty thereafter. It would seem to be clear that if a royalty is granted from the start, it should only be a proportion of what would be paid for an original work. In other words, there is no justification for paying a foreign author plus a translator more than would be paid for a corresponding work by an English author. This sounds obvious, but one constantly encounters publishers (American publishers in particular) who in the same breath admit that they cannot afford more than 10 per cent royalty for a work by an unknown writer, and that they have just agreed to pay 10 per cent for some translation rights of a work by an author of whom few people have ever heard. They seem oblivious of the fact that by the time they have paid the translator they are probably paying the equivalent of 20 per cent for authorship. One such publisher recently admitted to me that he had never yet made any money on translations. I am afraid he never will.

Series have disadvantages as well as advantages. Many of the best have grown out of some successful book, and were not planned as series at all. A publisher finding himself unexpectedly successful with a book entitled *Questions about X* will naturally follow it up with a book *Questions about Y*, and almost before he knows it the 'Questions' series is in existence. Others, however, are planned and carefully thought out from the start, but many of the most pretentious schemes of that kind have come to an end with the failure of the first half-dozen titles. The existence of a series gives the publisher opportunities of publishing books which, issued by themselves, would be foredoomed to failure. An isolated volume on, let us say, Obadiah would stand a poor chance of success, but as one of a series of small books on the Minor Prophets it might receive attention. It is a very great temptation to a publisher to include a volume in a series, even if it is not entirely suited to it, because by so doing he knows he will be giving the book a better start. Probably this is partly responsible for the deterioration there is in almost every series. But even worse are the volumes which authors have no urge to write but are persuaded to contribute to a series. There are indeed few in which deterioration is not noticeable. One of the exceptions is the Muirhead Library of Philosophy, and the high standard that has been maintained is due not only to the discernment of the editors, but to the fact that the publishers left them entirely free to veto the inclusion of any work that was not up to the required standard.

Censorship (except for the First World War, when we were *all* under the tutelage of DORA) is a trouble with which British publishers are fortunately not afflicted; but the very absence of a censorship throws grave responsibilities upon the publishers themselves. The best firms use most careful judgment. Few who have not had the responsibility thrust upon them know how difficult it is to decide exactly what will be regarded at any given moment as permissible. Some things are a matter of custom, and customs change rapidly. Ideas which are universally accepted today would have horrified a previous generation. The publisher whose aim it is to cater for tomorrow rather than yesterday, and to give opportunities for the expression of new ideas, is confronted with the whole problem in its acutest form. Most publishers are extremely timid in facing authority; but if you are satisfied that what you are doing is right and fully justified, there would seem to be no reason, in England at any rate, for timidity, whatever governmental pressure may be brought to bear.

One of my own experiences in this connection was amusing. Shortly after the *Rainbow* prosecution, I was visited by an emissary from Scotland Yard, who said they had received a complaint concerning one of our publications. He mentioned, I remember, that our author had overstepped the mark, and added that he had been instructed by his chief to call and see whether we would withdraw the book. I immediately took a piece of paper and pencil and asked the inspector if he would be good enough to let me know what the exact message was—were we instructed to withdraw it, requested to do so, or was it merely a polite hope that we might? I then warned him that what he said would be brought up in evidence against him. The effect of that last statement was instantaneous. The inspector had evidently been so accustomed to say these words to other people that he was painfully disturbed at having them administered to himself. He was visibly relieved when I later suggested that I had better see his chief. Before his departure, I had taken the precaution of transcribing into a copy of the book the markings which had been made in the copy in his possession. These markings were most instructive. Most of the passages were single lined, a few double lined. One of the latter passages puzzled me greatly, because I could not see upon what ground even an official could take exception to it.

At Scotland Yard I produced the paper on which I had taken down the message given me by the inspector and inquired whether it was correct. I was informed that the inspector had overstepped the mark, which, as I was able to point out, was precisely what he said our author had done. I then inquired whether it was realized:

(a) That the offending book had been published seven years.

(b) That it had been published by two other firms before we took it over.

(c) That it was in its third edition.

(d) That the author had only recently received from nearly all the leading literary people in the country a most wonderful testimonial on the occasion of his birthday.

I then asked what was wrong with the particular passage that had been doubly underlined. The official read it and replied that he regarded it as very serious, and when I asked him why, found that he had attributed to it precisely the opposite meaning to what the very clear wording indicated. When I pointed this out to him he at once admitted the mistake, and was honest enough to add that he was dealing with so much evil that he tended to see it where it did not exist. When he added that he did not intend to prosecute, I am afraid I replied that I wished he would, as I should like the people who had signed the testimonial (of which I then handed him a copy) to know what he thought about the book. Half unconsciously he added that if it came under the Defence of the Realm Act he would prosecute. But it did not come under DORA. The probable explanation of the incident, which was very instructive, was that the absence of any legal or other difficulty in securing the immediate suppression of the *Rainbow*, and the consciousness of DORA in the background, led the authorities to act a little more rashly than they would have done in normal circumstances. They were taking anonymous complaints much too seriously, and had succeeded with some publishers in getting books suppressed without anyone hearing about it, a real grievance, by the way, for the authors, who were surely entitled to be heard. In our case nothing further happened, save that, as the result of my call, the waiting-room accommodation at New Scotland Yard was improved, and visitors are no longer kept standing in a cold and draughty corridor.

I have dealt with the problem of obscene libel in Chapter IV. Here I will merely add that it would be a splendid thing if officials, and for that matter all those who call out from time to time for censorship, could be made to learn Milton's *Areopagitica* by heart. For the rest, public opinion will do all that is necessary as far as serious publications are concerned. Apart from all other considerations, it never in the long run pays a reputable publisher to 'overstep the mark'. Both the book trade and the public would soon let him know if he did, and as often as not before the authorities had time to intervene.

At this point a reference to the so-called 'banning' of books by the circulating libraries is appropriate. Both the extent and the effect of the action taken by these libraries are apt to be exaggerated. In the management of their business they have to consider the requirements of their customers.[1] If a given book is likely to offend the large majority of their clientele it is obvious that they must take steps to see that only the small minority see it and that no copy inadvertently reaches any of the others. This is achieved by the simple expedient of deciding that such a book shall not be supplied unless specifically asked for. It certainly limits the circulation of such a book to those likely to appreciate it, but cannot be termed a censorship. There is no ground for the suggestion often made by authors that the fate of their work will necessarily be made or marred by the attitude of the circulating libraries, most of which are merely seeking in this matter to carry out their customers' wishes.

The Methods of Attracting New Business are manifold, but the best of all is the recommendation of satisfied authors; it is the kind of testimonial that can be bought only with service—by work faithfully, conscientiously,

[1] And also, by the way, the law of libel.

315

and efficiently done. Some publishers feel it essential to take advantage of social functions of every kind to extend their connections. It is an excellent method, particularly for the bachelor publisher without home responsibilities. Another effective plan is, by wide reading of serious periodicals of every kind, to observe who are the coming men and what are the coming subjects before they have arrived. My predecessors published Freud's *Interpretation of Dreams* several years before psychoanalysis became a household word, and we more or less commissioned the first popular book on the subject over a twelvemonth before the boom came. When, during the First World War, my firm reissued Kant's *Perpetual Peace* and published books on the League of Nations, it was regarded as a pro-German activity. Scarcely any copies of Baudouin's *Suggestion and Autosuggestion* were sold during the first three months following publication. Brooks's *Practice of Autosuggestion* —of which about 185,000 copies have been sold here and in America—was definitely commissioned to meet the demand for a cheaper and more popular book that we were confident that Baudouin's would arouse.

Specialization often helps in the development of a business. It is comparatively easy, sometimes, to get a sort of 'corner' in the best books on a certain subject, and when once that is achieved most of the other good books on the subject are likely to come your way.

The starting of series, the commissioning of authors to write books for you, are other plans adopted to increase business, and there is also the alternative, more favoured by some publishers than others, of turning to literary agents for assistance. There remains also poaching—or paying others to poach for you if you have any qualms about doing it for yourself. No doubt I am old-fashioned, but this method seems to me to lower the dignity of the profession. The ideal to be aimed at is surely that described by the late Henry Holt, who, when speaking of American publishing in the 'seventies, wrote:

All those old publishers—Putnam, Appleton, Harper, and Scribner —were incapable of petty or ostentatious things, and were much more inclined to friendly co-operation and mutual concession than to barbarous competition. The spectacle of a crowd of other men making fools of themselves exercised upon them no temptation to do as the herd did. No one of them, or of a few more, would go for another's author any more than for his watch; or, if he got entangled with another's author through some periodical or other outside right, would no more hold on to him than to the watch if the guard had got caught on a button. They were wonderfully kind to me as a young fellow, and their kindness and example have been of inestimable value all my life.

If we cannot live up to such a standard today we might, at any rate, bear it in mind.

Valuation for Probate.—As an executor I have had to pay substantial fees for every valuation needed for the purpose of obtaining probate. As a publisher I find myself constantly expected to value, without fee, deceased authors' literary assets. I do not suppose that any publisher ever refuses to do this, but why they should be the only experts not paid for this technical assistance is not clear. Whatever adverse reputation publishers may have no one can suggest that in this matter they are ungenerous to their authors' heirs.

Unprofitable Books.—A problem that confronts every serious publisher is what to do with the many first-rate and learned books which cry aloud for publication, but which it is certain will have an insufficient sale to pay their way. In olden days, nearly all the better firms of publishers considered themselves under an obligation to issue such books so far as their means justified them in so doing. It was often possible for them to do much in this way to foster learning, because if any of their more popular books were particularly successful the bulk of the profits came their way. Today, with sliding-scale royalties, the author reaps the fruits of any exceptional success. This is quite as it should be, but it sets a very definite limit upon what even the most public-spirited publisher can do in the way of financing unprofitable undertakings. Moreover there is no longer any greatly increased margin on reprints and the sum needed to finance a learned work is now, alas! much greater.

CHAPTER XI

PUBLISHING AS A PROFESSION

'Aptly has it been said by one of the most brilliant writers of our day, that the great publisher is a sort of Minister of Letters, and is not to be without the qualities of a statesman.'
From John Morley's *Recollections.*

THE foregoing chapters will have convinced my readers that book publishing is not such a simple task as is usually thought. Despite the current impression to the contrary, neither an Honours Degree at a University nor even literary ability is a sufficient qualification. Manifold technical knowledge and commercial acumen are essential. Furthermore, it will usually be found that the most able and successful publishers have been right through the business from start to finish, and can therefore, from personal knowledge, check and follow all the work, including the various processes of production. The knowledge that is needed cannot be acquired in a day nor yet a year, and it is often not till after a wide experience of ten or fifteen years that a publisher realizes most keenly how much there is still to learn. It is only the man who has never mastered his job who is sure that he knows all there is to know about it.

The monetary return is in few cases commensurate with the labour expended. It is, in fact, much more difficult to 'make good' in publishing than is commonly supposed. The owners of well known and famous publishing houses are not necessarily the enormously wealthy people they are usually reputed to be. It is probably true that anyone who could make money at book publishing could make more in other businesses; and to the beginner who asks for advice, one is safe in replying, 'Do not go into publishing, if money-making is your chief objective. Publishers who regard their job merely as a means of making money give one the feeling that one has about doctors whose sole concern is their fees. Publishing has rewards to offer far greater than money. A decent enough living can be made at it, if you have really mastered the technique and have the necessary aptitude; but your day's work will never be done, and it is possible that the better work you do, the less *monetary* reward you will receive.'

It seems necessary to emphasize this side of publishing, because of the exaggerated ideas that are prevalent. Fortunes made by publishers in other days are attributed to the present time, when quite other conditions prevail, and it is wrongly assumed that what happened in the past or may happen in war-time happens in the present. But there is likewise exaggeration of the opposite kind. The view of those who have put their money into publishing and lost it, that in no circumstances can a publishing business be made to pay its way, is as erroneous as that of the disappointed author who regards every publisher as a potential millionaire.

Many publishing businesses are endowed by foolish people. If a publisher who is in low water advertises that a directorship or partnership is available to anyone introducing capital, he will be inundated with offers, mostly from fond parents who want their sons to start as directors instead of going right through the business.

The number of publishing houses of any real importance in England, or even in such a big country as America, is extremely limited, but the attractions of publishing as a profession are such that scarcely a week goes by without every firm of repute receiving applications from men just down from the universities, anxious to adopt it as a career. In common with most publishers, I have interviewed scores of such applicants. A few are genuinely keen, and are ready to make some sacrifice to qualify themselves, but for the most part they appear to think publishing a 'soft job' which consists of reading an occasional manuscript. In practice, what seems to happen is that the young man is asked by his father what he would like to be, and replies that he does not know. When questioned what he is interested in, he perhaps replies he likes reading. It is then assumed he ought to be a publisher.

I emphasize the point, because its effect upon publishing is, in my judgment, disastrous. It enables the most hopelessly inefficient and incompetent firms to prolong their existence and confront the efficient publisher with the most difficult form of competition. There is the case of the firm which had over £60,000 poured into the business by a succession of partners. These sudden accessions of capital, on which interest had to be paid, prompted the undertaking of many doubtful ventures, and necessitated the payment of a substantial salary to the incoming partner, who, in most cases, brought no qualifications with him other than his money. Regarded from the purely financial point of view, this is apt to be a most extravagant way of raising capital. The partner contributes, let us say, £5,000, and is given 6 per cent debentures, calling for £300 per annum interest. In addition, he is paid a salary of £500 or £600 a year, whereas on his own merits he might not be worth anything at all. Thus over 15 per cent may be paid for the additional capital, a rate that is obviously crippling. After the lapse of a few years the partner may have learned something about the business and be able to earn his salary, but by that time most of his £5,000 will have been paid out in interest and salary, and the firm will once again be complaining of lack of capital. Another partner is then sought and the process is repeated. Among those to introduce money in this way will be bankers, solicitors, and business men. They will take what seem to them to be the very greatest precautions, the books of the firm will be examined by chartered accountants and a certified balance-sheet demanded; but, as will have been seen in the last chapter, it will be of no avail if the valuation of the stock, plant, and copyrights has not been carefully checked. That is a problem beyond the competence of an ordinary chartered accountant, and even the certificates of some of the professional valuers are worse than useless. A point to be remembered is that *bona fide* openings seldom occur. The firm that is prosperous and well managed does not, in normal circumstances, require additional capital. The firms that most want it are usually among those to whom it is least safe to entrust it.

So much for the difficulties of entering already established publishing businesses; there remains the alternative of starting a fresh one. To judge by the number of firms that spring up like mushrooms, it might be thought the easiest method. In fact, the difficulties are overwhelming. Of the many that start, few survive seven years, unless the founder had already made a success of the management of some other firm. Of the others, practically none hold out beyond seven years without obtaining further capital to carry them along. The reasons are obvious to those with publishing experience. The working expenses have to be borne by a very small list of books, mostly obtained in keen competition with older houses. It is almost inevitable that some of the books will be failures; and, unless there is some exceptional piece of good luck, the profits on the others will not meet the office expenses—without taking into consideration the drawings of the partners or interest on capital. Unless the amount provided is much more than is usually the case, this process and the cost of producing new books will soon exhaust the initial capital, and from that moment onwards a struggle begins, which may be temporarily mitigated by the securing of additional money, on which further interest has to be paid. When the end comes, the founders realize, though all too late, that they have merely been living on their capital.

In practice, it may often be less risky to purchase the assets of an existing business, however derelict, provided the price paid is not too high; because, if the business has been established any length of time, it will have accumulated at any rate a few publications with a steady sale, and these, together with the profits on the disposal of the old stock (if bought at a reasonable figure), should go some way towards meeting the working expenses while a new list is being built up. Here again, however, experience is essential, because so much turns upon the ability to realize old stock to the greatest advantage. Lest there should be those who think it is merely a case of providing enough capital, I may be forgiven for mentioning a recent instance where over £30,000 was put into a new firm and irretrievably lost in less than three years and another in which over £90,000 was dissipated. There is no short cut. In recent times, at any rate, no successful business has been established by any publisher who has not first acquired the necessary technical knowledge. This is a point that has to be emphasized to all entering a publishing office.

Those who have read the earlier chapters will have gained some idea of the many qualifications which contribute to a publisher's success. Here I will merely refer to two which might otherwise be overlooked: both are of great importance. The first is experience of the actual selling of books to the public (in a retail bookshop) and to booksellers (as a publisher's traveller). The publisher who has had neither of these experiences is sadly handicapped in gauging either trade requirements or the commercial merits of manuscripts which come his way.

The second is memory, which occupies a more important place in a publisher's work than in most other businesses. However carefully the business is organized, however perfect the systems introduced, much will depend upon the publisher's memory. The value of his experience rests largely upon his recollection of the literature of any subject and the record of success or failure that has attended, not only his own, but other people's publications. There is all the difference in the world between a decision based upon your own prejudices and one founded upon an accurate recollection of the history of a number of other books on the same subject and a knowledge of the markets requiring them. In brief, however many precautions are taken to avoid any reliance upon memory, there can be few occupations which tax it so greatly or in which it is such a valuable asset.

Book publishing is a very personal business, and that is one of its fascinations: the personal element therefore is one of the biggest factors. We have already seen that a publisher's own inclinations determine the selection of the manuscripts chosen for publication. They will likewise have a decisive effect upon the character of the business. The publisher who rates size above quality, outward success above the judgment of the cultured minority, and who regards publishing as primarily a commercial venture, will inevitably gravitate towards what are known as 'big fiction' and 'big memoirs': in other words, the publication of works by authors whose reputations have been made and whose works are certain to have a large sale. Seeking to reap where others have sown, such firms tend to be less scrupulous in the methods they adopt to secure the transfer of competitors' authors to their list, and it is to them that some literary agents most readily turn. At one time the current flowed strongly in their direction, but the tide has now turned, and many of the more discriminating authors have come to realize that better service can be obtained from publishers who can give personal attention to their work than from firms where it will of necessity be merely one of a long list. The day of gauging a publisher's merits by the extent to which he will gamble on 'advance payments' in anticipation of royalties is passing. As Charles Morgan rightly said, 'a publisher's steady confidence is worth all the advances in the world'. Big fiction and cheap fiction certainly figure largely in most people's minds; but, judged by any other standard than 'turnover', they form but a small proportion of books published.

The control of a publishing business gives unique opportunities for self-expression. If the publisher happens to be interested in technical matters, it is very easy for him to develop a technical side to his business; again, if he is interested in medicine, law, architecture, or any other subject, his business can be led into these channels. But for the most part each house has its own tradition behind it, and any sudden departure from that tradition is likely to prove disastrous. If a firm which for several generations has specialized in nothing but theology suddenly takes to the issuing of fiction, the result will not be good either for its theological list or for its fiction. On the other hand, the merging of several publishers' lists will leave a firm with several traditions behind it, of each of which advantage can be taken.

Probably the most satisfactory feature of any publishing business is a good educational side, because, if the list contains many books that are 'set', or firmly established, those books will continue to sell almost regardless of how the business is run. Many a firm must have depended for its very existence upon its educational list. But there are grave disadvantages as well as advantages in connection with educational publications. In the first place, the work comes in spurts: the orders pour in at certain periods of the year; at these times the publisher's staff has more than it can cope with, whereas a few weeks later there may not be enough to do. Then again, although all is plain sailing when once a book is established, it is apt to be extremely difficult to get a book adopted, and the margin on new educational books is too meagre to cover many failures.

In England (not in America), 'juveniles' were until recently one of the most unsatisfactory branches of publishing. Competition was particularly keen, and there was a deplorable tendency to judge the value of children's books by their bulk and the number of illustrations, rather than by the intrinsic merits of the text or the quality of the artist's work. Many of the big buyers of 'juveniles' purchased them in hundreds assorted at a given price, and would not be bothered with isolated books. It is, of course, only by production in large quantities that such astoundingly good value can be given. This makes it difficult for the publisher who eschews mass production and aims at high quality of text and illustration to publish at a price which will stand comparison with the results of mass production. Fortunately parents are beginning to give as much thought to the mental food of their children as they do, let us say, to the choice of a new dress or a new suit of clothes, and in consequence the courageous publisher of really good children's books is coming into his own. Children themselves are seldom as hypnotized by bulk as aunts and nurses and the many Children's

Book Weeks and other facilities afforded them to see the best enable children to clamour for the better type of juvenile they so very much prefer.

As I have mentioned the extent to which a publisher's personal inclination may influence the character of his list, I should like to refer to the all-too-prevalent idea that a publisher must, or should, approve of all the opinions expressed in his publications. This is an absurd notion, and if carried to its logical conclusion would reduce a publisher to issuing nothing but multiplication tables and books written by himself.

Censorship (except of the libellous and obscene) ill becomes a publisher; the more limited responsibility for seeing that the matter is reasonably well and clearly expressed is quite sufficient. In fact, I regard the publication of controversial books as a specially important part of a general publisher's function. What better way is there of securing deliberate and thorough investigation of new ideas and unpopular opinions? The enemy of subversive thought is not suppression, but publication: truth has no need to fear the light of day; fallacies wither under it. The unpopular views of today are the commonplaces of tomorrow, and in any case the wise man wants to hear both sides of every question. Publication winnows the grain of truth from the chaff of prejudice and superstition, and it is the publisher's duty to help this process by maintaining an open forum.

Partly perhaps because of my interest in controversial literature, the lot of the general publisher with a varied range of interests seems to me the most enviable one, particularly if his list is dominated by the ideas of tomorrow rather than those of yesterday. His work brings him into close touch with the intellectual life of his time, affords wide scope for initiative, and gives endless opportunities to help the cause of progress. Much is written of the power of the Press, a power which may last but a day; by comparison, little is heard of the power of books, which may endure for generations. The feeling that one may be building with permanent materials, the knowledge that one's name is associated with books that enshrine profound thought and the triumphs of the creative imagination add a fascination to the best publishing. To offer the public just what it wants, to pander to the worst prejudices of the moment, may be the speediest way to profits, here as elsewhere; but it is a dull road to follow. Publishing has far more thrilling adventures to offer the man who is ready to accompany pioneers along fresh paths; eager to help overcome apathy, ignorance, and prejudice; anxious that, above all, the lamp of truth should be kept burning. It may not yield the same monetary reward, but it will afford a satisfaction no money can buy. If you are a student and lover of human nature in all its amazing variety, where will you have such an opportunity of gratifying your desire as in publishing? Among authors, you will meet the very perfect gentleman and his exact reverse; you will encounter the colossal egotist who acclaims his manuscript as opening a new era, the learned man of humble spirit, and all shades and patterns between. As the years pass, some of your clients become your personal friends, and to their confidence you are able to respond in ways that surpass the strict limits of business.

Is it surprising that so many active minds with an

idealistic strain should hasten to join our ranks? But I must repeat what I have been saying all along, that the man who enters upon book publishing without being well grounded in all its prosaic and tedious details, complex organization, and financial bearings, is only inviting disaster. Such a grounding cannot be acquired from a book. My object in any case is not to teach publishing, but to give, out of a somewhat varied and unusual experience, some information that authors and all concerned with the book craft should possess. There is much more that might be said, and probably much that might be said better, but I hope that I have in some measure succeeded in my task.

Learning hath gained most by those books by which the printers have lost, whereas Foolish Pamphlets prove most beneficial to the printers.
THOMAS FULLER

ORGANIZATIONS CONNECTED WITH THE BOOK WORLD

(*a*) OFFICIAL BODIES

  (1) The Incorporated Society of Authors, Playwrights, and Composers, 84 Drayton Gardens, London, S.W.10.

  (2) The Publishers Association of Great Britain and Ireland, 19 Bedford Square, London, W.C.1.

  (3) The Booksellers Association, 14 Buckingham Palace Gardens, Buckingham Palace Road, London, S.W.1.

  (4) The Library Association, Chaucer House, Malet Street, W.C.1.

  (5) The International Association of Antiquarian Booksellers.

  (6) Aslib (Association of Special Libraries and Information Bureaux), 3 Belgrave Square, S.W.1.

  (7) The International Publishers Association, Morgartenstr. 29, Zürich, Switzerland.

(*b*) OTHER ASSOCIATIONS.

  (8) The National Book League, 7 Albemarle Street, W.1. (Objects: *The promotion of book reading and the wider distribution of books*.)

  (9) The Publishers' Circle. (*A Club confined to members of the Publishers Association, which meets at irregular intervals for the discussion of subjects of interest to members*.)

  (10) The Society of Bookmen, 7 Albemarle Street, W.1. (*A group of 75 Authors, Publishers, Booksellers, Printers, Binders, and others, whose object is to initiate schemes for the advancement of the book trade*.)

  (11) The Publishers' Advertising Circle.

  (12) International P.E.N., 62 Glebe Place, London, S.W.3. *World association of writers, editors and translators whose aim is to promote friendship and intellectual co-operation between men of letters in all countries in the interests of literature, freedom of expression and international goodwill.*

PROOF READER'S MARKS

∧ The caret-mark—insert matter indicated in margin.

/ Sign to show that marginal mark is concluded.

ℐ Delete—take out.

ℐ̶ Delete character indicated and close up.

stet Let cancelled words, dotted underneath, remain as printed.

⸗ cap Change to capital letter.

= s. cap Change to small capitals letters underlined.

l.c. Change to lower-case (encircle letters to be altered).

ital Change to italic letters underlined.

rom Change to roman type (encircle letters to be altered).

w.f. Wrong fount—change to correct fount.

ᓂ A letter inverted—reverse.

✕ A broken letter.

c Remove space and close up.

Insert a space between the words or letters indicated.

 # > Space between lines or paragraphs.

⌴ Less space—reduce space between words.

eq# Unevenly spaced—make spacing equal.

⌒ Transpose letters or words as marked.

▢/ Indent one em.

⌐ Move lines to left.

¬ Move lines to right.

═ Straighten lines.

⌡ A space to be pushed down.

⌐ n.p. Begin a new paragraph here.

run on No new paragraph here.

⊙ Insert full stop.

,/ Insert comma.

;/ Insert semi-colon.

⊖ Insert colon.

-/ Insert hyphen.

⊢—⊣ Insert em rule.

ᵌ/ Insert apostrophe.

PROOF MARKED FOR
CORRECTION

It is not often that a printer has an opportunity
of guiding authors in the manner in which they should
prepare their copy for the press. Usually he has to
suffer in silence and do his best to cope with copy as
it is sent in.

On many occasions a few minutes conversation
between author and printer would save much labour
and expense to say nothing of the fraying of tempers
on the part of both parties. I am, therefore, particularly
glad to have this opportunity of discussing the matter
with the members of your Society, many of whom
have a good good deal to do in one way or another
with the placing of copy with the printer.

Many of the points I to wish make may seem elementary; but it is more often than not the lack of
attention to these very details that cause so much
trouble when the work actually gets under way. with
the aid of illustrations I hope to make clear any
technicalities touched upon.

The Beginning.

The beginning of all things, as far as the printer is
concerned, is the actual Manuscript.

At the present time practically all mss. are typed,
and this is obviously a wise procedure, unless the
author happens to possess a particularly readable
handwriting even then the possibility of mistakes is
endless, especially when the matter consists of mathe-
matical formulae where the misinterpretation of an
algebraical sign can alter the sense of a whole equation.
The typed MS. should be compared with the original.

NET BOOK AGREEMENT '1957'[1]

WE the undersigned several firms of publishers, being desirous that in so far as we publish books at net prices (as to which each publisher is free to make his own decisions), those net prices shall normally be the prices at which such books are sold to the public as hereinafter defined, and in order to avoid disorganization in the book trade and to ensure that the public may be informed of and able uniformly to take advantage of the conditions under which net books may be sold at less than the net prices, hereby agree to adopt and each of us does hereby adopt the following standard sale conditions for the net books published by us within the United Kingdom:

STANDARD CONDITIONS OF SALE OF NET BOOKS

(i) Except as provided in clauses (ii) to (iv) hereof and except as we may otherwise direct net books shall not be sold or offered for sale or caused or permitted to be sold or offered for sale to the public at less than the net published prices.

(ii) A net book may be sold or offered for sale to the public at less than the net published price if

(a) it has been held in stock by the bookseller for a period of more than twelve months from the date of the latest purchase by him of any copy thereof and

(b) it has been offered to the publisher at cost price or at the proposed reduced price whichever shall be the lower and such offer has been refused by the publisher.

(iii) A net book may be sold or offered for sale to the public at less than the net published price if it is second-hand and six months have elapsed since its date of publication.

(iv) A net book may be sold at a discount to such libraries, book agents (including Service Unit libraries), quantity buyers and institutions as are from time to time authorized by the Council

[1] It has been registered as a Restrictive Practice desirable in the public interest.

of The Publishers Association of such amount and on such conditions as are laid down in the instrument of authorization. Such amount and conditions shall not initially be less or less favourable than those prevailing at the date of this Agreement.

(v) For the purposes of clause (i) hereof a book shall be considered as sold at less than the net published price if the bookseller

(*a*) offers or gives any consideration in cash to any purchaser except under licence from the Council of The Publishers Association or

(*b*) offers or gives any consideration in kind (e.g. card indexing, stamping, reinforced bindings, etc., at less than the actual cost thereof to the bookseller).

(vi) For the purposes of this Agreement and of these Standard Conditions:
Net book shall mean a book, pamphlet, map or other similar printed matter published at a net price. *Net price* and *net published price* shall mean the price fixed from time to time by the publisher below which the net book shall not be sold to the public.
Public shall be deemed to include schools, libraries, institutions and other non-trading bodies.
Person shall include any company, firm, corporation, club, institution, organization, association or other body.

(vii) The above conditions shall apply to all sales executed in the United Kingdom and the Republic of Ireland whether effected by wholesaler or retailer when the publisher's immediate trade customer whether wholesaler or retailer, or the wholesaler's immediate trade customer, is in the United Kingdom or the Republic of Ireland.

We the undersigned several firms of publishers further agree to appoint and each of us does hereby appoint the Council of The Publishers Association to act as our agent in the collection of information concerning breaches of contract by persons selling or offering for sale net books, and in keeping each individual publisher informed of breaches in respect of such net books as are published by him and we further hereby undertake and agree that we will each enforce our contractual rights and our rights under the Restrictive Trade Practices

Act, 1956, if called upon to do so by the Council of The Publishers Association, and provided that we shall be indemnified by The Publishers Association if so requested by us in respect of any costs of such action incurred by us or by the Council of The Publishers Association on our behalf.

APPENDIX IV
TURNOVER STATISTICS
OF THE BRITISH BOOK TRADE

Year	Total	Export (Including the Dominions and India)
1937	£10,507,204	£3,146,175
1938	£10,706,018	£3,171,018
1939	£10,321,658	£3,154,599
1940	£ 9,953,196	£3,517,335
1941	£13,986,700	£3,983,900
1942	£16,735,900	£3,608,700
1943	£19,290,800	£4,469,600
1944	£20,500,516	£4,895,349
1945	£21,979,554	£5,139,222
1946	£26,961,622	£6,715,212
1947	£30,203,763	£7,412,905
1948	£33,241,431	£8,739,236
1949	£35,297,252	£9,798,838
1950	£37,158,652	£11,394,220
1951	£41,553,760	£13,740,322
1952	£42,790,387	£14,482,036
1953	£44,892,291	£15,566,874
1954	£46,270,953	£16,527,054
1955	£49,439,087	£18,156,084
1956	£56,659,484	£20,870,597
1957	£60,456,095	£22,505,440
1958	£63,608,654	£23,817,453

THE NUMBER OF TITLES ISSUED*

Year	Totals	Reprints
1939	14,904	4,493
1940	11,053	3,530
1941	7,581	2,326
1942	7,241	1,499
1943	6,705	1,201
1944	6,781	889
1945	6,747	921
1946	11,411	1,508
1947	13,046	2,441
1948	14,686	3,924
1949	17,034	5,110
1950	17,072	5,324
1951	18,066	4,938
1952	18,741	5,428
1953	18,257	5,523
1954	19,188	5,846
1955	19,962	5,770
1956	19,107	5,302
1957	20,719	5,921
1958	22,143	5,971
1959	20,690	5,522

* According to *The Bookseller's* compilation. (See also page 342.)

APPROXIMATE SCHEDULE OF A BOOK PUBLISHER'S WORKING EXPENSES

	Per cent of total turnover
Wages and Salaries, including Pension schemes ...	13·00
Travelling and Commission	3·75
Carriage and Packing, etc.	1·50
Light, Heat, Water, etc.	0·35
Rent, Rates, etc.	1·80
Outside and Specialist 'Reading' Fees	0·60
Insurance	0·20
Postage, Telegrams, Telephones	2·10
Stationery, etc.	0·70
Warehousing	0·40
Sundry Expenses, including Audit	0·60
Motor Expenses, including Depreciation	0·50
	25·50
Advertising	5·00
	30·50

The above figures are based upon such limited information as I have been able to obtain. All the available accounts showed great variation in detail, and the total working expenses, excluding advertising, fluctuated between 22 per cent and 36 per cent; most of them were over 26 per cent of the turnover.

It is unwise to draw any hasty conclusions from individual percentages given above, e.g. Travelling and Commission are mostly incurred in connection with *new* books, but the average cost shown in the schedule is calculated upon the publisher's *entire* turnover. Were it confined to that part to which it is applicable the percentage would be more than doubled. The same remark of course applies to advertising.

No allowance has been made for two important factors which because of their inevitability might justly be termed running expenses. Major Putnam described them as 'publishing fallibility', that is the cost of some proportion of 'publishing failures', and 'manufacturing fallibility', that is the cost of over-supplies which may occur even with successful books. (See pages 192–3.)

APPENDIX VI—TYPICAL (1959) PROFIT AND LOSS ACCOUNT OF A MODERATELY WELL SELLING FIRST NOVEL OF 95,000 WORDS

(3,000 COPIES, 288 PAGES Cr. 8vo, 15s).

Dr.	£ s d	£ s d		Cr. £ s d
To Composition at £22 10s per 32 pp., including small type and make-up ...	202 10 0		By Sales:	
" Machining at £3 7s 6d per ream ...	91 2 6		Circulating libraries and wholesalers ... 1,000 at 9/6	475 0 0
" Paper, 27 reams Antique Wove, 80 lb., at 1/4 ...	144 0 0		Ordinary sales, including repeats from libraries ... 650 at 10/-	325 0 0
" Author's corrections 10% ...	20 5 0		Other ordinary sales on varying terms ... 150 at 10/-	75 0 0
Gross sheet cost ... 3/0½		457 17 6	Colonial ... 600 at 7/6	225 0 0
" Three-colour blocks for jacket	23 0 0		Total sales ... 2,400	
" Artist's fee for design ...	12 12 0		Review copies ... 100	
" Binding at 1/7½ ...	243 15 0		Stock ... 500	
" Binder's brass ...	4 0 0		3,000	
" Jackets including paper and printing ...	40 0 0			
Gross binding cost ... 2/2		323 7 0		
" 36 paper bound copies for travellers and publicity ...	7 0 0			
" Postage on Review copies ...	2 5 0			
" Advertisements ...	140 0 0			
" Author's Royalty if at 10% ...	157 10 0	306 15 0		
" Insurance ...	—	—		
" Working expenses ...	—	—		
		£1,087 19 6		
		12 0 6		
" Gross Profit ...		£1,100 0 0		£1,100 0 0

N.B.—In the above account *not one penny* has been allowed for the publisher's 'working expenses' which exceed 25 per cent of his turnover (see Appendix V). The cost of composition, jacket design, blocks, etc., has been spread over double the number of copies shown in the 1939 account—3,000 as against 1,500—and much larger sales have been assumed. But for the increase in the size of the edition a published price of over 21s would have been necessitated. (See page 33.)

THIS TYPICAL (1939) PROFIT AND LOSS ACCOUNT, NOW COMPLETELY UNREALISTIC, IS INCLUDED FOR HISTORICAL COMPARISON

(1,500 COPIES, 352 PAGES Cr. 8vo 7/6)*

Dr.	£ s d	£ s d	Cr.	£ s d	£ s d
To Composition, including small type and make-up (352 pp.)	7 0 0		By Sales:		
" Machining 16½ reams (1,500)	22 0 0		Circulating libraries ... 230 at 4/9	54 12 6	
" Paper, Antique Wove, 30 × 40, 70 lb. for 1,500 copies	18 0 0		Ordinary sales, including repeat orders from libraries ... 220 at 5/-	55 0 0	
" Author's corrections 10%	14 4 0		Other ordinary sales on varying terms ... 210	56 0 0	
Gross sheet cost ... 1/7½		121 4 0	Colonial editions 376 at 3/3	61 2 0	
" Tri-colour blocks for jacket ...	5 10 0				226 14 6
" Artist's fee for design ...	6 6 0		Total Sales 1,036		
" Binding ...	45 0 0		" Review copies 100		
" Binder's brass ...	2 0 0		" Stock ... 364		
" Jackets, including printing tri-colour blocks	9 0 0		1,500		
Gross binding cost ... 11½		71 16 0			
" 36 copies, wrapped, on proof paper for Colonial buyers ...	1 16 0		" Deficit (as against which there is surplus stock valued as 'Remainders' at say £11 10s and possibly a small share in American or other rights)		69 11 0
" Postage on Review copies ...	1 3 0				
" Advertisements ...	55 0 0				
" Author's Royalty, if at 10% ...	29 6 6				
" Moulds (if taken) ...	16 0 0				
		103 5 6			
" Insurance ...	—				
" Working expenses ...	—				
		£295 5 6			£296 5 6

N.B.—In the above account *not one penny* has been allowed for the publisher's 'working expenses', which almost invariably exceed 25 per cent of his turnover. (See Appendix V.)

* The war completely invalidated these figures.

341

SOME INTERNATIONAL STATISTICS OF BOOK PRODUCTION, 1927–1957

(For fuller information, covering 64 countries, see *Basic Facts and Figures*, 1958 and *The United Nations Statistical Year Book*, both published by UNESCO.)

	1927[1]	1938	1948	1957
Bulgaria	2,379	2,750	2,371	3,615
Czechoslovakia[6]	5,162			7,187
Denmark	3,293	3,423	4,054	3,062
France[1]	11,922	15,894	16,020	11,917
Germany[2]	31,026	25,439	18,090	15,710
Great Britain	13,810	16,091	14,686	20,719
Holland (*Nieuwsblad*)[3] ...	6,103	8,096	8,047	7,284
Hungary	4,424	3,136	5,804	3,456
Italy	6,533	10,648	7,685	9,320
Japan	19,967			25,299
Norway	1,238	2,384	2,548	3,021
Spain[5]	2,374		3,693	4,248
Sweden	2,652	2,834	3,288	5,663
Switzerland	1,909	2,162	4,691	4,216
United States of America ...	10,153	11,067	9,897	13,142

[1] The figures for 1927 are those of the *Bibliographie de la France*.

[2] The German figures for 1927 and 1938 include all the German-speaking countries (Germany, Austria, German Switzerland); those for 1948 and 1957 merely the West German Republic and West Berlin.

[3] According to the *Nieuwsblad* the 1927 and 1938 figures include periodicals.

[4] Includes musical publications with and without text.

[5] Includes musical publications.

[6] The figures for Czechoslovakia in the column 1927 relate to 1926.

N.B.—The methods of compilation vary greatly in the different countries.

INDEX

INDEX

The Truth About a Publisher
Publishing in Peace and War
Best Sellers: are they Born or Made?
Book Trade Organization in Norway and Sweden
Book Trade Organization in Denmark
How Governments Treat Books
The Book in the Making
On Translations

JOINT AUTHOR
Two Young Men See the World